HIGH PRAISE FOR

THE PARIS SECRET

"Lester's magnetic characters, lyrical writing, and extensive historical research breathe life into this riveting tale. This is a stunner."

—*Publishers Weekly*, starred review

"A stirring portrait of a daring and courageous group of women willing to risk it all in a time of war, *The Paris Secret* is historical fiction at its best. A beautiful love story coupled with an intricate mystery, richly detailed and impeccably researched history, and an homage to the strength of the human spirit make this a poignant and powerful read. Natasha Lester has done it again!"

—Chanel Cleeton, *New York Times* & *USA Today* bestselling author of *The Last Train to Key West*

"Extraordinary!"
　　　　　　　　　　　　　　　　　　　　　　　—*Marie Claire*

"A dazzling marvel of storytelling, a perfect blend of action, history, and emotional depth. Unforgettable."

—Erika Robuck, bestselling author of *Hemingway's Girl*

"Lester is a master storyteller. In only the way Lester can do it, these seemingly unlinked stories come together in a gorgeously satisfying way that will have you wiping tears from your face in the final pages."

—*Daily Telegraph*

THE PARIS ORPHAN

"Rich and riveting…Readers will become engrossed from the very first page as mystery and romance are expertly combined into one emotionally charged, unforgettable story."

—*Publishers Weekly*, starred review

THE
PARIS
SECRET

OTHER BOOKS BY
NATASHA LESTER

THE
PARIS
SECRET

NATASHA LESTER

FOREVER

New York Boston

Copyright © 2020 by Natasha Lester
Reading group guide copyright © 2020 by Natasha Lester and Hachette Book Group, Inc.

Cover design and illustration by Daniela Medina. Cover photographs © Trevillion; Shutterstock. Cover copyright © 2020 by Hachette Book Group, Inc.

Forever
Hachette Book Group
1290 Avenue of the Americas, New York, NY 10104
read-forever.com
twitter.com/readforeverpub

Originally published in March 2020 by Hachette Australia
First US edition: September 2020

Forever is an imprint of Grand Central Publishing. The Forever name and logo are trademarks of Hachette Book Group, Inc.

The publisher is not responsible for websites (or their content) that are not owned by the publisher.

The quotation on page 5: from *Circe* by Madeline Miller, copyright © 2018. Reprinted by permission of Little, Brown and Company, an imprint of Hachette Book Group, Inc.

The quotation on page 45: from the book *Spitfire Women of World War II* by permission of HarperCollins Publishers Ltd © 2007 Giles Whittell.

The quotation on page 337: from *A God in Ruins* by Kate Atkinson copyright © 2016. Reprinted by permission of Little, Brown and Company, an imprint of Hachette Book Group, Inc.

The quotation on page 413: from *A Life in Secrets: The Story of Vera Atkins and the Lost Agents of SOE* by Sarah Helm is reprinted by permission of Little, Brown Book Group Ltd © 2005.

Every effort has been made to contact copyright holders of materials reproduced in this book. If anyone has further information, please contact the publishers.

The Hachette Speakers Bureau provides a wide range of authors for speaking events. To find out more, go to www.hachettespeakersbureau.com or call (866) 376-6591.

Library of Congress Control Number: 2020935796

ISBNs: 978-1-5387-1728-8 (trade paperback), 978-1-5387-1727-1 (ebook)

Printed in the United States of America

LSC-C

10 9 8 7 6 5 4 3 2 1

To Audrey, the dark-haired heroine in my life.
You are boundless. I hope you always believe this.

PROLOGUE

In a grand townhouse at 30 Avenue Montaigne, Margaux Jourdan is helped into an ivory silk shantung jacket with a padded and flared peplum, and a pleated black wool skirt. The skirt falls, shockingly, all the way to mid-calf—such an excess of fabric for a post-ration world. A strand of pearls is placed around her neck, and she is finished off with a wide-brimmed hat and black gloves. Even after the desecration of war, a woman's hands are still too startling to be left unclothed.

Madame Raymonde spins Margaux around as if she were a ballerina in a music box and allows her chin to fall just once into a satisfied nod. She indicates with her arm that Margaux should step through the doorway of the *cabine* and into the salon.

Thus, the legendary Dior Bar Suit is conveyed via Margaux's body to an unsuspecting world.

In the grand salon, a crowd of elegant Parisians—Jean Cocteau, Michel de Brunhoff from *Vogue* and Marie-Louise Bousquet from *Harper's Bazaar*—sit shoulder to shoulder with barely any room between them for breath. Some people are standing against the wall, and others line the staircase—such has been the demand for tickets to this show, which canny profiteers have sold to the clamorous for more than it costs to buy black-market butter.

The salon wears its muted palette of pearl gray and white as subtly as a concealed zipper. The Louis XVI medallion chairs, the gilt picture frames topped with fontanges bows and the Belle Epoque chandeliers all seem to declare that time has stopped and it would be best to pay attention. Unfurled fans rustle like premature applause, and the air is scented with perfume and Gauloises and anticipation. Everywhere, skins are atingle.

As Margaux glides along she hears gasps, sees heads lean forward and hands twitch as if they wish to skim the *en huit* curves of her suit. She completes her circuit and passes through the gray satin curtain, behind which stands Christian Dior—the man who stitches seams with magic, whose gowns transcend fashion. Eighty years hence, should one be asked to name a couturier, his will be the first name spoken. But that is all still to come.

Christian gifts Margaux a smile. The show continues. Nobody needs to declare that it is spectacular; it is a fact known without words.

The finale is, naturally, a wedding gown. Margaux stands perfectly still while she is dressed. Then she steps back into the salon and the collective intake of breath is so violent it almost depletes the room of oxygen. For Margaux appears to be wearing a full-blown white rose plucked at its moment of true perfection. Or at least that is the illusion she purveys in her voluminous skirt: a lavishness—no, a prodigality—of silk billowing like optimism around her before funneling in at the waist to a span of just twenty inches—a requirement for any Christian Dior model.

Of course, none of the spectators know that Margaux only possesses such a waist because of years of deprivation; that it is a legacy of a time when such a gown would have been as shocking as the sun appearing in the midnight sky. But it does no one any good to recall what can never be undone, so Margaux concentrates on her feet, walking slowly enough for the crowd to apprehend that what they are seeing is extraordinary, but also fast enough that she is gone too soon, leaving yearning cast behind her like a shadow.

There is hardly enough space amongst all the people for the gown's stupendous skirt and it brushes against one of the tall, white columned ashtrays. Nobody except Margaux notices the ash spill to the floor. Nobody notices either that it is minus fourteen degrees outside and that Paris has been shivering through a winter of postwar electricity rations and coal shortages. Christian's dress has the power of erasure.

As she exits the salon, the applause is so thunderous it could rouse the dead. But Margaux knows nothing will ever rouse her dead.

The mannequins return to the salon and stand in a line. Christian— or Tian as he is known to Margaux and a few select others—bows and accepts his congratulations.

He singles out Margaux, still wearing the wedding dress despite the fact that she will never be a bride, raises her hand to his lips and kisses it. "*Magnifique*," he says.

Christian's sister Catherine Dior kisses Margaux's cheeks. "You were *magnifique, chérie.*"

Carmel Snow from American *Harper's Bazaar* steps forward. Her fingertips whisper rapturously against the silk of Margaux's skirt. "Dear Christian," she says, "your dresses have such a new look."

And Margaux knows, as if she were suddenly able to divine the future, that this is how Christian's collection will be spoken of from now on. A New Look, for a new world. A world in which death and loss and heartbreak will hereafter become muted emotions rather than a rawness tearing always at one's skin. They will not be a way of life, as they have been throughout these last years of war. The New Look will be the perfect amnesiac for a generation that has survived the war and does not wish to recall anything of it.

Margaux is the only one who remembers. Skye and Liberty and Nicholas and O'Farrell are all gone now, in different ways. She will never say their names again, not to anyone. Nobody wishes to hear the names of the victims. Just as nobody wishes to understand that Margaux's waist is tiny because she is a victim too.

Catherine slips her arm into Margaux's. "Here, *chérie*. Let us raise a glass of champagne to . . ." She hesitates. "The future?"

That word will always have a question mark after it. So Margaux does not drink to the future. Instead she lifts her glass to all of them—herself, Catherine, Skye, Liberty, Nicholas and O'Farrell. As she does so, she feels the spirits crowding around her, pleading with her, as they do every night in her dreams. But just as there was nothing she could do the last time she saw each of them, there is nothing she can do for them now. Except drink champagne, smile and step forward with her New Look into this terrible new world that she cannot comprehend.

PART ONE
SKYE

. . . in a solitary life, there are rare moments when another soul dips near yours, as stars once a year brush the earth. Such a constellation was he to me.

—Madeline Miller, *Circe*

ONE

I can see your underwear."

Skye Penrose knew that the ordinary response of a ten-year-old girl to such a statement would be to stop cartwheeling along Porthleven pier like a gamboling star and restore her skirt to its proper position. Instead she paused to change direction, then turned two perfect cartwheels toward the boy who'd spoken. In the rush of her upward trajectory, she lunged at him and gave his trousers a swift tug, dislodging them from his waist and popping at least one button in the process.

"Now I can see yours," she said, giggling. She'd meant to run away immediately to escape his likely anger, but his face was so astonished—eyes wide, his mouth a well-rounded "O," just the right size for throwing in a toffee if only she had one—that she grinned and said, "I'm Skye."

He reinstated his trousers, stuttering, "I'm Nicholas Crawford. Pleased to meet you." He spoke oddly: his words sharp-angled rather than round, emphasis falling on different vowels so that the familiar became strange.

"I thought it only fair, if we're going to be friends, that neither of us should know more about the other," Skye said. "So I had to see your underwear too."

Nicholas Crawford nodded as if that made perfect sense. He was taller than Skye, with near-black hair and striking blue-gray eyes, like the sea on an uncertain day. His clothes were clean and pressed, not grubby with play like Skye's.

"Friends," he repeated.

"As long as you can keep my secrets."

Curiosity shimmered aquamarine in his eyes. "What sort of secrets are they?"

"The best ones. Come on, I'll show you."

She grabbed his hand and took off. He didn't hesitate, didn't protest that he ought to tell his mother where he was going, didn't say he couldn't be friends with someone who'd robbed his trousers of a button or two. He ran with her, keeping pace, even though, given his accent and demeanor, he must be from somewhere far from Cornwall— a place where, most likely, one didn't often run free. Together, they turned right in front of the town hall and raced along the sand until an apparently impenetrable rock wall blocked the way.

"Through here," Skye said, showing him a gap just big enough to crawl through.

On the other side of the wall, his mouth opened again, and she knew he was wonderstruck, just as she'd hoped he would be.

"You're the first person I've brought here," she said.

"Why me?"

She considered how to say it: *I've never met anyone so wide-eyed*. It wouldn't sound right. "I thought you'd like it," she said.

They both turned full circle to take in the white-laced sea hurling itself against the cliff face to the left of them, the curve of the bay where the waves simmered in the dropped wind, the cave behind them, which was craggy and dark and promised feats of great derring-do.

"It's all mine," Skye said proudly. "See that house up there." She pointed to the clifftop, where a weather-thrashed cottage sank its toes into the ground, holding on, just. "That's where I live with my mother.

And my sister. The only way you can get to this cove is through the gap in the rock wall or the path that leads down from the house. So it's mine. And now yours too."

Nicholas furrowed his brow. His hand moved to his pocket and he pulled out a watch. "If you're going to share your cove with me, then I'll share this with you." He handed it to her. "It was my father's. And his father's too."

Skye ran a finger over the engraved gold of the case before opening the cover. Inside, she found dignified Roman numerals and a strangely misshapen half-moon.

"Where's your father?" she asked.

"Up there." Nicholas pointed to the sky.

"You don't need to share this." She passed the pocket watch back to him, understanding it was the most important thing he possessed.

"I want to. You can have it one day every week."

His tone was firm. This well-dressed boy who didn't seem to have ever set foot on a Cornish beach had strength of will. And he could run. And he liked her cove.

"That means you'll have to come back tomorrow to get it," she said.

He nodded.

"Do you want to see inside the cave?"

He nodded again.

* * *

Skye stood on the clifftop, Nicholas's pocket watch tucked safely inside a handkerchief, and watched her new friend squeeze through the gap in the rocks and trudge along the sand below. Just before he turned toward town, he looked back and waved. Skye performed a rapid series of cartwheels that she thought might make him smile. Then she went in to dinner.

Her sister, Liberty, who was younger than Skye by one year, pounced on her the moment she entered the cottage.

"Where were you?" Liberty whined.

"At the beach," Skye said.

Liberty screwed up her face. "You're always at the beach."

"Then you could easily have found me."

"I'm hungry."

Before she could remind her sister that the kitchen, not Skye, was the source of food, she saw, over Liberty's shoulder, the Snakes and Ladders board set out on the table. Gold and green snakes wriggled toward illustrations of naughty children and Skye realized, her stomach twisting like the snakes, that she should be the subject of one of those drawings. She'd promised Liberty a game of Snakes and Ladders that afternoon. But she'd forgotten about it in the thrill of finding someone who loved the cove as much as she did—unlike her sister.

Liberty followed Skye's eyes to the game. She flounced over and thrust it off the table. The dice clattered to the floor, momentarily obscuring the gentle hum of voices from the room next door where their mother was busy with one of her clients.

"I'll make you a cup of tea," Skye said. "And then we can play."

Liberty didn't reply and Skye thought she might march upstairs and sulk in her room as she was wont to do. But then she nodded and peace was momentarily restored. They sipped their tea as they played and Skye said nothing when Liberty, in order to ascend a ladder, miscounted the number of squares she was supposed to move. She said nothing either when Liberty protested that Skye had miscounted and needed to slide down a snake. Liberty won.

* * *

The following morning, Skye was up at dawn and in her swimsuit, waiting impatiently for Nicholas, his pocket watch held tight and safe in her hand. She sat in the window seat in the parlor, staring at her beloved ocean, willing him to ignore propriety and come now, although it was too early even for breakfast. When Liberty appeared downstairs an hour later, she scowled at Skye's swimsuit and let fly with a spiteful foot, which Skye—who'd had plenty of practice—dodged. Then there was a knock at the door and Skye beamed. He too must prefer her cove to breakfast.

"See who it is, darling," her mother called from the kitchen where she was standing at the chipped blue Royal Windsor stove, stirring a pot of porridge. "I'm not expecting anyone until ten."

Skye was already sprinting down the hallway and throwing open the door. Nicholas stood there, alongside a woman with a possessive hand clamped on his shoulder. Skye's smile faltered.

"Is this the girl?" the woman asked.

"This is Skye," Nicholas replied.

"I would like to see your mother," the woman told Skye.

"Come in," Skye said politely. As she held the door wide, the cottage's colored glass oil lamps—they were too far out of town for electricity—flickered with the ill wind the woman had brought with her.

In the kitchen, which smelled as always of woodsmoke, French cigarettes and coffee, Vanessa Penrose turned to greet the visitors. She was resplendent in her long and gloriously ruffled black silk embroidered nightgown, which had draped sleeves and a low neckline. The woman beside Nicholas stared as if Skye's mother were cartwheeling through the house with her knickers showing.

"Have you come for breakfast?" Vanessa said, which made the woman wrench her eyes away from the nightgown. "You must be Nicholas," Vanessa continued. "Skye told me all about you. I'm Vanessa, or Mrs. Penrose, whichever you prefer. Do you like porridge?"

Nicholas smiled at last. "I do."

"He does not," said the woman.

"I do and I'm hungry," Nicholas said with the same quiet determination Skye had heard in his voice when he'd said at the door, *This is Skye*.

"Skye has hollow legs," Vanessa said to Nicholas, "which means she's unable to stand up until she's eaten. You'll simply have to join us."

Skye giggled and Nicholas sat down.

"I am Finella Crawford and your daughter owes my nephew an apology." Nicholas's aunt had a voice like a fishhook: sharp and designed to hurt. It was accented like Nicholas's, but from her mouth it sounded abrasive rather than interesting.

"She ruined a perfectly good pair of trousers and stole a very valuable item," his aunt continued.

Skye reached under the table and pressed Nicholas's pocket watch into his hand, hoping it would help.

"Thanks," he whispered.

Vanessa took an orange from the bowl, cut it in half and juiced it. She poured the juice into a glass and passed it to Nicholas. "Skye told me about the trousers. I can mend the buttons. But Skye doesn't steal."

"You're wrong. She stole my nephew's pocket watch, left to him by his dear father, my brother." Nicholas's aunt dabbed her eyes with a handkerchief but Skye rather thought she was enjoying her performance.

"I have the watch," Nicholas said, holding it up.

"Mystery solved." Vanessa made quick work of three more oranges before sitting down.

"I'm sorry for making a button fall off your trousers," Skye said to Nicholas, using her best manners.

"Buttons and Skye go together like the sea air and smooth hair," her mother said, glancing at Finella's wind-ruffled coiffure.

Nicholas's aunt changed direction. "I was told that you divine the future."

"I do," Vanessa replied.

"My sister-in-law would like a reading." The words squeezed from Finella's mouth as if the idea were as repugnant as animal droppings. "She has suffered a great loss—the death of her husband, Nicholas's father. I've brought her from New York to the country of her birth under the instructions of my doctor; she requires sea air and repose. Given what she's suffered, I'm prepared to allow her to indulge this whim."

Skye's mother poured honey onto Nicholas's porridge. Liberty's eyes widened at the quantity and she opened her mouth to protest, but Skye shook her head furiously at her sister. That honey offered a solidarity that could not be spoken of, yet. Like Nicholas, Skye and Liberty did not have a father.

"I will take your sister-in-law on for readings provided you let Nicholas continue to play with Skye," Vanessa said. "I think they'll be good for one another."

Nicholas's aunt acquiesced with a nod, then turned to leave, forgetting her nephew, but Skye solved that problem by calling out, "Nicholas will be home in time for dinner."

* * *

Over the next month, Skye introduced Nicholas, who was a year older than her—eleven, rather than ten—and who came from a far-away city of skyscrapers, to her world. The world of rummaging in rock pools for hermit crabs and hairy crabs and seeing whose would scuttle away the fastest once put down on the sand. The world of scraping mussels and limpets from rocks, working alongside the red-billed oystercatchers. Of searching for cowrie shells, the fairy-sized, peach-colored slivers that were so easy to miss and therefore all the more precious, to add to Skye's collection.

Initially, Liberty joined them, trailing behind as they skidded down the path to the cove, bargaining with Skye. "I promise I won't kick you if you stay home and play with me."

"Come and play out here instead," Skye said, knowing she could usually avoid her sister's feet anyway and that summer wasn't a time to sit inside.

But rock pools and shells weren't to Liberty's taste. She sat on the sand, back turned toward her sister, glaring at Nicholas when he tried to give her the biggest and fastest crab to race. Eventually, Skye forgot that her sister was there and, hours later, realized Liberty had gone back up to the house to talk to her collection of dolls, who all preferred tea parties to limpets.

One morning, Liberty was particularly annoying on the way down to the beach. "Don't leave me alone," she whined, over and over.

"If you come with us, you won't be alone," Skye reasoned.

So Liberty did, but once on the sand, she shoved a crab down the back of Skye's bathing suit. It nipped Skye in fright.

"You're a beast!" Skye shouted at her sister.

Liberty threw a fistful of sand in Skye's face and burst into tears.

Skye watched Liberty run home. The sand scratched her eyes in the same way the words she'd yelled at her sister scraped her conscience. She would play two games of Snakes and Ladders with Liberty that night, she promised herself.

"Let's go in the cave," she said to Nicholas.

He nodded and followed her in.

They lay on their backs in the darkest, deepest part, where nothing could be seen. They were silent for only a moment before they began to tell stories that couldn't be told out in the light. Nicholas's story was about his father, who had died from "an excess of emotion," whatever that meant. His mother had then suffered an excess of emotion of a different kind, but hers had sent her first to bed and then back to England—where she had lived before her marriage—rather than up into the sky to join her husband.

"So my aunt looks after me now. My mother doesn't go anywhere, except to see your mother for readings," Nicholas finished, and Skye heard in his voice that he hated it: the loss of his father, the vanishing of his mother, and being subject to the custody of his aunt.

The Penroses would care for him, she vowed. But first she needed to tell him who the Penroses were.

"None of the children in town will play with me. Or with Liberty," she said. "It's because my mother tells fortunes." A gust of wind screeched into the cave, forcing more of the truth from Skye's mouth. "And because Liberty and I don't have a father. Not in the way that you don't have a father. We've *never* had one. My mother has never been married. But you're meant to be married if you have a baby."

All her life Skye had been told by sneering adults and jeering children that it was a sin to lose one's father in the way that hers and Liberty's had become lost. To die was heroic; to be merely absent was ungodly.

Nicholas said, "I like that your mother tells fortunes. I like your mother. And you're my friend."

* * *

Not long after, Skye was able to show Nicholas the best thing of all. Early one morning, Vanessa drove them to a grassy paddock that served as an airfield and pointed to a de Havilland Gipsy Moth.

"It's a beautiful day for flying," she said.

"Flying," Nicholas repeated, eyes fixed to the canvas biplane before them.

"You can go first," Skye told him.

"Don't leave me here by myself," Liberty sulked but Skye had no intention of sitting in the car with a sister who hated flying. Instead she ran beside the Moth as it bounced and then leapt into the sky. Nicholas, helmeted and scarfed and jacketed to withstand the chill, waved down at her from the front seat of the open cockpit, and her mother sat at the controls behind.

Then it was Skye's turn. Once the Moth ascended, Skye took over; her mother had started teaching her to fly six months ago. Vanessa's voice gave directions through the Gosport tube that connected front passenger to back, although Skye hardly needed them anymore.

She handled the turn, and then did what she'd seen her mother do hundreds of times before: she flew into the wind, giving the Moth full throttle, then climbed vertically until the plane inclined onto its back and she felt the stomach-roiling thrill of looping the loop.

She heard Vanessa say in a bemused voice, "Let me know if you get into trouble." But the Moth anticipated Skye's every move. At the right moment, she eased off the throttle and adjusted the ailerons to keep herself vertical. The plane arced downward like a gentle dove to complete a perfect circle.

Skye wanted to cartwheel along the wing, looping her own loop, but she'd pushed against her mother's equilibrium enough already. She let Vanessa take the rear controls to land.

As soon as the plane had come to a halt, her mother lifted her out, saying, "I don't know whether to shout at you or to laugh."

"I prefer laughing," Skye said. Then she called to Nicholas, "Did you see me?"

"That was you?" he said admiringly.

"That was most definitely my daughter," Vanessa said. "Trying to show me she's more than ready to handle a takeoff and a landing. Perhaps next year we'll have you looping the loop too, Nicholas."

Nicholas placed both hands on the canvas wing of the plane. "Do you really think I could do that?" he asked.

"I'll teach you," said Skye's mother. "I think you have the right temperament for flying—levelheadedness is actually more important than daring, no matter what Skye thinks. I'm sure you could teach her a thing or two."

"I don't think anybody could teach Skye anything," Nicholas said, whereupon Vanessa laughed, ruffled his hair and said, "Unfortunately I think you might be right."

* * *

All too soon summer was over and school interfered with their days at the beach and their flying lessons, but even school was tolerable now that Skye had Nicholas as her friend. That fact was confirmed at the end of the very first day when they were walking out of the school gates together and Skye heard a gaggle of children hiss their usual taunts: "Witch's daughter! She-devil!"

Skye drew her sister closer as the biggest boy, the butcher's son, knowing that Liberty was the weaker mark, picked up a rock and flung it at her. Skye deflected it with her arm, refusing to wince at the sting and the blood. Liberty started to cry.

Skye was unsurprised when Nicholas turned away from them and toward the taunters. She'd expected that once he saw how despised she was, he would make other friends; those whose lives weren't besmirched by illegitimacy and sorcery.

But Nicholas stood in front of the butcher's son and said, politely, "Legend has it that every time you say the word 'she-devil' in the presence of one, your teeth will turn gray and then fall out."

The butcher's son put his hand up to his mouth to cover the gap of a missing tooth on one side and a graying tooth on the other.

After that, it was accepted that Skye and Nicholas were inseparable friends. And because Nicholas was the smartest kid at school, nobody wanted to risk disbelieving what he'd said.

In the afternoons, they would walk together to Skye's house, where Nicholas would do more schoolwork in the kitchen. The first time, Skye had questioned him about it, telling him she never even bothered to look over her spelling words.

"But don't you want to escape?" he'd asked, then shook his head. "You don't need to. But I need to know I can go anywhere I want to when I'm old enough."

Escape. Skye had dropped into a chair, understanding hitting her forcefully as she realized how much he hated being trapped with an aunt who spared him no love, waiting for his mother to recover. After that, she not only sat beside him and did her spelling words but tackled some mathematics too.

In that way, the year passed quickly by and summer came again. Days were once more spent at the cove, or the airfield with both Skye and Nicholas taking lessons from Vanessa, or exploring the downs and moors behind the house. Occasionally, Skye's mother held weekend house parties and fabulous people descended upon Porthleven, some staying at the house, others cramming into any available room in town. Skye didn't know most of the people, but that didn't matter. The parties were a spectacle, like a sudden summer storm: electric, skin-tingling, alive.

Vanessa would talk Nicholas's aunt into letting him stay the weekend and Skye, Nicholas and Liberty would camp in the garden, having surrendered their rooms to the guests. They'd bathe and dress in the best clothes they owned, and Skye would actually brush her tangled knot of dark brown hair. Then she and Nicholas would slip into the window seat from where they could see everything.

Liberty, who adored the parties, would circle the room, studying the women's clothes, eavesdropping on conversations, staring at people with pleading eyes until they beckoned her over. She would beam and chat—and nobody would ever guess that she was disposed to slipping crabs down people's backs—until the adults bored of her and returned to their grown-up circles. After those parties, Skye would hear her sister reenacting the evening with her dolls; the dark-haired doll called Liberty would always be given the starring role at the center of everyone's devoted attention.

At one such party, a year after Skye first met Nicholas, Vanessa Penrose entered the room later than most of her guests, looking like someone Skye had never met: a woman with curled and shining near-black hair, and the reddest of red lips. She wore her "French dress," as she called it: a cream silk bodice with a deep V-neckline, and a skirt made entirely of ostrich feathers dyed in various shades of cream and gold. The exposed skin of her décolletage was supposed to be partially concealed with a matching scarf but Vanessa never bothered with the scarf. The combined effect of her lustrous hair, glossy lips and the unexpected gold feathers was that Vanessa Penrose spent the whole night dancing.

There was one man who came to every party and who was always allocated more than his fair share of dances with Skye's mother. Skye watched Vanessa smile at him—a smile unlike that which she bestowed upon her daughters or any of her other guests. They danced beautifully, like movie stars, and even Liberty sat quietly, entranced by their magnificent mother.

The man's lips whispered against Vanessa's ear. Skye didn't want to watch anymore. Liberty had leaned her head against the wall and her eyelids drooped so Skye tucked a blanket over her legs. Then she led Nicholas outside, sighing.

"I wish I could dance like that," she said.

"I can show you."

"You can dance?"

He shrugged. "My parents made me learn. They said all gentlemen danced."

Skye laughed. "If you're a gentleman, you'll need a lady to dance with. We both know that, according to the town of Porthleven, the Penrose women aren't ladies."

"I think you are."

He bowed to her with a flourish and a grin, which made her feel less awkward. He didn't tease her for her clumsiness but moved them both through the flawless full-moon night, showing her what to do. In accompaniment, silver ribbons of light waltzed across the sea below them.

"We'll have to do this again when we're older," Skye said, once she had the basics under control. "The clifftop deserves a more splendid dress." She indicated her white dress, which was simple and clean but lacked the panache of gold ostrich feathers.

"What if we're not friends by then?" Nicholas asked, stopping suddenly.

Skye just missed squashing his foot. "Why wouldn't we be?" She stood beside him, both of them facing out to the ocean.

"My aunt says that we'll go back to New York soon. I have to go to school there, the same school my father went to. We'll leave as soon as my mother's better."

"Will she get better?" Skye asked. She only saw Nicholas's mother when she came to the house for Vanessa's prophecies and she always seemed wraith-like; a creature who might simply slip into the sparkling waves and disappear.

"I don't know," Nicholas said.

It was the first time Skye had ever seen him hesitate. She took his hand and squeezed it. "You'll stay here forever," she said. After all, she had a mother who told the future so she could claim some authority on this.

"I hope so."

TWO

The following weekend they explored the moors rather than going down to the cove as the wind had blown up into a tempest, threatening to pick up slightly built Skye and carry her away. The moors stretched on uninterrupted for almost half a mile behind Skye's house and she and Nicholas tramped for longer than they normally would, discovering a broken wall at the far boundary of Vanessa Penrose's land.

Skye scaled the wall and stood atop it, reciting lines from *A Midsummer Night's Dream*, a play they'd studied at school. As she was declaiming Hermia's angst at Lysander's apparent betrayal—*O me! you juggler! you canker-blossom! / You thief of love! What, have you come by night / And stolen my love's heart from him?*—and reveling in the sound of the canker-blossom insult, resolving to use it with Liberty the next time they argued, she fell off the wall and over the other side.

Luckily she landed in a thicket of overgrown bushes but was still badly winded.

Nicholas's face appeared at the top of the wall and he started laughing. "That's the first time I've ever seen you speechless."

She managed a smile and rasped, "Are you coming over?"

He lowered himself down to land beside her.

As Skye sat up, she realized that before them stood a lost garden; a place that time and overgrowth had hidden from the world. If there was a house to which the garden belonged, it was out of sight, which meant there was no chance of them being discovered.

A statue of a giant-sized woman lay on the ground in front of them, but she hadn't fallen there; she'd been designed in repose, one hand resting beside her sleeping face. Moss and leaves clothed her body, and her hair was a tangle of ferns. She was possibly the most beautiful thing Skye had ever seen.

"She looks like you when you sleep," Nicholas said unexpectedly.

Skye shook her head. Nicholas had seen her asleep when they shared the tent with Liberty on the night of the party but the very inelegant Skye was nothing like this bewitching stone maid lost forever in a lovely dream.

Then her attention was caught by something beyond the statue: a lake, almost oceanic in size, over which stretched a rope bridge. The water was sheltered by a drapery of branches that looked to be fishing for gold.

Skye raced over and placed her foot onto the bridge. The rope creaked; it obviously hadn't been used for some time. "What do you think is at the other end?" she asked, avoiding the obvious question: *Is it safe?*

"The other side of the sky," Nicholas answered, and Skye smiled.

They'd found a hidden world atop their own; a world without sick mothers and kicking sisters and whispering townsfolk and a school in New York, beckoning.

They were halfway across the bridge when it happened.

Skye heard a tearing sound and whipped around to see the rope beneath Nicholas's feet cleave apart. He plunged down, one hand grasping the rope as he fell. Skye did the same as the entire floor of the bridge disintegrated.

Luckily the sides of the bridge remained intact, giving them something to cling onto. Their legs were in the water, their torsos and heads above it.

"We'll have to jump in," Skye said prosaically, as if her heart weren't thudding faster than the Moth's propeller at takeoff. "We'll just pretend it's the sea, rather than slime." She cast her eyes over the thick layer of green muck that hid who knew what horrors beneath.

Nicholas's face was pale, his knuckles whiter than bone. And then he said it. "I can't swim."

Her insides sank into the water. "Of course you can. I've seen you."

Only then did she realize that no, she hadn't ever seen Nicholas swim. Even though they spent so much time at the cove, he was always engrossed in the rock pools when she dived out into the waves. She'd seen him in the water up to his knees, but never any farther than that.

"I'm going to fall in," he said.

Skye heard fear in his voice for the first time ever. So she did the only thing possible. She let go, dropping into the water, keeping her mouth firmly closed.

"You can go hand over hand along the side ropes until you can stand," she said firmly, as if she were certain it would work. "It'll hurt and you'll get blisters, but it's the only way. I'll swim beside you."

She didn't mention the unmistakable dangers.

Nicholas began to move as if he were swinging himself across the climbing frame in the school playground. He was good at that, so he'd be good at this too, Skye reasoned. She swam beside him just as she'd promised, her eyes fastened to his, brown locked with blue, wanting him to know that he could do it. His gaze assured her that he believed her.

They were still a way from the shore when he began to wince; the rope was tearing away the skin on his palms. Skye stretched down with one leg but couldn't feel the bottom.

"Not much farther," she said, and he kept going, hand over hand, not stopping to catch his breath even though he must have been exhausted and in agony.

Of all the people Skye knew, Nicholas was the one who could do this. Liberty wouldn't; and nobody from school had the stomach for it. Perhaps not even Skye herself. But Nicholas woke up each day in a house without love and, despite that, was the best friend Skye had ever had. If he could endure that kind of pain, he might just make it to shallow water before he reached his limits.

Soon Skye realized that the sandy bottom wasn't far from her feet. "You can let go now," she said with relief. "Then bounce along like you're on a pogo stick. It'll keep your mouth above water."

He dropped the instant she spoke. Being taller than her, he only had to bounce a few times before he could walk. Soon they were out of the lake, where they fell panting onto the bank.

"I don't know why I'm out of breath," Skye said at last, turning her head to look at Nicholas. "How are your hands?" He held them up and she grimaced. "We're going to be in so much trouble."

But Nicholas just smiled. "At least now I can ask you the thing I've been wanting to ask since last summer. Can you teach me to swim?"

"Lessons start tomorrow," Skye said decisively. "Whoever heard of a person who can dance but not swim?"

"In New York one dances," he said, putting on a posh voice so she relaxed into a smile. "In Cornwall, we swim. I'm glad I'm in Cornwall."

"Me too," she said. Then, "Why didn't you tell me?"

He inspected the chafing on his palms. "I thought you'd think I was an idiot."

"An idiot would have been so scared they'd have fallen in and drowned. I never thought you'd do that."

His mouth turned up and Skye felt her heart glow in the sunshine of his rare and exceptional smile.

She stood up. "We'd better get my mum to dress your hands. We'll swim tomorrow."

Fortunately, Vanessa Penrose could be relied upon not to tell her daughter off as long as she was honest. All she said was, "You can't teach Nicholas to swim, Skye. I'll take him to the beach each morning for half an hour. You can stay at the house and mind your sister. I'll also tell Nicholas's aunt that he scraped his hands while chivalrously chopping logs for me, rather than by rescuing himself from a lake in a place where you probably shouldn't have been. I know it's futile asking you both not to go back there, but I will ask you not to return until I'm satisfied Nicholas can swim well enough to tackle the lake, should he chance to find himself in it again."

They spent the rest of that afternoon inside, resting Nicholas's hands, listening through the wall to Vanessa with her clients.

The last client of the day was Nicholas's mother and, when she arrived with his aunt, Nicholas jumped up. "Let's go for a walk," he said.

"Don't you want to know your mother's future?" Skye asked.

He shook his head.

Skye frowned. If they stayed to listen, then all might be revealed about his mother's recovery. Skye hoped, on the one hand, that she would never recover because then Nicholas wouldn't go to New York. On the other hand, she hoped Mrs. Crawford would recover this very day because his mother was the only thing Nicholas never talked about. Skye knew, in her own childish way, that behind that reticence lay a deep hurt.

So she went for a walk with him down to the cove until his aunt appeared at the top of the cliff, hands on her hips, glaring at him and his bandaged hands and saying, "I did not agree to being your nurse."

Skye watched Nicholas leave with the two women, his mother walking alongside but saying nothing, not defending her son from his aunt's tongue, just smiling beatifically as if she'd been blessed.

"Will you tell me my future? And Nicholas his?" Skye asked her mother when she returned to the house.

Vanessa shivered. "Not ever, Skye. So you needn't ask me again."

"But why?"

"I can't tell you anything you don't already have inside you. The future isn't a promise yet to be kept. It's an act waiting to begin. Perhaps it's already begun."

Skye shivered too. It had never before frightened her, this gift her mother supposedly had for looking into what hadn't yet happened and placing it before those who asked, like a fingernail-sized cowrie shell, its pearly lips whispering its secrets.

* * *

Another year passed. Skye turned fourteen and began to bleed every month. Her legs lengthened, her chest and hips curved, and the only places she felt at home were in the sea, swimming, or in the sky, flying.

She swam with Nicholas all the time now. And she began to take the Moth up on her own. Soon Nicholas did too. More parties were held, and Skye's mother continued to dance with the man who whispered in her ear.

Liberty's kicks became more accurate and bruising until she began to spend less time with Skye and Nicholas, rarely asking Skye not to leave her alone anymore. She only tagged along when they visited the lost garden. Even there, she mostly left them to themselves, preferring to sit and stare at the stone maid, entranced, wearing the same dreamy look in her eyes as when she watched Vanessa dance.

Once, Skye asked her what she was thinking. Liberty shrugged and said, "Life," as if it were obvious.

Rather than risk stirring Liberty's temper by saying what she thought—*life's in the garden or in the cove, not in a statue*—Skye shrugged too and joined Nicholas by the lake.

By now, Nicholas was fifteen and had been Skye's friend for four years but she felt as if she'd known him forever. She couldn't remember a time when he hadn't been the most fundamental thing in her life; her ocean and sky.

"Whenever I think of you, I think of the color blue," he said to her in a peculiar voice as they walked back to her house after the last day of school, ready for another long summer. "Water and air."

She smiled, accepting it as a compliment of the best kind. Then she saw his face and she stopped still.

"I'm going to New York tomorrow," he said miserably. "My aunt told me at breakfast. It's only for six weeks though. I have to take a test for school."

Six weeks. It might as well be a year. All the things she'd imagined they'd do together over summer vanished, like gulls taking off for a long migration.

Skye kicked at the ground, scraping the black from her shoe. The sun vanished, making manifest the dark shadow already cast by tomorrow.

"Come back," she said, suddenly afraid.

"I promise," he told her.

Skye watched him go, like she had the day she'd met him, and, just like that day, he turned back to wave before he moved out of sight. Even though she was far too old for any such thing, Skye flipped into a cartwheel as if to say: this doesn't change anything.

She tried to fly every day of the next month; she'd never been in a plane with Nicholas, so she didn't feel his absence so acutely in the sky. But as her mother couldn't take her to the airfield every day, she bought Skye a bicycle, and Skye cycled there instead. Even though she could fly almost as well as her mother, neither of them was sure what the other pilots would say if they found out that Vanessa had let her fly alone at age fourteen, although there were no rules to prevent her. So Skye, as tall as her mother now, wore Vanessa's helmet and goggles and pretended to be her; and Vanessa, as always, trusted Skye to stay within her limits.

But it was a wet and foggy summer, as if the sky were crying for the temporarily severed friendship, and Skye couldn't fly when visibility was poor. She spent many a day curled up on the window seat, scowling at the weather.

Liberty wanted Skye to sit with her on the floor, ear pressed to the wall, and eavesdrop on the futures of Vanessa's clients. Skye refused. What right did anyone else have to a future when all Skye had was this rainy, hazy present? Liberty, predictably, tried to pinch her sister in retaliation but then changed tactics and gazed unblinking at Skye, which was much more irritating than physical violence.

"Liberty, can you fill the wood basket," Vanessa said, after catching her in the act.

"Why do I have to do it?" Liberty complained.

"Skye filled it yesterday."

Liberty dispatched, Vanessa made Skye a cup of sweet, milky tea.

"Nicholas's father was a very wealthy man," she said as she measured tea leaves into the pot. "Nicholas will inherit his business when he is of age, and I think he'll soon be groomed to take it over."

"What?" Skye said, attention absolutely caught.

"His mother's condition has, at last, been declared untreatable and his aunt feels it's time to focus on Nicholas. She wants him to be properly schooled, and to reestablish herself in New York. With Nicholas's mother so ill, his aunt becomes, in effect, his mother. He must do as she says."

"Why didn't you tell me this before?"

Her mother smiled. "I was trying to put off the future. But of course it's the destiny Nicholas has always had in him. He's fifteen now. An age when birthright and tradition matter."

Skye felt her eyes tear up. At the same moment, Liberty returned with the wood. She gaped at Skye, dropped the basket on the floor and said, "I won't stare at you again. I promise."

Skye swiped her eyes. "I'm not crying because of you."

Liberty scuttled over and sat beside her in the window seat, and Skye felt a wave of affection for her sister who, despite having tempests to rival those of a Cornish winter, could occasionally show such kindness too.

"He said he'd come back," Skye told her mother.

"I don't know that he will, Skye."

"Nicholas *never* lies."

Her mother sat at the table then, an unrecognizable expression altering the familiar features of her face.

Skye clutched Liberty's hand. Liberty's fingers closed over hers.

Their mother's mouth twitched strangely when she saw their joined hands. "I thought to send you to France, to stay with your aunt for six months or so," she said suddenly. "You could go to school there. Learn all the things I'm not very good at teaching, but which she excels at." Vanessa leaned over and fingered Skye's unkempt hair. "I've never cared about things like hairdos and wealthy families, but now, looking at your face, I think that perhaps I do."

"I don't want to go to France," Skye said.

Liberty cuddled in closer.

They'd only met their "aunt" twice before, when they'd been to France as children. But as Vanessa had never actually married Skye and Liberty's father, this woman in France wasn't really bound to them. Skye shook her head.

"And," Vanessa continued, "I'm tired of seeing everyone's future and doing nothing about my own—one of the few futures, like yours, I will never foretell. I'd like to do what Amy Johnson did and fly to Australia. Just take off and go. I want to see if I have anything more to me. Do you understand?"

"I'll go with you," Skye said.

"I want you to look after Liberty for me. If you stay here in Cornwall without Nicholas, you'll only miss him all the more."

"But why fly to Australia?" Skye demanded.

"I need to know that I can. I once knew Amy. I was a better flier than her. But she's just claimed a record to Moscow, and to Cape Town. What have I claimed?"

Skye felt it then: pain of a kind she'd never known as she understood that her mother's life in Cornwall, with its occasional parties and two daughters, had its own shadow—a restlessness, a void, an unfilled space.

"But . . ." Skye couldn't articulate what she wanted to say. "I thought it would be like this forever," she managed eventually.

"You can't look for cowrie shells forever, Skye."

* * *

Six weeks after Nicholas had left, Skye was surprised one morning to see a man picking his way down the path to her cove. Only when the man reached the sand did Skye realize it was Nicholas.

How had six weeks wreaked such change? He was taller, broader, and his face had hardened, all traces of the boy vanished. She stood still, the water taunting her ankles, and folded her arms across her chest.

"Let's sit in the cave," she said when he was close enough to hear her.

He nodded and followed her to the cave, where she lay on her back in the darkness and he did the same beside her.

"I start school in New York next week," he said, his voice deeper now, masculine. "My aunt was going to have someone pack up the house here, but I threw a Liberty-sized tantrum and convinced her to come back for our things."

"Well, if you copied Liberty, I'm not surprised you won," Skye said, keeping a smile on her face so it would show in her voice.

The sounds of their shared childhood filled the cave: the ceaseless roll of the ocean toward the sand, the violent unfurling of water, the crash as it spilled. The wind blew in a squall of protest: this couldn't be happening. Salt water dripped silently over Skye's cheeks, so many tears it was a wonder she didn't drown in them.

For a time, neither spoke. They lay on their backs, side by side, hands so close she could feel the electricity of his body buzz from his fingers and into hers. She withdrew her hand from the sand and made a circle with her thumb and forefinger, closing one eye so she could focus through the makeshift ring.

"When I did that cartwheel on the pier in front of you it was just one tiny moment. But now . . ." She faltered, then flung her arms apart, as wide as they could go. "This moment is too big. It's so big that I can't see all of it and I don't want to feel any of it. It's too big," she repeated.

She heard a soft thud, as if a cartwheeling girl had toppled to the sand right beside them. Their heads moved in unison toward the sound, but there was nothing there except a memory.

"I don't want to go," Nicholas said quietly.

Skye sat up, leaned over and gave Nicholas a hug that was ferocious and quite possibly painful. His arms closed around her too, and she felt that his cheeks were wet, like hers. Then she scrambled to her feet and ran away, feeling something rip against her chest, imagining that in her tear-blindness she must have scraped against one of the walls of the cave.

She ran fast, feet beating against the sand, up to the house and then over the moor beyond. Finally, at the top of the hill, she stopped and sank to the ground. From up here she could see everything, but she couldn't see Nicholas and that was how it would be from now on.

She touched her chest but found no graze from the rocks, yet it still hurt more than anything ever had.

* * *

Aunt Sophie was as vivacious as Vanessa, but more effusive in her affections: hugs and kisses ended her sentences, rather than periods. She was the most elegant creature Skye had ever seen, always dressed in Schiaparelli or Poiret. Liberty watched her with delighted eyes and even Skye, sitting in her bedroom at the apartment in Passy—the sixteenth arrondissement near the Bois de Boulogne—couldn't help but try to discipline her hair so it more closely approximated the lustrous upsweep of her aunt's chestnut coiffure. But that was a minor transformation compared to everything else that happened in Paris.

Liberty was the first thing to change. She forgot to kick Skye. She smiled. She woke up in the morning eager to go to school. Rather than staying inside all weekend, Liberty went to visit her new friends and ate ice cream with them while strolling through the Jardin du Ranelagh. She became a cool, elegant Parisienne, not unlike their Aunt Sophie.

Skye observed this metamorphosis with openmouthed astonishment.

The second thing to change was Nicholas. Skye wrote to him almost every day. He never replied.

She'd been wrong when she'd thought, atop the cliff on the last day she'd seen him, that her chest couldn't hurt more than it did in that moment. That pain had been a mere twinge. What she felt now, each day when she searched through the mail and found nothing, was a skewering—deep and raw.

Skye was the one who stayed inside now, lonely.

And then one terrible letter arrived, addressed to her. It came during the All Saints' Holiday when their aunt had taken Liberty and Skye on the train to Deauville in the hopes that being near the sea might cheer Skye up.

As soon as Skye stepped onto the beach, the clouds devoured the sun. The air gathered itself into such a furious wind that waves crested like phantoms, driving away the beachgoers until Skye was the only one left there, shivering, her aunt and Liberty urging her to come away.

She didn't know what was wrong, just that something was. The letter waiting for them on the hall stand when they returned confirmed Skye's premonition. Cloud, the kind that blanketed the sky and swallowed planes, had taken Vanessa Penrose. She was never coming back.

Every night thereafter, when Skye closed her eyes, she saw her mother plunging downward into brutal absence. She crawled into Liberty's bed, where they lay on their backs with their eyes wide open until sleep dragged them away into nightmares. They would wake crying, Skye hiding her tears in order to console her sister.

That all changed the day Skye resumed her flying lessons. Up in the air, she felt her mother all around her, even heard Vanessa's voice whispering through the Gosport tube: *I love you, Skye*.

Skye climbed into her sister's bed that night impatient to tell her what had happened, eager to persuade Liberty to come flying with her so that Liberty could hear it too. Liberty shoved Skye off the mattress and onto the floor.

"What was that for?" Skye demanded, rubbing the spot where her head had cracked against the wood.

"You can't come in here again until you give up flying," Liberty snapped.

"I'm not giving up flying," Skye said emphatically. "Let me show you—"

"Then get out."

Of everything Liberty had ever done to Skye—the kicks and pinches and stares and moans—those words hurt the most. She got up off the floor, stormed out of the room and went to sleep in her own bed.

After that, they returned to spending most of their time apart, Skye at the flying club and Liberty with friends who preferred gossip to airplanes. The year Skye turned eighteen, she told Liberty she was leaving Paris and returning to Cornwall.

Liberty turned into a demon.

"This is our home, Skye," Liberty screamed, face red, fists clenched.

"This is an apartment in Paris. Not home," Skye said quietly, trying to keep calm, expecting Liberty would have her tantrum and then settle down.

Instead Liberty flew down the hall, threw open their aunt's bedroom door and began to bellow at the top of her voice, demanding that Sophie force Skye to stay in Paris, that she fulfill her promise to Vanessa Penrose to look after Skye and Liberty. Liberty raged all night, relentless, hurling accusations and loathing at Skye in equal measure until, soon before dawn, sick to her stomach with fear that she might actually have driven her sister mad, Skye relented and said, "I won't go."

Liberty didn't say thank you, just returned to her room, fell into bed, and slept.

Skye lay on her own bed and cried until her eyes were so swollen she could no longer see, until the collar of her dress was so damp with tears she could wring her heartache out of it. The one thing she most wanted—to return to the cove in Cornwall—had just been taken from her.

She didn't get out of bed until the following day. Liberty spoke not a word to her. That night, when Skye returned to her room, her bed was soaking, as if someone had poured a jug of water onto it. She slept on the sofa.

The next day, the tires of Skye's bike were punctured so she couldn't cycle to the airfield. Liberty smiled at her over breakfast.

The following week, the two assignments Skye had completed for university—where she was studying history and languages—went missing before she could submit them and she had to stay up all night redoing them. Liberty invited a friend over and they laughed and talked so loudly in the room next door to Skye's that she could hardly concentrate.

One month later, after Skye had fixed the punctures in her bicycle tires, she found them slashed through with a knife.

"Oh dear. Not again," Liberty said when Skye pointed out the damage.

They had reverted back to their nine-and ten-year-old selves, except the crabs down the backs of bathing suits had become something crueler.

The day Liberty turned eighteen, Skye wrote a note to her aunt and, while Liberty was out, she collected her things in a suitcase, walked to the train station, and left for England.

PART TWO
KAT

THREE

CORNWALL, JUNE 2012

Kat's rental car bumped along a track that looked as if it had never welcomed a motor vehicle in its life, her destination her grandmother's uninhabited cottage. It sat atop the cliff, proudly unloved, wind, sea spray and gulls its only friends: banished to the very edge of the world. The downs behind concealed any neighboring properties which were, in any case, at least half a mile away.

The track deteriorated further so Kat parked, stepped out and stumbled as the wind grasped her, pushing her back; for a moment she thought she heard it hiss that she shouldn't be there. She rubbed her arms, regretting both her journey and the very Australian summer dress she'd chosen.

She hurried onto the porch, where the boards complained beneath her feet. She inserted the key in the lock and jiggled the door until it gave way. The smell of decades of neglect hurtled toward her, winding her. What had she just unfettered?

Don't be silly, she chided herself, first in her head and then aloud, hoping to make the unsettled history retreat and the present reassert itself.

Kat pressed on into the kitchen, which looked out across a magnificent expanse of wild sea. The window seat in the sitting room beckoned, and she thought she might sit there, despite the dust, and have a cup of tea. But she discovered that the kettle was the old-fashioned sort that needed to be heated on the stovetop, and the stove was ancient and fueled only by wood. Better to get on with what Margaux, her grandmother, had rather unexpectedly asked of her.

Kat traveled to Europe from Sydney a couple of times a year to meet with fashion conservation colleagues at the Victoria and Albert Museum, and to deliver papers at conferences and symposiums—just as she had done this past week—but she had never made a trip to Cornwall to look in on this house. Because she hadn't known it existed until three days ago.

Margaux had called her in London and told her that the caretaker in nearby Porthleven, who apparently checked the house regularly, had grown too old and ill to do anything for months. Would Kat mind taking a look?

Kat had been so dumbfounded at the idea of her grandmother owning a Cornish cottage that she had spluttered inarticulate and half-started sentences into the phone, extracting very little information beyond the fact it had been purchased decades ago, and the location of the key. Now, she felt that same dumbfoundedness fix her in place in the parlor as she realized the house was fully furnished and fitted out—but like a museum.

Everything around her was from the 1920s and early 1930s, as if the occupants had gone out for the day, intending to come back, but had somewhere been lost forever. An Art Deco red celluloid hair-comb sparkling with rhinestones; a fantastic enamel clothes brush in sea green; paste rings tumbling out of a case; sheet music on the piano waiting to be played. Kat stroked the horn of the gramophone affectionately; marveled at the delicacy of a cloisonné pendant on a crimped brass chain; blew a flurry of dust off a lovely collection of glass kerosene finger lamps in various shades of green. Everything laid out, ready for a moment in history that had, perhaps, mattered to someone.

She briefly imagined lighting the lamps, placing a recording on the gramophone, securing the pendant around her neck and returning to a time long ago when she hadn't made any mistakes and could relive the past few years with the benefit of wisdom. Something made her shiver, as if just thinking of enkindling the items around her had made the ghosts stir. Why had those ghosts run away? she wondered. And why had Margaux bought this place that was more mausoleum than home?

Kat made herself move into the next room, opening and shutting cupboards and checking inside drawers. She found no evidence of animal habitation and only a few spiders, most long dead, and was soon drawn back into a vortex of questions. Why keep a cottage that was never used? Had her grandmother ever visited? Certainly not in the thirty-nine years Kat had been alive. She should, Kat reasoned, persuade her grandmother to sell it.

She was thinking about real estate agents and international removals when she reached the very last bedroom, empty of everything except a couple of wardrobes. She opened the door of one and a blaze of bright red caught her eye, followed by a shimmer of pink, a beam of sunflower-yellow. Slowly, she reached in. Her hand touched fabric. Expensive fabric: a froth of tulle, a glittering of sequins, the purr of velvet.

She lifted down one of the hangers and what unraveled before her was, quite simply, astonishing. A long red dress—no, a gown— strapless, the bodice shaped to fit perfectly over the swell of one's breasts, the waist nipped in, an homage to the New Look. Tumbling down from the narrow waistline was a skirt that had a life of its own; a skirt that wanted to dance, to spin around and around in a wild and romantic rush of red. Her right hand stroked the silk, as soft as newly born skin beneath her fingers.

Impulse made Kat hold the dress up against her body as if she were contemplating buying it from a store. She turned to face the mirror and was stunned. Even though she hadn't yet stepped inside the dress, she was no longer Kat. She was the woman she had always meant to be, the woman she'd forgotten to become beneath the demands of working full-time and having two children and divorcing one husband.

Then she glimpsed the tag inside: *Printemps-Été 2012 Christian Dior Paris* and a series of numbers. Kat was holding an haute couture gown, which was what she'd suspected when she first saw it. But why—and how—did her grandmother have a Dior couture gown hidden in the wardrobe of a house Kat had never known she owned?

Kat pulled out more hangers. Each bore something almost as remarkable as the red gown. A dress made from silk rainbows—Kat knew it was called Hellebore—from Galliano's 1995 collection for Dior. A fabulously fun pink dress, strapless like the red, but with a mass of fabric at the back shaped into a flower-like bustle.

Kat stopped taking garments out of the wardrobes and instead flicked through them. They were mostly dresses, but also some suits, skirts and jackets, moving from the easily recognizable 1950s fit-and-flare silhouette to the shorter skirts of the sixties, the fluidity of the seventies, the just-reined-in garishness of the eighties, the glitz of the nineties, and then on to the classically modern styles like the red gown she had first held. Every piece had a numbered Christian Dior label stitched into its back.

There was one more gown that had her stretching up to the rack, to bring it down and hold it against her body. She had never seen anything like it. A dress of brilliant azure blue, as close to the color of the sea outside as anything man-made could ever be, and with the same prismatic quality, as if the sun sparkled on the rippling skirt even inside this dark room. It was made from an exuberance of silk and tulle, the lavishness of both fabric and color declaring that this dress was epoch-making, one of a kind—a gown her grandmother could never afford and would never have the occasion to wear. It was almost too magnificent for a princess.

Kat sat down on the bed, shut her eyes, then opened them slowly. The dresses were still there. She reached into her pocket, withdrew her phone and dialed Margaux's number. The call rang on and on, unanswered. She tried again. Nothing.

So she stood up, laid each dress on the bed one by one—sixty-five in total—and photographed them like the impartial and rational fashion conservator she was.

It was late when she finished. She locked the house, returned to her car, expelled a long breath and was unable to banish the questions any longer. Why were the dresses there? And had her grandmother intended for Kat to find them?

PART THREE
SKYE

They knew, if they stopped to think about it, that they were operating at the very limit of what society could tolerate even in war. But they weren't much interested in society either, or . . . their place in it, and they were so used to being unusual that anything else would have been . . . soul-destroyingly dull.

—Giles Whittell, *Spitfire Women of World War II*

FOUR

L unch in Paris with a melange of British and French pilots turned into dinner in Paris, as well as too much champagne.

"We'll have to stay the night," Skye said as the sun hid itself away and the sky became too dark to fly through.

"We will," Rose agreed, clinking her glass against Skye's and then against the glasses of the others at the table.

Valentin, a Parisian, offered a toast: "To peace. And may Monsieur Adolf give himself a deadly apoplexy from too much vigorous Nazi saluting."

Everyone laughed and drank to it so enthusiastically that Rose gestured to the waiter for yet more champagne. And so they drank their fears about Hitler's ruthless and bloodless purloining of Europe into submission, and Valentin draped his arm over Skye's shoulders as she entertained them all with stories of the acts she performed in the flying circus in England each summer, acts that helped pay her bills.

"The anticipation of a dreadful accident is what brings people to the circus," she told them. "I can feel them holding their breath every time I turn the plane over. They want a sensational story to share at the pub: that they were there when the sky let go of the plane and it fell to the ground"—she let her hands fly up into the air, mimicking an explosion—"and the lady inside died a tragic death." She smote her hand dramatically across her forehead. "I never oblige them, of course."

Laughter and glasses were raised once more, toasting the crowds Skye had disappointed by living through her aerobatics.

"I hear you can wing-walk," Valentin said.

"She made a jolly good display of it at last year's Magyar Pilots' Picnic," Rose said, referring to the annual gathering of pilots just outside Budapest which she and Skye regularly attended for more uproarious lunches.

"I couldn't go to that one," Valentin said regretfully. "I was doing my military service. You must need extraordinary balance for such a thing."

"And damn-fool pluck," Rose added.

"Or an 'incurable reckless streak' and 'a lack of concern for keeping her head attached to her neck.' That last one's my favorite," Skye said, accepting the cigarette Valentin passed her. "The blue bloods at the Civil Air Guard wrote all that and more into a report about my suitability to instruct for them. Luckily there are so few qualified instructors in England, and pilots are needed so desperately to bolster the RAF in case of war, that they employed me anyway in spite of my careless attitude toward my body parts."

"To Skye's head," Valentin said, raising his glass. "Long may it be attached to her neck."

Skye laughed and joined in the new toast.

For it didn't matter a bit to anyone at the table that Skye was the least wealthy flier there and possibly in England too. Her pilot friends were a group of the very early fliers who flew for love rather than because it had lately become an exclusive and voguish pursuit. They were too raffishly bohemian to ever mention money and were more than happy to pay for the champagne at this impromptu lunch that

Rose had organized just yesterday. Skye was lucky to have inherited her plane from her mother and could thus fly all over Europe with these people, to Cairo too, and even South Africa once. So long as she took up the opportunities that presented themselves to earn money during the flying circus season in England, or instructing for the Civil Air Guard, which she would do again on Monday after she'd slept off her Parisian all-nighter, she'd been able to keep her little plane airworthy and herself fed and clothed.

Midnight approached and some of the party began to drift away.

"My apartment is nearby," Valentin whispered to Skye.

She considered his invitation, but she hadn't drunk so much champagne that she believed indulging in a meaningless physical encounter with a charming Parisian would be a balm against the threat of war. So she refused, and Rose refused a similar invitation from the man at her side, but they both offered the consolation prize of dancing to the music of Django Reinhardt at a jazz club off Rue Pigalle. There, Skye twined her arms around Valentin's neck and he wrapped his around her waist and she let him kiss her, because sometimes it was nice to have the kind of casual intimacy that came without the prospect of heartache.

The night turned into a perfect Parisian dawn, where rain cascaded like velvet from the sky but the sun shone through too, arcing a double rainbow over the Sacré-Coeur. Surely it was a promise of a future without warfare—except that Valentin pointed to the morning newspaper and its headline that read: *Hitler Invades Poland*. The rainbow fell from the sky.

The drive to the airfield was silent. Until Rose said, "I feel as if today is a day for grand gestures."

"It is," Skye agreed, and she let Rose take the front seat in the Moth while she took the rear. After they'd leveled out, Skye climbed onto the wing and proceeded to perform the stunt they'd spoken of at lunch: wing-walking.

She saw the open and gasping mouths of Valentin and the others as Rose flew in low enough to show them that yes, Skye was walking along the wing of the plane, her cerulean scarf streaming behind her and her hair flying too. She flipped into a simple handstand—she'd always wanted to cartwheel on the wing, but even she wasn't quite daredevil enough for that—then waved to her friends on the ground.

They came in to land, and Valentin, who really was exceptionally charming and handsome, kissed her goodbye. Skye promised nothing in the way of correspondence—Nicholas had cured her of that.

Back in the air, she waggled her wings at Rose and the others lined up for takeoff in their newer and faster planes, before soaring upward and away, propelled by a tailwind and laughter and possibly still a few bubbles of champagne, trying hard to forget the headline in the newspaper.

But she could no longer ignore it once she landed at the flying club outside London where she taught cocky young men to fly in readiness to join a vastly undermanned and desperate RAF. She parked the Moth in its usual place and climbed out to find Ted, one of her pupils, waiting for her.

"It's over," he said.

"What is?" Skye asked.

"Civilian flying. It's banned after tomorrow. The Civil Air Guard's being disbanded too. A declaration of war is likely any day, and everyone's grounded, unless you're an RAF pilot. They now own the skies."

Ted's words made Skye stagger backward, as if a plane had run right through her. She closed her eyes. *Everyone's grounded, unless you're an RAF pilot.* As a woman, she could never be an RAF pilot. Which meant it really was over.

* * *

Two days later, determined to prove Ted wrong, Skye dressed in her most demure navy suit, hoping the dramatically puffed sleeves, nipped waist and flared peplum wouldn't be considered too modish for an earnest pilot like herself. She walked through an anxious London, where everyone seemed to be searching the skies for signs of the war they were supposedly engaged in, but the only evidence Skye could see was the closed cinemas, the absence of children—they'd all been exiled to the countryside—and the red pillarboxes with yellow squares painted on them to detect poisonous gases.

When she arrived at the Air Ministry, she explained her flying experience to the young man before her.

"Join the WAAF," he said. "Women's Auxiliary Air Force."

"That sounds perfect," Skye said. "Will I be instructing? Or flying—"

The man interrupted. "The WAAF don't fly. They pack parachutes and monitor aircraft movements. Or chauffeur the pilots. You'd be good at that," he said, a suggestive glint in his eyes. "In a car," he added, as if he needed to underscore the fact that she was bound to earth.

"I've never learned to drive," Skye said flatly.

She visited the Air Ministry every day for a fortnight. Each day, the same man, or sometimes a different man, told her the same thing. At the end of two weeks, she came to a halt in the ministry's foyer at the sudden and painful understanding that she would never be allowed to fly.

Her cerulean scarf sagged from her neck. She made herself walk back to the desk. "May I have the application form for the WAAF, please?"

The man smirked. "They urgently need typists for the typing pool."

Skye pictured herself stuck inside a cavernous room with a hundred other women, their typewriters clacking out the frustrations hidden behind their red-lipsticked smiles. She left London then, unwilling to type her way through a war.

Was this the future her mother hadn't wanted to tell her? That war would come and men would die; and Skye would too, from the inside, cobwebbing over like her grounded plane.

* * *

In the quiet of Cornwall, she would be able to think about what to do. Skye caught the train to Helston and the bus to Porthleven and walked up the path from the village to the cottage. It was her legacy from her mother, along with the Moth, an estrangement from Liberty and enough years in France that Skye had become as close to a Frenchwoman as one born elsewhere could possibly be. Even now the accent clung to Skye's words.

Atop the cliff, she stared out over the sea. It was white today, bridal, lace frill after lace frill coursing down from the horizon. The sound of a motorcar made her turn around and as soon as she realized the driver was Pauline Gower, Skye cursed herself for not having thought of her sooner. Of course Pauline would know if there was any chance at all of Skye or any other woman flying while this strange war vacillated on with hardly a bullet fired.

Skye and Pauline had flown together during Skye's first season in Tom Campbell Black's Air Display. Next to Amy Johnson and perhaps Skye herself, Pauline was one of the most experienced female pilots in the country. Her father was also an MP, which meant Pauline knew everyone who mattered and, as a consequence, knew *about* everything that mattered. She was like Rose—a blue blood who couldn't have cared less that Skye's blood had no blue in it at all.

Pauline climbed out of the car and smiled at Skye. "I expect you're the annoying woman who won't leave the chaps at the Air Ministry alone?"

Skye grimaced. "Yes, that's me." She led Pauline to the old swing seat on the porch that looked across to France. "I've spent the past year at the Civil Air Guard reciting my number of hours' flying experience to the men I was supposed to be teaching, men who refused to go up with me because I was a 'girl.' I didn't let it get to me because the greater good of them learning to fly was more important. The ones who did submit to going up with me behaved as if an hour together in the cockpit gave them permission to inspect my wings at close quarters. I never complained. But I'm going to chew my tongue off very soon if I have to keep pretending to be demure and compliant."

"Then you mightn't be interested in my invitation," Pauline said. "It will certainly require demureness and compliancy."

"How about a drink? Then I can fortify myself into the right level of decorum."

Skye went inside, found one of the bottles of champagne she'd brought back with her from Paris and poured out two glasses.

Pauline raised hers. "Bottoms up."

"You look too jolly," Skye said, tucking her legs up beside her. "Surely you're grounded too?"

"For now. But I'm recruiting." The sudden flash of satisfaction on the older woman's face was like sun after a week of fog.

"What for? Do the RAF want women wearing feathers to perform some kind of stationary aerobatics to entertain the men in their downtime?"

"You'd suit feathers better than I," Pauline said, chuckling. "No. I've been given permission to recruit twelve women for the Air Transport Auxiliary. It's a civilian flying service that will take planes from factories and maintenance units to RAF bases. They don't have enough pilots; you have no idea how many planes are being manufactured, planes that need to be moved around the country. So we'll have a women's division too."

Ted was wrong. Skye *would* fly. And, what's more . . . "Does that mean I'll get my hands on a Spitfire?" Skye said, beaming, swallowing champagne and euphoria.

"Before you start dreaming of being the first woman to fly a Spitfire, I need you to understand that I have to do things formally. Lunch with twenty women—which is about the sum total of women in England who've ever flown a plane—then a test flight. Even for you," Pauline added before Skye could protest. "Not at Central Flying School though. The RAF, in a fit of pique that this unsavory scheme has been thrust upon them, have refused to allow women to sully their elite school."

Skye exhaled. "Thank goodness for their pique. I have more chance if you're the one doing the selecting. So yes, I will do a test flight. And I *will* be one of the twelve women chosen. I have to be."

* * *

"Skye!" Rose, more sober than the last time Skye had seen her after their Parisian all-nighter, greeted her with a smile at the airfield at Whitchurch.

Skye kissed Rose's cheek. Her friend's light brown hair was set in uniformly arranged curls, and her green–gray suit was respectable, and Skye suddenly felt that she hadn't given enough thought to her own costume. She was wearing trousers for a start, along with a red sweater and her usual cerulean scarf, all of which drew too much attention. She patted her hair, which she had made an effort to curl, but it had emerged from the rollers more mane than coiffure.

"The RAF have sent someone along to watch," Rose whispered to Skye, pointing to an air marshal who'd just arrived.

"Then he'll see a show he's not expecting," Skye replied stoutly.

And she believed he would. She knew most of the twenty women gathered there, at least by sight. Each had at least five hundred hours' flying experience under her wings. It was ridiculous that the RAF wanted them to prove they knew their way around a plane.

Then, with a jolt, Skye realized she knew the air marshal. He was an older version of the man who'd once come to the Cornwall parties and whispered in Vanessa Penrose's ear in a manner Skye could now describe as intimate. For a moment Skye wanted to step over to him, to ask him how he knew Vanessa, to revel in the bittersweet joy of talking about her mother. But she turned away before he saw her and slipped on her helmet and goggles, which would make it impossible for him to recognize her. Because the fact that she was Vanessa Penrose's daughter was something she should keep from the RAF. Her illegitimacy would most likely bar her from even taking the test flight.

She moved to stand as far away from the air marshal as she could, watching Rose take off into the sky. Rose landed precisely and, yes, demurely, and Skye felt apprehension push into her stomach like a storm front. Many of the women there, like Rose, were minor aristocracy—they had even been presented at court—giving them the manners and the demeanor and the connections that Pauline needed. Marion Wilberforce was the daughter of a laird. Gabrielle Patterson was the first woman in England to have gained her instructor's license. Margaret Fairweather had a viscount for a father and her brother was the managing director of the British Overseas Airways Corporation. And then there was Skye, with a dead mother, no legitimate father and a few air pageants in her past. Her heart performed its own stall turn, and she wondered if she'd even be able to climb up into the plane, let alone fly it.

Luckily muscle memory took over and she performed her test flight well. But she couldn't see why Pauline would choose her. Besides her history of wing-walking, there was her youth: she and Joan Hughes were by far the youngest at only twenty-one. And the promised twelve women had been cut back to only eight. Skye's chances were less than fifty percent.

She waited until the very end and then blurted out her question to Pauline. "How will you decide?"

"I haven't a clue," Pauline said tiredly, and Skye could see how hard Pauline had fought to get to this point. How important it was that she make the right selection and not run the risk of proving to the RAF that their reluctance to take on women was justified.

Skye thought quickly. She had to give Pauline the evidence that would allow her to place Skye's advantages right beside those of a viscount's daughter.

"I never thought I'd see this as advantageous," Skye began, ideas forming as she spoke, "but I have no real family anymore, as you know. When I'm in an airplane, I'm not distracted by the people I love. Worrying over fathers and brothers and husbands who could lose their lives might interfere with the single-minded concentration that makes one a good flier. I would never suffer from those distractions."

"War changes things, doesn't it?" Pauline smiled gently, the first time that day her face had relaxed at all. "If there's one thing I know about you, Skye, it's that while you might appear to be a careless daredevil on the surface, you've sacrificed a mother to the sky so everything you do up there is impeccable. Trust," she said, as if the conversation had given her clarity. "Perhaps that's how I decide. Who can I trust up there when all is said and done?"

* * *

On the first of January 1940, as the war floundered on with much in the way of preparations and little in the way of battle, Skye became one of the first eight women to join the Air Transport Auxiliary—

the ATA. She was made a second officer, starting at the very bottom, based out of the Hatfield airfield.

Austin Reed in London made up their uniforms: a dashing navy-blue skirt and jacket decorated with gold bars. Or it became dashing once each woman had altered it. The tailors at Austin Reed had never outfitted women before and had been overly careful not to touch anything untoward when taking their chest and inside leg measurements. The result was trousers with elongated crotches and blouses that could have accommodated two women. Skye hoped it wasn't a sign of what was to come.

Women didn't receive a billeting allowance and were required to arrange their own accommodation, unlike the men. Rose, Skye and Joan Hughes, who had perfectly appled cheeks and the dimpled adorableness of a baby, found rooms at the Stonehouse Hotel within walking distance of the airfield. This further sign that things were different depending on one's gender didn't especially alarm Skye, until she arrived with Rose and Joan for their first day of work.

They stood in the doorway of their new headquarters, staring into the muddy hut that was to serve as the operations office, the mess, everything.

"This is glamorous," said Rose.

"Are there enough chairs for all of us to sit down?" Skye asked.

"No." Pauline's voice came from behind them. "You either have to get here early or perch on an armrest."

At that, Rose, Joan and Skye scooted inside and claimed one of the too-few seats, whose split cushions and uneven legs made it apparent that the women's hut was viewed by the RAF as a garbage dump.

For the next few days, various newspaper headlines alerted the nation that something out of the ordinary was taking place. The final straw was one that read: *8 Girls "Show" RAF*. Skye winced when she saw it, knowing the RAF would be furious.

Clever Pauline invited the press to Hatfield to introduce this set of eight "girls" to the general public, reasoning that it might be easier to win over the broader sweep of opinion first, which might then soothe the tempers of the elitist men of the RAF.

At the press call, Skye was told to arrange herself alongside the other women around a tea table, as if finger sandwiches and sponge cake would make them more conventional. The photographers snapped pictures of the silent group, then asked for some "action."

The women hoisted up their chutes and ran to the planes, only to be asked to do it again because the photographers hadn't got quite the right shot. Decorum, Skye reminded herself, smiling grimly. But after six such sprints lugging a heavy parachute and for no good reason that Skye could see other than the photographers were incompetent, she felt her patience fading. So when Pauline asked Skye and Rose to each take a Moth up into the sky, Skye flipped the plane into a single flawless and very demure loop-the-loop in order to show the press that women didn't need six attempts to fly an airplane properly. Upside down, she felt the joy that ordinarily swept through her when she flew, but that she hadn't experienced since she'd seen the dilapidation of the women's ATA headquarters.

Rose grinned at her as they landed.

Skye jumped down from the wing and pulled off her helmet, smiling at the sensation of the midair pirouette still swirling through her. She ran a hand through her hair, combing it into a less wind-blown state—as befitted newspaper photographs of serious young women doing an important job—and saw the combined blaze of a dozen flashlights. She thought nothing of it; was proud of herself for demonstrating the capableness of the ATA women—until the following day when the pictures appeared in the newspapers. Every paper who'd sent a photographer ran a shot of Skye's plane upside down and, beside it, a picture of her, hand in hair, which was swept back becomingly off her beaming face as if she were a model posing for *Vogue*.

"Oh no," was all she could think to say when Rose showed it to her; and "Oh no," again when Pauline called her into the office.

The newspapers sat open on Pauline's desk, displaying Skye's seemingly model-like stance and her stunt, which now looked like the action of a devil-may-care woman who flung airplanes upside down one minute and simpered for the cameras the next.

"How bad is it?" Skye asked, sitting down before she was invited to because she honestly didn't think she could stand. "I didn't mean it to turn out like that. I never thought they'd be able to catch a plane upside down."

"That's right, you never thought." Pauline's words were ice. "This is a letter *Aeroplane* magazine has warned me will be published in their next edition. *I think the whole affair of engaging women pilots to fly airplanes when there are so many men fully qualified to do the work is disgusting! They are contemptible show-offs.*"

Disgusting, Skye thought. Hitler was disgusting. Not women flying airplanes.

"But there aren't enough men," she protested. "It's not as if we're stealing their jobs. We're helping," she said, voice trailing off as Pauline continued to read.

"*The trouble is that women insist on wanting to do jobs which they are quite incapable of doing. The menace is the woman who thinks she ought to be flying a high-speed bomber when she really has not the intelligence to scrub the floor properly,*" Pauline finished.

Shame burned through Skye. She closed the newspaper, unable to look at herself, understanding that her tendency to solitariness might be useful when flying an airplane but on the opposite side of it lay a propensity to think only of herself. Which one didn't do when part of a team.

"Are they going to shut us down?" she asked, then stopped. Shut *us* down. No, shut *her* down. It was the only solution. Rose, Joan and the other five women had done nothing to be ashamed of.

"I'll resign," Skye said, trying to block out the image of a future devoid of flight because of her own incurable rashness.

Pauline sighed. "I'm not supposed to tell you this, but enough of the general public are so enamored of you and your derring-do and rather gorgeous face that the RAF have had to chew on their fingernails rather than on us. It would be more of a public relations disaster to close us down now than it would be to let us continue. The press is fascinated. Every man and woman on the street is fascinated— especially the men," she added. "You're the poster girl for the ATA, like it or not. And the RAF is smart enough to realize that firing their new poster girl is unlikely to win them any friends. But I'm giving you an official warning. Get another one and you're out."

"Thank you," Skye whispered. "I'll apologize to everyone. I've learned my lesson."

Which was: don't be Skye Penrose again. Not *ever*.

"Good." Pauline's voice was firm. "We only just landed on the side of good fortune this time. So the warning stands, as does me begging you to fly the planes with nary a smile nor a wing-waggle until this settles. Don't bugger everything up."

Skye returned to work determined to never get another warning, to forget she knew aerobatics at all, and to tame every maverick part of herself.

FIVE

On their first real day of flying, the ATA women juggled themselves into the few chairs—Skye perching on an arm and letting Joan take the seat—and Skye saw that Pauline looked tired again. As if she'd been fighting through a hailstorm and had acquired a lot more bruises.

"Tell us," Skye said, and she felt Joan shift closer to her, as if they might need to be braced for whatever Pauline would say.

"This won't be like any flying you've done before," Pauline began, somewhat carefully. "You'll rarely be able to take a direct route to wherever you're ferrying as you need to avoid barrage balloons, anti-aircraft guns, coastal defenses and restricted flight zones. But you won't have any instruments for navigation. Instead, you have to fly by dead reckoning, using only maps, a compass and your watch, flying in sight of the ground at all times—that's the only way you'll know where you are. You have to become expert in identifying railway lines, Roman roads and other landmarks as those are the navigation aids that will get you from the start to the finish of your route."

Skye found herself squeezing Joan's hand and avoiding Rose's eyes entirely because she didn't want to see the incredulity she knew she'd find there. But, she reasoned, if they got lost while taking a plane from one side of Britain to another with only a watch and a railway line to guide them, they could always radio in to check both their position and what obstacles—like a German Messerschmitt—might be lying in wait for them along the flight path.

Then Pauline said, "You're not allowed to use radio. Ever. Which means you can't fly if the cloud base is less than eight hundred feet. If it's lower, it's scrub for the day. No going up into the clouds and trying to find a way over the top. Without radio and navigation aids, that would be suicide."

"But . . ." Skye couldn't form the words. She could scarcely believe what Pauline had said. They might as well be flying with blindfolds on.

"Righto," said Rose, and Skye could hear the effort it took for her to be her usual chirpy self. "No instruments. No radio. Are we allowed a little luck?"

Nobody smiled. What they were being asked to do was not just risky but possibly deadly. Skye could easily set out on a day that looked clear, only to run into cloud fifty miles farther along and be stuck in the thick of it, like her mother had been, unable to see the railway lines on the ground and flying blind into a hill, with no way to call for help. Or losing her way and ending up somewhere over the North Sea with no fuel left.

Pauline allowed them a moment before passing them each a map. "You'll notice," she said drily, "that it says on your maps: *Areas dangerous to flying not marked on this sheet.* You're not allowed to mark the location of hazards like barrage balloons in case your plane goes down and you and your map are taken by the enemy, thus giving them valuable intelligence."

Skye couldn't bear it anymore. She let a little of her old self escape. "As the editors of *Aeroplane* magazine don't ascribe to us any intelligence, it shouldn't matter what we write on our maps."

Rose was the first to laugh, then Joan, then Mona and the others. What else was there to do?

"And these are for you." Pauline handed Skye a pile of letters.

"Me?" Skye tore one open to find a request from a pilot to accompany him to dinner and a dance. The next was a similar request, this time from an engineer. And so it went on, through the pile.

"Your picture in the newspaper has made you somewhat sought after," Pauline said.

Nary a smile. "I'll decline them all, of course," Skye said, pushing to the back of her mind the Skye who had danced all night in Parisian jazz clubs with handsome Frenchmen. She dropped the letters into the nearest rubbish bin.

"Quite," Pauline said. "You'll need to save your strength. Nobody will let us touch operational aircraft, which means the only planes the women of the ATA will fly are Tiger Moths. To Scotland."

"Bloody hell." Rose said what everyone must have been thinking.

Tiger Moths had open cockpits. It was winter. The air over Scotland was not even warm enough to be considered freezing. It was arctic.

The women were given fur-lined boots, a Sidcot flying suit and a leather helmet for protection. But when you were flying for four hours in minus thirty degrees windchill, it was like being naked in a snowstorm, Skye reflected through chattering jaw on her very first flight. She could barely concentrate enough to fly the plane as her body shut off every function besides keeping the blood moving through her.

She almost didn't register the RAF base when she saw it, almost flew on, over the North Sea and into oblivion. She could see that her hands were still attached to her, but she couldn't feel them. Somehow they moved, muscle memory still functioning, and she slowed the Moth for her final approach, thankful that some guardian angel ensured she landed safely.

She taxied the Moth after the follow-me car to dispersal, and at last heard the sound of the chocks being placed under the wheels. It was time to get out. But her legs wouldn't work. Pauline needn't have bothered to forbid her from smiling. She simply couldn't.

An engineer climbed onto the wing and stared disgustedly at her. "The only good thing about having women in the ATA is your weight," he snapped.

He reached into the cockpit and lifted her out, bodily. It was the most mortifying thing that had ever happened to her.

After he put her on the ground, she held on to the wing for dear life, knowing that if she fell down right now she would cry, not because she was hurt, but because she had never, in all her life, imagined having so little dignity.

"I'll have to quit flying and become an engineer," a pilot called out as he walked past. "Isn't that two for today?"

The engineer laughed, and Skye understood that Mona or Joan or someone else had landed before her and had also had to be removed from the aircraft. It didn't make her feel any better to know she wasn't the first whose body had so let her down. Nobody, not even a man, could survive such a flight in bitter cold and be capable of movement at the end. But the men were ferrying closed cockpit planes to bases farther south where the air was milder, so it was just the women who looked weak.

The engineer threw her parachute down at her. "Don't forget that," he said.

It slipped through her arms. While she might be slowly defrosting, she didn't yet have the range of movement needed to catch a heavy parachute when thrown at her from above. He tossed her bag down after it.

"Thanks," she mumbled as she bent to pick it up. Then she forced one foot in front of the other so she could find somewhere to change, to abide by the ridiculous regulations that stated she must take off her much warmer flying suit immediately after she had landed and put on her skirt.

Once she'd pulled on thin lisle stockings and her skirt, she had to catch the overnight train from Scotland to St. Pancras. Still colder than she'd ever been in her life, Skye found a blue-lipped Joan on the platform, and was momentarily grateful for her prewar habit of swimming most days, even in winter, which had perhaps made her more robust.

On the train, Skye boosted Joan up into the luggage rack where she could at least lie down. Skye sat on the floor, head resting against a pole, eyelids closing occasionally but flying open with every noise and movement around her.

They arrived at St. Pancras in time to catch the train to Hatfield to start a new day's work, barely thawed from the previous evening. Pauline handed Skye and Joan hot cups of tea that they swallowed gratefully.

"Sorry," Pauline said grimly.

Then Rose appeared with a pile of fur and wool, which she dropped on the table. "I phoned Mummy and asked her to bring some things from home."

Each woman took a garment. Skye passed Joan a fur stole and selected a heavy shawl for herself. Once they were all wrapped in fur and cashmere and mink, as glamorously attired as if they were attending a winter ball, it was time to leave, to face a day that was forecast to be colder than the previous one.

"Look at this," Pauline said, holding up a newspaper.

Pictured there was of one of the ATA women—taken from the rear so it was hard to tell who it was—parachute bumping against her behind as she walked, accompanied by the caption: *How d'ye like the togs, girls?* The answer to that question, according to the newspaper, was: *We LIKE you in your harness, and the bustle, which is a parachute. We like your air. In fact, we LIKE you flighty!*

Skye's eyes met Joan's, then Rose's, and finally Pauline's. She saw in them the anger that burned empyrean, a realm of pure fire, in them all.

"You are being given every opportunity to give up, to retire to life as a flighty bird who entertains men in her bustle, to prove that women cannot fly planes," Pauline said plainly. "I will not judge you if you choose an easier life. But if you stay, know that this is how it will be. You must deliver every plane intact, in dreadful conditions, and you must never make a fuss. Here are the chits for those who decide they will do just that."

Every single woman in the unheated, muddy hut took a delivery chit from Pauline and marched outside. Skye marched with them, knowing none of them would ever give in.

She never discovered if the Scotland route was punishment for her loop-the-loop escapade, or whether the RAF had planned it all along. She supposed they couldn't have known it would be the worst winter England had seen for decades. But the RAF did coordinate the ferrying movements and so could dictate what the women flew and where. And they flew those Tiger Moths right the way through the record-breaking winter to Scotland. Two thousand planes. Two thousand arctic journeys in all.

* * *

The summer of 1940 brought with it the fall of France to the Nazis, followed by the Battle of Britain and the Blitz, which turned England into a nation determined to keep calm and carry on in spite of the fact that everyone believed the Germans would arrive on their shores at any moment.

Summer also brought the news from Skye's aunt in France that Liberty had been persuaded to leave for England before the German occupation. Skye was so thankful her sister had escaped. They hadn't seen one another nor spoken for three years, and Skye's letters to her sister always remained unanswered. Now she waited, braced, for her sister to come and find her, but Liberty remained stubbornly absent. A small and terrible part of Skye was relieved—she wasn't sure she wanted to discover whether Liberty's malice had developed from punctured tires and stolen assignments to something worse—but another, larger part of her shed a tear or two in bed at night at the awful possibility that Liberty might stay away from Skye forever.

Through August and September, as the bombs fell like a vicious and unrelenting rainstorm, Skye, Rose and Joan spent every night huddled in the Anderson shelter, resurfacing when the all clear sounded at dawn. The acrid stink of incendiaries hung in the air like fog and it seemed as if all of England were alight. Everywhere, ordinary people died, people who had nothing whatsoever to do with Hitler and war.

Following one such night, and after only an hour's sleep, Skye found herself readying a Magister to land at RAF Biggin Hill. She tried not to think about what Rose had whispered to her the day before: "One of the RAF boys decided to do some fancy low-flying past his friend's house to show off. Broke the plane and his leg. They forgave him, of course."

They forgave him. What if, right now, Skye decided to do some fancy low-flying of her own? What if she decided to buzz through the arches of the Severn Bridge, a dare undertaken—but without punishment—by so many RAF pilots that a guard had been posted by the bridge to prevent such escapades. What if she stopped being so twisted up with fear that flying to Scotland in the Siberian nightmare of a winter they had just been through had been a punishment for the photograph of Skye that had turned so much attention their way? What if she put the plane into a spin and didn't just smile but laughed for the full-body thrill of it?

Skye clenched her hands on the stick. She would do nothing of the sort. She would fly perfectly and never smile again. Being joyless was easy when everything she could see below her—ruined houses, parts of cities obliterated, ever-expanding cemeteries—reminded her that it didn't matter a bit what the RAF boys did. The nation needed them to get in their planes every night to stop the Germans taking England for themselves.

Skye lined up behind a squadron of Spitfires coming back from a sortie to land, then put her plane down, taxied to a hangar and waited for an engineer to climb onto the wing and unbuckle her.

It was Ollie, one of the men she'd come to know over the past couple of months, one who treated her like a human being rather than a hindrance. She said hello—but didn't smile—climbed out, and was about to leave the hangar when something flashed gold on the ground at her feet.

She bent to pick it up and what she found knocked her back into the past with all the force of a hurricane. A pocket watch made of gold with a misshapen half-moon on the face that Skye now knew was called a chronometer. It looked so much like Nicholas's father's watch that Skye couldn't breathe.

"Do you know whose this is?" she asked Ollie when at last she straightened.

"Nope. But if it's his good luck charm, he'll be hopping mad he's lost it. You should see the stuff the pilots carry—letters from their sweethearts, their baby's socks, the scarf their mum knitted them. That," he tapped the watch knowledgeably, "is going to have some pilot turning his squadron's flying suits inside out."

Skye felt a thump to her chest at the idea of a tiny sock sitting in the pocket of a jittery pilot who wanted only that most basic of things—to live.

"I'll ask around, see if anyone's lost it," Ollie said. "A squadron came in ahead of you so it could be one of theirs."

He left Skye staring at the watch. She jumped when, a moment later, a distinctly American voice called out, "Ollie? I dropped my watch."

A man rounded the nose of the plane—and there stood Nicholas Crawford.

SIX

Skye stared, speechless.

Nicholas did the same.

She felt her mouth move, forming shapes that didn't become words. There were too many things to ask: *How did you get here? Why didn't you write?* And, *Is it really you?*

That last question was the most troubling of all because it both was and wasn't Nicholas. This man was tall, well-built, his dark hair cropped, and his blue eyes held a kind of sensual intensity that was—she couldn't halt the thought—awfully alluring.

Finally her mouth escaped her constant self-regulation. "Nicholas?" she said. "It can't be. You're handsome."

Immediately she stepped back, wishing the airplane might take off with her clinging to its wing. If she wasn't allowed to smile, she was definitely not allowed to call anyone handsome.

"Skye?" Nicholas said, seeming not to have heard her reckless words. "What are you doing here?"

"Flying planes," Skye said stupidly, as if that wasn't obvious from the fact she was dressed in flight overalls.

Nicholas took a hesitant step toward her but Skye didn't move away from the safety of the plane. If anything, she pressed her body closer to it, not trusting herself to speak lest she say or do something else that might cause trouble.

He studied her face, which she imagined must look as bewildered as his but also more guarded than he'd ever seen it. "What's wrong?" he asked, skipping over all the ordinary pleasantries people might exchange after a long separation and cutting straight to the heart of the matter.

"Everything," she said quietly, eyes fixed to the ground. When she looked up, she realized that his face was shadowed by sadness too. "Don't you think?"

Nicholas ran a hand through his hair in frustration. "I just heard that one hundred and three RAF pilots died last night," he said, his voice disbelieving, wild, trying to make sense of the incomprehensible.

"One hundred and three," Skye repeated. "In one night?"

"And now they're rushing in men to replace the ones who've died. Most of them haven't even finished their training courses; they have less than twenty hours in the air. *Twenty hours*. We'll be lucky if there aren't two hundred and three dead tonight."

The sun slipped behind a thick bank of clouds and the light vanished. Darkness descended upon the hangar, transforming it into a space like the cave of their childhood, where they had lain on their backs sharing secrets. And she felt now as she had back then: that Nicholas was the one person in the world who wanted her to speak the truth. So she did.

"That's why I've never spoken of the fuss that was made about the women flying despite our hundreds of hours' flying experience," she said urgently. "It's why I fly wherever and in whatever weather I'm told to and never complain. It's why I'd never say that if *I* so much as looked sideways at the Severn Bridge, let alone flew through it, I'd be fired. It's why I'd never point out that the men of the ATA have had accidents and the women have had none and yet we're still only allowed to fly non-operational jets. Because none of it matters when set beside one hundred and three men dying."

Nicholas didn't interject. That had never been his way. Nor did he leap to the defense of the RAF and thus dismiss everything she'd said.

You haven't changed, she wanted to say, based on the evidence of nothing other than the way he was listening to her.

His attentiveness made her offer her most secret thought. "If they let the women fly more than just trainers, if they let us fly Spitfires and other operational jets, then the men in the ATA would be freed up to fly for the RAF. You'd have all of those experienced pilots. Why doesn't anyone think of that?"

Nicholas's reply was brief, and serious. "So what are you going to do about it?"

Skye stared at him, a punch of disappointment robbing her of breath. He hadn't been listening to her at all. How had she missed the moment when the conversation turned from the confiding of unsayable things to the asking of preposterous questions? Because the answer to his question was, obviously: *nothing*. She could do nothing about any of it.

The sun shouldered ahead of the clouds, spilling blinding light into the hangar. Ollie's voice, as confounding as the sun, made them both whip around.

"You found it. Brilliant. You'd better shift yourself," he added to Nicholas. "Your squadron leader's waiting to debrief and he's hopping mad you've disappeared."

Nicholas swore.

Skye remembered the watch and passed it to him.

"I'll write to you," Nicholas said. "Where are you?"

"Skye's at Hatfield," Ollie said, as if the question had been asked of him, and then Nicholas was gone again, just like eight years before.

As he left, she saw the eagle on his uniform, which meant he was with the newly formed American Eagle Squadron serving with the RAF. It also meant he'd defied America's Neutrality Act, and jail if he'd been caught, to get himself to England and into combat. Of course he had. It was Nicholas.

Skye felt her disappointment of moments ago turn into something else: an understanding that he *had* listened to her. When he'd asked her what she was going to do about it, he'd been telling her that he still believed in her, in a Skye Penrose who, if facing a battle, would do something.

And so she would.

She pushed herself away from the plane.

But then Ollie said, "Your ATA compatriot Mona Friedlander burst a tire on a Lysander. They've grounded all the women until further notice."

* * *

So, rather than doing something, Skye, and every woman in the ATA, was evaluated over the following month. They were subjected to leg-strength tests. An assessment of their ability to concentrate. Measurements of their reaction times in wind-shear. All because one plane in twelve months had been damaged by a woman. Several men in the ATA had wrecked planes but the strength of their legs had never been examined.

Skye, more serious than ever, was called into the medical examiner's office at White Waltham for her test.

"You can place your uniform on the chair," the doctor said.

"Pardon?" Skye said.

"Your clothes," he said impatiently. "Put them on the chair."

"Why?" she asked, unable to imagine why assessments of her cognitive powers had to be conducted while she was nude.

But even as she asked the question, she felt her hand stray to her jacket as if she was really going to remove it. As if she was going to do just what she was told to, even though all she wanted to remove right now was the doctor's head with her bare hands.

"It's for the inquest, as you know," he said, and waited, not even drawing a curtain.

What are you going to do about it? Nicholas's voice sounded in her head.

"Do you really not know how to report that my legs are strong enough to fly a plane without seeing me naked?" she heard herself ask coolly.

"It's protocol."

"Are the men told to strip too?" Her voice was louder now.

"The men don't require such testing."

This was what it came down to, thought Skye. A small room with a small man who reported to other small-minded men. And the question of whether she was willing to take off her clothes in order to keep her job. No wonder Joan had returned from her examination yesterday unsmiling, unspeaking. And Rose the same, the day before.

So Skye, at last, did something. She turned on her heel and walked out.

Outside, under a dirty sky, as if the world were reflecting back at her the filth of what it had become, she walked, unseeing, to the nearest aircraft. She held on to the wing with one hand and wrapped her other arm across her stomach, as if trying to hold herself together.

It was over. By walking out of the medical examination she'd ensured that she would, at last, be fired. Were her principles really so important?

A scream of fighter jets flew over, coming back from defending her country against a man who took whatever he wanted whenever he wanted, grinding to blood and bone beneath his heel anyone who stood in his way.

So yes, principles mattered. They mattered more than anything right now.

Skye would pay whatever it cost to keep hers intact.

* * *

Pauline Gower was the first to come looking for Skye. She pulled up in her car and said, grimly, "Hop in. We're going to lunch."

"Lunch?" Skye repeated, sure she'd misheard.

"Yes. I'm supposed to be speaking at a luncheon in London about what the ATA women are doing. I rather think you should speak instead. Reapply your lipstick and get your hair under control. If there was time, I'd order you to cut it to regulation length, rather than turning a blind eye to the fact that you tuck it up and pretend it's shoulder length."

Skye's hands obeyed even as her brain struggled to comprehend. "You know what happened at my medical examination?" she asked.

"I know what happened." The stern set of Pauline's face didn't alter. "But you're the girl from the newspapers. The face of the women's section of the ATA. The one everyone wants to see."

Skye was sure that the unflappable Pauline Gower had become delusional. The constant smoothing of paths until they were so sleek they could be skated upon had finally got to her.

As they drove toward the Mayfair hotel, Skye's despair worsened. London was shadowed by barrage balloons: gray planets that crowded out the light. On the ground, sandbags held up the city, and maimed buildings, gutted by the Luftwaffe, spilled their insides into the streets. War had scrubbed all color away so the landscape was an achromatic murk of navy, khaki and brown clothing. The sudden appearance of a red double-decker bus was a laceration across the gloom, as preposterous as a belch at a suddenly silent dinner party.

When they arrived at the hotel, waiters served ration meals on fine china as if that might transform the food into haute cuisine. Rows of helmets and gas masks sat stoically by the door, ready for the guests if the air-raid sirens sounded.

Somebody spoke and Skye heard herself introduced to the gathering. Eyes glanced in her direction.

"There are MPs here today," Pauline whispered to her. "People who want to let us fly Spitfires and Hurricanes. People who understand it's a waste to use fighting men to ferry those planes across the country when we could be doing it. It's do or die, Skye. Right here, right now."

Do or die. Skye's feet carried her toward the microphone. She kept her fingers curled tightly into her palms to stop herself from shattering the glasses and china plates against the walls, all of them, so that the room would ring with the sounds her unscreaming voice wished it could make.

At the microphone, she stared at the mass of people who wanted chucklesome stories to distract them from the bombs that might fall on them tonight.

Then she saw a face she recognized: the air marshal who'd scrutinized the women's test flights; who had been to the Penroses' Cornish cottage and danced laughingly and too often with her mother. Her mother. Whom the people of Porthleven had whispered about because she was a woman who preferred flying airplanes to hosting tea parties. Skye's fists clenched tighter, nails cutting her palms.

What are you going to do about it? The words were so loud in her head it was almost as if Nicholas were in the room.

Her anger flared. Her head lifted.

I'm sorry, she mouthed to Pauline.

"It can be hard to be alone, to be silent," she said, a little too softly. She shifted closer to the microphone as the murmuring quieted. "But every day, for a good part of my day, I am alone and silent in the cockpit of an airplane. In the sky above you. In the clouds. Well," she amended, "I'm supposed to be below the clouds, but cloud isn't always predictable, nor does it behave as the meteorologists think it should."

There was a gentle titter from the crowd. The air marshal stared at Skye, forehead creased, as if trying to fathom her.

"My mother taught me to fly when I was only ten years old," she continued. "I'm sure I'm not supposed to tell you that either." Another laugh, louder this time. "Her name was Vanessa Penrose, and what she loved about flying was the aloneness. The silence."

The air marshal flinched as if the words *Vanessa Penrose* had hit him square in the jaw. Now he was staring at Skye with a mix of anger and dismay.

"There's more to flying an airplane than the ability to master the controls and to understand weather and navigation," she said. "It takes more than strength in your legs; it takes strength of mind. Character. Things that can't be measured and assessed by doctors and air marshals. Things you don't know you possess until you're tested."

She knew what she would say next: something she'd been told by Pauline; something she'd been told not to speak of. But she *had* to speak of it. "The Prime Minister recently visited Fighter Command and, as the German planes threw everything they could at us, he asked why we were sending no more planes into the sky to fight them off. Our Prime Minister was told that every available pilot was in the sky. That the RAF's strength had been cut by one quarter since the start of the Blitz. That they were running out of pilots. But that isn't true."

Whispers flitted around the room, everyone clearly wondering whether the censors were about to sweep in and carry Skye away. Even Pauline was looking at her with concern.

"There are many other men who could fly Spitfires to fight off the Luftwaffe," Skye said. "But they're busy ferrying airplanes from maintenance units to RAF bases, doing the work I do every day. Except I'm not allowed to ferry operational planes like Spitfires because I'm a woman.

"I know many people think it's shameful and disgusting that women like me wish to fly airplanes. But all I want is for our country to win the war. And to help make that happen, I want to fly a Spitfire from a factory to an RAF base so a male pilot can get into that same Spitfire and chase away the Luftwaffe when they come to drop bombs on us tonight. How is that shameful and disgusting?"

She spoke directly to the air marshal now, shutting out everyone else in the room. He at least had the guts not to look away from the tears that formed in her eyes when she said that final word: *disgusting*.

"Today I was asked to do something that I think is disgusting: to present myself naked to an older male doctor in order to prove my ability to do something I've already shown, day in and day out, over many long months, that I can do. *That* is disgusting," she repeated. "Putting me in the cockpit of a Spitfire so that a man might be freed to fight for us is simply common sense."

Skye stepped down from the podium, meaning to make her way outside, to sit down, to rest her shaking legs before they collapsed underneath her. But a sound so deafening that it made her duck, thinking it was a bomb dropping from the sky, crashed over her. Then she realized it was applause.

She caught Pauline's eye. Pauline was smiling in a way she'd never smiled before, and her eyes were filled with tears too.

Thank you, Nicholas, Skye thought. She wouldn't wait for his letter; instead she'd write to him first and tell him what she'd just done.

* * *

The next morning inside the hut at Hatfield there was a buzz of conversation to rival a Merlin engine.

"You're in the papers again," Mona told Skye, holding up a copy of the *Evening Post*.

"And I heard the MPs were talking about you in Parliament yesterday," Rose added. "What did you say at the lunch? And why were you there?"

"Can I see that?" Skye asked, and took the newspaper from Mona.

They had reproduced the photograph of her stepping out of the plane with her hand in her hair, the sunlight falling on her face in a way that made her look young—which she supposed she was—as if she knew nothing of cynicism, as if she were barely old enough to have finished school, let alone be asked to remove her clothing. And that, thankfully, was the point. The newspapers had taken her side.

The MPs at the lunch had been outraged by what Skye had said and they'd taken her case to Parliament to argue that there was a very simple solution to the problem of not having enough RAF pilots: let the women of the ATA ferry more types of aircraft in order to free up the men to fight. The debate had raged for hours, with many still convinced that it was unnatural for a woman to sit in the cockpit of an airplane, and others unable to see how it was any different to allowing a woman to sit behind the wheel of a car. But nothing had been resolved, except to bring the nation's spotlight back onto Skye and her fellow ATA women.

"I'm sorry," she said. "I've done it again."

"You have to be joking," Rose said crisply. "You said what everybody in this room has been wanting to say since the day we started."

At that, Skye sank into the nearest chair, rested her elbows on the table, covered her eyes with her hands and started to cry.

The women gathered around her. Joan offered a clean hanky, Rose held Skye as if she were her mother. Mona, who had started the whole thing off by landing awkwardly in the Lysander, made Skye a cup of hot, strong tea just the way she liked it, using at least two days' worth of the precious rationed leaves.

Then Pauline Gower and the air marshal from yesterday's lunch entered the hut.

"Skye, I'd like to see you in five minutes, please," Pauline said, before ushering the air marshal past, even though no amount of hurrying could make him oblivious to the fact that Skye was bawling and nobody was doing any work.

Rose broke the silence. "Right, wipe your face, Skye. I'll do your hair. Joanie's best at powder and lipstick."

Before Skye could blink, all hands in the hut had turned their full attention to her face, her uniform and her coiffure.

"He's come to fire me," Skye said, clutching the ends of her cerulean scarf.

"Then he'll have to fire us all," Joan said firmly.

"No," Skye protested. "You can't."

"Nonsense," Rose said. "Otherwise it's like saying we agree with them. And I am never again taking off my clothes for a medical examination."

"It's funny, isn't it," Joan added pensively, "you think if you're being asked to do something by someone so senior, it must be all right. Even though you know it isn't. But you convince yourself that *you're* the one who's wrong."

Heads nodded in agreement and Skye saw cheeks flush pink as the women remembered what they'd been asked to do, and that they'd done it, unwillingly, hating it, but believing they had no choice. Rose whisked away a tear, then resumed work on Skye's hair.

Within five minutes, Skye was declared ready. She tapped on Pauline's door.

"This is Air Marshal Wylde," Pauline said, introducing Skye to the man she knew from childhood. "And this is Second Officer Penrose."

Wylde nodded.

"Air Marshal Wylde believes there has been a communication error," Pauline continued. "As a result, a new doctor is conducting the medical assessments. Yours has been rescheduled for this afternoon. You are to wear your uniform at all times. Once your medical examination is complete, the inquest will be concluded. Then I will be selecting four pilots to attend training at White Waltham to fly Spitfires and other Class II jets for the ATA."

Skye felt her mouth fall open. There were many things she'd thought Pauline might say, but the news that four of her pilots were to fly Spitfires was not one of them.

"We need a statement from you for the press noting that there was a communication error," Air Marshal Wylde said, his eyes drilling through Skye. "And you will agree to be photographed at a press call with one of the Spitfires."

Skye nodded. She would concede to a communication error in order to gain so much more; not just for herself, but for every woman waiting outside. And she would swallow the question filling her mouth— *How did you know my mother?*—because her personal curiosity—or fear—meant nothing when set beside the momentous victory that had just been handed to the women.

She gave Pauline a huge grin.

She, a woman, was going to fly a Spitfire.

SEVEN

Flying a Spitfire was even better than Skye had imagined it would be. It was snug in the cockpit, just the right size for a woman, and every time she slid into her seat she felt like she'd slipped on a silk evening gown. The aircraft moved through the sky like a dolphin through water: playful, powerful, and responding to the lightest of touches. She sometimes wondered if she could move the throttle with just the exhalation of her breath.

The change in policy allowing women to fly operational jets created many other changes. An all-women's ferry pool was opened at Hamble, near Southampton, close to the Spitfire factory at Eastleigh. Skye, Rose and Joan were moved to Hamble, where they found a cottage together, near the water.

Two years of relative bliss passed by—well, as blissful as wartime life could be. For thirteen days straight, Skye would fly planes—mostly Spitfires, but often Hurricanes, Typhoons, Tempests, anything that needed to be moved around the country. Then she had two days off to laze around Hamble, eating lobster dinners at the Bugle Inn, or to go to London, where she danced all night at the Embassy Club on Bond Street with a pilot or two, before catching the early train back to Southampton in time to start work in the morning. She was no longer afraid to smile. The RAF appeared to soften, not mounting overt opposition to the women, and RAF pilots and ground crews became more used to occasionally seeing a woman step down from a plane.

In all that time, Skye didn't hear from her sister. She didn't even have news of Liberty secondhand from her aunt as it was impossible to get letters out of France. Skye had never been taught to pray yet, most nights, she found herself thinking in a prayer-like way about Liberty, even though she suspected her sister's ongoing silence was meant to communicate the fact that she had not forgiven Skye for leaving France.

Each morning, Skye walked to Hamble—which was a vast improvement on the muddy hut at Hatfield—and waited with the ATA women in the lounge for the weather to clear, or, if it was already clear, to collect their delivery chits. The ferry pool resembled a compressed world with women of almost every nationality working there: American, Canadian, Chilean, South African, Australian, Polish. The radio was always on, tuned to the BBC, and posters of prim Prudence with whom they were all supposed to fly—no matter that Prudence looked like just the sort to turn to jelly in an airplane—covered the walls.

Jackie would be upside down practicing headstands; Honor would be waiting to battle Skye in backgammon; Chile, affectionately nicknamed after her homeland, would be writing letters; and Diana would be discussing her latest beau, or saying that she really ought to learn to knit so she had something to do to pass the time. Rose would roll her eyes, knowing that Diana, beautiful, rich Diana, would never learn to knit.

One morning in late 1942, while waiting for the call over the tannoy that signaled the start of the day's ferrying, Skye and Rose attacked a jigsaw puzzle that was trying to get the better of them, while Joan took over from the unusually silent Diana and complained about the faithlessness of her latest RAF pilot.

"They're all faithless," Rose said knowledgeably. "Better that way, then you won't miss them when they die."

"You're so jolly unfeeling," Joan said, as near to cross as someone who inhaled optimism instead of oxygen could be. "Between you and Skye, you'll have been taken out by almost every man in the RAF before the war ends."

Skye smiled at Joan. "You each want different things. You want a lifetime; Rose wants a diversion."

Skye was unequivocally of the same mind as Rose. It might sound unfeeling, but a long life and being an RAF pilot were not compatible, and everyone, especially the pilots themselves, knew it. It was best to stick to diversions if one wanted to survive the war with only a few scratches to the heart.

And Rose was right about the faithlessness of pilots: Nicholas had proved himself to be as capricious as the worst of them, never sending Skye that promised letter. She'd written to him at RAF Biggin Hill but had received no response. She'd written again in case her letter had been lost but there was no reply the second time either.

Their strange encounter now seemed like a dream, as if she'd conjured up his ghost because it was what she'd needed at the time: someone who knew her from before the war, and before the RAF had almost ground her down. What she'd understood in the hangar that day to be the unbroken bond of their remarkable friendship had obviously been, to him, just a brief encounter, quickly forgotten.

She'd asked Ollie, the engineer, about Nicholas after the months of silence had dragged on, but all Ollie had been able to tell her was that Nicholas had been transferred; he didn't know where. Short of asking about him at every RAF base she flew into—which she gathered Nicholas didn't want, otherwise he'd have written to her—she had no idea how to find him. She'd tried to forget about him, but it was as difficult this time as it had been when she was fourteen.

The call sounded, returning her to the present: "Will all pilots report to the operations room for chits."

Immediately everyone crossed to the hatchway, where they were handed slips of paper to tell them what and where they were flying that day. Skye had a routine delivery of Spitfires, three in all if the weather held.

She took her maps from her locker, collected her compass and her overnight bag in case she was stuck somewhere for the night, then wound her cerulean scarf around her hair. Then she went outside, smiling. It was a perfect day for flying: autumn, light cloud, sun shining.

Joan was flying the taxi plane that day and she dropped Rose, Skye and Honor at Eastleigh, before taking off again to deliver the remaining pilots to their pickup points. Skye found her Spit and patted it on the flank. Then she climbed onto the wing, placed her parachute on the seat and herself upon it.

She let the throttle open slowly, gently, letting the Spit know she was in charge. A delicate flick of the wrist had the plane banking smoothly, the perfect dance partner. She squeezed her way through the corridor of barrage balloons and then hit the open skies, checking her map, setting her compass and settling back for an easy flight.

It was on her last flight for the day, less than an hour away from RAF Stanbridge, where Joan would pick her up in the taxi plane and take her back to Hamble, when she caught a glimpse of something to her right. She thought nothing of it at first; with Luton and other bases nearby, it was feasible that this part of the sky might have a little traffic.

Then something flashed past her nose. If there'd been room in the Spitfire, she would have jumped. But as the plane fitted over her as tightly as a shell, the only part of her that could move in response was her heart, which gave her a swift kick. She'd just been shot at.

She waggled her wings, expecting that some overzealous and obviously blind RAF pilot had mistaken her for an enemy plane even though she didn't have a swastika painted on her tail. But it happened again, and this time her heart didn't thud against her chest; it stalled. Because the plane was a German Me 110 and it had her in its sights.

What the hell was she supposed to do? She had heard of this happening, but so rarely that there was no accepted protocol to handle the situation. And how on earth was she supposed to handle it without guns? She felt her breath coming fast, the joy from earlier evaporating like mist.

Think, Skye told herself. *And quickly*.

The Messerschmitt fired again: one shot grazed her wingtip and the other embedded itself into her flank. Her Spitfire lurched, and so did her stomach.

Despite the fact that aerobatics were *strictly* forbidden, she pushed the Spit into full throttle, roaring ahead, not horizontally but vertically, aiming for the base of heaven.

The German plane hesitated: it had expected her to engage or to race away, not to attack the sky. She was counting on the fact that, given the rate at which the Germans went through pilots, the man on her tail had never performed an aerobatic maneuver in his life.

She executed the stall turn expertly: the engine speed dropped to zero and the plane stopped. A moment alone in the sky in an airplane that was precisely perpendicular to the ground, without acceleration to hold her there, engines silent. Just Skye Penrose and the beautiful blue nothingness of air.

But then she had to right herself, and face the fact that the other plane was still nearby. She readied herself to climb once more.

Suddenly and appallingly, the sky filled with more planes. She was in the middle of an ambush and she understood for the first time that true fear was not expressed in a racing heart and a sheen of sweat; it manifested itself in a perfect stillness. She didn't blink, didn't think, was certain she didn't even breathe. Her eyes locked like radar on the approaching planes and she wondered if she would die like that: a statue, already lifeless.

A sudden, urgent inhalation of air made every part of her body start working again, her gasp one of astounding relief now, not horror. The new arrivals didn't have swastikas on their tails; they were on her side. Thank God.

She pulled her Spitfire around in time to see the Me 110 screaming off across the sky. The RAF pilots, obviously realizing from the fact that she'd discharged no weapons—and had instead resorted to circus tricks—that there was some kind of difficulty, came up alongside her to escort her into their base.

She wasn't allowed to fly at night and it was getting dark so she flew in formation with four Lysanders—the modified and top-secret black Lysanders she'd seen once at RAF Tangmere on the south coast. She'd asked about them and been told they were used by the Special Duties squadrons, but for what purpose she had never discovered. Unlike most other Lysanders, these had ladders fixed to the rear cockpit, metal cylinders attached to the fuselage, the rear guns removed. One of the Lizzies had a mermaid emblem painted on its flank, above which were at least a dozen stars signifying completed missions. Another bore a curvaceous Betty Boop.

They descended into a fiery orange Belt of Venus that had slung itself above the horizon. Looking down through the dusk, Skye could hardly believe they were at an RAF base.

She landed on a narrow, boggy runway cut through a derelict farm. Cattle wandered around the perimeter, ducks flapped forlornly beside a swampish puddle in the eastern corner, and thatch-roofed outbuildings sagged in a forlorn huddle along one side. But Skye's eyes were sharp and she began to make out the Nissen huts designed to look like cowsheds, the hardstandings, the fire and ambulance garage, the outlines of more black Lysanders.

As she taxied after the follow-me car, safe now, the sensation of the bullet lodging in her Spit's side played over in her mind. She made herself breathe slowly, suddenly too aware of her vulnerability; a vulnerability that she and the other ATA women chose not to contemplate. Some of them had died over the past year; among them the famous aviatrix Amy Johnson, lost in cloud so dense and vast that she'd only fallen out of it, to her death, when she ran out of fuel. Skye had been lucky so far: no drowning sea, no murderous hillsides, no disastrous mechanical failures like others had experienced. She'd been lucky again tonight. For how long would that luck hold?

Don't think about it, she told herself for the hundredth time that year.

She sat still, waiting for the ground crew, but her fingers worked her scarf this way and that. Even though everyone had the impression that the RAF and the ATA women were getting along, Skye knew it would take only one slip-up for the fragile peace to be broken. It was entirely possible that she would be reported for her forbidden aerobatics. She needed her wits about her. She climbed out of the cockpit and jumped to the ground, pulling off her scarf to reveal her long, dark hair.

The pilots from the squadron of Lysanders were also out of their planes now, and they all stopped dead in their tracks in a manner decidedly slapstick, as if there were some kind of invisible wall in front of them. And there was, Skye supposed, just not one of bricks and mortar.

"You're a woman," one of the pilots said in a noticeably American accent. "And beautiful." He grinned.

"I certainly was a woman when I dressed myself this morning," Skye replied, glad that her voice was steady and that she had, by now, become expert in these types of conversations. She knew to fire back from the outset or else suffer a barrage of commentary and innuendo. "And you're obviously an excellent flirt."

All the men laughed, the American loudest of all.

Skye had heard stories about the Special Duties squadrons, of which this must surely be one; there were a few other camouflaged airfields in England but not like this one. Special Duties pilots were the glamour boys of the RAF: the best and bravest of them all, and, apparently, they always had plenty of French perfume and champagne. The American certainly looked the part: so tall that Skye had to tip her head back to meet his gaze, hair the sandy color of a Cornish beach, eyes a warm shade of honey, smile perfectly shaped for making knees go weak.

"Thank you for frightening off the Me 110," she said, nodding around the now very close circle of men. She wondered if she could perhaps charm them into supporting her report about the incident. "Women aren't to be trusted with guns, which leaves me with nothing more than aerobatics to protect myself."

"They were some damn good aerobatics," her American admirer said. "Do you give lessons?"

And they thought women were the flighty ones. "I'd say you've had lessons enough of the kind you're referring to," she countered.

Hoots of laughter followed, and the American—a squadron leader she noted from his insignia, so he couldn't be half bad at flying— looked a little abashed.

"Quit it, O'Farrell." Another voice broke into the jocularity. The men stepped aside to let in their wing commander. "Are you all right?" he asked Skye.

Skye turned and then stopped, as if she were the one walking into an invisible wall.

"Skye?" the man said.

As soon as her legs had recovered from the shock, and despite her disappointment that he hadn't written, she did what she should have done the last time she'd seen Nicholas. She crossed the space between them in an instant and wrapped her arms around him.

"It's so good to see you," she cried, giving him a tight squeeze in case he vanished again, a squeeze that he returned with equal fierceness.

When she stepped back, she saw that his mouth had opened in astonishment. It wasn't quite the perfect circle of surprise she'd been struck by when they'd first met on the pier at Porthleven, but in that expression she saw, unmistakably, her friend. She grinned.

Nicholas didn't. A cloud passed over his face. It became suddenly closed, unfamiliar.

Behind her, Skye heard the murmurings of the men. And she realized what she'd done. In an organization known for discipline and rank, one didn't throw oneself on a wing commander in front of all his men, even if one had known that wing commander when he was eleven.

"I mean it's good to see you, Wing Commander Crawford," Skye amended. "It's Captain Penrose now," she added, realizing that with her sheepskin flight jacket on and rank insignia hidden, he would have no idea what to call her.

Then Nicholas smiled at last and she lost the very few words she'd been able to gather together. The force of that smile alone could have sent the Me 110 screaming back to Germany. Not to mention the eyes, blue and startling and looking right at her. She shook her head in bemusement, blushing as she remembered what she'd said to him the last time they'd met: *You're handsome.* The same thought crossed her mind now: *how* had Nicholas Crawford become so handsome?

"Captain Penrose," he said teasingly. "It's been a while." He turned to the assembled men. "As much as you'd all like to watch Captain Penrose and me catch up on nearly ten years of estrangement, I'm sure you have better things to do. O'Farrell, see if Skye can stay at the Waafery tonight. Jenkins, let the station commander know we have a visitor."

As the men set off, Skye heard another voice call out from behind them: "Sir, your fiancée's here."

And Skye saw Nicholas, the "sir" whose attention was required, whip around. Before he did, she caught a look of immense relief on his face, as if this arrival was something he'd been waiting for with a fervor ordinarily reserved for more momentous news, like the end of the war.

A woman crossed the hardstanding toward them. She wasn't beautiful but striking, like a light pillar in a night sky—that spectacular clustering of ice crystals into columns of fire. She was immaculate in her Women's Auxiliary Air Force uniform, her glossy deep brown hair set in a perfect victory roll, her lips painted a dark and stylish red, her face barely animated by a smile. She attracted the combined gazes of everyone there.

She slipped her arm into Nicholas's.

As the pilots dragged themselves away, Skye heard one of them mutter, "Christ, if I hadn't thought our wing commander had the dishiest piece in the land, now he's got another one who's just as much of a doll."

"Jenkins!" Nicholas's voice fired.

The men quieted immediately.

The fiancée spoke in French-accented English. "How are you, Nick?"

"This is Margaux Jourdan," Nicholas said to Skye. "And this is Skye Penrose. A friend from childhood."

The strangest sensation swept over Skye—a narrowness in her throat that made it hard to speak. She remembered feeling like this once before: when her mother had told her she was sending Skye and Liberty to France for six months. Bereft. But what had she lost? Nicholas's words were correct: she *was* a friend from childhood. But his words were devoid of everything she'd thought their friendship had been.

"Did you know each other well?" Margaux inquired, as if she didn't really care and was only making polite conversation.

Margaux's uninterested tone caused Skye to recover her voice. "Well enough for him to have seen my underwear," she said. "And me his."

She left Margaux to swallow that and, buoyed by Nicholas's laugh, followed the men across the airfield.

But as she walked into the darkness, Skye understood what she'd lost, finally and forever: the shining idea of Nicholas, the boy with whom she had, once upon a time, discovered a lost garden, and danced on a clifftop, and lain in a cave in the dark, silently weeping. He was never coming back.

EIGHT

After Skye had found somewhere to change into her skirt and jacket—RAF rules forbade her from wearing her flying suit in an officer's mess—O'Farrell, who said that even he couldn't remember his first name, so long had it been since he'd heard it, was more than happy to escort her to the mess. He pulled out a chair for her.

"You were on the cover of *Picture Post*," O'Farrell said knowledgeably.

"I was," she said, stabbing her fork into the bacon and eggs—real eggs, not the powdered kind—and smiling, always smiling.

"We don't get many ATA pilots here," another man said. "Wish we did," he added wistfully, only to be silenced by a look from O'Farrell.

"Where exactly are we?" Skye inquired. "I've ferried to almost every RAF airfield in England, but not this one."

"They've found a place for you at the Waafery tonight," Nicholas Crawford cut in. He stood before her again, having momentarily divested himself of his fiancée.

Skye felt the sudden alertness in the room, an alertness she recognized from spending time in other RAF messes: the poised-on-the-toes responsiveness of a squadron before their leader. But this wasn't the fearful vigilance of a team whose wing commander ruled with threats and violence; it was the eager reverence of a group of men who respected their commanding officer.

Nicholas had, it seemed, done everything he'd wished for when they'd sat together at her mother's kitchen table doing homework. He'd well and truly escaped his past. His American accent had returned; all the smoothness his vowels had acquired during four years in Cornwall gone. With the accent had come a confidence of tone and manner that she supposed he'd always possessed but, because it was more innate and quiet than O'Farrell's cockiness, it had been easy to overlook. Not anymore.

She wanted to ask him how he'd done it, to talk to him properly. She was about to invite him to sit down when he said, abruptly, "You have everything you need?" He gestured to her overnight bag as if he expected her to put down her fork and leap to attention. It was impossible to imagine this man asking *What's wrong?* and her telling him.

"Do you mind if I eat first?" she said lightly. "I haven't had anything besides a chocolate ration since breakfast. All that corkscrewing has given me an appetite."

"I'd rather you came now."

Skye matched her tone to his—cool, impatient. "I need to file an incident report with the CO. I'm assuming that's you."

"I'll write it for you."

"But I need to see it. Not everyone reports incidents that women are involved in accurately."

She thought she saw a flash of anger then—that she would doubt his integrity—but he was behaving like a stranger, so she had to assume she knew nothing about him.

"Finish your supper." He extracted a pen from his pocket and summoned the appropriate piece of paper. Nobody spoke as he scrawled a few lines across it. He handed her his pen and the report. "If you're happy with that."

She read the account. It was a fair summary, so she signed her name at the bottom. Then she stood up. "Sorry, boys, seems I'm not wanted."

She smiled at the men, paying special attention to O'Farrell, ate a last mouthful of egg and picked up her jacket.

O'Farrell stood up. "Why don't I walk you out too?" he said.

On the way to the Waafery, Nicholas said nothing but O'Farrell cajoled from Skye which pool she worked out of, when her next days off were, and tried to find a time when their respective leaves coincided. He was the epitome of the brash American flyboy and she knew her counterparts at Hamble would be swooning by now. But he was also funny and nice and had rescued her from an awkward situation.

"You don't need to accompany me," she called out to Nicholas, who was striding a little ahead. "I know you both need to eat and debrief. And," she added as Nicholas turned around, "that you have a fiancée somewhere who must be eager to see you."

"Peggy!" O'Farrell hollered, and a young woman in a WAAF uniform came running over. "Can you walk Captain Penrose to the Waafery?"

Peggy batted her eyelids at O'Farrell, and then at Nicholas. O'Farrell grinned at the attention and engaged her in conversation, whereas Nicholas appeared not to notice Peggy was even there.

"You're at Hamble now?" he said quietly to Skye, obviously having overheard her conversation with O'Farrell. He caught her at the exact moment she was flicking her scarf carelessly over her shoulder in the same way she'd once flung beach towels. He must have had the same thought because he shook his head. "You know, in some ways you're so exactly the same as you used to be that it's like stepping out of now and into then. And in other ways, you are absolutely and completely different."

There it was at last: the empathy she'd expected. And it *was* strange, seeing flashes of their childhood ghosts in the adults they'd become. Perhaps that accounted for his behavior.

"I'm sure you're very different in some ways too," she said mischievously, hoping to reestablish a status quo between them.

Nicholas rubbed his hand on his jaw and then spoke determinedly. "I hope one of the things that's different is you're not so much of a daredevil. Jesus, Skye, you're flying without radio, without weapons, without instruments—what if my squadron hadn't been around tonight?"

Skye halted, anger stirring. "Would you say that to me if I were a man?" she asked casually.

"I'm saying it because I used to care about you, and that history means I still care about you." His tone was flat and emotionless, as if he were trying to pretend, by using words like "care," that he wasn't giving her a ticking-off.

"How dare you."

"What?" he said, head jerking back as if she'd slapped him, which she certainly felt like doing.

"I'm a captain," she snapped. "I've worked my way up from second officer. I was offered a promotion to flight captain, which I declined because it meant being desk-bound. I've landed planes without landing gear, navigated through storms without instruments, watched the propeller fall off my plane and still managed to bring it down safely. I have never once damaged a plane through my own actions. The RAF needs planes to fight a war and it's my job to deliver those planes intact so we can win that war. A 'daredevil' would think of none of that. Please take your chauvinist concerns and apply them to the men in your squadron who have less experience than I do, and who are the daredevils who try out their first stall turn in an RAF plane, crash and take that plane out of action, so I have to ferry it around for repairs without a radio and without any instruments."

She stalked over to the waiting Peggy and said, "Let's go."

* * *

Nicholas swore as he watched Skye walk away. *Why* did that have to happen the way it had? Why did she have to appear again tonight, without warning, looping back into his life the same way she'd twirled into it fourteen years ago, upside down and with a smile brighter than anything he'd ever seen exploding into flames against a midnight sky.

Margaux appeared at his side. "Are you ready? Or do you still have to debrief?" Then, "Do you think she'll say anything about where she ended up tonight?"

"I think that after I practically threw her out with what she thought was a reprimand, she'll do her best to forget she was ever here."

"You couldn't have done anything else."

Margaux lit a Gauloise and offered him the pack. He took one gratefully. She was right. But it didn't make him feel any better.

"You look like you just shot your best friend in the back," Margaux said now. "How close were you two?"

"I haven't seen her for years. Besides one quick meeting at an airfield in 1940."

It wasn't an answer to her question, but it was all he could say at that moment.

If he'd been asked the same question ten years ago, he would have said that Skye was like his breath: essential. It was unthinkable that he would ever be without her. But he had been without her for a long time. He hadn't written to her as he'd said he would the last time he saw her because it was too damn hard. In the passage of years she'd become, unquestionably, a woman. He hadn't quite realized that when they last spoke, so intent had he been—and she too, he thought—on disburdening their pent-up fears. Perhaps she also had a fiancé. Although the way she'd let O'Farrell flirt with her suggested she didn't.

He ground his cigarette butt beneath his boot. Margaux slipped her arm into his.

"How are you?" he asked softly. "Sorry I couldn't pick you up. Engine trouble."

She shrugged. "I'm tired. Like you. Which means we both need a drink."

He tossed her a smile. Say what you would about Margaux—that she was cold, ruthless, marble-hearted—but she was always practical. "That sounds like a very good idea."

They walked to the Unicorn, deep in conversation, and drank more whiskey than they should have and smoked too many Gauloises, because what else was there to do?

In the morning, Nicholas walked over to the Waafery to inquire about Skye and was told she'd already gone.

This time, he would find her. He couldn't explain most of his behavior, but perhaps he could explain enough that she wouldn't hate him.

PART FOUR
KAT

NINE

When Kat arrived back in Sydney, rather than going home from the airport to shower and change and switch her jet-lagged brain to the higher-level functioning required to wrangle a five-year-old and a three-year-old, she collected her daughters from her ex-husband in a smother of hugs and kisses.

She didn't step into the house, hoping to avoid Paul, but divorce was the gift that kept on giving: pain, guilt and anger its usual offerings. Indeed, hardly any time passed before she was drawn into a not-quite argument, carried out in calm tones to disguise the petty words.

"You didn't tell me the girls were having French lessons," he said.

"They're not," she replied, immediately on the defensive. "I speak French with them occasionally. My grandmother does too. You know that."

"And you know as well as I do that bilingual children struggle in the first few years of school. We wouldn't want them to fall behind just for the sake of learning a few French words."

"Then you must also know that bilingual children more than catch up by middle primary school," she countered, "and usually move far ahead of their peers. Plus they have the added benefit of speaking two languages. I don't see the problem." She caught herself about to cross her arms and dropped them back to her sides, not wanting to appear vulnerable. "Besides, Daisy's only in preschool; it's not as if she can fall too far behind in coloring."

Paul leaned against the door frame and smiled as if his next words would secure victory for him. "Elizabeth can't even spell 'cat.' At first she said it was K-a-t and then she said it was c-h-a-t."

A small laugh escaped Kat. "Lisbet," she called. "How do you spell 'cat'?"

Five-year-old Lisbet reappeared, dragging her backpack behind her. "It's c-a-t, Mummy. You know that."

"*Et voilà*," Kat said to her ex-husband. "I don't think that a child who knows how to spell cat three different ways is having any trouble at school."

Daisy skipped after her sister, pink galoshes in hand, dripping muddy splashes across the hardwood floors.

Paul snapped at Kat as if that was her fault too. "I'd prefer you consult with me about any extracurricular activities you involve the girls in."

Kat could feel the girls' eyes fixed on their parents. "Lisbet, take Daisy to the car," she said. "I'll be there in a minute." As the girls trotted down the path, Kat spoke to Paul. "I'm not going to call you every time I use a French word or two with them. Nor is my grandmother. You were once excited by the prospect of having children who knew languages other than English. Try to remember that."

She left, sensing Paul watching her before he went inside to his new family, which Kat hoped wouldn't break apart like theirs had. Divorce wasn't something she'd wish on anyone, even her ex-husband.

Lisbet and Daisy chattered excitedly all the way home. They were, as always, thrilled Kat was back, and her heart hurt from the quantity of love they showered upon her. Their enthusiasm dimmed a little when Kat told them she was taking them to visit their great-grandmother at Pambula Beach on the weekend, but she knew it was just because they hadn't been home for ten days and wanted the security of their own rooms and their toys. Both girls loved Margaux Jourdan, although they would never appreciate her the way Kat did. To Lisbet and Daisy, their great-grandmother was an old woman who was often too pointedly accurate in her remarks. But for Kat, Margaux Jourdan was a surrogate mother, a woman who'd unquestioningly taken on the care of a week-old baby when Kat's mother, Margaux's daughter, could not.

Kat decided not to mention the visit again as she drove to the little cottage in Birchgrove that she'd bought after she left Paul. She ordered pizza for dinner, let the girls have a bubble bath, and read them their favorite story—"Ali Baba and the Forty Thieves"—for the hundredth time, lingering over their favorite part—when the thieves were boiled in oil. Then she tucked them into bed and gave them their special kisses: one on the forehead, one on the tip of the nose, one on each cheek, and one final kiss over the heart.

Once the girls were asleep, tired though she was from jet lag, Kat turned on her computer and studied the pictures she'd taken of the dresses she'd found in the Cornish cottage. Open on her desk was a book about Christian Dior, full of beautiful images of his gowns, and she used that and the internet to prove a suspicion that had formed as she'd puzzled over the strange treasure on her flight home.

The first photograph was easy for Kat, as a fashion conservator, to identify: the glamorous red of the Aladin cocktail dress from 1947. From 1948, the chocolate-brown panache of the Bon Voyage travel dress. 1949: another one Kat recognized on first glance; the froth and sparkle of the sequinned silk scallops on the Venus ballgown. 1950: more white, another ballgown; the Francis Poulenc in pleated taffeta.

The dresses in her grandmother's mysterious cottage were not just a random selection: there was one gown for every year from 1947, when the House of Dior opened, through to the present. Sixty-five gowns in all, chosen carefully to represent the best and most timeless pieces.

Kat pressed her hand to her forehead and tried to think. When Margaux had inherited Kat, she'd started trading secondhand couture gowns so she could afford the expense of raising a child, transforming the front room of her Potts Point terrace into a salon. Before all of that, when Kat's own mother was small, Margaux had modeled for local department stores. It meant she knew the right people for her new business and could buy dresses from the women she'd once modeled for, women who wore their couture once or twice and had no further use for it. Then other women, those on the next rung down on the social ladder, would visit the terrace and purchase the gowns for about half the price of a new one.

Kat had grown up surrounded by gowns, and thus had been born her love of fashion; a love that had proved more enduring than that which she'd shared with Paul. As a child she'd sat in her grandmother's lap when the buyers and sellers came, delighting in the faces of the women as they stepped into a couture gown for the first time; it was as if they'd been plugged into the stars.

Margaux had always said that nobody could own the magnificence of the Sainte-Chapelle in Paris: it was a work of art that could only be visited, its memory taken away in a photograph. But a dress was a work of art to both lift the spirits and be taken home, to be worn whenever one felt like it, even to make the breakfast if that was what was required to revive the heart. Indeed, Dior had always maintained that his gowns endowed one with poetry, and with life, and her grandmother had agreed. "You're not just sewing a seam," Margaux would say, "but fashioning a new life."

Kat had believed her then and she believed her now. But how many new lives did her grandmother have hidden in wardrobes on the other side of the world?

For it was impossible to imagine that the gowns in the cottage were a leftover from her grandmother's business venture. Margaux hadn't started it until 1973, and she had closed the business in the nineties. Kat had helped her sell off everything. The dresses in Cornwall spanned a much larger timeframe, and were Paris-made originals, rather than the licensed models that would mostly have been available in Australia during that time. Indeed, Kat would certainly remember if her grandmother had ever received anything as remarkable as the Venus dress to sell.

So where *had* they come from? And why keep them so far away and in such substandard storage? Kat's conservator's soul ached at the thought of what the salty wind creeping in through the cracks in the doorframes might be doing to decades old, museum-quality pieces. It was one of the reasons she'd purchased an extra suitcase and brought some of the dresses home with her.

And then there was that most spectacular piece of all: the jaw-dropping blue. It had no label. Kat, despite searching for two hours, had found nothing like it in a multitude of Dior images.

None of it made any sense. And she was so tired she hadn't the energy needed to keep her eyelids open. It was time for bed. She would ask her grandmother about the gowns, and the cottage, on the weekend. There had to be a simple explanation, although Kat couldn't conceive of what it might be.

* * *

The next day, ignoring the lingering jet lag in the same way that mothers ignored every perpetual tiredness, Kat dropped the girls at school and caught the ferry to King Street Wharf. She noticed a few women on the ferry running covetous eyes over her dress and she wanted to invite them to touch it, to look inside to where Dior's true artistry was most evident, knowing that most people would only ever see such a dress behind the glass wall of a vitrine case in a museum. Her heart had overruled her conservator's head that morning and she'd worn the 1948 Dior Bon Voyage dress from her grandmother's wardrobe. It was made of deep-brown wool, belted at the waist, and had a collar that wrapped around into a beautifully draped scarf, then tucked under the belt and flared out like a peplum over the skirt. She knew that light, air, even the oil on her skin were making the museum-piece dress deteriorate second by second, but sometimes clothes were meant to live rather than be entombed in boxes inside a climate-controlled storage facility.

As she walked around to the Powerhouse Museum, she made the mental adjustment from a person whose head was full of school lunches and uniforms and where on earth Lisbet had put her library book to Katarina Jourdan, the fashion conservator who reveled in coaxing centuries-old dresses back to life. It was to be a particularly exciting day, one that would definitely make her forget both fatigue and what had happened in Cornwall, and she wanted to make sure she was focussed enough to enjoy it.

At the museum, she greeted Annabel, her assistant, who exclaimed over Kat's dress. Once it had been thoroughly inspected, Kat asked expectantly, "Are they here yet?"

Annabel nodded, her face shimmering with the kind of excitement Kat could feel emanating from her own fingers, which were itching to don gloves, dive into boxes and travel back in time.

"I had them brought straight here," Annabel said, indicating five long boxes on the workbench in the middle of the room.

"Five?" Kat queried. "I thought there were only four."

The objects she was about to unbox had been donated to the Power-house by one of their generous benefactors, a woman who'd bought them at the Paris Fashions For All parade at David Jones in Sydney in

1947. They were the first four Christian Dior designs to ever be shown in Australia and the museum was delighted to take possession of them. As was Kat. While she could make herself fall in love with almost anything in the Powerhouse's costume collection, Dior had always been one of her favorite designers. Getting these pieces ready for display would be the best thing she'd done all year. And she couldn't help but send the universe a wry smile for endowing her with so much Dior to marvel over right now.

She snapped on her gloves, removed the lid from the first box and parted the tissue paper to reveal a lustrous black ankle-length cocktail gown. She lifted it out and the skirt unfurled, silk blooming gracefully to swathe the hips, then billowing into elaborate folds at the back. Kat and Annabel sighed in unison.

"Can we get them all out?" Annabel asked. "See them together, rather than just one at a time?" She was hopping from one foot to the other, reminding Kat of her daughters in an ice-cream shop.

"Let's," Kat said, feeling the frisson of an unrepeatable and extraordinary moment spangle the air.

She opened the next box. Inside was a silk afternoon dress in navy blue, which mimicked the lines of the renowned Bar Suit. Then a wool suit with a jacket drawn in by a cummerbund to exaggerate the inward curve of the waist. But it was the skirt that stole all of Kat's breath: it cascaded down to reveal, beneath its black and white diagonal check, its padding and its boning, an astonishing sixteen gores, which created a perfectly parabolic shape.

"How that must have swirled," Annabel said wistfully.

Kat stroked the skirt. "Imagine being there in July 1947 at the parade."

"It must have been like . . ." Annabel cast around for a suitable comparison. "Like Paris Fashion Week being held here instead of in France."

Kat laughed. "Maybe something like that. They transformed the entire fourth floor of David Jones into a French salon so the models could parade around the tables, rather than along a raised platform, wearing pieces from Paquin, Balenciaga and Maggy Rouff. And just these four from Christian Dior."

Annabel closed her eyes and Kat knew she was visualizing the spectacle. It might sound underwhelming to modern ears, but to Australians who'd never seen anything like it before, it had been breathtaking.

"Go on," Annabel urged.

"Well," Kat said, closing her own eyes as she recalled everything she knew about the parades, "the walls were decorated with oversized images of models wearing the gowns in Paris—you couldn't escape the fact that this was all about fashion. Beautiful fashion, never before seen or imagined fashion—the skirts were all four or five inches longer than anything sold in Australia for years. David Jones held two shows a day over two weeks, each with eight hundred spectators; all sold out well beforehand. Australians suddenly and unbelievably had clothing directly from France and within the same season. There was nothing separating them from the Parisians."

Annabel sighed feelingly, then opened her eyes, leaned in closer to the black cocktail dress and indicated the waistline. "It's tiny."

"I remember reading that the models' waists had to be eighteen to twenty inches," Kat said.

"Twenty inches!" Annabel gasped. "They must have starved themselves."

"The French *had* been starved for most of the 1940s. Paris was still on rations in 1947. I'm sure the mannequins would have much preferred food to their twenty-inch waists."

Kat moved over to the last, unexpected box and opened it. It was like taking the lid off the sky and having it pour down upon you, showering you in a bright, mid-afternoon lapis hue.

"Wow!" Annabel said.

Kat didn't exclaim. She dropped the lid on the floor with a crash that she didn't hear. Her hands forgot how to work and remained fixed in place, clawing at the empty air where the lid had been.

But inside her whirled every conceivable emotion—shock, disbelief, a strange, bubbling hysteria—so fast she couldn't respond to any of them. She could only stare into that magnificent, prismatic blue. It was the same blue she'd seen in her grandmother's desolate cottage in Cornwall, a color that made mouths gape and eyes round, a color more hypnotic than any mythical Siren.

Sounds began to filter back into Kat's ears: Annabel still rhapsodizing, mistaking Kat's confusion for dazzlement. Kat extended her arms forward, into the box, knowing exactly what she would withdraw from within.

A dress with no label. A fantastically wanton full skirt, a little like Dior's Adelaide ballgown with its incredible seventy-seven yards of tulle skirt, weighing in at a total of one hundred pounds. A nipped-in waist and seams stitched with haute couture precision.

"Was there a note with the boxes?" Kat asked, mind jumping from question to question and settling on one that was the most innocuous.

Annabel cast around, then retrieved an envelope. She tore it open and read aloud. "*I remembered I had another dress. I've never worn it—a friend gave it to me. I thought you would like it. I've never known who the designer was. Madeline.*"

"She thought we'd like it?" Annabel repeated. "That's got to be the understatement of the year. We *love* it!"

Kat shivered. If she hadn't ever seen the twin dress in Cornwall, she'd be in complete agreement with Annabel.

"Is it Dior?" Annabel asked, noticing the absent label. "I've never seen it before."

And that was just one of the problems. A Dior gown so sensational would certainly be featured in any book on the fashion house, would have been displayed proudly by any museum, would be almost as well known as the Bar Suit. But, as far as Kat was aware, nobody knew anything of this beautiful blue dress. Why? Did it somehow mean that only two had ever been made? The one in Cornwall and the one in Kat's gloved hands now? Impossible. How would her grandmother have ever come by such a unique piece?

"Could you pass me a magnifying glass?" she managed to say.

Annabel did so and Kat bent her head over a small tag she'd found sewn into the side seam. There appeared to be traces of ink on it, handwritten letters. She held the lens closer but the letters had faded with age and dry-cleaning. She could possibly make out the tail of a "g" and the circularity of an "a" near the middle of what had once been a word. Or perhaps a name.

Kat's phone buzzed, making her and Annabel jump.

"The debrief," Annabel said.

Kat remembered she was supposed to update everyone on her recent visit to the belly of the V&A Museum and what she'd learned about preventative conservation and new methods of object storage. She returned the blue dress to its box.

All she could be certain of was that Dior mysteries were following her like insistent children. And none gave the impression of being easily solved.

* * *

On Saturday late morning, Kat's car drew up at the cottage that sat on one of the highest points of Pambula Beach, overlooking Haycock Point. Margaux Jourdan stood waiting on the veranda, lacking the straight-backed elegance of twenty years before, but still upright, although she held on to the railing. Her navy suit was immaculate, her face was powdered and her lips were colored—a softer hue than the red she'd once worn; the always impeccable Margaux acknowledged that an aging face and deepest red lipstick were not the best of friends.

Kat wondered if her grandmother arranged herself like this every day or if she only did it for her visitors' benefit. She knew it was a throwback to a time when women always wore makeup and stockings, and tracksuits were unheard of, but her heart throbbed a little at the thought of her grandmother waking up early, readying herself for this visit.

"Hug your great-grandma gently," Kat said to the girls as they bounded out of the car like puppies who'd been cooped up too long.

They obliged Kat's request by resting their heads on their great-grandmother's legs, which was as high as they could reach. Margaux stroked their hair. "There's a present for each of you on your beds," she said to them.

Both girls beamed and ran into the house. Their great-grandmother always gave them the most precious and thoughtful gifts: a scrapbook of photos and stories recounting what they'd done together the last time the girls had come to the beach; a quilt made of squares cut from clothes the girls had loved but sadly outgrown; a carved wooden box filled with ribbons and sequins and colored feathers for them to play with. Discovering a new gift was one of their favorite parts of each visit.

Kat smiled at her grandmother and studied her face. With every day that passed, age gouged markings more deeply into Margaux's skin. But there was nothing to unduly alarm Kat so she wrapped her arms around her grandmother and kissed both of her cheeks. Margaux shook her head and pretended the show of affection was too much, although Kat saw the curve of her smile beneath the protestations.

"Anyone would think you hadn't seen me for two years instead of two weeks," Margaux said.

"Sometimes when I'm away it feels more like two years," Kat

admitted. "I miss the girls so much. I feel as if they grow and change entirely, and that one day they'll turn around and berate me for the things I didn't notice because I wasn't there."

"Mothers worry too much these days. You love your children, and they know you love them. Simply being present doesn't make them feel more loved."

Kat nodded and let her grandmother go on ahead into the house, knowing that to offer assistance would be the equivalent of implying she was incapacitated. Margaux shuffled along, not moving too badly for someone aged ninety-four.

Inside, the house was austere, almost as if nobody lived there. It was a holiday cottage, meant for a family to summer in, and Kat had never understood why Margaux had insisted upon buying it soon before Kat married Paul, moving so far away from her granddaughter and civilization. But Margaux had always been detached from everyone except Kat, and the house added another bulwark of distance.

Once her grandmother was settled in a chair, Kat ferried the girls' belongings from the car into the house. Then she took Lisbet and Daisy to the beach, where she reveled in the simple joy of swimming— ignoring her chattering teeth.

Lisbet climbed onto Kat's back and took innumerable rides out into the deeper water. Daisy dug through the sand. Kat watched them, wanting to stretch out this span of time when there were no conflicts except those easily solved by making sure both girls found an equal number of shells.

Toward late afternoon, Kat took the girls back to the house, showered them off, made pasta and then Margaux volunteered, as she always did, to tell Lisbet and Daisy a story. It was another thing they genuinely loved about their great-grandmother—her ability to weave a story like no other. She usually recounted the tales from Jules Verne's *Extraordinary Voyages*, narrating mostly in English but with a smattering of French, and quite possibly an overlay of fabrication as she took the story where she preferred it to go.

Tonight the girls sat on the rug before the fireplace and stared expectantly at the old woman. Margaux's eyes looked suddenly far away as if she were searching out the right story to tell at that particular moment.

She settled on *A Floating City*. Lisbet and Daisy listened with not just their ears, but with rounded eyes and open mouths, as Margaux recreated a ship so big that it had streets and buildings upon its decks. As the story flowed on, Kat sat in a chair and let the words and the contentment swaddle her.

After the girls were in bed, Kat prepared to wash her grandmother's hair, a task that Margaux's ancient arms and uncertain balance made difficult. Kat readied the jug, the shampoo and conditioner that her grandmother liked, made sure the water was warm, then waited while Margaux draped a towel around her shoulders, leaned back and closed her eyes.

Kat unbound her grandmother's thick, white hair and poured the first jug of water over it. Neither spoke for a time, Kat content to massage her grandmother's head, wishing she had time to drive here each weekend and give her grandmother this half hour of complete repose.

The years fell away from Margaux's face and Kat could imagine her as a young and beautiful woman whose life was perhaps more extraordinary than Kat had ever credited. Moving to Australia from France, an unmarried woman with a young child, must surely have been, back in 1948, a stupendous thing.

"Do you miss France?" Kat heard herself ask, surprising both herself and her grandmother, and she knew her subconscious was trying to find a way to begin a conversation about the mystery of the astonishing wardrobes in Cornwall.

Her grandmother's answer was quick and emphatic. "No. The war ruined it for me."

Kat toweled off Margaux's hair, which, as it dried, felt like the softest cashmere scarf. She combed the strands gently, knowing her grandmother enjoyed the sensation of the brush on her scalp. They had both lapsed into French; they often did when it was just the two of them. The language suited Margaux's voice, which had never acquired an Australian pitch but had instead blurred into an unidentifiably cosmopolitan accent.

"I went to the house in Porthleven," Kat said.

Her grandmother nodded.

"I didn't realize there would be so much furniture there," Kat said, delicately advancing on the subject. "Household items. Jewelry even. Whose is it? Don't you worry about thieves?"

"It came with the house," was her grandmother's uninformative answer. "And thieves want flat-screen televisions, not ancient vanity sets."

"When did you buy it? And why do you keep it?"

Margaux's eyes opened and she studied her granddaughter's face. "A whim. Surely I'm allowed one at my age."

A whim. Were the dresses a whim too?

"I also found some wardrobes full of Christian Dior gowns. Haute couture, not off the rack. I don't suppose you know anything about that?" Kat asked softly.

Her grandmother's eyes took on that same lost or far-reaching look they'd worn when she'd thought about what story to tell her great-granddaughters. "I wanted you to have them," she said, voice very thin. "Dior's gowns once helped me when I was starting over. I thought they might help you." Her tone changed, becoming sharper and more purposeful. "They deserve to be worn—which means you need to go out more. On dates. Life isn't over for you, Katarina. I hope you brought some of them back with you."

Kat felt her mouth drop open. Margaux seemed to be saying that the dresses had been hers, and were now Kat's. "Did I bring any of the dresses back with me?" she repeated, rubbing her finger over the two fine lines she knew were creasing the space between her brows. "Where did you get them?"

Margaux's eyes closed and her face turned the color of bone.

Kat dropped to her knees before her. "Put your head down. No, breathe. I'll call the doctor."

"Don't," Margaux rasped, opening her eyes. But no blood recolored her cheeks; they remained that ghastly, ghostly white.

"Are you all right?" Kat asked urgently. "Come and lie down."

Margaux shook her head.

The bathroom wheezed with the sound of Kat's grandmother's shallow breathing.

Then Margaux spoke. "I thought I could tell you. But I . . . I can't. I'm sorry."

Kat was horrified to see that her grandmother was weeping: silent, aching tears. "Don't be sorry," she cried, wrapping her arms around Margaux, panic of a kind she'd never felt before making her hold on tight—like a child herself—to the only mother she'd ever known.

What she'd seen on Margaux's face after the bloodlessness passed was a terror so stark Kat never wanted to see it again. It was as if her grandmother had witnessed death itself, as if the dark angel had reached for Margaux with outstretched arms.

Kat didn't ever want to unravel herself from her grandmother. But that was, of course, impossible. Instead she would wear Margaux's dresses and not ask another thing about them.

At last Margaux extracted herself and kissed Kat's cheek. "I'm being a fool," she said. "The dresses are from my modeling days. A perk of the job, I suppose you could say." Then she dragged herself up from her chair and shuffled along the hallway.

Kat stayed where she was, kneeling on the floor. She didn't know what was worse: her grandmother's initial distress or the lie that had followed.

Besides perhaps the first ten dresses, the vast majority of the sixty-five gowns were not from the period when Margaux had modeled. And local department stores in Australia would never have had such dresses to give away to their models. All Margaux had proven was that Kat's initial conjecture—that the dresses couldn't have come from the secondhand couture business—was right. That would have been the easier story to massage into believability, yet Margaux hadn't done so. And nor had Margaux given any satisfactory answer about the cottage.

It was Kat's turn to shut her eyes. Why would Margaux lie like that? Kat recollected the look on her grandmother's face and knew she would never ask.

TEN

The following week at work, Kat had just pulled the mystery blue gown out of its box so she could stare at it some more when her phone rang.

"Katarina Jourdan speaking."

"Hello." A voice with an English accent rolled charmingly through the phone. "I'm Elliott Beaufort. You're probably busy so I'll keep it brief. I'm a historian and author, and I'm currently researching a book about a family of women who did some remarkable things during both world wars."

At the man's name, followed by the word "author," Kat felt a flash of recognition. She searched her memory and recalled that, about a year ago, her book club had gone to hear an author speak about his latest book. She hadn't been able to go herself, and at the next meeting her friends had giggled like teenagers with a crush on a boy band about the witty, erudite author. They'd all agreed they'd happily leave their husbands for him. Kat, recently separated, hadn't listened to the rest of the conversation, but she was almost sure the author's name was Elliott Beaufort.

"I understand you're possibly related to a Margaux Jourdan," he continued. "I found the connection in some bio details of yours on the internet. I'm trying to work out if your Margaux Jourdan is the same one I'm looking for. And I'm sorry for the strange call," he added. "People usually hang up on me because they think I'm trying to sell them a computer virus. Maybe we could arrange a time to talk properly, when it's convenient. I can email you some information about me too, so you can make sure I'm not trying to scam you."

Kat laughed. "You don't sound like a telemarketer. But I'm pretty sure my grandmother isn't the woman you want. What kind of remarkable things did this Margaux Jourdan do?"

"She supposedly worked for an auxiliary service of the RAF where women did things like packing parachutes. But she really worked for a government organization called SOE—the Special Operations Executive. She was sent to France throughout the war to gather information from the Nazis and pass it on to the Resistance. She was a spy, in other words."

"Then it's definitely not my grandmother," Kat said confidently, ready to hang up and let him go and give his spiel to a relative of a different Margaux Jourdan somewhere else in the world. "She was in England during the war but she didn't do anything like that."

"What did she do?" Elliott asked.

Kat cast her mind right back to a school assignment, a family tree, when everyone had had to write down the names of their relatives, important dates and what their occupation had been. Kat's tree had looked like the scene of a massacre—beside almost everyone's names, including those of Margaux's parents and brothers, were the words: *died during the war*. And besides Kat's mother's name: *died 1973*. Kat had thrown the tree in the bin and not handed it in because hers was so different to everyone else's in her class.

"I don't know. She doesn't talk about it," Kat said, voice no longer confident, each word dressed with uncertainty. Cottages, dresses and now a man trying to pass her grandmother off as someone who'd spied. *Oh, Margaux*, Kat thought, *what's going on?*

"That's very common." He sounded as if he were trying to reassure her but Kat's unease clung to her like latex.

Was it also common, when talking about the past, to have a face white as bone, for eyes to turn black with fright?

"Well, this next question will definitely exclude her," Elliott said in that same gentle tone and Kat had the feeling he could sense her disquiet. "Do you know if your grandmother was born in France?"

"Yes, she was. On the first of November, 1918."

"Really?"

Now Kat heard both surprise and hope in his voice. She wanted to hang up the phone and not hear his next words.

"It makes her the only Margaux Jourdan—not that there are many of them in the world—who has the same birth date as the woman I'm looking for. Was she born in Lyon?"

"I'm not sure," Kat said slowly. It would have been on the family tree she'd thrown away but a detail like that had been unremarkable to her when set beside the word *died* repeated so many times. "I'd have to check."

"I could talk to her, if that's easier for you," he said.

Kat shook her head emphatically. "She won't talk to you. She's . . ." Kat searched for the right words, knowing she had to keep this man away from her grandmother so he didn't frighten her the way Kat had with her questions on the weekend. "She's a little reclusive."

Elliott's sigh expressed his disappointment. "Is there any chance you could find out if she was born in Lyon? And maybe answer some more questions?"

Annabel's voice returned Kat to her workroom at the museum. She sat up straight, drawing professionalism around her. "I'm at work. So I can't right now. Are you in Sydney?"

"London."

The words fell from her mouth. "I'll be in London next month," she said. It might be the wildest of goose chases, despite a coincidence of birth dates. Or it might somehow give Kat the answers to her questions about the cottage, the gowns and her grandmother's visceral, animal fear.

"Brilliant!" Elliott said, and Kat found herself agreeing to ask her grandmother whether she had indeed been born in Lyon and also scheduling a time to meet Elliott in London.

She hung up the phone, shaking her head. Going back to London was something she'd organized only yesterday as the V&A Museum's French couture expert was eager to discuss Kat's potential Dior discovery—the blue dress—and it so happened that one of the House of Dior's archivists would be visiting the V&A at the same time and wanted to talk to Kat too.

She felt herself childishly crossing her fingers—perhaps Margaux would tell Kat she'd been born in Paris or Marseilles and then Kat could forget all about Elliott Beaufort. But that wouldn't banish the memory of her grandmother's bone-white face, Kat knew—nothing ever would—and so she wasn't at all sure if that was the outcome she really wanted.

* * *

When Kat's phone rang again, it was the childcare center calling to tell her that Daisy had been complaining of a sore stomach for the past hour.

"You took her to the toilet?" Kat asked desperately, knowing that of course they would have tried all the obvious things. She couldn't afford another afternoon off work. But nor could she ignore her possibly sick child. She felt tension creep up her neck and across the top of her head. "I'll be there as soon as I can," she said.

She wouldn't be solving any dress mysteries today. Instead, she'd have to grovel to her boss to ask for the afternoon off, and possibly the next day too, depending on how sick Daisy was.

Daisy greeted her with a wan smile and a clinging hug that told Kat she wasn't feeling her best. All of Kat's irritation dissolved with the whispered words, "Can you carry me, Mummy?"

Kat scooped her daughter up into her arms and carried her to King Street Wharf where they caught the ferry home. Once Daisy was settled on the sofa, tucked in a blanket, Tylenol administered, the Wiggles singing too-bright nursery rhymes on the television, Kat dialed her ex-husband's mobile.

It was answered by an intern at the children's hospital's emergency department, who asked her to hold. As Kat waited, the sounds of monitors and pain and crisis brought back with too-sharp force the weekend that finally ended her marriage.

Paul had been attending medical conferences with greater regularity in the year after Daisy was born, which Kat understood—even though it made the childcare juggle a nightmare. Conferences were important for someone like her husband who was both emergency physician and researcher. But then Lisbet had fallen very ill on a Saturday night— Why did these things always happen on Saturday night?—and Kat was sure she had appendicitis. She'd taken her to the hospital and run into Simon, a doctor and friend of Kat and Paul's since medical school. When she saw him, she'd said, unthinkingly, "I thought you were at the conference with Paul." Simon looked so completely blank that Kat knew at once the conference was fictitious. And Simon's face, moving from confusion to horrified comprehension, told her he'd arrived at the same conclusion.

All that weekend, while Lisbet had her appendix taken out and Kat and Daisy slept by her bedside—Daisy was still being breastfed and couldn't be left with anyone—Kat seethed at her husband for what she imagined must be an affair with a colleague or perhaps

even a medical student. When he arrived home, she discovered it was
something far worse.

"I'm not having an affair," he'd said belligerently. "I just need
some time out every now and again. To play golf and eat normal
food instead of pasta all the time. So I take weekends in Queensland
occasionally."

Time out from what? Kat had wanted to scream. All he had to do
was work and look after the garden and change the goddamn toilet
roll when he'd finished with it; she had to work and cook and organize
cleaners and know when the girls needed to go to the dentist or when
they needed injections, had to organize childcare and costumes for
Book Week and haircuts and new shoes and all the other things that
children required, and which threatened to make her head explode.

And then he'd said, "If I asked you for a weekend off to do nothing,
you'd act like the world's biggest martyr because you'd never take a
weekend off from being a mum."

That was when she knew their marriage was over. He was right.
She *would* have been furious at him for wanting a weekend away
from the demands of family. But what kind of person would slink
off anyway, while she'd juggled emergency surgery for one child and
the demands of caring for another who was still just a baby. She told
him she wanted a divorce and had felt ever since the sure and certain
knowledge that he would never forgive her for leaving him, which
was how he saw it.

"What is it?" Paul's brusque voice came over the line.

"I'm really sorry and I know it's inconvenient but can we work
things out so I can go to London next month?" she asked.

She hoped that apologizing up front would enable them to amicably
work out the arrangements for the girls while she was away.

"Again?" Paul complained. "Kat, I can't drop everything to look
after Elizabeth and Daisy every time you go away."

He said it as if she were taking a holiday and she bit back the retort: what about the unspoken expectation that she would take a day off work whenever one of the girls was ill, like now? If Paul had them overnight and they fell ill, he simply dropped them at her house the next morning along with the words, "She threw up," or "She has a fever," and left it to Kat to gather up the wan child and tuck her into bed and call the museum to say she couldn't come in, while Paul drove off to the hospital.

Paul's reasoning was that he was saving lives while Kat was just mucking about with dresses. It didn't matter a bit to him that, over this past year, all the articles she'd written for journals and all the papers she'd presented at conferences were paying off and she was becoming something of a spokesperson on fashion conservation.

Her resolve to remain calm collapsed like a snagged hemline.

"I've made the next trip as short as I can," she said. "It's very hard to get to London and back in just a week or two, but that's what I do every time. Would you prefer that I didn't work and asked the court to increase your child maintenance payment instead?"

It was a cheap shot and they both knew it. Kat loved her work too much to ever quit.

She tried to regain the high ground she'd leapt off. "I can get in a nanny. Or the girls can stay with friends for a night or two. There are lots of options. They don't have to stay with you."

"You'd love that, wouldn't you? Telling everyone I'm too selfish to look after my own children? Of course they'll stay with me."

"No, I wouldn't love it," she said sadly. "What I would love is for none of this to ever have happened."

A sound made her spin around. Poor Daisy was scrambling for the kitchen cupboard where they kept the bucket they used if someone was sick. But she didn't quite make it, and now the floor was a mess and Daisy was sobbing.

"I have to go," Kat said.

Daisy reached out her arms and, despite the mess, Kat picked her up and held her tight and kissed her hot little forehead and told her it didn't matter. Intermingled with Daisy's tears were tears of Kat's own.

Later, when Daisy had dropped into sleep, her hand still holding her mother's, Kat tried to tap out a one-handed email to friends to arrange weekend sleepovers for Lisbet and Daisy. Then she emailed Paul the remaining dates, trying not think about the fact that her life was made up of beads of guilt strung together with the certainty that she wasn't doing right by anyone, least of all herself.

* * *

Later that night when both girls were asleep, Kat rang her grandmother. "I was wondering if I should pop over to France while I'm in London next month," she said, lying. "But not Paris. Somewhere else." She paused, as if thinking. "Where were you born, again?"

"Lyon," Margaux said. "But I was only there as a young child before we moved to Paris. I don't remember enough about it to give you tourist advice."

Lyon. Kat froze. *Keep going*, she told herself.

"I had a call from an author earlier today," she said as casually as she could. "He's looking for a woman called Margaux Jourdan. He's interested in what she did during the Second World War."

The ensuing silence spun on and on, stretching Kat's nerves so thin they almost snapped.

Then her grandmother said, "I never thought anybody would come looking for Margaux Jourdan."

What to say in response to that?

Finally her grandmother added, "I worked during the war, like every woman did. Packing parachutes at an air base, I think. I don't know. There's a lot your mind loses, like socks in a washing machine, when you're as old as I am."

"If you can remember anything more," Kat said almost pleadingly, "then I can tell him and he'll see that you're not the Margaux he's looking for." *Even though you have the same birthdate. And the same birthplace. And you said you packed parachutes, which Elliott mentioned too.*

"I didn't do anything worth remembering during the war," her grandmother said. She hung up the phone.

ELEVEN

Kat walked hesitantly into the Beaufort Bar at the Savoy Hotel. It had been a long time since she'd met a man in a bar for a drink, and while this was a business meeting rather than a personal one, she still felt like an awkward teenager as she stepped past groups of impeccably suited businesspeople.

She'd arrived in London two days ago at the break of dawn and had driven to the house in Cornwall to pick up some more of the dresses. They didn't belong in an isolated cottage and were in excellent condition so she'd convinced herself that wearing them only a few times would be less of a sin against the tenets of conservation than leaving them abandoned in musty wardrobes. Besides, she hadn't been able to stop thinking about them, wondering if, away from her life as a Sydney mother, they might suit a Katarina Jourdan who could actually have a drink at the Savoy Hotel at six in the evening without having to move heaven and earth to make it happen. Nor had she been able to stop wondering about where they'd come from.

The one she'd chosen to wear today was from the 1953 Tulip line. It was black, with a wonderful bodice designed like a collared shawl that gave the dress a completely unexpected and rather flattering touch. Her hand strayed up to smooth down the collar as she took in the jet-black walls and curved alcoves lined with gold, the moody opulence of the bar. Throughout the room, people relaxed in brown leather armchairs and black velvet sofas and Kat realized she'd been so busy getting herself to Cornwall and then back to London that she'd forgotten to do any research on Elliott Beaufort. She hadn't even googled a picture of him.

A rather handsome man stepped forward, toward Kat. He had dark hair and incredibly dark brown eyes, a color she didn't come across too often, if at all. Her scientist's mind wondered how that intensity of color might hold over a life span; in a fabric, it would certainly fade. His smile was especially prepossessing and in the dim lighting of the bar it was impossible to tell how old he was. Anywhere from mid-thirties to forties, she thought. She was suddenly very glad of her Dior.

"Kat?" he asked.

"Elliott?" she said, and he nodded.

She shook his proffered hand and followed him to two empty stools at the bar.

"What can I get you to drink?" he asked. "If you've been to London often you've probably been here before, but they're very good at cocktails."

He passed her what looked like a book and she was gratified that he imagined she might be the kind of woman who often found herself in the bar at the Savoy Hotel.

She opened the menu and laughed delightedly when Coco Chanel and an elegant bouquet of camellias leapt up off the page, as if Kat were perusing a children's pop-up book rather than a cocktail menu. On the next page, Ernest Hemingway's head burst forth. "It's fabulous," she said, looking up at Elliott.

He grinned. "I think I come here just for the menu."

"You realize it's going to take me forever to choose a drink?" she said, turning to the next page.

"Take your time." He sounded as if he meant it. As if here, in this luxurious bar, hours were inconsequential.

And Kat remembered she had nowhere she needed to be, no obligations at all except to enjoy herself. She settled in to select a drink. Normally, she'd have a gin and tonic, but the classic cocktails caught her eye and she remembered that, long ago, before marriage and children and divorce and work, her grandmother had sometimes made her a negroni on summer nights when she was on a break from university.

"I'll have a negroni," she said at last.

Elliott ordered negronis for them both, then asked her, "Are you over here for work? You're a fashion conservator, right? How'd you get into that?"

"The long way around," she said, reaching for the drink the barman placed in front of her. "I originally studied medicine—I always loved science. I was, in fact, the nerdy math and science whiz at a time when girls who were into math and science were called freaks. Well," she amended with a smile, "a freak was probably the nicest thing I was called. But I quickly realized I'd be a terrible doctor—too soft, my . . ." She paused. She'd been about to say, *my ex-husband said*, but didn't want the shadow of Paul to darken the conversation.

"My friend said I was too soft," she said instead. "I sidestepped into a science degree, discovered I enjoyed materials science and, most especially, textiles science. When I finished the science degree, I sidestepped again into a Master of Conservation at the Sorbonne in Paris. I love fashion history and I've been lucky to be able to mix that interest with science."

"That definitely makes you the most interesting person I've spoken to all day, if not for months," Elliott said.

She laughed. "I'm sure authors must meet much more interesting people than me."

"Modest, as well as smart and beautiful. A rare combination." He smiled at her.

Kat knew she was blushing. He sounded sincere, not as if it were a well-practiced line, but surely it must be. Most people heard the words "textiles scientist" or "conservation" and thought her job dusty and dull rather than worthy of interest. "Hardly," she managed to say. And then, with negroni courage, "Is flattering your interview subjects the way you ordinarily extract information from them?"

It was his turn to laugh. "I was being honest. You are all of those things. And given that my usual interview subjects are over eighty years old, all I need to do to get information from them is profess to enjoy overbrewed tea and let them talk about their Highland terriers' ailments. I rarely comment on anyone's appearance because I've learned that you can never form a true picture of a person based on what they look like. I've interviewed women who look too frail even to pick up a toddler, only to discover that they withstood torture from the Gestapo for weeks on end." He paused. "But you're a busy woman and you've taken the time to meet me. I'll move on to business."

He opened a notebook and Kat was fleetingly disappointed. It had been a long time since she'd been called beautiful by anyone except her grandmother or her children and she rather liked it. But his comments about the Gestapo, and torture, made her shiver.

"You must hear some terrible things," she said quietly.

"Enough to make me very glad I'm alive now, rather than then."

Kat nodded in agreement.

"You said in your email that your grandmother *was* born in Lyon," he continued. "Which means that, even though I know you're skeptical, it's becoming more likely that she is the woman I'm looking for. She has the right birthdate, birthplace and name. But she won't tell you much about her life during the war, except that she was in England?"

"She said she doesn't remember anything other than packing parachutes." Kat fidgeted with her almost empty glass, not wanting to tell him about her grandmother's silences, omissions and that terrible, unsettling fear.

"Packing parachutes," Elliott repeated. "Which would mean she worked for the Women's Auxiliary Air Force—the same organization my Margaux was commissioned into as cover for her real work as a spy for SOE."

Kat frowned, and Elliott mistook it for confusion.

"I know there are a lot of acronyms," he said. "WAAF; that's the Women's Auxiliary Air Force. It wasn't a secret department; lots of women worked for it. SOE—that's the Special Operations Executive, the organization nobody knew about. It sent agents into France to work with the Resistance, sabotage strategic targets—"

Kat interrupted. "Why is finding Margaux Jourdan important for your book?"

Elliott swallowed more negroni. "Margaux Jourdan isn't the subject of my book, but she knew two of the women who are, which is why I'd like to speak to her. I'm researching three women from the same family: Vanessa Penrose, and her daughters, Liberty and Skye. Each worked in intelligence during their respective world wars. One family with three women over two generations who worked as spies."

Even Kat, whose interests were more scientific and less literary, could tell it would be a fascinating book. "I've never heard of them," she said. "And despite not knowing what she did during the war, I know a lot about my grandmother." She pressed on, despite her subconscious reminding her of all the mysteries and unknowns her grandmother had thrown up lately. "She was also my mother, you see; she looked after me from the time I was just a week old. Margaux took me on because my mother . . ." Kat tried to think how to explain it in a way that wouldn't invite questions. "My mother couldn't care for me."

"I'm sorry," Elliott said. "You must think I'm prying, but as time goes on and so few people from the 1940s are still here, research becomes harder and harder. I have to use whatever or whoever is willing to help. I really am grateful for your time, even if it comes to nothing."

"Well, at least you've reminded me how much I used to like negronis," Kat said, smiling a little.

"Speaking of which, I'll get us another."

She shook her head. "I'm a bit too out of practice for that. I definitely cannot have two negronis on an empty stomach."

Elliott glanced around the bar, and pointed to one of the alcoves, which was now empty. "If you claim that for us, I'll get them to bring us some food and then you can have another drink."

"You don't have to do that," Kat protested, horrified that he might have thought she was angling for an invitation to dinner.

"I'd like to."

"All right," she said, somewhat doubtfully.

As she made herself comfortable on the sofa and waited for him to join her, she realized the negroni had reached her head. Despite the gentle probing about her grandmother, she was feeling delightfully carefree for once; perhaps too carefree if she'd just agreed to spend another hour or so with a man who was certainly more good-looking than anyone she'd spoken to in ages.

Elliott returned with a smile and two more negronis. "Do you mind if I show you some photos?" he asked, opening a satchel.

"It's the least I can do in return for the drinks."

He passed her a couple of blurry black-and-white pictures. "This," he said, pointing to one, "is Margaux Jourdan. Any resemblance to your Margaux? I know seventy years have passed and the quality is poor but . . ."

Kat examined the photograph closely. In the low light of the bar, she could make out a dark-haired, unsmiling woman in a uniform, cigarette gripped tightly in her hand.

"This woman was, what, in her twenties?" she said. "My grandmother is ninety-four. Her cheeks are wrinkled; this woman's are smooth. Even if the quality was any good, I'm not sure I'd be able to see Margaux in her. Because it's black-and-white, I can't even tell what her eye color is. All I can say is that she's about the right size: petite. And it seems like her hair is dark; so was Margaux's. So I guess this looks as much like my grandmother as any other petite, dark-haired woman from that time."

Elliott sighed. "I know. It's like trying to see a pearl through an oyster shell."

"You said you've met frail women who don't look as if they could ever have done anything extraordinary," Kat went on. "But my grandmother has very little interest in the world. She definitely wasn't a spy."

Elliott didn't try to contradict her. Instead, he took out another photograph. "There are no pictures of Vanessa Penrose. She was taught to fly by an intelligence officer who then set her up in France with his sister during the so-called Great War. The two women sent information about German activities back to the Intelligence Office in London. But this is Liberty Penrose, her daughter. She worked for SOE, just like Margaux Jourdan."

Elliott handed Kat a photograph of a dark-haired woman standing in a group, each face too small to see the features properly. "And this"—he passed Kat a much folded and faded copy of a page from a newspaper—"is Skye Penrose."

A waiter arrived with the food. Kat examined the second picture too; it showed a woman stepping out of a plane, her hand in her hair.

Elliott leaned back in the sofa, negroni glass held in his fingertips. "Liberty worked on the sabotage side of things for SOE. By all accounts, despite her superiors commenting on her emotional volatility, she was very effective at her work. And Skye gathered information that helped bring about the relatively peaceful fall of Paris to the Allies in August 1944. Before that, she was one of only a handful of women who flew planes for the Air Transport Auxiliary. Not in combat; she ferried them around England to air bases and maintenance units."

Kat felt affinity bind her to the woman Elliott was speaking of. "That must have been very unusual for a woman back then," she said.

"It was. By the end of the war, only around one hundred and fifty women worked for the ATA, compared to thirteen hundred men. Probably the same gender split as in a university science class in the nineties."

She found herself smiling at him again. "Well," she said, trying to hide her pleasure at his intuition under cover of selecting some food from the delicious morsels before them, "how else can I convince you that my grandmother isn't the woman you want?"

"Why don't you want it to be her?" he asked, studying her face as if he wanted to read her, to see what was inside her.

She shivered a little because nobody had looked at her that way for years. She shrugged. Sipped her drink. Ate an oyster as prevarication. Decided to give Elliott some of the truth, but not all of it, yet. "My grandmother is one of the most precious people in the world to me," she said quietly. "You're telling me I know nothing about her. That's . . ." She searched for the right word. "Frightening. It means she shut me out. Or that she lied to me. I'm not fond of liars."

An understatement, but she wasn't about to tell him the details of her divorce.

"I can't fault you for that," he said softly. "But I also know this is a book that needs to be written and I want to write it. So few people know what these women did. Partly because women rarely speak of their achievements, and partly because they grew up in an environment of 'stiff upper lip' and 'get on with it.' The fact that three female spies came from the same family is extraordinary, but for people like the Penroses—and Margaux Jourdan, whoever she is—the terrible things they saw and perhaps had to do mean they're even less likely to speak of them. They helped give us the freedoms we have today, Kat. So someone has to speak of the heroic things they did. I'd like to do it."

He was certainly beguiling. And right. Without these women, who knew how the world might have ended up? Kat felt some of her resistance begin to dissolve. She nodded. "What else do you want to know?"

"What about your grandfather?" Elliott asked. "What do you know about him?"

"Not a lot," Kat said, understanding for certain now that her family tree was as full of holes as a pair of 1980s jeans. "He was an American named O'Farrell. A pilot. He and Margaux weren't married and you know what a scandal it was to be an unwed mother at the time. I'm sure it's why she doesn't talk about that part of her life."

"I didn't know that Margaux Jourdan and O'Farrell were lovers," he said, as if he'd heard the name O'Farrell before.

He riffled through his satchel and produced another photograph. It showed a man and a woman dancing closely together in a way that suggested they were more than foxtrot partners. It was difficult to tell whether it was the same woman as in the other photograph, but when Kat flipped it over she saw perfectly formed cursive handwriting declaring that the people in the photograph were Margaux Jourdan and the man without a first name, O'Farrell.

"I guess that kind of evidence is a little hard to refute," Kat said slowly, all the while thinking, *Don't turn into a stranger, please, Margaux. I couldn't bear it.*

"It is," Elliott said quietly, as if proving the point he'd been trying to make since he'd first spoken to her on the phone wasn't really such a big deal. "Do you mind me asking when your mother was born?"

"Third of January 1945."

"This photograph of O'Farrell and Margaux was taken in late March 1944."

"About nine months prior."

"Yes."

Like buttons slipping into buttonholes, Kat could see the pieces of Elliott's puzzle were fitting together. It made her admit aloud the absolute truth. "I didn't want any of this to be true because when I spoke to my grandmother about it she sounded so afraid."

The words sounded stark against the buzz of conviviality in the bar.

"I really am sorry if I've stirred things up," Elliott said.

It wasn't a platitude. Kat could tell by the way he looked directly at her, eyes gentle on her face, that he meant it.

His phone buzzed, making them both jump. He glanced at it as if he planned to ignore it, then said, "Sorry again; it's my daughter. I have to get it. Hey . . ."

He winced and pulled the phone away from his ear and even Kat could hear the wailing sounding from it. Elliott rolled his eyes at her and she understood that, whatever was going on, it wasn't to be taken too seriously.

"You're deafening me and the other person here," he said, and the wailing diminished. "You're supposed to be staying with your mother tonight." A pause. "Fine. I'll help you. Let me pick you up in a bit . . . You're already in a cab? Brilliant. Well, I'll just leave what I'm doing and come home and meet you, shall I?" Another pause. "No, it's fine. I'm sure Kat will understand. See you soon."

Elliott put the phone down. "For the millionth time tonight, I'm sorry. I have a fourteen-year-old daughter, which is a bit like having a moody royal living in your house. Everything is about her, and everything is a catastrophe, no matter how many times I tell her about actual catastrophes from the past. Tonight's drama is a history assignment that's due tomorrow. I should tell her I'm not going to help her with it. Instead, I'll probably point her in the direction of the right research sources and proofread it for her, and hope that by not actually writing it for her I've found the right balance between spoiling and neglect. Although she'll see it as neglect and I'll see it as spoiling. Also," he added, "she hasn't been getting along well with her mother of late. I suspect something's happened and that's the real reason she's already in a cab to my place." He hesitated. "We didn't get to finish our conversation. I don't suppose you're free tomorrow night?"

"I am." The words were out before Kat had time to think.

"I'm going to a party where I've planned to spend the evening in a corner catching up with a couple of friends who are over from France. Would you like to come with me? It might be fun."

A party? With Elliott's friends? It was Kat's turn to hesitate.

"We can finish this another time," she said. "You'd rather see your friends, not listen to me telling you nothing useful for your book."

"I'd love you to come. My friends, Josh and D'Arcy, are great people but they're also very . . ." He stopped and thought. "Overwhelming. It would be nice to have company. And not just that—it would be nice to see you again."

At his last words, a warmth Kat hadn't felt for a long time pulsed inside her. "All right," she said. "I'm staying at the Sofitel. What time . . ."

"I'll pick you up at eight. See you then."

Kat watched him walk into the lobby, where a group of women stopped him. He smiled at them restrainedly, not the way he'd smiled at Kat, while the women summoned a receptionist and arranged themselves around Elliott with beams on their faces. They giggled instructions at the receptionist, who took photos of them on five different phones. Elliott continued to smile politely throughout and finished by scribbling something on a piece of paper for each of them—even the receptionist. Finally, with a wave and a collective sigh from the women, he was gone.

Kat snatched up her phone and googled Elliott Beaufort. She didn't even have to finish typing his name before Google understood what she wanted. Hundreds of brooding pictures appeared, along with just as many pages of search results. Apparently, the man who'd been sitting opposite her was something of a celebrity. Elliott Beaufort had cut his teeth on writing pop stars' biographies before turning, over the past decade, to more serious nonfiction—or "popular history for the masses" as one reviewer snidely put it. He took historical events people thought they knew about and retold them from the perspective of someone unexpected or overlooked—hence, Kat thought, him writing about a family of female spies during the world wars.

She read on to discover that his name on a front cover ensured bestseller status, his queues at writers festivals were always the longest, his appearances on various television programs about books or history—thankfully not reality television—had given him more visibility than authors usually attained. He'd studied history and languages at Cambridge, so clearly he wasn't stupid.

A longer bio piece revealed that he was born in 1972, had recently turned forty—which made him a year older than Kat—had been married and divorced three times, and had a daughter from his second marriage. Three times! Once was bad enough, but to have made the wrong choice three times could only mean that he made incredibly bad decisions and never learned from them. But who was she to judge—her decision to marry Paul had been the wrong one too.

Regardless, Elliott Beaufort wasn't the kind of person she should be going to parties with. His attention span when it came to women was obviously shorter than 1960s hemlines. Luckily she wasn't looking for anything from him other than a fun night out—and, she hoped, a chance to prove that her Margaux wasn't his Margaux. After that, she'd never see him again.

PART FIVE
SKYE

The RAF certainly did not welcome us into their entirely male and combatant world. Of course at that time it was never envisaged that we would fly their beloved fighters and bombers but they saw no reason why we should contaminate even their elementary trainers ...

—Rosemary du Cros (née Rees)

TWELVE

When Skye returned from the Bedfordshire air base where she'd rediscovered Nicholas and then shouted at him, she received news so huge it was almost unbelievable. She was to be transferred to RAF Leavesden for four months of training.

"You've been selected to learn to fly Class V planes," Pauline told her.

Of all the ways the women had gained ground, this was the most unbelievable: the one Skye had never thought would happen. She was going to fly the largest planes of all—enormous 65,000-pound Halifaxes and Lancasters—and she'd be the first woman to do so.

Even the less-than-friendly welcome she received from the CO at Leavesden didn't dampen her spirits; Skye had long since lowered her standards and expected only civility. Besides, Dluga, the Polish pilot who'd taught Skye on previous conversion courses, was to be her instructor again and he was waiting for her with his usual friendly smile.

"Ready to lift a rhinoceros into the air?" he asked.

Skye grinned. "Absolutely. I've been training with hippos."

She spent a glorious afternoon being grilled by Dluga, and at dusk she went back to the office to collect her things, to move into whatever accommodation had been found for her, and then to eat. But when she arrived at the office, her bag wasn't there.

"I'm not allowed in the mess in my flying suit," Skye said, gesturing at her overalls. "I need to change."

A flight captain was eventually located, who told Skye she'd been billeted in a cottage off the base and that her bag was there. She was given a set of directions, which led her to a junkyard containing all the detritus of an operating airfield. She received the message loud and clear.

She returned to the ferry pool and entered the mess.

The flight captain accosted her. "You must change," he said.

A lightning strike of fury flashed through her. "Certainly. If you'll find my bag and my accommodation."

"You must have written the directions down incorrectly," he said.

"Of course I must have," she said, sarcasm icing every word.

He gave her more directions, very different to the last set, and Skye made a show of writing them down. "You're too kind," she said.

He stepped aside, obviously expecting she would leave, find her billet, change and then come all the way back. Instead she brushed past him and collected a food tray, still in her forbidden flying suit.

"You must change," the flight captain repeated.

"I must," she agreed. "But first I must eat."

She sat at a table, quite alone. The silence was appalling and hostile and told her with painful clarity that she could not make a single mistake for the next four months. The RAF had long put it about that women hadn't the strength to fly four-engine bombers. She mustn't prove them right. The burden sat on her shoulders more heavily than a parachute, and she tried not to think about Rose and Joan and how terribly long her time at Leavesden would be without companionship.

After supper, she was ordered to the CO's office. She went slowly, trying to reignite the fire of half an hour before, to gather the strength to stand her ground in the face of the dressing-down she was about to receive after her stunt in the mess.

But it wasn't the Leavesden CO who greeted her in the office; it was Air Marshal Wylde, her mother's friend, the man she'd seen three times since childhood: first at the test flights, then at the lunch where she'd given a speech and lastly in Pauline's office at Hatfield. She stared mutely at him.

"Captain Penrose," he said. "I believe you were involved in an incident with an Me 110 three nights ago."

"I was."

Skye made herself stand tall, even though her stomach had plummeted to the floor at the realization that her aerobatics had not gone unnoticed. If Wylde added to that her earlier defiance in the mess, at best she'd be booted back to Hamble and no woman would *ever* fly a four-engine bomber. Skye would have ruined everything, again.

"I read the incident report," Wylde said.

"If you read Nicholas's . . ."

She halted. *The "incident" report.* It wasn't an "incident." Skye had been shot at by the Luftwaffe. If she hadn't cartwheeled her plane, she might have been killed. She directed her anger into her gaze, which she fixed to Wylde. "If you read Wing Commander Crawford's report, you'll know that I can hardly be blamed for anything—except being an unarmed woman. I know the RAF tries to make my gender into an offense, but as far as I'm aware it hasn't yet succeeded."

Wylde sat heavily in a chair. "Deference is not part of your makeup, is it?"

"Sorry, I should have appended 'Air Marshal Wylde' onto my sentence." Skye pressed her lips together. She'd gone too far. How was it possible for her to have such impeccable control of herself in the sky and to have none whatsoever on the ground?

Wylde gave her a half smile. "Yes, that would make what you just said more deferential."

Even though she tried to suppress it, the unexpected joke made her lips curve into a smile. She felt the tension in the room ease a little.

"I'm here to order you not to mention your . . . your adventures in Bedfordshire to anyone," Wylde went on. "They should have had you sign the Official Secrets Act. I don't know what they were thinking. It's unlike Wing Commander Crawford to be so forgetful."

He produced a piece of paper headed *Official Secrets Act* and indicated that Skye was to sign it.

"What—" Skye began, then stopped herself. Wylde would never tell her what Nicholas and his squadron were doing. But it must be terribly important if an air marshal, of all people, was here to tell her to keep her mouth shut about that strange and secret air base.

She signed the paper, frowning, and passed it to Wylde.

He stood up. "You should get an early night. You've a tough couple of months ahead of you." Then his demeanor changed, as if he'd somehow taken off his air marshal persona and had stepped into the role of some other, slightly less intimidating man. He spoke quietly. "You're very like your mother. But I would have thought that, knowing what happened to her, you'd be the last person to take on new challenges in the air."

"It's my job," Skye said simply.

Before she could ask any more about his connection to her mother, he turned to leave. At the door he stopped. "You fly well. As did Vanessa. I wish that knowledge had been enough for her, and that it would be enough for you."

The door closed and Skye dropped into a chair. There was no mistaking the regret in Wylde's tone. As if he mourned not just the loss of Vanessa, but the manner of losing her. Skye pressed her hands over her eyelids until mini auroras were all she could see, rather than Wylde dancing with her mother. Rather than Nicholas, and the fact that whatever he was doing was classified, which perhaps accounted for his behavior the other night. She shouldn't have lost her temper at him, especially if—her eyes flew open—all the secrecy meant he was doing something decidedly unsafe.

* * *

The day came when Skye was to fly the Halifax by herself: a simple takeoff, circuit and landing.

She spent the morning as second officer on an unfriendly flight where the pilot completely ignored her and returned to Leavesden at lunchtime, too nervous to eat. Dluga, the instructor, found her in the mess staring at her empty tray. "Skye," he said somberly.

"What?" she asked.

"It's been requested that you do ten takeoffs and landings before your conversion course is completed," he said.

She didn't say, *But the men only have to do seven*, because she knew it wasn't Dluga who required it. She didn't speak at all. Instead she felt her head nod, as if she agreed it was fine for her to be made to do more circuits, simply because she was a woman. In that action, she knew being at Leavesden was causing Skye Penrose to seep out of her body. She needed to recover herself before her solo flight or else she'd never pass.

"Penrose! Office," someone called and she jumped like a guilty person.

She dragged herself to the office, mind turning over her morning as second officer. She was certain she'd made no mistakes and couldn't possibly be in trouble. Perhaps they were going to tell her she had to do twenty circuits now. Or some impossible number she'd never be able to achieve. Would she just nod again? Or would she find the courage to protest once more.

But in the office she came face-to-face with Nicholas.

Her hand reached for the edge of the desk and curled around it.

"I've been trying to get across here for the past month," he said quickly. "I owe you an apology. What I meant to say and what I actually said when I last saw you were two very different things." His brow furrowed and Skye stood still, listening.

"I wanted to say that I was so happy to see you again," he continued. "And finally explain why I hadn't written to you. I was transferred to Special Duties not long after I saw you at Biggin Hill in 1940. To anyone else I could have pretended I'd been transferred to another base. But you're ATA—you know all the bases. You'd have known I was lying. And obviously I'm not allowed to go around telling everyone I'm in a Special Duties squadron. Which meant not writing to you. But after what happened last month, I can explain that much, at least. And hopefully convince you I'm not one of the chauvinist idiots in the RAF who think women can't fly planes. I know you can fly better than most men, including me."

He paused for breath and Skye found herself forgetting Leavesden and how many circuits she had to do and actually laughing.

"Why are you laughing?" he asked, brow furrowing still more.

"Because I don't think I've ever heard you say so much at once in your life."

She moved around the desk that separated them and saw that it wasn't just seriousness on his face but worry too, as if he'd also lost sleep over their last strained conversation. "Apology accepted," she said. "It seems that circumstances contrived to make me think you'd turned into a pipe-smoking, mustache-sporting, awfully superior RAF commander." She grinned.

It was Nicholas's turn to laugh. "Well, I definitely don't have a mustache, although," he touched the dark shadow above his upper lip, "I could probably do with a shave. And I've never smoked a pipe—the New Yorker in me rebels at even the thought of it. These are more to my taste."

He pulled a packet of Gitanes out of his pocket.

"My favorites," she breathed. "I haven't seen them since the war started."

"Then you'd better have them."

He tossed them to her, and she extracted one and had it lit and inhaled within seconds.

"I'm not sharing," she said.

"So you've become someone who goes around yelling at her old friends and not sharing her cigarettes?"

She was mid-inhale when he spoke and her ill-timed laughter made her start coughing.

"I suppose I deserved that," she managed at last. But there was something more serious she needed to say and she studied the lit tip of the cigarette as she spoke. "I had a visit from an air marshal to ensure I don't tell anyone about a mysterious RAF base and its squadron of Lysanders. If you're doing the kind of special duties flying that requires an air marshal to warn me to keep my mouth shut, then it's more dangerous than what I'm doing. Does that mean I should give you a ticking-off too?"

He was silent, but from the sudden hardening of the muscles on his face she understood two things: that he couldn't say any more, and that she was right.

Her hands lifted to her neck and she tugged off her cerulean scarf, holding it out in front of her. "Like I said, or rather shouted at you last month, I have flown through almost every kind of mechanical failure and something is keeping me alive. This is my good luck charm, but you need it more than I do. Not because you aren't an excellent pilot, but because secret special duties must be risky at best, deadly at worst."

Nicholas stared at the scarf, and then swept his eyes upward to meet hers, and she saw that they were a wistful, liquid blue.

"I can't," he said, one hand touching the scarf then falling away. "If anything happened to you and I had your scarf..."

Skye hastily withdrew her offering. Of course he couldn't accept it; he was engaged to another woman. "Do you at least have your watch?" she asked.

He nodded. "I'm sorry you've had air marshals hunting you down. And I really am sorry about what I said to you. I was so dumbstruck at seeing you that my behavior thereafter can only be described as dumb."

"And I'm sorry I told Margaux I'd seen you in your underwear," Skye said sheepishly.

He laughed. "Luckily Margaux isn't..." He hesitated. "The jealous type."

What to say to that? He said his fiancée's name casually, as if they'd known each other a long time and were completely comfortable together. Yet another reminder that Skye needed to get used to thinking of Nicholas as the person he was now, not the person he'd once been.

Then Nicholas turned to the window, glancing sideways at her. "O'Farrell's been asking about you. I told him he wouldn't find a better woman in all of England to spend time with."

"So he's worth spending time with?" she asked, squashing her cigarette into the nearest ashtray with a nonchalance that she hoped hid the fact that talking with Nicholas about O'Farrell was, for some reason, bizarre.

"He is. He pretended to be Canadian back in 1940 so he could get over here and fly with the RAF."

"That was a brave thing to do," Skye said.

For the United States had passed a Neutrality Act in 1939, which meant any Americans caught trying to get across to England to help at that time were liable to be jailed. With America's entry into the war, that had of course been revoked. But it meant that beneath O'Farrell's cocky exterior might be a man more intriguing than she'd thought. What if, when she returned to Hamble, rather than limiting her encounters with men to just one dance at the clubhouse or one supper at the Embassy Club in London, she allowed for more?

As she considered what Nicholas said about his friend, she passed the Gitanes back to him. "If you were here in 1940, it wasn't only O'Farrell who did a brave thing."

Nicholas's cheeks colored a little and he took out a cigarette. "O'Farrell and I met at university," he said. "We were both members of the Harvard Flying Club. It was so damn frustrating sitting in America knowing there weren't enough pilots over here and having the skills the RAF needed, but being told, for no good reason, that I couldn't use them. One night I thought, to hell with it. O'Farrell came too. We'd probably both had too much whiskey," he added, as if trying to minimize their actions.

"I imagine the whiskey had worn off before you got to Canada," she said quietly.

Nicholas's cheeks pinked still more and Skye felt an almost unbearable urge to throw her arms around him, to squeeze him as tightly as she'd done in the cave the day he left England, both to thank him properly and to give expression to everything she felt right then: pride in her friend and the overwhelming fierceness of affection she'd always felt for him. Back then she expressed it by giving him her cove, her mother, the Moth, and occasionally the fastest hermit crab to race. Now, she had no idea how to express it.

"I wouldn't have O'Farrell in my squadron if he wasn't brave,"

Nicholas said, turning away from the window to face her and bringing them back to where the conversation had started. "And I'd definitely have you if I could."

His sincerity had her staring at the Halifax on the runway outside rather than at him. "That would be fun," she said, voice small. "And much better than being here."

Nicholas walked to the end of the table and picked up a jar. "This would have to be the toughest assignment of all," he said. "I know what they're like here, and that this is probably a bit insignificant set beside you wanting to give me your scarf, but I brought these for you." He passed her the jar.

It was full of the tiny cowrie shells Skye had used to collect. They shone in the sun like childhood and summer and a prewar world. She looked at Nicholas, unable to speak, every tear she'd been too stubborn to cry over the past month threatening to break the dam of her self-control.

"I've had them since I left Cornwall," he said, lifting one finger to touch, so quickly, her cheek. "I thought something of home might help."

It took her a minute to speak, and when she did she gave him the truth, like she always had. "I'm doing my first solo in the Halifax today. All day I've been thinking I need something to remind me who Skye Penrose is so I don't crash and ruin any chance of a woman flying a four-engine bomber again. This," she looked down at the jar, "is just what I needed."

"I'm glad it was my day off then."

He smiled at her and she smiled back, and somehow it wasn't just a simple action of the mouth. It was an entire bodily feeling that her feet wanted to move to as if it were music.

"I have to go," Skye said reluctantly, clutching the jar.

She walked out of the office, leaving behind the boy she'd been mourning for ten years. But she no longer wanted that boy back. She wanted the man Nicholas had become, and with whom she hoped she had a new kind of friendship.

Her first takeoff in the Halifax was as smooth as a cowrie shell's surface. The landing was another matter. It wasn't graceful, but she'd seen plenty of Halifaxes thunder to the ground over her time in the ATA. Then, instead of climbing out, she fired the Halifax up and taxied back to the runway and, to Dluga's astonishment, did her ten takeoffs and her ten landings all in a row, each better than the last.

* * *

The new year had advanced onward and winter was almost over when Skye returned to Hamble, eager to see all her friends. Cloud mantled the sky quickly and unexpectedly as her train drew into the station and she hoped none of the ATA women were trapped in it.

Rose was the first to sweep Skye into a hug when she appeared in the lounge. "I forbid you to ever go away again," Rose said. "Now, tell us when we'll be able to get our hands on a Halifax."

"I'd rather get my hands on something with warmer blood," Diana said, and the eruption of laughter made Skye beam for the first time in ages.

But it couldn't last, not when the war thundered on and even God seemed to have withdrawn his protection and left them all as vulnerable as ants scurrying across a busy runway. Pauline's voice sounded over the tannoy, summoning them all into the lounge.

Joan, who must have just landed, arrived white-faced. "Honor's dead," she said baldly.

"No." Skye shook her head. "She can't be. Not another one."

"She is." Pauline, her voice strained, strode in behind Joan.

"Someone's always flying into a hillside lately." Joan whispered the terrible truth.

"Five ATA pilots died this morning," Pauline continued. "Honor, plus four of the men."

"Five?" Skye repeated, wanting Pauline to contradict her; to agree that Skye had misheard.

But Pauline only said, "An unforeseen inversion layer is covering most of England. It's impossible to fly out of."

As with so many things, Honor's death wasn't to be spoken of again. While the women's training on how to fly new classes of airplanes involved overt instruction, their training on handling death was unexpressed but somehow known to all. They could not talk about a friend dying in a plane one day and then go out and fly the next. It would break them all. But weren't they all, right now, a little broken, Skye thought.

As the women left the ferry pool that evening after a long and silent afternoon, Joan said, "I can't stand everyone sitting around and not talking about it."

"Talking won't bring her back," Rose said.

Outside, day submitted to night and everything in that predusk slip of time turned ashen; a hue that matched Joan's face exactly.

"Come with me," Skye said, walking not to the main gate but to the runway, the place where flights began and where they were supposed to end.

Skye took Joan's hand in her own, and Rose's too, and the three women stood on the tarmac looking up at the sky to which they had given Honor. A gift the sky did not need but had taken all the same.

A light shower began to fall, the kind of rain that gentled down sometimes on a sunny July day, the kind of rain that was always followed by a rainbow. It dampened their faces in a way that tears could not.

The rain stopped as abruptly as it had started, but there wasn't enough sun for a rainbow, and the crescent moon hadn't the power to create any such phenomenon. So Rose began to sing a song about that wondrous place over the rainbow where there were only clear blue cloudless skies.

If only the skies *were* always blue, Skye thought as she tightened her grip on her friends' hands. If only there were no clouds and no storms and no inversion layers, just stars and bluebirds and a lullaby land where war never happened, and nobody died and everyone's dreams came true.

She closed her eyes and listened to Rose's voice fading as her throat tightened over the words. All their faces were wet now, but not from the rain.

THIRTEEN

The following week, Rose urged them all to go out to a night of movies and dancing at RAF Tangmere, which had installed a brand-new cinema in one of the hangars. She thought it might be the thing to cheer them up. So they cycled to Southampton, then caught the train to Chichester. It was an uncertain night, the full moon hidden behind thick clouds that threatened rain, and the women prayed they'd make it to the base without a soaking.

They were lucky. They made it through the main gate and found the sports hangar where the cinema was located before the deluge started.

Joan immediately paired off with a flight sergeant, but Rose and Skye did what they always did: deflected some familiar attention so they could watch the movie in peace, reasoning there was no need to couple themselves off until the dancing began.

They were about to sit down when Skye heard her name called. She turned to see O'Farrell grinning at her.

"This is a nice surprise," he said.

Skye remembered that she'd decided to give O'Farrell a chance. "Come sit with me," she said. "But make sure Rose isn't lonely."

Rose smiled winningly and O'Farrell hollered for one of the men Skye had seen at the secret base in Bedfordshire to join them, which he did, plying Rose with charm.

"What are you doing at Tangmere?" Skye asked O'Farrell as he maneuvered them toward some empty chairs.

"A few of us are here for a couple of weeks." O'Farrell indicated the doorway.

Nicholas Crawford and Margaux Jourdan were walking through it. Nicholas offered Skye a stiff nod and didn't wait to see it returned. Skye only just swallowed her "Oh" of disappointment. It was as if their conversation at Leavesden had never happened; as if the man she'd shouted at that night at the base in Bedfordshire was the real Nicholas, and the other—the one she'd hoped she'd reignited a friendship with—had been a figment of her overtired and, at the time, overemotional imagination.

"What's the deal with you and Crawford?" O'Farrell asked, noticing the awkward greeting.

"I knew him when I was ten," Skye said. Then added, trying not to sound sad, "That's all."

"So I won't be stepping on any toes if I claim the first dance with you later? It's not a good idea to get on the wrong side of your wing commander."

"He has a fiancée, so I don't think he's in a position to object if you dance with me."

"Good." O'Farrell dropped his arm over the back of her seat. Skye settled back against it, determined to enjoy herself.

"Not flying tonight?" she asked offhandedly, hoping he might say more, still wondering what on earth his squadron did that was so important she had to sign the Official Secrets Act.

He shrugged. "Grounded tonight because of the weather."

Which didn't tell her anything.

The movie started. At the bottom left corner of the screen, three rows in front, Skye could see Margaux's head resting on Nicholas's shoulder.

"Smoke?" O'Farrell offered her a Lucky Strike and she took it even though she hated American cigarettes. He lit it for her, the flame illuminating the contours of his sharply handsome face and also the couple beside him who were familiarizing themselves with one another's lips.

O'Farrell stood up. "Let's go sit down in the back. Otherwise I'm going to have to start correcting their technique."

Skye laughed. "That I'd like to see."

She followed him to the other side of the room, where she could no longer see Nicholas's head or Margaux's. She felt her shoulders drop down from around her ears.

"This is better," she said as she sat down.

"You didn't seem too interested in the movie," O'Farrell said, studying her face intently. "You sure are beautiful."

He leaned over and kissed her lips gently, not at all how she'd imagined he would, and she was momentarily charmed.

When he drew back, he said, "You know, I'm not looking for someone to marry, and I'm not looking for someone to warm my bed for a night or whenever it suits me. Dance with whoever you want, whenever you want. I'm not a cage. I'm just looking for someone who's also fighting a war and who sometimes needs something to get them through it."

As he spoke, Skye felt a sharp stab of loneliness, a loneliness she could hear mirrored in his words. Of course they were both surrounded by people every day, her at the ferry pool at Hamble and him at his own base; but up in the sky there was nobody around, and it must be worse for him because his friends must die more often than hers did. He probably saw them blown up right before his eyes, whereas she only heard about it in the aftermath. An empty bed after a night like that must feel like the loneliest place of all.

So she tucked her head onto his shoulder and he draped his arm around her, fingers lightly tracing over her neck as they watched the movie together.

* * *

When the movie was finished and the gramophone wound and the dancing began, an unquiet energy filled the room.

As O'Farrell led Skye out to dance, they passed Margaux and Nicholas, whom O'Farrell acknowledged with a "Sir."

Nicholas nodded at him and said Skye's name, and Margaux ignored them both as Nicholas drew her in to dance.

Skye managed two dances with O'Farrell before he was claimed by one WAAF, and then another. It didn't pay to choose such a good-looking man to distract oneself with, she thought wryly.

Nicholas was just as popular, and Margaux seemed perfectly at ease with him dancing with every mooning female whose interest in him outweighed her fear of Margaux. Nicholas chatted and laughed with each of them easily and they all walked away looking lovestruck, even as he returned to Margaux's side after every dance.

Skye was similarly blessed with dance partners and the music was suitably inspiriting—"I'll Be Home for Christmas" and "When the Lights Go on Again All Over the World." But would they, Skye wondered, and she wished for a song that wasn't about war and absence.

She excused herself for the next dance. As she was coming back from the bathroom, she found Margaux leaning against the wall, red-lipsticked mouth drawing on a cigarette, dark brown hair set with precision, self-possession radiating from her like a searchlight even in her WAAF uniform.

"Gauloises?" Margaux asked, proffering the pack.

How the hell had Margaux managed to get hold of French cigarettes? But then, how had Nicholas? Amid the melange of feelings she'd experienced when she last spoke to him, Skye realized she hadn't asked him that most obvious of questions.

She shook her head. "No, thank you."

"You prefer Players?" Margaux's tone was sardonic, and her words accented enough to suggest she'd been born in France and must therefore wake up every day knowing that her country and her kinsmen and possibly her family were suffering the wretchedness of German occupation.

Skye relented. "Nobody with any taste prefers Players. I dream of Gitanes but this is close enough." She took the cigarette and then felt she couldn't really walk away. "Are you based at Tangmere?" she asked. "Or up in Bedfordshire?"

"I move up and down with the pilots," Margaux replied. "They're here for a fortnight, so I am too."

"You're lucky you get to work so closely with your fiancé."

Margaux shrugged. "You're the first female pilot I've met," she said, turning the conversation.

"We do exist," Skye replied lightly, wondering how much more small talk she needed to come up with to pay for the cigarette.

"Where did you learn to fly?" Margaux asked, walking toward the hangar as if she expected Skye to accompany her.

Skye explained about her mother, curious as to why Nicholas hadn't told Margaux that Skye's mother had taught him to fly. "And then I had lessons in France for a few years. I lived there after my mother died." She switched the focus away from herself. "You're obviously French. And your name . . ."

"Yes, the name." Margaux blew out a long, thin and elegant stream of smoke. "It's like wearing a badge that declares me an exotic species. *Margaret*, people always say after I'm introduced to them. Or, *Can I call you Meg?*" She lifted one acerbic eyebrow. "The English are the only people in the world who could get Meg from Margaux."

Skye laughed. There was no way she would ever dream of calling this poised and aloof woman Meg.

"Skye. How are you?" Nicholas's polite voice broke in and Skye's mirth creased at the edges.

She managed a "Fine, thank you," and a "Thanks for the cigarette. Excuse me" to Margaux before she slipped outside. She walked past the Belfast hangars where the Tangmere squadrons' Spitfires, Hurricanes, Mustangs and Typhoons were waiting; past the main store, the engine workshop and the parachute store—all the flat-roofed, boxy and ill-featured buildings that Skye adored because, without them, planes couldn't fly. Fuel and oil and damp scented the air as she reached the armory.

On the grass behind it, hidden away, she found the black Lysanders lined up like abandoned dragons. It had stopped raining so she clambered up onto the Lizzie with the mermaid painted on it and, with her back leaning against its body and her legs stretched out over the wing, she smoked two Players in a row. After the Gauloises, they tasted like discontent.

She heard footsteps and expected it was O'Farrell come to find her, but the head that rounded the nose of the plane was dark, not blond.

"Skye," Nicholas said, starting. He studied her face with a quizzical intensity, then ran a quick hand through his hair. "Every time I see you, it's like falling through time and being eleven again, and war is something from a long time past. But then I remember the war is now, and I'm not eleven and you are . . ."

He paused and she wondered if the stiff greeting in the sports hangar was simply an expression of the same disturbance she felt when she saw him; a disturbance arising from an inability, despite what she'd thought at Leavesden, to finish that sentence. *You are . . .* what?

An old friend? A new friend? Some other unnameable and unknowable thing?

The music waltzed toward them as the breeze picked up. Skye concentrated as ferociously on her cigarette as if it were the first time she'd ever smoked. Nicholas studied the ground with the same intensity until the clouds thinned to wisps and the moon glimmered through, lightening the night.

He looked back up at her. "Mind if I join you?"

"Sure," she said lightly, mimicking his accent, and he grinned and swung himself up beside her, reaching into his pocket and pulling out a cigarette—another Gauloise.

"Margaux's?" she queried, and he nodded.

"Who would have thought," he mused as they both watched smoke drift like tendrils of cirrus into invisibility, "that we'd both finally be old enough to fly airplanes by ourselves, smoke cigarettes and," he pulled a flask from his pocket, "drink whiskey."

"And get engaged," Skye said breezily. She accepted the flask and took a long drink. "When are you getting married?"

"I don't know. We haven't decided."

Skye felt her eyebrows quirk up in surprise. "Really? I thought engagements were either superfluous or else a quick step from a bed to the altar these days. That marrying was the point, given how precarious life is."

"We aren't in a hurry," was all he said. Then, "I'm sorry about your mother."

He sounded genuine, as if he truly understood the breach Skye's heart had endured when her mother died. She felt her eyes tear up and she stubbed out the cigarette, finding it impossible to inhale, let alone suck in air filthy with smoke. His next words were so surprising that they stole even more of her breath.

"I read about it in the newspaper," he said. "A woman dying in an airplane was such a strange thing back then that the news made it into the *New York Herald Tribune*. I decided to steal money from my aunt, escape from school, fly to England and come to the memorial service. I only made it as far as the subway station before I was taken back to school and caned."

"I didn't know," she whispered. "I thought that because you didn't write . . ."

"I wrote to you every damn day for two years," he shot back.

"You didn't," she insisted. "I wrote to *you* every damn day for two years and you never once replied."

"Believe me, if I'd received even one letter, I would have more than replied; you'd have heard me shouting with joy all the way over in France." His words rang with the adamance of absolute truth.

"Oh," was all she could say, silenced by the revelation that Nicholas hadn't gone off to New York and tossed her aside like an under-sized fish.

"I can't believe you thought I didn't write," he said quietly. "I guess my aunt told the school not to pass on or post any letters."

"I was never her favorite person," Skye said, remembering the woman with the fishhook voice. She sighed. "Let's not talk about her. Tell me about you instead. You're a wing commander. And you have a DFC and a DSO." She pointed to the decorations on Nicholas's uniform, awarded to those for distinguished and exemplary service. "Congratulations."

He moved before answering her, and she did too, both of them angling their bodies toward the other so they no longer had to turn their heads to talk and Skye could now see his face and the play of expressions across it as he spoke.

"I wanted to continue my flying lessons in New York but my aunt wouldn't allow it," he said. "So I didn't fly for a couple of years and it was like I'd lost everything of my Cornwall life: your family, swimming, flying. When I went to Harvard though, there wasn't anything she could do to stop me. I didn't get my inheritance from my father until I was twenty-one so I didn't have the money for flying lessons. I worked at one of the bars in Cambridge every night till closing, studied until dawn, slept for two hours, went to classes and did it all over again, and paid for my flying lessons and my membership of the Harvard Flying Club with the money I earned. Then O'Farrell and I came over here. We joined one of the Eagle Squadrons first. Now I'm in Special Duties. Having an English mother and an American father means I can work just about anywhere in the RAF. And the decorations are," he shrugged, "strokes of luck."

"I doubt that," Skye said. "You always worked hard at anything you wanted. And decorations like yours are given for acts of bravery, not luck."

"You must have worked hard too," he countered. "You don't get to be a female captain in the ATA too easily. If the ATA gave out DFCs and DSOs, you'd have more than me."

Nicholas shifted again, propping one elbow up on his bent knee, inhaling smoke. In his RAF uniform and with his beautiful blue eyes and jet-black hair, he looked like a propaganda poster for the armed forces.

Skye snatched her eyes away, caught off guard by the sudden jolt inside her. She had spoken to men aplenty over the past two and a half years, seen a thousand ways to combine different features—eyes and hair and face and physique—and none of those combinations had stirred anything in her. But at least twice now, Nicholas, her friend Nicholas—when he'd smiled at her, or sat as he was now, spotlit by moonshine—had caused her body to respond in a way she didn't understand. Friends were like kittens: they did not cause feelings other than a comforting, contented warmth.

"How's your mother?" she asked, needing to fill the space between them with words rather than her peculiar thoughts.

"Worse," he said, reaching for the flask. "Sometimes it's like . . . I don't know; it's like she's barely alive. I write to her. But I doubt she knows who I am anymore."

"I'm so sorry," Skye said, unable to stop herself from touching his arm—how could she listen to him speak so bleakly and not offer any comfort? "And I'm sorry again," she said, removing her hand.

"Don't be. Like I said before, Margaux wouldn't mind." He turned the conversation. "What about Liberty? Is she still an amateur prize-fighter?"

"My turn for the whiskey," Skye said abruptly.

Nicholas watched the emotions she couldn't hide transcribe them-selves on her face. "What happened?" he asked.

Skye sipped from the flask, not feeling the burn of alcohol in her throat, just the warmth and the promise of forgetting, for one night, all the things she tried not to think about.

She started by telling Nicholas about Liberty's astonishing transfor-mation in Paris. "Then," Skye said, "when I was eighteen, I wanted to leave France and go home. I'd waited until Liberty was seventeen and able to look after herself. I honestly didn't think she'd care if I left; we spent hardly any time together. And Paris was never home for me." Skye's voice faltered on the last sentence.

"I'm prying," Nicholas said in apology. "It's just so strange that I knew everything about you for four years and now I feel as if I know nothing at all."

"You're not prying. I mightn't talk about her much but I think about Liberty all the time. I tell myself not to though. I feel . . . guilty."

There it was: stark fact, spoken aloud for the first time.

"You'd never do anything to hurt your sister." Nicholas examined the gray flecks of ash on the tip of his cigarette. "I know that."

"But I did," Skye said. "After I told her I was leaving, Liberty screamed at me. She said . . ." Skye breathed in smoke, then released it. "She said that if I broke my aunt's promise by running away then our mother would haunt us forever. I told her it was my dearest wish to be haunted by my mother."

"Skye," Nicholas said, but she shook her head.

"Don't," she said, blinking hard. A tear spilled out anyway.

Above, the clouds shuffled restlessly, obscuring the starlight. The music from the sports hangar crescendoed, and Nicholas stood up on the wing.

"In there," he pointed in the direction of the hangar, "it looked as if your dancing might have improved over the past ten years. But I won't know for sure until you dance with me." He jumped to the ground and held out his hand. "Please?"

"All right," she said, confused. Then realization hit her: she'd bored him by talking about Liberty.

She slid off the plane and, to hide her embarrassment, busied herself with squashing her cigarette beneath her shoe. She'd dance with him once—he'd danced with other WAAFs in the hangar so that would be fine—but she wouldn't mention Liberty again.

He took her hand and her eyes skittered up to meet his. She saw in them an expression of such tenderness that it made even her bones hurt; it was tenderness of a kind she hadn't realized she craved.

His other hand touched her back. "I couldn't just sit there and listen to you when you sounded so sad," he whispered. "Tell me the rest."

She finally understood. The only way he could offer her comfort was like this: dancing as men and women did all the time, whether they were engaged or not. And so, in the familiar circle of his arms, as they moved to the distant music, she told him what she had never spoken aloud to anyone. She told him that she'd stayed in Paris for

Liberty, who'd repaid Skye by soaking her bed in water and puncturing the tires of her bike.

"So I left the following year without telling her," she finished.

Nicholas's hold on her hand tightened.

"Now I wonder if all those things were just her way of begging me to stay," Skye said in a low voice. "Doing what she could to get my attention. She didn't want to come back to England. But I missed Cornwall so much. Maybe so much that I chose it over my sister. That's why I feel guilty. She's never written to me since. All I know is that she's in England somewhere. I think she hates me."

"She has no reason to," Nicholas said softly. "You wanted to leave; she wanted to stay. You told her your plans. She was eighteen, not a child."

"But I promised my mother I'd look after her." Her voice was so close to a whisper that she thought Nicholas might not hear. But he did.

"Your mom knew how much you loved Cornwall," he said, narrowing the distance between their bodies by just an inch but increasing five hundredfold the empathy contained in that space. "She, more than anyone, would have understood. I understand. Those years in Cornwall were the best gift of all: my family had been taken from me, but then, somehow, this other family, this incredible family, was given to me instead. It made my childhood something to remember rather than something to forget. If I'd been able to escape from New York and go back to Cornwall, I would have."

Nicholas looked down at her and she saw him unshielded. Not the wing commander in charge of a squadron, but a man who, despite the missing years, knew Skye Penrose better than most people did. A man who was doing something secret and dangerous for her country, and for his too, but who still had time to listen to her. A man who wasn't afraid to let her see all the different pieces of him concealed behind the uniform.

Their dance slowed to a drift.

"You know," he said, concern on his face, "if the war doesn't end soon, you're going to fade away. Dancing like this I can feel that you're almost as skinny as you were when you were twelve. Do they feed you in the ATA? You didn't really mean it when you were up at my base and said you'd only had a chocolate ration since breakfast, did you?"

Skye, on the other hand, could tell that Nicholas wasn't skinny. Rather he was well-built and muscular—a man, of course—as if flying and exercise took up his time between suppers. He wasn't fueled by adrenaline and cigarettes as she and the other ATA women were.

"We don't get bacon and egg breakfasts or suppers when we return from a day's flying," she said lightly.

"So you did mean it?"

She didn't answer.

He frowned. "How often don't you eat?"

His tone was gentle rather than interfering, and suddenly she wanted to move closer still, to place her head on his shoulder while they swayed to the music. To feel his voice slide softly past her ear.

She inhaled sharply. She'd obviously had too much whiskey if she was thinking about resting any part of her body on Nicholas Crawford. "Let's talk about something less serious," she said, searching for diversions. "Something funny would be perfect."

"Okay," he said, thinking, then smiling a little.

"What?" she said, her mouth lifting up at the corners in anticipation of his next words.

"Talking about your mom made me remember something I never told you. Something funny. Although I didn't think it was funny at the time," he added.

"You have to tell me now," she said.

"Well, when she was giving me swimming lessons, she sat me down and talked to me about the birds and the bees, about how my body would change and how yours would too."

He gave a wry smile at the look on Skye's face and she thought she saw his cheeks flush, just a little.

"Back then, I had no real idea what she was talking about," he went on. "But I realized, the day I left Cornwall, that what she'd been trying to tell me was to make sure I never took advantage of you, of the closeness of our friendship. She didn't know I'd be leaving before either of us was old enough for that and we need never have had that excruciating conversation."

Skye found herself back in Cornwall one summer morning, arm bruised from Liberty's pinching fingers, about to defy her mother's orders and march off to the beach to escape her sister. Nicholas had returned from his swimming lesson monosyllabic and had remained so for the best part of the day.

"I remember one day you came back so red I thought the sun must have baked you," she said. "You wouldn't look at me, even though I wanted to show you how impressive my bruises were. Was that the day?"

He nodded. "She told me you'd grow breasts and I was too afraid to look at you in case it happened right before my eyes. I didn't quite grasp that it was a more gradual process."

Skye doubled over with laughter. "Oh God, you didn't?"

Nicholas began to laugh too and for a time neither of them could speak.

"We've covered the full range of emotions tonight, haven't we?" he said at last when they'd recovered.

"We have."

And then they both seemed to realize that they were no longer dancing, or laughing, just standing together in the darkness of an airfield. In that darkness, her eyes held by his, Skye felt like she was caught in a plane spinning aerobatically and unstoppably toward him. Her fingers curled into her palm so they wouldn't, on terrible impulse, reach out to touch him.

A movement behind Nicholas. Another man walking toward them. His hair glimmered gold in the moonlight and Skye knew it was O'Farrell and that it was time for her to leave.

Nicholas leaned back against the Lizzie and lit another cigarette. Before O'Farrell was close enough to hear, he said, "I missed you, Skye."

"I missed you too," she said. Then she walked over to O'Farrell and slipped her arm through his.

FOURTEEN

Nicholas finished his cigarette, had another decent slug of whiskey, then returned to the sports hangar to find Margaux. She was watching Skye dance with O'Farrell.

"She looks like a fairy dancing with a giant," Margaux said when Nicholas joined her.

"More like a selkie dancing with a giant," Nicholas replied, seeing again what he'd sensed outside: that Skye's regime of working hard and forgetting to eat made her look tiny compared to the well-built O'Farrell.

"I don't know what that is."

"A mythological sea creature. Skye's mom used to tell us stories about them."

Margaux faced him, no longer watching Skye and O'Farrell. "You must have been in England for quite some time as a child if you knew her mother well enough to have listened to her stories."

"Four years."

"I should probably know that." Margaux's smile was, as always, a smooth curve of lip that didn't touch her eyes.

"You probably should." He smiled at her too, and they stood in companionable silence for a few minutes.

"You know," he said suddenly, as one dance ended and another began and Skye remained in O'Farrell's arms, "I'm going to send her some of the oranges I got last week in Algiers. 161 Squadron is more than well-fed. We don't need them."

"Why don't you take her out for a meal too? If tomorrow goes well, I won't be here for at least a couple of months, perhaps longer, and it will give you something to do besides drinking too much whiskey." She cocked an eyebrow at him and Nicholas gave her a half smile because Margaux always knew everything and could somehow tell he'd been emptying his whiskey flask that night. "The moon period's almost over," she finished. "Which means you'll soon have time."

"Maybe I will," he said.

No, he *would*. It had been the most difficult thing of all not to write to her after he'd seen her at Biggin Hill two years ago; like pushing against gravity and hoping to win. So often he'd sat down to write a letter in which he didn't tell her anything about where he was or what he was doing, but he knew that would be like standing on a roof-top and shouting it all out, thus breaking the Official Secrets Act—Skye would have known something was amiss. But he could send her oranges and take her to dinner, as Margaux had suggested. He felt himself smile the way he only did when he was with Skye.

Then he saw O'Farrell draw Skye in closer, whispering in her ear, and the two of them disappeared outside. He couldn't shift his eyes from the doorway through which they'd left, even though he could feel Margaux watching him.

* * *

Later, as Skye, Rose and Joan cycled through the sightless blackout to their cottage, their head-flashlights providing three slivers of light, the distant boom of flak and fighters over France faintly heard, Joan said to Rose, "You're smiling so hard your teeth will light a path for the Germans. Don't tell me you're falling for someone?"

Rose laughed. "Perhaps," was her coy answer.

"The pilot from Nicholas's squadron?" Skye asked. "Really?"

"Richie Jenkins," Rose said. "He was nice. And that squadron seems to have made its way into a few of our hearts."

"What do you mean?" Skye squeaked, only just avoiding a pothole.

"O'Farrell," Joan said. "Something has gone terribly wrong in the world—apart from the obvious," she added as more enemy gunfire sounded in the night—"if you two are returning smitten from a night out, but my heart is undisturbed."

"O'Farrell," Skye said faintly as they drew up at the cottage, her mind playing over her final dance with him, recalling the way he'd led her outside and kissed her, and how it had felt somehow less than she'd wanted it to.

* * *

Even though it was March, for two days snow had been falling to earth in a great purging deluge. For those two days, Skye had been sitting in a freezing hut in her flying suit and sheepskin jacket, having been assigned a priority-one wait. It meant she had to remain with the Spitfire she was to ferry from Chattis Hill to Colerne until the very first sign of improvement in the weather. Then she was to get in the plane and deliver it. It was the only time they were allowed to ignore the eight-hundred-foot cloud base rule—a priority-one wait meant that lives were at stake and every second's delay was another blow to the still-floundering Allies.

But with the weather the way it was, even Skye, their so-called fog-flier, hadn't managed to get airborne. And waiting meant doing nothing, which meant thinking. She remembered waking up the morning after dancing with Nicholas, a whiskey-headache pounding her skull. At first she'd been relieved because it meant she *had* drunk too much. But the next moment, she'd recalled Nicholas's smile, how he'd looked sitting on the wing of an airplane with his elbow propped on his knee and her whole body had felt suddenly and unacceptably warm.

She stared out the window, needing to let the memory go. She could just see the trees now, and the runway. It was time to forget about Nicholas and to fly.

It was the most difficult flight of her life and considering she'd been shot at by enemy planes and had propellers fall off while airborne, that was saying something. She had to stay beneath the soggiest blanket of thick black clouds, the base of which was only three hundred feet from the ground. It forced her to fly as low and as slow as she'd ever flown in her life, sticking to every sleeper of the railway track that was her marker, shaving the trees with her jet stream, knowing that to lose sight of the ground in a snowstorm like this would be fatal. When the railway did a double loop in Savernake Forest, she didn't fly over the loop—picking up the point where it headed north—as she ordinarily would. She looped with it, and was never so pleased as when she knew she was only a couple of miles from her destination.

Then she saw a shape dead ahead and coming straight for her. A Lancaster, an elephant in the sky, on course for a collision.

She heard herself swear as she hauled the Spit onto its tail and gave it full throttle. She almost ducked, as if that would help, horrified to see the disbelieving face of the Lancaster's rear gunner almost within handshaking distance of her.

Then she was in the cloud, and she braced herself for the tail of the enormous plane to clip her underside, thanking God it had dived down while she had instinctively gone up. Nothing happened. But now she was stranded in the blindness of cloud.

Don't panic, she told herself.

It was impossible to describe what it felt like to be adrift in cloud, with no way of knowing in which direction lay the earth or the heavens, as discombobulated as if thrown into the deepest part of the ocean, tumbled around, and then let loose with no guiding light. Her heart was giving the engine stiff competition for both pace and volume and she clutched at the collar of her suit, desperate for air.

The only thing she could do was take the Spit straight back down and pray that what she thought was down was not, in fact, up. Below her, if she was very lucky, would be the airfield rather than a forest or the Lancaster or the edge of the world.

Was this how her mother had felt? Fatalistic, knowing there was only one possible choice, and that was to plunge, sightless, and hope.

The cloud thinned. There was a flash of green. Stray tufts of cloud. More green. An airfield, too close.

She landed heavily but didn't care. She was alive.

They had the blood cart and crash wagon ready for her but thankfully she didn't need either. She sat, incapable of movement, as the Lancaster crew and the engineers rushed out to greet her.

A thumping noise alerted her that someone had climbed onto the wing. A man unbuckled her straps, held out a hand and said, "Can I help you?"

"I could have done with some help ten minutes ago," she said shakily, hoisting herself up.

"I told you it was a woman," she heard someone say and she looked down and saw the gunner who had passed her by so near in the sky.

She shook her head, unable to believe that her gender was still the most surprising thing about what had just happened.

"We had no idea you were coming in," the engineer said. "The Spit that took off after you turned straight around and went back to base. Your ops officer at Hamble thinks you're dead. You'd better give her a call."

"Have a cup of tea first," the Lancaster pilot added.

"And maybe a cigarette," Skye said wryly.

* * *

News of what happened reached Pauline's ears and Skye's ferrying schedule was lighter for the next couple of weeks. So much lighter that one afternoon she finished a rare hour early, but had to wait at the base in case anything came up. A beautiful April sun shone; the snow had obviously been winter's last flourish before spring unleashed her magnificence upon a weary England. Skye took herself outside, smiling at the warmth, so glad to still be alive that she decided to do something she hadn't done since autumn.

She made her way to the far reaches of the airfield, behind one of the hangars, where a couple of Spitfires sat. She climbed onto a wing that had been warmed to just the right temperature by the sun. Then she unbuttoned her blouse, slid it off and lay on her back in just her skirt and brassiere—which was pale blue silk and had come with her from France. Every time she put it on she prayed it would outlast the war so she wouldn't have to resort to ration lingerie. For most people, it was probably too cold for sunbathing. But to Skye it was glorious. She let the heat sink into her and the tension of her near-miss melted away.

She didn't hear footsteps, only heard someone say her name. She sat up, startled, to find a man in an RAF uniform turning away from her when he saw what she was wearing.

"What are you doing?" Nicholas demanded, his back to her, voice half an octave higher than the last time she'd heard it.

Skye lay down again, mouth twitching, trying not to laugh. "Sun-bathing," she said demurely.

"On the wing of a Spitfire?"

"It's actually very comfortable. You should try it."

She heard him laugh, which made her laugh too. She imagined a row of RAF pilots lined up on the wings of their planes, sunbathing. That would definitely give Diana's heart something to flutter over.

She reached for her shirt and slipped it on. "You've seen me in my swimming costume."

"You looked a little different the last time I saw you in your swimming costume," he said, voice not quite steady, and Skye's hands on her buttons faltered.

"People change in ten years," she said, her voice altered too. She smoothed down her shirt. "You're safe; I won't scald your eyes anymore."

He turned back and smiled, and Skye almost fell off the wing. If O'Farrell's smile made a woman weak at the knees, Nicholas's smile made her forget she had knees.

"It seems you haven't broken your habit of showing people your underwear," he said, then his cheeks colored and he swore softly. "I didn't mean that the way it sounded. As if—"

"As if I regularly lie in wait for pilots on the wings of planes wearing only my brassiere?" She couldn't maintain her faux-annoyance for more than a few seconds before she started to laugh again.

He ran a hand through his hair and gave her a rueful grin. "I thought you were about to start yelling at me again. But hopefully you won't yell when you see what I've brought you." He held up a bag.

"Oranges?" Skye stared in disbelief, then slid down to the ground, needing to inspect them at close range to make sure they were real. She hadn't seen an orange for two years.

"I remember you used to like orange juice for breakfast," he said.

"I did. Thank you."

"And I'm taking you out for dinner. I was telling Margaux how lucky we are to have a mess and cooked meals after ops and that

I wanted to bring you some oranges and she said I should buy you dinner as well."

Skye tried not to let her mouth fall open. Margaux had told her fiancé to take Skye out for dinner. She really wasn't the jealous sort.

"You don't have to do that," Skye protested, even though she wanted to have dinner with Nicholas. She'd had fun talking with him at the dance. Conversation between them was effortless, and it made her stop thinking about the war and remember another kind of life.

"I want to," he said. "I'm not flying tonight because I'm going back to Bedfordshire tomorrow, so I caught a ride here on the taxi plane with one of your friends. I'll stay the night at an inn in town and catch a ride back tomorrow."

"Who was flying the taxi?"

"Rose."

That at least meant a more subtle level of questioning about Nicholas than if it had been Diana flying the plane. And Rose's questions could be easily answered by reminding her that Nicholas was a childhood friend. That was all.

"Dinner would be lovely," Skye said. "Thank you. Let's take these to the lounge first though." She indicated the oranges.

Nicholas followed her across the airfield to the lounge, where the oranges were leapt upon by Rose and Diana as if they were foie gras.

"Are you going to save any for yourself?" he asked Skye, and she heard exasperation in his voice.

"I've got one," she said, holding it up. "Let's go." She wanted to slip out while the fuss over the oranges was at its peak and nobody would see that she was leaving with Nicholas.

They walked past her cottage, where she dropped off her orange, and then to the Bugle, where Nicholas booked himself a room for the night. They found a table inside, and Skye hoped that tonight everyone from the ferry pool would stay home and not dine at the Bugle too.

Mrs. Chambers, the wife of the owner, greeted Skye. "Hello, love. Who's your handsome fellow then?"

"This is my *friend*"—even Skye could hear her emphasis on the word—"Nicholas. I've known him since I was young."

"Well, any friend of Skye's is always welcome," Mrs. Chambers said. "I've managed to cobble together a chicken pie out of nothing but it'll be gone before long. How about I get you some now?"

"Yes please," Skye said, and heard her stomach rumble loudly.

Nicholas laughed. "And that is why I'm taking you to dinner."

Skye laughed too and relaxed at last, sitting back in her chair, sipping the wine Mrs. Chambers had somehow found for them. "Cheers," she said, raising her glass. "Here's to . . ." She considered what would be appropriate, then came up with, "Surviving."

Nicholas grimaced. "A macabre toast, but given the circumstances I'll raise my glass to it."

Mrs. Chambers brought their chicken pies, and Nicholas carved off half of his and added it to Skye's plate despite her protests. Then he looked at her, as serious as she'd ever seen him.

"While we're on the subject of surviving . . ." His fingers turned a pack of cigarettes over and over. "Skye . . ." Another pause and then it all came out. "I saw a friend from Colerne last week. He entertained everyone with a tale of a 'beautiful dark-haired dame' who'd not only ventured out in the filthiest weather we've had when almost every other plane in England was grounded, but that a Lancaster had almost landed on her and she'd bounced out of the plane asking for a cigarette as if nothing was the matter. I know it was you. Don't," he said vehemently, "don't fucking die."

He didn't apologize for swearing. He didn't appear to realize how he'd spoken, seeming only to care that Skye heard him and made him a promise. She put down her fork, her throat now too tight to swallow anything.

"I was so scared," she said quietly, seeing again the Lancaster, just an arm's length away, and the crew's faces so close.

"I know," he said, and in his eyes she could see his RAF dead, just as her ATA dead lived in her despite her stubborn pretense. She and Nicholas were separated from those souls by simple luck, not the power of pocket watches and scarves.

And she felt it then, like the kick in the back from a Merlin engine suddenly throttled up: the absolute certainty that Nicholas could not die either. If he did, it wouldn't matter if there was a war or not. Her world would end.

If they were still ten and eleven, they might have pricked their fingers to seal the promise. All she could do now was stretch out her hand across the table, hoping that a handshake had an effect as binding as a blood vow.

"Don't you die either," she said.

As their palms met, Nicholas's thumb slid over the arch of skin where her forefinger curved around to her thumb. His fingertips brushed against the back of her hand. She had shaken hands a thousand times before but she had never shaken hands like this.

"I'm glad I found you again," he said.

"Me too."

* * *

After dinner, they went for a walk along the river.

"Do you miss swimming every day?" he asked.

She grinned. "What makes you think I don't still swim every day?"

He laughed. "Of course you do. Even though no one in England is allowed to swim in the sea, Skye Penrose manages to breach the coastal defenses and convince everyone in the village of Hamble to turn a blind eye to her rule-breaking. Is that about right?"

"I didn't have to convince everyone," she said. "Just those who get up early, like the baker. Half of Hamble beachcombs for souvenirs and debris so I'm not the only one. And it has its benefits. The beachcombers found a crate full of wheels of Camembert washed up last year and I came home with two. No growling stomach that week."

"After all that pie, it shouldn't make a noise for a week this time either," he said, smiling.

"Maybe a couple of days at least."

Others out walking nodded as they passed and Skye wondered what they must look like: a man and woman in uniform, out together, but not together in the way that most men and women walking at night in uniform were. Their hands weren't joined and there was a decorous space between their bodies. Only their eyes touched fleetingly every now and again, before pulling quickly away.

"I miss the water," Nicholas said. "I can't remember the last time I swam in the sea." He stopped and leaned his forearms against the river wall, and Skye sat atop it, facing him. "Do you still have the house in Porthleven?" he asked.

"Yes. But I haven't been there for two years. Two days off isn't quite enough time to take the train and I don't have a car, so I've never learned to drive."

"I'd love to see it again. Find out if it's the same as I remember or if..." He hesitated. "If I've somehow made it into more than it was. Or if I haven't quite made it into enough."

"Every time I go back, I find the reality far surpasses my expectations."

"That cove," he said wistfully. "There's no other place like it."

"There isn't," she said, smiling to think that he still adored her home the way she did, that his New York City and Harvard upbringing hadn't ruined the unelaborate for him. "We were so happy, weren't we? Sometimes, now, I forget that happy exists. And I feel guilty, when so many people are dying, for coveting it. Do you think it will all end—the worry, the fear? No," Skye corrected herself, "the need to not feel the worry or the fear, because if we did, how would we ever fly an airplane again?"

"It will end," he said grimly. "I don't know how, or whether the end might be worse than now. Sometimes I don't even know whether to pray for the end or not."

"That's why I swim," she said as she contemplated the future that lay out there, somewhere beyond reach, beyond prophecy. "When someone dies, or nearly dies, and I can't talk about it, I can at least hit the water as hard as I like and it doesn't complain. What do you do?"

"At the risk of sounding like the clichéd American pilot, I guess we drink whiskey, O'Farrell and I." He straightened up, turned to lean his back against the wall and rubbed a hand tiredly over the back of his neck. "Special Duties is a place of well-curbed and bridled emotion. It has to be. Except if it's midnight and we're not flying, you'll find the younger ones and the new recruits so full of whiskey that they'll try to walk across a ceiling beam and fall off and break their arm, and various other stupid dares. O'Farrell and I watch with resignation, because if you tell them to stop they think you're doubting their courage and that only makes them do something even more stupid. That's when you know their emotions are only just in check. I started a football competition because there was no goddamn way I was going to play cricket, and I try to make them dare one another on the comparative safety of the field. O'Farrell and I run circles around them while they try to make sense of the rules." He grinned. "It makes me a terrible person that I make them play American football instead of cricket, doesn't it?"

She laughed. "I'd say that if it stops them falling off ceiling beams it can only be a good thing." She almost didn't ask because they'd moved from seriousness to lightness, but she had to. "How old are those younger ones?"

"Special Duties doesn't take eighteen-year-olds. Our youngest is twenty-three."

Nicholas was twenty-five. "Only two years younger than you. And you're in charge of a squadron."

"I feel a thousand years old inside, Skye."

His voice was low and she had to lean in close, too close, to hear it. *Don't*, she wanted to whisper. *Don't talk like that*. Because right now, all she wanted was to slide off the wall, step in front of him and lean the back of her body into the front of his, to feel his arms wrap around her, his chin rest on her shoulder, his breath warm against her cheek as she held on to him and he held on to her. To stand like that all night long and not let go.

"I wish I could fix that," she said softly.

"You do," he said, his lips so near her ear. "You always do."

A raucous group of ATA pilots swept past then, bringing with them the sharp sting of reality and leaving behind them the echoes of common sense.

As they passed, Skye did slide off the wall, but she faced the water, shaking off her strange imaginings. "How's O'Farrell?" she asked, in order to move the conversation into less turbulent space.

"Same as always."

"Flirting with every WAAF who crosses his path then?"

Nicholas didn't answer.

"It's all right," she said. "I know what he's like. I'm not looking to him as a safe harbor for my heart or my feelings. You're lucky you've found someone for that," she added, as much a reminder for herself as anything. "Will you and Margaux go back to New York after all this is over?"

"I don't know. We don't do a lot of future planning."

"Do you think your mother will be able to attend the wedding?"

Nicholas stared fixedly at the ground. "Margaux doesn't know about my mom. We don't talk about the past. My relationship with Margaux is . . ."

He met her eyes at last and Skye braced herself for what he was about to say. A physical thing? She couldn't help the involuntary shudder as she thought about Nicholas engaging himself to someone out of pure lust. But that wasn't Nicholas. Except neither was it Nicholas to keep so much to himself, to give Margaux nothing except who he was right now, which was only half of the Nicholas Crawford Skye knew.

"Unorthodox," he finished, which told Skye nothing beyond what she already knew. That Margaux didn't get jealous. That she was happy for her fiancé to take other women out for dinner. That she was the most unknowable person Skye had ever met.

Nicholas lit two cigarettes. As he passed one to her, their fingers touched. His eyes followed her hand up to her lips.

Somewhere above them, a gull squawked. The water in the river rustled impatiently. Skye didn't hear any of it. Nicholas was the only thing in her world right then. On the wall, her other hand sat beside his, a half-inch between them. A sliver of emptiness in which sat the most spectacular and untraversed sky, somewhere she would never return from if she entered it. A place that lived in her own mind and certainly not in that of Nicholas Crawford, who was so very at ease with his unorthodox fiancée.

She pushed herself away, began to walk, and heard Nicholas clear his throat behind her. She drew on the Gitane and it whispered something to her. *French cigarettes*. It was impossible to buy French cigarettes in England. And oranges.

She whipped around to face him. "You've been on the ground in France." Her heart shuddered in her chest, then thumped ferociously, wrathfully hard. "Of all the stupid and dangerous things to be doing. Nobody goes on the ground in France. Everyone stays in the sky.

Except you. How can you promise me you won't die when you're doing that?"

His silence said everything. "O'Farrell . . ." he said, then stopped.

What had he been about to say? O'Farrell is too? "I don't care about O'Farrell!" she cried.

She pressed a hand to her forehead. Of course she cared about O'Farrell! "Thank you for dinner," she said formally. "The inn is that way. Goodnight."

Then she left, feet striking against the ground, trying to drown out those terrifying words: *How can you promise me you won't die when you're doing that?*

FIFTEEN

It was two months before Skye was at Tangmere again, delivering a plane. She hadn't seen O'Farrell since the dance, although he had telephoned her once and she knew he was at Tangmere for a week or so and that she might see him. Which meant she might also see Nicholas. She had a present of sorts for him, to apologize for the way she'd ended the dinner he'd been kind enough to invite her to. She planned to leave it with one of the engineers to pass on to him, and to try to find O'Farrell, a man whom it was permissible to always have in her thoughts.

She flew over a cottage that was hidden by a screen of hedges from the airfield. She was low enough that she could see three people in the garden: one dark head, one fair, and a woman's perfect, straight-backed poise. Skye waggled her wings, knowing they probably wouldn't have any idea who was in the plane, but hoping O'Farrell, if indeed it was him, might come to investigate.

The circuit was busy. And she soon saw why. A Beaufighter, which should have returned hours ago, was limping in, riddled with holes. Skye saw the blood cart and fire engine waiting and she knew it meant somebody on board had holes in him too. She watched the pilot jump out and shout to the medics, who pulled out not a man but a body.

Skye's hands tightened on the stick as her throat tightened around her breath. She turned her plane around, circling, not looking at the scene on the ground, wishing she could keep her understanding of death to abstract noun rather than reality.

It didn't take long for the Beaufighter and its awful cargo to be cleared away and she was soon able to land. The roof opened, an engineer's face appeared and it was one she recognized—her friend Ollie.

"I need to leave this for Wing Commander Crawford," she said, indicating the box under her arm.

"I just saw him," Ollie said, before hollering across the runway. "Sir!"

"If you could just give it—" Skye began. Too late. Nicholas was there and Ollie had gone to deal with another plane.

"I thought it might have been you," Nicholas said with a smile. "O'Farrell's coming too, although he said I was nuts to think that just because a plane waggled its wings, it meant you were flying it."

Skye thrust the box at him, on which she'd written: *Delicate and quite possibly nippy*. "To thank you for the oranges," she said. "And to apologize."

"You don't need to apologize. I remember yelling at you for doing dangerous things. We're even." He opened the box and laughed. "Hermit crabs."

"You have no idea how long it took me to find two at Hamble," she said, laughing too. "If we'd been at Porthleven..." *Everything would have been different*. She didn't say it. "I thought they might be a better distraction than whiskey when there aren't enough pilots available for football."

He laughed again. "They will. Thank you. Do you have time to come to the mess for coffee? I think O'Farrell and Margaux will be there," he added.

"Just let me get changed."

"Before you go . . ." He put out a hand to stop her. "I saw Liberty," he said.

So many questions tried to tumble out of her mouth all at once. "Where? How is she?"

Nicholas's face was more guarded than England's coastal defenses. "She's the same as I remember."

Liberty wasn't even there but Skye still felt the blow. "You mean she doesn't want to see me."

"That's what she said. But Skye . . . you know with Liberty it's never about what she says or does."

"No, it's about how hard she kicks." Hurt shaped those words. Her next were formed from fear. "Or it's about what's making her kick."

"Yes."

"What's she doing?" Skye asked, remembering lying beside her sister in bed in Paris after their mother had died. "Does she think I'm mad at her? I'm not. I wish she knew that." The last sentence quivered in the air.

"If I run into her again, I'll tell her that." He stepped closer to her, gathering her eyes in his, just as he'd gathered her into his arms the night they'd danced on the airfield, and Skye saw on his face that same tenderness: a compassion she would gladly fall into, if only she could.

Then she recalled that he'd said Margaux was waiting for him and she knew she'd taken too much of his time already. "Perhaps I'll see her somewhere too," she said, steadying her voice so Nicholas would think she was fine. "Then she'll have to talk to me." She picked up her bag. "See you in the mess."

* * *

Skye sat on a bench in the changing room, still in her flight suit. Nicholas had seen Liberty. Which meant she was safe and well. Thank God. Relief hit Skye now and she exhaled loudly, resting her elbows on her knees and her chin in her hands. In wartime, it should be enough to know that someone you loved was alive. But it wasn't. And there was nothing Skye could do to make Liberty come and see her, except, of course, to hope that they might bump into one another some day soon.

She stood up, changed, composed herself and walked over to the officers' mess. O'Farrell, who was lurking by the entrance and tossing casual smiles at the WAAFs, waved Skye over and led her to a table near the window. Through the glass, Skye saw Nicholas step onto the porch and stop to talk to a white-faced pilot whose hand shook around a cigarette. She wondered if it was the man from the bullet-scarred Beaufighter who'd flown home with a dead body beside him. As Nicholas spoke to him, the pilot's lips formed into the ghost of a smile and a touch of color returned to his face.

Margaux smoked impatiently by the door, watching three WAAFs making eyes at her very handsome fiancé, who was oblivious to all but the man he spoke to. Then Nicholas joined her, following her over to where Skye and O'Farrell sat.

"How do you learn to fly so many planes?" O'Farrell was asking Skye.

From her pocket Skye produced a rectangle of paper the size of a folded handkerchief. The heading at the top read *Lancaster and Lancastrian*.

"With this," she said. "They're kind enough to give me notes. So I can look up the stall speed rather than having to work it out for myself." She grinned at the look on O'Farrell's face.

"Notes?" he said incredulously. "But how the hell does a woman who weighs at best one hundred and ten pounds get a thirty-ton Lancaster into the sky?"

"Given I'm planning to fly the Lancaster rather than carry it on my back, my weight hardly seems relevant," she said coolly.

"O'Farrell, if you want to finish the day with your head still on your shoulders, rather than bitten off, I'd probably start talking about something else," Nicholas broke in.

Margaux, watching, looked mordantly amused.

"Can I come up with you?" O'Farrell asked Skye.

Before she could say no, Ollie reappeared. "I've got something for you."

The way he said it made Skye shake her head. "What? A Meteor without an engine? A Typhoon without wings?"

"The Beaufighter that just came in. It's NEA."

The plane a man had died in just hours ago. His blood would still be inside it. And it was NEA—Not Essentially Airworthy—damaged so badly the RAF didn't want to risk any of their pilots in it. It would be flown only one more time, by her, to a maintenance unit to be broken up.

Skye stood. "Are you still coming up?" she asked O'Farrell.

"I think I'll let you take this one on your own," O'Farrell said sheepishly.

She couldn't help it. She started to laugh at the look on O'Farrell's face—the tough American pilot who didn't want to take a chance on a beaten-up plane flown by a woman. But she sobered up when she saw Nicholas frown, heard him mutter, "Jesus, Skye," and realized Margaux was looking at him as if she'd apprehended something that made her a little unhappy.

* * *

Nicholas sat on a chair in the garden of the cottage opposite the main gates of RAF Tangmere. Six pilots were there for the full-moon period, housed in relative luxury compared to the Nissen huts on an air base, although Nicholas still had to share a room with O'Farrell. They had their own flight sergeants, who acted as mother hens cum cooks cum security, and who attended to the pilots' every need: plying them with eggs and bacon at breakfast—an extravagance in ration times—and making sure only those with clearance entered the cottage. It was like being back in boarding school, Nicholas sometimes thought. Impossible to be alone.

He lit what was possibly his hundredth cigarette for the afternoon and knew he would wake up tomorrow with a throat as raw as if it had been used as a runway. He should be getting his maps ready. He should look over the briefing folder. He should at least check the latest weather report. But he couldn't concentrate on a damn thing besides Skye walking off, laughing, to fly a plane that could very well collapse into pieces eight hundred feet above the ground.

The back door of the cottage opened and Margaux came out, hands occupied as always with a cigarette. She passed him a coffee and sat down in the chair beside him, letting the silence linger, giving him the chance to say something. But he had no idea what to say.

Margaux did. "You can't fly tonight with your head full of whatever is occupying it. If you don't want to tell me, then tell someone else. But if you're going to say what I think you will, then I expect I'm the best person."

"I'll be fine by tonight. In fact," he stood up, "I was about to get ready."

"No, you weren't."

Margaux never let him get away with avoiding the issue. It was why she was so good at her job: her ability to see inside people and not let them know it at the time, but to have them understand later that whatever they'd thought they'd hidden, they had not, and she was about to use it.

He sat down abruptly.

"Is it because she's letting O'Farrell pay court to her, or because she's up there in a plane that's all but broken?" Margaux queried.

Of course she didn't make the vastly less pointed inquiry—Is it about Skye?—thus giving him the opportunity to deflect. She went straight in for the kill, knowing it was about Skye and only trying to determine if it was jealousy or fear that had made him so uptight.

"The latter," he said shortly.

"You know she's been taking up planes like that for the past couple of years and you didn't know anything about it. Which means you worrying about her isn't what's keeping her alive. The only thing you have even a little control over is tonight's mission."

"The moral of your story is to pay more attention to my job and less to hers."

Margaux gave him one of her uncommon and charming smiles. "You know I don't do morals. But if I did, the moral of my story would be to work out exactly why you're so bothered about her flying into danger when we do it every full-moon night and you don't worry about anyone in Flight A in quite the same way as you're worrying about her."

"I do worry about my squadron. And the agents. And you." He met her eyes at last.

"I know you do. But as I said, not in quite the same way. I'll call Hamble and find out if she's back. Get your maps organized. I'll see you in the lounge."

* * *

Nicholas stood in the cottage's ops room—a former chapel. The walls around him still bore penciled numbers of the stations of the cross, although one was now papered with a huge map of France and the table in the center of the room was littered with even more—maps being a more reliable survival tool than prayer. Beside him on the mantelpiece, empty champagne bottles stood in their dozens; every reception committee in France sent Nicholas and his fellow pilots back to England with more champagne than even they could drink.

He opened a folder and studied a photograph that showed an almost perfect landing field—treeless and wide, not cut through with cart tracks or bogged with mud. The river alongside it was the ideal marker for his plane to follow, under cover of night and without anything more than the light of the moon and a folded map to guide him, to the pinpoint.

Then he read the Air Transport form. It was typed in black, which meant it came from SOE—the Special Operations Executive: the organization nobody knew about, whose mission was to coordinate espionage and sabotage behind enemy lines, and which Prime Minister Churchill had charged with setting Europe ablaze.

Tonight's mission was named Operation Peaceful; some wag at HQ obviously had a sense of humor. The operation was a double: he and O'Farrell would each fly a Lysander carrying one SOE agent and six hundred pounds of cargo—Sten guns, money, radios, pamphlets—to a tiny field in France, and land on a flare path just one hundred and fifty yards long and lit by only four pocket flashlights. They'd bring back four passengers, who could be SOE agents—civilians who could pass as authentically French and who worked with the local Resistance cells—or members of de Gaulle's Free French Forces, or Allied pilots who'd evaded capture. Tonight, the reception committee waiting for Nicholas at the field would flash the Morse letter "S" to indicate it was safe to land; "S" for Skye. Nicholas hoped it was auspicious.

He took out a 1:500,000-scale map of France and cut strips from it, making sure the route he needed to fly along, with approximately fifty miles extra on either side to allow for error, was squarely in the middle of each strip. He mounted them on cardboard, and folded everything down until what he had was about the same size as the notes Skye had produced earlier, able to be held in one hand, with two strips viewable, while he flew the Lizzie with the other hand. As there was barely enough room in the cockpit to stretch, a large map was out of the question.

O'Farrell worked beside him, both of them silent. A double pickup, which they'd done before, required even closer attention to detail than a lone mission.

When Nicholas had finished, he committed the route to memory, testing himself until he could scan the map in his mind as easily as his times tables. Everything told him that tonight's mission should be easy. Although easy wasn't quite the right word to describe flying a plane into German-occupied territory in the dead of night to deliver a spy and ammunition to the French Resistance. Since the British retreat at Dunkirk three years ago, only the pilots in his squadron, and one other similar squadron, ever landed in France. Almost nobody knew they did anything of the sort, or that it was even possible.

"I think we'll be on," Nicholas said to O'Farrell before picking up the scrambler telephone and calling the station commander at Tempsford, their home base. They used Tangmere, which was closer to France, as their forward base for two weeks every month—the full-moon period—when there was a better chance that they might actually be able to see where they were going.

The station commander agreed with Nicholas that even though there was a chance of fog in low-lying areas, the mission should go ahead.

Nicholas nodded at O'Farrell and both men went upstairs to change.

Nicholas put on a navy-blue roll-neck sweater whose labels had been cut off. Over that went black flight overalls. Into his pockets went a specially designed miniature saw, a compass, maps for use on the ground should they have the bad luck to be stuck there, a fountain pen that released tear gas, and a beret. He pulled on his RAF escape boots, which looked from the outside like the usual fleece-lined boots all pilots wore but which had detachable uppers and transformed into a pair of civilian shoes. Last to go on his body was his gun: the single piece of defensive equipment, besides fists and feet, that he and O'Farrell would carry.

The purr of engines told him that the staff cars from London had arrived with more agents, or Joes as they were called. Some were already at Tangmere, having been set to go the previous evening when all ops had been canceled due to bad weather and poor visibility. It was time to go downstairs for the last supper.

Margaux came over to him immediately. "She's at Hamble. The starboard engine failed as she was coming in to land and the plane tried to dump her onto the ground, but she got it down in one piece and with only a scratched underside. It seems a shame she didn't at least dent *le connard* given it tried to do her in."

Nicholas actually found himself laughing. "That would have been a very good idea. Are you ready? Shall we eat?"

Margaux nodded. She was wearing a gray skirt, a navy blouse, and the silk stockings her Nazi target had bought for her the last time she was in Paris. It always amazed Nicholas that the minute she put on her costume, her face changed too. She was a beautiful woman, but that beauty was usually edged with hardness, as though cynicism beat in her veins. Now, she had relaxed her face so it looked innocent and lovely, and Nicholas wasn't at all surprised that her Nazi fed her a steady diet of useful secrets.

Soon, their driver took them to the hidden dispersal point where Skye and Nicholas had danced. Nicholas's Lizzie had a dark-haired mermaid painted on the side; O'Farrell's sported an impossibly busty Betty Boop.

Their ground crew greeted them warmly, and the full moon shone convincingly above them as if letting them know that tonight would be a good night. That the fog would dissipate, that they would find the field and it would have a properly lit flare path, that their reception committee would be waiting, that no Germans would hear the sound of a lone plane falling from the sky into the heart of France.

Margaux put a hand on Nicholas's arm. "I'll just be a minute."

She walked across to O'Farrell's Lysander where his agent was waiting to climb aboard. Nicholas watched as the agent smiled at Margaux and then, thankfully where nobody could see and thus ruin Nicholas's and Margaux's cover, he bestowed on her a passionate kiss that suggested he and Margaux had been comforting one another beneath the sheets.

Being Margaux, the kiss didn't last long, and she was soon back by Nicholas's side.

"Is that a good idea?" he asked.

"If I'm going to die, I might as well have enjoyed myself the night before," she replied. "One of us has to, and I know you're not about to indulge. Not until your mind catches up with your heart."

"What do you mean?"

"Skye."

Nicholas shook his head. He was used to her blunt attacks disguised beneath a matter-of-fact tone, but didn't understand this one. "What about her?"

Margaux sighed. Then she reached up and kissed his cheek. It was their ritual: they never took off without that one simple kiss. "See you in a couple of months. I'm hoping that this time Oberführer Dietrich's pillow talk will be even more enlightening."

"How does it feel?" he asked before she turned away.

"I have a very long shower when I return to England," she said quietly.

"I wish there were some other way. Or someone else to do it."

Margaux allowed herself a small laugh. "We all know why SOE chooses women whose looks don't fail to make one's captain salute. I knew what I was getting myself into when I signed up."

"He obviously isn't the jealous sort," Nicholas said, nodding toward the agent she'd kissed.

"A night or two with him has nothing at all to do with a couple of months with a Nazi."

Her candor made Nicholas tell her his own truth. "You asked me if I was behaving like a bear because of Skye and O'Farrell and I said no. I think I lied."

"You should tell O'Farrell."

"Tell him what?"

"That you love her. That you adore her." The same cool voice. The same composed face. Margaux's, but not Nicholas's.

The silence following her words was a tangible thing. Like cloud the second before the rain fell: sodden, heavy, suffocating. He felt as if he could reach out and grab great fistfuls of it.

His hand reached up to the wing, holding on. "Fuck." He could *not* be in love with Skye. He shook his head, trying to dislodge the brutal truth.

"It's why you're not an agent," Margaux continued prosaically. "Your face is too easy to read. I suspected it after the dance, but I knew it for certain this morning. I wasn't going to say anything, as I thought the knowledge might be too distracting to take into a plane. But now I think it might give you the best reason in the world to concentrate. You can only tell her how you feel, that this—us—is a lie, if you survive the war."

If he survived the war. If Skye even felt the same. If she didn't fall in love with O'Farrell first. *God dammit.*

He'd signed the Official Secrets Act. Nobody was allowed to know what Margaux did: that a *woman* was being sent to France as a secret agent. If anyone outside their small group of privileged insiders ever found out that a woman was being used as a spy, there would be uproar all over Britain, and perhaps the world. So he'd agreed to

SOE's idea of an engagement cover story to explain to everyone why he and Margaux spent so much time together. He was absolutely not allowed to be in love with Skye. There was too much at stake. If he told Skye anything at all about what he did, he'd be court-martialed. His grip on the wing tightened, knuckles white.

"I can't tell O'Farrell," he said, as if that were the most important part of the conversation. It was the only part he could even begin to deal with. "What if . . . what if she's meant to be with him? I can't ruin that in exchange for the nothing I can offer her right now."

Margaux clicked her tongue impatiently. "O'Farrell was at the pub last weekend with at least four WAAFs. You know he doesn't do commitment. He would have told Skye that too."

"There's also the fact that she most likely thinks I'm a jerk," Nicholas said. "I keep coming across to her like a disapproving father. What I said to her at Tempsford. And when O'Farrell kissed her cheek in the mess, she saw me frown but it was only because I was thinking that I'd never be able to kiss her cheek; it would be too . . ." He couldn't finish the sentence. Didn't even know what he'd meant to say. Dangerous. Explosive. Perfect. Insufficient.

"You seemed to be getting along well enough at the dance." Margaux lit up a Gauloise and offered him one.

He shook his head. He couldn't comprehend how to smoke right now. "We'd both drunk too much whiskey, that's all. Drunken camaraderie."

"Nick, you never drink too much whiskey. You always drink right up to the edge but never beyond. Same as the way you push a plane right to its limits but never too far. Or the way you press for each and every moonlight op to go ahead and only relent if you think someone might get hurt. You're the most controlled person I know. But that must be exhausting."

"If I'm not," he said grimly, "people die. I can't manage a team of pilots doing work that makes every nerve in their bodies scream like a Stuka bomber if I'm not in control of myself all the time."

"Being in control of yourself around Skye is going to be the most exhausting thing of all."

The accuracy of her words hit him like a payload of bombs. It *would* be the hardest thing of all. Margaux understood because she had to climb out of a plane in a dark field in France, get herself to Paris and the Hotel Meurice, find her Nazi and smile just enough to titillate him, then bite back the disgust that must surely rise in her throat when he kissed her and took off her clothes. The whole time she had to be in the most perfect control of herself.

"If you can do what you do," he said, "then I can manage myself around Skye until this goddamn war ends so that nobody suspects you and I aren't really engaged, or that I have any feelings for Skye beyond the brotherly."

Margaux regarded him for a moment, then gave him a full and suddenly brilliant smile. He'd only seen that smile once before: when he'd picked her up from France after the first time she'd spent two months there with the Nazi.

"I'm not Skye," she said, "and it won't be the same, but I still care about you. Come here."

She opened her arms and he walked into them, holding her the same way she was holding him. As if they were each trying to reassure the other that everything would be fine, but knowing that neither of them believed it.

An engineer—not one of their squadron's—walked past as they were embracing, and whistled. "Shouldn't you two lovebirds be doing that somewhere more private?"

After the engineer's footsteps had faded, Nicholas smiled. "That should keep our cover going for a bit longer."

"It should." Margaux pulled back so she could see his face. "They told me more women will be joining SOE. They'll have to come up with a better way of managing our cover stories. Perhaps soon . . ."

Soon. Maybe the war would end soon. That's what they all used to say. He'd long ago stopped believing in soons. There was only one thing he could do right now.

"Let's fly," he said. "Let's survive."

SIXTEEN

Nicholas left the coast near Bognor Regis and climbed up to eight thousand feet. It was safer up there, and visibility was so good he could easily see the French coastline in the moonlight. Once he'd crossed into France near Cabourg, he took himself down to a thousand feet, not even wincing at the arc of enemy flak tossed into the sky, possibly at him, possibly at O'Farrell. Both of them were too good to be hit by flak and they passed safely through.

Inland, mist began to drift up from the ground. Despite that, Nicholas felt secure enough to let his mind drift backward to a point approximately nine months ago when he'd first met Margaux, not long after he'd joined 161 Squadron.

Margaux Jourdan was a bit like the mist below: slippery, dangerous and beautiful to look at. The first time Nicholas had seen her, she was stalking across the field in Somersham, near Tempsford, cigarette in hand, dressed in trousers and a sweater. O'Farrell's and Richie's mouths had dropped open, and Nicholas could tell that O'Farrell was about to get himself into serious trouble.

The wind had blown Margaux's scarf away, revealing long dark hair like Skye's. Margaux even stood in the same confident way, as if nothing could ever hurt her, and he'd wondered if it was a damn good act, like Skye's had always been. He was so distracted by Margaux's hair, and her stance, that he hadn't even thought to chase after her scarf—luckily O'Farrell had that in hand.

Both Richie and O'Farrell had called Nicholas a lucky bastard when he was paired up with Margaux—each pilot was allocated an agent to train—but Nicholas had shrugged them off. Life was complicated enough without adding to it the potency of romance with an SOE agent.

He'd set to work in a field that had once grown crops, showing two new French operators and Margaux how to set up a flare path. "You have three minutes after the plane has landed," he told her. "The pilot won't get out of the plane. Let's practice."

So Margaux had practiced climbing down the ladder from the plane, climbing back up the ladder, handing down the luggage, boarding, disembarking. Everything was practiced many more times than necessary because not a single mistake could be afforded in that slim and tense three-minute margin. Throughout, Nicholas could hear O'Farrell laughing with his Joe, using humor and high spirits to get the training done.

After one particularly raucous barrage of laughter, Margaux said impassively to Nicholas, "I heard that 161 is a squadron of charmers, all too good-looking, hard-drinking and hard-playing, and with access to enough French perfume and champagne to seduce the entire WAAF population of England."

It wasn't clear if this was an accusation or a statement.

"You'll be hard-drinking too in a few weeks. If you aren't already," Nicholas responded prosaically.

He knew what people said, but everyone liked a story. Apparently a group of men doing secretive and dangerous things wasn't interesting enough on its own; it had to be spiced up with half-truths.

"I think he," Margaux nodded at O'Farrell, her face remaining inscrutable, "would have taken what I just said as an invitation to prove me right. You seem to use very different methods of working."

"We each use what we think is best," Nicholas said. Flirtation and joking would not, he sensed, motivate Margaux. Hard-drinking might, he thought wryly. "We have a competition at the end," he added. "We'll be able to see whose methods were better."

He thought he saw Margaux smile and knew that she wanted to win.

She continued pulling herself up and down the ladder, but he saw that her hands were forming blisters. She didn't wince but she slowed and Nicholas frowned; she'd be furious if he told her to stop.

The next time she came down the ladder, he said, "When I was twelve, I had to swing across a rope bridge for such a long way that it tore the skin off my hands. A very wise woman told me that aloe vera was the thing to fix them. The Waafery has aloe vera."

He'd made sure they stocked it after the first training sessions when the same thing had happened to the other Joes.

"I might visit the Waafery later," was all Margaux said in reply, but she picked up her pace and Nicholas knew she'd be one of the best agents he'd have the luck to train.

Later, when they timed the Joes, Margaux won. If they'd been on the ground on a real op, they'd have taken off in less than three minutes.

O'Farrell groaned, then offered Margaux his congratulations. "I'll buy you a drink at the pub."

"I'm not your consolation prize," she replied, before walking away, still holding her body confidently, still bewitching to look at despite the fact she must be exhausted and her hands must hurt like hell.

"Thank God she's on our side," Nicholas said.

"Thank God she's yours and not mine," O'Farrell retorted. "If you fly into a trap, I bet she'd push you out of the plane and into the arms of the Germans, and then fly away without a thought for anyone else."

Nicholas didn't believe it though.

It was impossible, in those circumstances, not to become close to the person you were training. So he and Margaux formed a strange kind of intimacy in which they spoke little but intuited a lot and worked together well.

Margaux had initially been sent to France as a courier, but when SOE discovered that information-gathering was her special skill, they decided to use it. It meant she had to fly in and out more than most SOE agents, as it wasn't safe for her to radio back everything she learned from the Oberführer. Once this had been ascertained, SOE had suggested that Nicholas and Margaux pretend to be engaged. It allowed them to work and train together in close proximity while keeping everyone outside the close circle of 161 Squadron and SOE ignorant about what Margaux did. Nicholas was used to keeping secrets—nobody was allowed to know what 161 Squadron did either—so he'd figured one extra layer of secrecy wouldn't matter.

At the time, SOE had had a discussion with Nicholas about his "needs," and he'd almost laughed. He wouldn't be able to openly date other women if he was supposed to be engaged to Margaux, they said. He told Margaux about it later—of course nobody had had a discussion with her about her needs—and she laughed and said she didn't plan to be celibate for the entire war, but would be discreet.

Since the cover story had been put in place eight months ago Nicholas hadn't met anyone worth the bother of a secretive affair. But now there was Skye.

She had too much integrity to come near him in that way while she thought he was engaged. And he wouldn't love her the way he did if she didn't have that integrity. In return, he couldn't make any kind of physical contact with her because he never wanted her to think he was that kind of scoundrel.

There was also the very real likelihood that she wasn't interested in him. She seemed to be happy enough with O'Farrell. O'Farrell knew that Nicholas's engagement to Margaux was a sham. Nicholas could, as Margaux had suggested, tell O'Farrell he was in love with Skye, but what right did he have to prevent Skye from dating O'Farrell when all Nicholas could offer her was friendship? And maybe not even that if it proved too difficult to maintain without exposing everything he felt. To reveal anything at all meant putting Margaux at risk, meant exposing SOE, meant breaking the law, meant placing his personal feelings above the freedom of every country invaded and occupied by the Nazis.

He could never do that. And Skye would never want him to, of that he was sure.

The only thing he could do was fly by moonlight into France every month, trying to bring this war to an end as soon as possible. The only thing he could do was look down at the ground and curse because the fog had become thick and limitless and he could no longer find a landmark against which to check his position.

He flew on anyway, hopefully with O'Farrell and his Joe behind him, all of them sure to be thinking the same: that after the previous night's aborted mission due to fog, and the full moon set to waning, and the reception committee having come out each night to wait for them and leaving disappointed, all any of them wanted was for tonight's mission to go off without a hitch.

* * *

The cumulus dropped to one thousand feet. There was so little moonlight penetrating below it that Nicholas continued on blind, relying on compass and memory. He was supposed to rendezvous with O'Farrell at Blois, but it was impossible to see Blois so he kept going, hoping O'Farrell would do the same. Finally, just when he thought he'd have to abort, the fog lifted enough that he could see a river and a church, and he realized that luck was with him and he was no more than a couple of miles off course.

Fog floated past in patches, and only the thinnest feather of moonlight brushed the ground. It didn't make for ideal landing conditions but nothing was ever ideal. He flew around once to be sure, but he definitely had enough visibility. He saw the Morse letter "S" flashed to let him know that everyone was ready on the ground.

On his second circuit he saw O'Farrell's Lizzie with Betty Boop brazenly flaunting herself on the tail. He let O'Farrell make his own lap above the field, then he waggled his wings at O'Farrell, who waggled in response to let Nicholas know he was also happy to attempt the landing.

O'Farrell went in first, as was the plan, and Nicholas, watching, swore.

"What happened?" Margaux's voice sounded in his ear through the intercom.

"I don't know," he said. "But a Lizzie shouldn't land like that unless there's something on the ground."

He could see O'Farrell climbing out, which never happened unless there was trouble with the plane. Nicholas was supposed to wait, but he couldn't, not when he might be able to help.

"We're going down," he said to Margaux.

"Of course we are," she replied.

It made Nicholas smile. The four of them—O'Farrell and Nicholas, and Margaux and O'Farrell's Joe—Luc was his name—were as close as anyone could be in the circumstances, ever since Margaux had made O'Farrell swear he wouldn't flirt with her again. Margaux wouldn't leave any of them on the ground if she could help it, and nor would Nicholas.

But tonight disaster found Nicholas too. He felt the Lysander protest as soon as it hit the ground. His rudder was completely stuck and the stick wouldn't move at all. Even though the photograph he'd checked at the ops room in Tangmere had looked fine, there must have been a deeply gouged track running across the landing strip. While the reception committees were briefed about the kinds of hazards that could damage a plane, it often happened that a field that was perfect one day might be plowed or soaked with rain or scoured with machinery the next.

"God dammit!" he swore and jumped out of the plane.

The reception committee rushed over, all too aware that he was supposed to be off the ground in another two and a half minutes— and they hadn't even started unloading the cargo. But at this rate they wouldn't be going anywhere. The tail unit was broken and the rudder needed to be freed. Nicholas kicked it as hard as he could but it didn't budge.

At last, with a resounding crack, the bottom struts of Nicholas's Lysander snapped, freeing the rudder. He raced across to help O'Farrell do the same.

"Will we still be able to fly?" O'Farrell asked, no longer the cocky pilot he tried to be but scared, Nicholas could tell, scared that they were two American pilots stuck in France for the Nazis to find. Or that their broken planes would fall out of the sky and so would they.

It was Nicholas's job to resurrect O'Farrell's confidence, to make him believe they could do whatever they had to do, even though Nicholas's own doubts were huge. The friction between the two opposing choices—stay and find shelter until they could be picked up tomorrow night perhaps; or fly and hope—abraded his nerves like the scraping of cold air against warm in a thunderstorm.

"This is what we're going to do," Nicholas said decisively, as if he knew it would work when the reality was that he had no idea. "We mightn't be able to move our elevator controls, but with any luck—and we deserve some—if we throttle it up, it should ascend. I think you'll have to cut the engine to get the nose to descend when you get too high and too cold up there. We might be able to make it all the way home by alternating between climbing and falling."

O'Farrell looked at him incredulously. "You're kidding."

"Maybe I'm wrong. But if it won't fly level, that's what you need to do."

From the trees at the far end of the field came the sound of gunshots. The Maquis guarding the perimeter had obviously run into trouble, and the trouble was, most likely, headed their way.

"Back on the planes!" Nicholas shouted.

He grabbed Margaux's arm, made sure that O'Farrell had Luc and was racing for the Lizzies too, and then propelled the other waiting passengers toward the crippled plane—the plane he didn't know he would be able to get off the ground.

He, Margaux and O'Farrell reached the Lizzies, but Luc was too slow. An explosion of machine-gun fire threw bright spots of red into the air, like a handful of rubies, and Luc fell to the ground.

"Fuck." There was no way Luc could have survived those shots. "You have to leave him," Nicholas called to O'Farrell.

He pushed down the nausea rising in his throat at the thought of leaving Luc behind but it was Nicholas's job as wing commander to get as many people as he could out of there alive, without worrying about the fate of dead bodies. He wanted to punch the plane because Luc deserved more than that, but Margaux and O'Farrell and the other passengers deserved to live too and he couldn't justify putting all of their lives at risk for the sake of a corpse, even if the man who had once inhabited the corpse had been his friend.

Nicholas shoved his passengers into the plane, climbed in too and throttled up, cursing. "Come on, you bastard, fly!" The plane bounced out of the rut, following orders, taking off steeply.

He heard the sound of machine-gun fire chasing him into the sky and he pushed the Lizzie almost to its limits, but not to the very edge because he still didn't know the extent of the damage. Nicholas knew O'Farrell would follow his lead so he needed to judge not only what his plane was capable of but O'Farrell's too.

He circled to the right to make sure he could see O'Farrell. When he did, he felt a lungful of air escape but it was still too early to relax.

He didn't say a word to anyone while he tested his plane. Just as he'd suspected, the Lysander wouldn't fly level. It would climb beautifully, but there was a point at which it got too damn cold and he had to throttle back, sinking to the lowest point he could risk before he let the plane climb once more. They would fly all the way to England like some kind of ludicrous roller coaster in a dangerous carnival whose particular amusements were flak and enemy planes.

When he was sure that he had within his control every risk he could manage, he spoke to Margaux through the intercom. "Hey."

Her response was similarly brief: "Not now."

So he didn't say anything else and neither did the passengers, who, he imagined, were all white-knuckled and incredulous at the way he was flying.

Pushing the throttle forward the whole time exhausted his arms and, only halfway to Tangmere, they were shaking so badly he had to use his knees. The stick scraped away his skin through his suit, but the pain gave him something to feel other than shock. He finally touched down at Tangmere, inelegantly but grateful that the blood cart wasn't required.

His ground crew rushed over, concern plain on their faces as they unstrapped him. The passengers climbed out and one of them, a man about Nicholas's age, fell to the ground and kissed it as passionately as if it were his lover.

"Hallelujah," he said in a noticeably American accent. "I've been hiding for a month since my plane went down and didn't think I'd ever get out."

Nicholas understood that the man was a pilot too, with the U.S. Air Force, and that he must have been harbored in safe houses after being shot down. They'd exchanged one SOE agent for one American pilot, and three others. Was it worth it?

Nicholas ran a hand through his hair in frustration, then turned to look at what the ground crew were pointing out. The undercarriage of the tail had been pushed right up inside his plane like a bone breaking through skin. It was a miracle he'd flown anywhere.

Margaux stepped in beside him and he turned to her, but she shook her head and he knew they would never speak of Luc's death. If she did, then how would she ever do the work she had set herself to do?

"One of them," she murmured, eyes fixed on the passengers they'd brought with them, "is Jean Moulin, head of the Resistance, de Gaulle's right-hand man. You didn't hear it from me, of course. But yes, it was worth it."

The hardness on Margaux's face had returned, but harder still. A dead lover, and dead parents and brothers, and a murdered country making it impossible, he knew, for her to be anything other than closed off. He took her hand in his and felt her squeeze it, hard, not to give comfort but to take it for once.

She released his hand as O'Farrell came to stand beside them, face white.

Nicholas took out three cigarettes and lit them, passing one to Margaux and one to O'Farrell, and the three of them stood leaning against the broken plane, none of them speaking. All of them, Nicholas thought, seeing the splash of red against the black-gold sky, Luc falling onto his face in a field in France.

He stubbed out his cigarette. "I won't be able to sleep."

"I won't either," Margaux said.

"Nor me." O'Farrell began to pace. "Let's go see Skye."

"It's four in the morning," Margaux said incredulously.

"She always used to be up at dawn," Nicholas said without thinking.

"We'll be there after dawn," O'Farrell said, as if it were perfectly reasonable to visit someone not long after sunup. "I'll take champagne."

"And Gitanes," Margaux added.

"And oranges," Nicholas said.

"And silk stockings and perfume." O'Farrell brightened as he said it.

They did have all those things, incredible spoils from previous ops so far into the South of France that they'd had to overnight at Algiers. And every reception crew in France—besides tonight's—sent them back to England with champagne and cheese and Chanel perfume.

"I'll swing it," Nicholas said, knowing that after the debrief, they were supposed to eat and sleep, not go for drives. But he'd find a car and some fuel at the air base and he'd get permission for them all to disappear for a few hours to settle their nerves.

Margaux shrugged. "Then let's go visit Skye."

So O'Farrell collected the fripperies, Margaux the cigarettes, and Nicholas the oranges, and told O'Farrell to bring his swimming trunks—if he had any—and packed his own, thinking that O'Farrell was right: the only thing Nicholas wanted right now was to see Skye. To hold her. But of course O'Farrell would be the one holding her, not him.

SEVENTEEN

S kye woke with the sun, threw on her swimsuit and walked through the village of Hamble, whose ordinary inhabitants—yachtsmen, rather than the staff of a frontline airfield—were not yet awake. Only Clarke's, the baker on the High Street, showed signs of movement: the smell of fresh bread was intoxicating.

It was almost possible to believe that here, with water all around—the river on one side and the Solent on the other—in a town adorned with the white sails of grounded boats and trellised porches and salt-scented breezes, she was having a holiday; that Hitler had been captured, or the war had never happened. Until she turned her eyes to the omnipresent glint of the silver barrage balloons jostling for space in the Southampton Defense Corridor; so many it seemed as if they were holding England up and, should one burst, the entire country would sink into the sea.

She stepped through the not-so-secret opening in the barbed wire fortifications and sank straight into the water, the shock of cold waking her up properly. She stroked out from the shore, then floated on her back, staring up at the sky, her second home, no matter that, lately, the planes she took up there seemed determined to toss her back down to the ground. The starboard engine failing yesterday had been almost comical in the end—once she'd got the damn thing on the ground and herself out unhurt. She smiled ruefully as she imagined what O'Farrell's face might have looked like if he had come up with her and put his life in the hands of a female pilot flying a gargantuan bomber with a broken engine.

O'Farrell. He'd been pleased to see her yesterday and that was nice. Nice. Such a bland word. What was nice about the ocean, or about the sky? Nothing. They were either wild or magnificent with nothing in between. But nice was safe. Nice didn't come hand in hand with the kind of discomposure she'd felt yesterday when her eyes had circled, in a fixed orbit, around Nicholas. Talking to him the night they'd had dinner had been like glimpsing a shape far out to sea behind a curtain of mist and rain. Skye knew she should turn her back and walk away before she understood whatever it was about Nicholas that lay just out of sight.

She hit the water with her hands and rolled over, closing her eyes, kicking her legs, letting the water engulf her. Only when her lungs burned did she shoot back up to the surface. Then she left the water, dried herself off and returned to the cottage. She was hungry now and happy to concentrate on that mundane sensation, something easily solved with toast and a hot cup of tea.

Rose was still asleep and Joan had gone to London the previous night to see her latest beau, so Skye didn't bother to bathe and change. Instead she gave Rose's cat a pat on the head, took out the teapot and was spooning in precious leaves when she heard a knock on the door. Expecting Mrs. Chambers from the Bugle gifting them some extra food, she froze when she saw O'Farrell, Nicholas, Margaux and another pilot, the one Rose had been goggle-eyed about, on the doorstep.

"What are you doing here?" she asked, hardly aware, in her surprise, of what she was saying. "Is it even seven o'clock?"

O'Farrell looked uncharacteristically abashed. "We were too edgy to sleep. We brought champagne." He handed her a bottle.

"I'm not exactly dressed for a champagne breakfast," she said.

Which was something of an understatement. Her swimming costume was a black Lastex halter-neck with a white tiger crawling over her belly and hip. She'd brought it with her from France, never expecting to be wearing it and nothing else when she opened her door to a coterie of pilots.

"I'm not complaining," O'Farrell said, grinning.

She looked past him to the others and caught Nicholas, his eyes tracing the outline of the tiger down her chest and across her stomach, resting for a moment on the bare skin at the top of her leg. Skye's hand found the doorframe and closed tightly around it.

The next instant his eyes flicked away, brushing like feathers past hers. He flushed when he understood she'd noticed, and the color of his cheeks matched exactly the color of everything he'd lit up inside her. She shivered.

"Here's some more oranges," he said quickly, holding up a bag to shield his face.

O'Farrell started talking but Skye hadn't a clue what he was saying, just that his words were coming out fast and his hands were jumpy. Even Margaux seemed tightly strung, the cigarette barely leaving her mouth for the exhale before returning relentlessly for the next inhale. Skye knew the feeling of coming down after a day of flying and not being able to switch off, of lying in bed and staring at the ceiling, sleep a stranger. So she stepped aside to let them in.

She led the way into the kitchen and tipped the bag of oranges onto the countertop. Nicholas pushed several boxes of Gitanes her way and Skye knew he must have been in France again. He wouldn't look at her.

Behind Nicholas, O'Farrell exclaimed in bemusement over the tiny cottage, where the bath was in the kitchen with a lid on top to convert it into a table. Everyone began to move chairs around and, somehow, they all squeezed in.

While Skye juiced the oranges, Nicholas cooked the eggs he'd brought with him.

"You cook?" she asked, and he nodded and smiled at her for the first time and she couldn't help smiling back.

O'Farrell toasted bread, badly judging by the smell of scorching, and the other pilot, Richie, laid the table. Rose appeared, yawning, and made tea, and Margaux leaned against the counter, smoking and watching them all.

O'Farrell touched a hand to Skye's back. "I wanted to see you," he said.

"I'm glad you came."

And she was. How much better to be thinking of breakfast and orange juice rather than the sensation of almost falling out of the sky yesterday.

"I would have arrived a lot earlier if I'd known you were wearing that," he said with a grin, his golden hair as sunny and shining as hope, his finger caressing the bare skin at the top of her back.

Skye laughed. "Take those for me." She passed him two glasses of juice and he carried them to the table.

"Champagne in yours?" he queried, holding up the bottle.

Skye shook her head. "I'm not spoiling my juice with champagne."

O'Farrell frowned and glanced at Nicholas, who was suddenly very busy with the eggs. And she understood that O'Farrell had brought the champagne and Nicholas the oranges.

"I'll have some after my juice," she said gently, sitting beside O'Farrell and he dropped his arm onto the back of her chair.

Margaux took a cup of tea and sat down, Nicholas too. Margaux refused the eggs. "I don't think I can stomach any food."

Skye caught the look that passed between Margaux and Nicholas; one of sympathy, she thought, and understanding.

"Hard night?" she asked and Margaux nodded.

Skye didn't ask any more because she knew someone must have died and that's why they were keyed up. She stood and opened one of the high cupboards, reaching right into the back for a *coffret* of Cazenave chocolates she'd hidden there for just such an occasion. Margaux would be the only one who'd know what they were, and Skye thought she might appreciate them. She placed the box on the table in front of the Frenchwoman and sat back down.

Margaux stared at the chocolates for a long moment before meeting Skye's eye. "You really are as nice as everybody says," she told her. Then, before Skye could work out whether that was complimentary or not, Margaux added, "Thank you."

This time, Skye couldn't interpret the look that passed from Nicholas to Margaux—a warning perhaps. Margaux selected a chocolate, bit into it, and the tension in the room from whatever had happened overnight eased back like the tide.

They talked about O'Farrell, who'd grown up in Chicago before he went to Harvard, and had never wanted to be caged in an office in a skyscraper, he said, so he became a pilot, taking flying boats into the air for Pan Am before coming to England to help out with the war. He didn't divulge what Nicholas had told Skye: that he'd come while the Neutrality Act was still in place, risking imprisonment.

"You could have stayed in America," Skye said, not wanting to break a confidence but also wanting to let him know that she respected what he'd done. "It would have been safer."

O'Farrell reached into his pocket for a Lucky Strike, lit it and inhaled before answering. "But that'd be like looking over the fence at a bully terrorizing a child and walking away because it's happening in somebody else's yard."

Skye leaned over and kissed his cheek.

"Thanks," he said, flushing, and trying to refill everyone's still-full champagne glasses to cover the collapse of his worldly facade.

"So we've established that O'Farrell's a hero," Margaux said drily. "What about our wing commander? What was he like as a boy?"

It was Skye's turn to inhale smoke before answering. *Is this the girl?* a mean woman had once asked, as if Skye were worse than the smell of rotting fish skeletons on the pier. *This is Skye,* Nicholas had replied, not allowing his aunt to demean his new friend.

"He was loyal," she said as one memory dissolved into another. Nicholas telling her he couldn't swim, and then pulling himself hand over hand along the rope bridge even while the skin was ripped from his palms. "And very brave."

She dared to look up then and caught Nicholas's eye. His face was as red as O'Farrell's had been a moment before, but Nicholas didn't shield himself by pretending to refill glasses. He let the moment sit, leaving himself unguarded and exposed to the likely ribbing of O'Farrell and Richie. But nobody scoffed or jeered; they nodded instead, as if they knew Skye had told the absolute truth.

"Then he hasn't changed," Margaux said, smiling at him; one of those infrequent lapses into warmth that she seemed occasionally capable of.

Skye jumped up and began to clear away the plates. As she ran water over them, she felt Nicholas slip in next to her and, under the pretext of passing her the teacups to wash, he murmured, "Thanks."

Before she could reply, he said, "Are we going for a swim? And if you still have more swimming costumes than clothes, would you mind lending Margaux one? You and she look as if you're about the same size."

"Of course." Skye turned off the tap.

"Swimming?" said O'Farrell. "I thought you were joking. No one's allowed to swim."

"Even if the beaches are all closed, you don't visit Skye in a house by the sea and not bring your trunks," Nicholas said. "I know the night she outran the Me 110 it looked as if her natural habitat is the sky, but it's really the water. And it's the perfect day for it."

It was. It had turned into a beautiful summer's day, too precious to waste.

"You go on ahead, Skye," Rose said as Nicholas left to get changed. "You're ready; there's no need for you to wait."

Skye looked distractedly around the room. "I just need to find my cover-up."

"Cover-up?" Nicholas repeated, reappearing in his trunks. "Skye Penrose doesn't mess around with cover-ups—unless she's a completely different person to the girl I used to know. Besides, we're about ten steps from the water."

Quick as a fish, Skye ducked past him and out the door. "What are you waiting for then?" And she ran, laughing, down School Lane to the sand, but he overtook her near the water.

It took them some time to stride out far enough to be able to swim, but once they had, Skye caught up to him and stroked ahead. She swam on and on, out into the Solent, not even knowing if he was following, swimming away from the sight of Nicholas Crawford in his swimming trunks, legs strong and bare, chest bare too, a line of hair trailing down to his waistband. She stroked harder, swimming away from the treacherous warmth in her body that had nothing whatsoever to do with the sun.

At last her breath came too fast and she slowed and turned over, lying on her back, certain she'd got hold of herself, that the physical sensations in her body were the result of exercise, nothing more.

She should return to the shore. But Nicholas was beside her now, floating in the water, a thing they'd done together a million times before.

"This was just what I needed," he said quietly.

"Me too." She closed her eyes and saw a dream behind her eyelids.

"Imagine," she said, turning the vision into words, "if there was no war and we flew planes every day for fun, to France and Cairo and Cape Town. And every weekend there was the cove in Cornwall . . ."

Her voice died abruptly as she realized she'd inscribed him into her dream. But his dreams were joined together with Margaux's.

"And we'd swim and cook limpets for dinner and fall asleep on the sand." Nicholas's voice, which had picked up her unfinished sentence so eagerly, perished as suddenly as hers had.

Skye couldn't speak. Her words, and his unexpected continuation of them, had left her throat as scalded as if she'd just drunk an ocean of salt water. She stared upward at the blinding blue of the sky, which, right now, seemed a safer place than the sea. Because she mightn't be in Cornwall, falling asleep on the sand next to Nicholas, but she was lying beside him in the water, recalling the way his eyes had traced over her body on the doorstep of the cottage. And she needed to stop.

"What happened to your knees?" she asked, trying to find safe ground.

"Broken elevator controls."

"Ouch."

For a long stretch of minutes there was only the gentle plash of waves, the occasional shriek of a gull—until the current moved her sideways and her fingertips brushed against Nicholas's. It was a whisper, nothing more, over almost before it happened, but she felt the crackle of it everywhere.

The splash that followed told her plainly that she was the only one who'd felt anything. Nicholas had simply been waiting for the perfect moment to copy one of Skye's favorite childhood moves, which was to catch him off guard and drag him down into the water. He pulled her under by the arm, but because he'd learned the move from her she knew how to twist away and dive below him. He caught her ankle, not stopping her from getting away as she'd always done to him, but tickling her foot.

She kicked feebly while at the same time convulsing with laughter, accidentally opening her mouth and swallowing water. She rose to the surface coughing and gasping.

He grinned. "I've been waiting to do that since I was thirteen."

She laughed again, having finally caught her breath, but lost it once more as she and Nicholas trod water just inches away from each other. Water droplets caressed his shoulders, and it was impossible to look at anything other than him. Their eyes tangled together, his flaring the fieriest of blues, his mouth opening. Then his smile vanished and he turned his head away in so sudden a movement that it felt as if he had torn her skin.

"I'm going back in," he said.

He swam back to the group: Rose splashing Richie in the shallows; Margaux leaning glamorous and elegant on her elbows on the sand, surrounded by a cloud of smoke; and O'Farrell, his trousers rolled up, his shirt unbuttoned, alternating between kicking the water and looking out toward Skye. And Nicholas, stepping out of the water and dropping down beside Margaux. She offered him a cigarette but he shook his head.

A group of friends by the seaside. So normal. Nothing at all out of the ordinary. Except that the mist had lifted and Skye could see it now, the large and shining thing: she was wholly and overwhelmingly and undeniably in love with Nicholas Crawford.

Which was just about the worst thing that had ever happened to her.

* * *

Skye made her way back to shore slowly. When she stepped out, it was to hear Nicholas say, "We should go back if we're going to get any sleep before tonight."

"You're on ops again tonight?" Skye asked O'Farrell as they started back to the cottage.

He nodded. "While you were being a mermaid, I made a plan. Our flight has leave in June and two days of it coincides with your leave. Rose worked it out. We'll all go to London. Dance at the Embassy Club. Stay at the Dorchester."

She knew what he was asking her. She saw Nicholas glance over at her and O'Farrell, and then turn quickly back to Margaux.

O'Farrell was holding her hand, Skye realized. She hadn't noticed the moment he took it in his, hadn't felt the frisson of skin touching skin, a frisson she felt when Nicholas merely looked at her. But what good was that? What was the best way to forget someone you couldn't have?

"That sounds like fun," she said, and O'Farrell looked as pleased if he'd invented the airplane all by himself.

"We'll take care of the arrangements," he said, indicating himself, Nicholas and Richie. "You ladies need only turn up at the appointed time and a weekend of fun will await."

But Skye was no longer listening. On the steps of the cottage, a woman waited, black Sobranie in hand, smoke forming a halo over her dark hair. Skye stopped still and stared.

"Liberty," Nicholas said to Skye.

Skye's mouth began to smile but then her body braced as if it recalled that it was best to assume a defensive position when near Liberty. One of Skye's feet stepped forward but the other wouldn't move so she remained fixed to the spot.

"I didn't think . . ." Nicholas said.

In his voice, Skye heard both surprise and wariness and she knew he'd believed what he'd told her at Tangmere—that Liberty didn't want to see Skye. But now here she was and Nicholas was clearly worried about why she'd come.

The last thing Skye wanted was for everyone to witness a reunion between herself and her sister. Luckily, Nicholas understood. He roused, gave Liberty a brief wave, then shepherded O'Farrell and Margaux into the car, and steered Rose toward it too so she could say goodbye to Richie.

Skye was left to walk alone toward her sister.

Her sister. Liberty was here at last. All of a sudden, Skye's heart hurried her feet along and she opened her arms, ready to embrace her sister for the first time since 1937.

Liberty raised her arm, bringing her cigarette to her mouth, deflecting Skye.

"Was that your friend Nicholas?" she said, her words inflected like Skye's with a rhythmic and husky Parisian accent of soft "t" sounds and an absence of the letter "h." "My, hasn't he turned out handsome? Although he's leaving rather than staying. And with a woman."

For Christ's sake. Liberty might not be hitting out with her fists and feet anymore but her blows were still brutal. And she hadn't finished.

"I'm surprised you've let him back into your life," she went on. "It took you ages to get over him leaving the first time."

The effort to keep her voice level, her face calm, was immense but Skye managed it. "Some people are always in your life," she said simply. She offered her sister a smile, hoping she would understand.

"What if he leaves again?"

Skye knew then that the worry she'd confessed to Nicholas the night they'd danced had been right. What she had seen as reclaiming her own life when she'd left France for Cornwall, Liberty had seen as abandonment. And after their mother's death, such departures smoldered deep in Liberty's psyche. Skye wished so much that she had known better when she was eighteen, wished she'd known everything that war and loss had taught her.

"I'm sorry," she said. "I didn't know how much I'd hurt you."

"You take a lot of credit for my feelings," Liberty said coolly.

It was the kind of kick that had used to precede an emotional storm. Skye accepted it and waited, ready, but the storm didn't come.

Instead, Liberty said, "I have a new job with the Inter-Services Research Bureau. The man I have to type papers for spends some time at RAF Tangmere. So I will too."

She smiled, and all at once looked so much like Skye's annoying little sister that Skye's heart contracted with both love and remorse, and the exquisite pain that only Liberty could inflict. She understood that—despite what Liberty had told Nicholas—Liberty had come to warn Skye, rather than letting their first meeting in six years play out on a runway with dozens of people around.

"Why don't you come in," Skye said. "We have a few years to catch up on."

"Yes, all those years since you left me in France."

That kick made Skye flinch. "I'm not sure we have anything to say to one another about the past, except things that hurt," she said. "And as war brings with it enough hurt, it might be better to call a truce and stay in the present."

This time, Liberty's smile was the same as the one she'd worn back in Paris when Skye had pointed out the damage to her bicycle tires— a smile that made Skye want to leave all over again, even though they were standing outside her cottage.

"You wear your emotions too obviously, sister dear," Liberty said. "That's why war hurts you."

Pain won out over effort at last. "I don't suppose you're ever afflicted with anything like hurt," Skye shot back.

The words hung in the air like the aftermath of an incendiary. Skye closed her mouth and pressed her lips together so nothing else so cruel could escape.

Liberty turned her back on her sister, which was what Skye deserved. But it meant that she didn't hear Liberty's next words properly. "I can't afford such afflictions," was what Skye thought her sister might have said.

But then Liberty shrugged and said loudly, "Someone's waiting for me." She pointed to a car parked farther down the road. A man in an RAF uniform sat in the driver's seat.

"But you've only been here for ten minutes," Skye said, and even she could hear the hurt in her voice. She *did* wear her emotions too obviously.

Perhaps it was the wind, or Skye's imagination, but Liberty's eyes appeared to shine with tears, and Skye couldn't help reaching out her hand, trying once more to mend the threadbare seams of their sibling bond before it finally unraveled.

At the same moment, Liberty pushed herself away from the door and clattered down the steps. "See you soon!" she called gaily.

And Skye knew she'd been mistaken; Liberty hadn't felt any emotion other than glee at the shock she'd caused. Skye was the only one with tears in her eyes.

And now Skye had two reasons to dread any flight that took her to Tangmere: the fact that Liberty might be there. And that Nicholas was, sometimes, too.

PART SIX
KAT

EIGHTEEN

LONDON, JULY 2012

For her meeting with Celeste, the director of conservation from Dior's archives, Kat wore another of her grandmother's dresses: a Marc Bohan design for Dior from 1961—the Green Park dress in scarlet wool.

"That dress was made for you," Celeste said, indicating the iconically sixties above-the-knee skirt and its delectable subtle flare. "But what I really want to talk about is your mystery dress—the blue. *C'est magnifique.* I'm convinced from your photographs that it is a Dior from 1947 or 1948. The covered weights in the back to make the dress hang correctly, the architecture of the internal corsetry, that minute row of hook-and-eye closures along the inside of the skirt tell me it is a Dior. But I know nothing of it." She finished with a dramatically raised eyebrow that perfectly complemented her striking mustard-toned strapless bodice and black-and-white houndstooth pencil skirt.

"You can't find a record of it then?" Kat asked.

"I have looked through all the archival drawings from that time, the extant photographs, Monsieur Dior's own notes and I can find nothing. Your dress was a secret. But why?"

"That's a very good question." Kat felt the buzz of finally talking to someone about the astonishing dress animate her. "And why a secret sent to Australia? I know Dior eventually had an excellent relationship with the country and Australians loved his clothes, but in 1947 he was just a rumor of brilliance, a discovery yet to be made."

"I want to start with the handwriting on the label that you mentioned," Celeste said. "Could it be a customer's name?"

"But why sew a blank label into a dress? And who writes their name on a couture gown? It's unlikely that whoever wore the dress was planning to keep it in a public changing room. You'd need a maid to help you undo all the fastenings for a start."

Celeste laughed. "Perhaps the words were written on the label at the atelier? I don't know why that would be . . ." She paused, thinking.

"The lady who donated it to the museum said that a friend gave it to her," Kat went on. "She didn't buy it from Dior. So I don't know who the original client was."

"I'll look through the records of Australian customers from that time and see if we can turn the fragments of letters from sixty-five years ago into words."

Then Kat confessed. "Actually, there are two dresses exactly the same."

"Two?" Celeste's eyebrows almost arched off her face.

Kat nodded. "The other one is here in England in a relative's collection. I'm going to look at it again on the weekend to see if it has a label with writing on it too."

"When you say they're exactly the same . . ."

"I mean they're identical." Kat took out her phone and showed Celeste the hasty pictures she'd snapped of the dress at the Cornwall cottage.

"Wow." Celeste couldn't take her eyes away from the phone and she looked as if she wasn't sure whether to faint from shock or laugh with delight.

"You wanted to see the fabric," Kat continued, trying to be the calm and rational one so that Celeste would shrug off her stupefaction and begin to flick through the exhaustive catalog in her mind of everything to do with Dior and thus help Kat with her quest.

She withdrew from carefully folded tissue paper a tiny sample of blue fabric snipped from one of the dress's seams—common practice for conservators when a deeper investigation was required. "I'll analyze this under the spectroscope. But I doubt it will tell me anything other than what I already know: it's silk."

Celeste reached out her hand for the sample. "I knew, when I saw your pictures, that I had seen this blue, this shocking and extraordinary blue somewhere before," she said slowly. "But I couldn't recall where. Seeing it now, in a tiny scrap, I have the same feeling . . . but this time I think I do know where."

"Where?" Anticipation filled Kat to the point where she thought she might burst the expertly stitched seams of her dress.

"Another secret. For now." Celeste smiled at Kat. "I could be wrong. I'll go back to Paris this weekend and see if I'm right. Then if I am, on Monday . . ."

"We might solve our mystery," Kat finished.

And she might have the answer to one of her grandmother's secrets.

Kat placed the small square of fabric under the spectroscope, shone light onto it and watched molecules vibrate with energy. An idea pulsed with similar intensity in her mind. She texted Elliott.

Are you able to check if there's any connection between your Margaux Jourdan and the House of Dior? I know it's a weird question but, depending on the answer, it might help rule my grandmother out or in pretty definitively.

He replied almost immediately. *No question is weird when you're researching. I'll check it out. Looking forward to seeing you tonight.*

And Kat realized she was looking forward to seeing him too.

* * *

Kat took off the dress, and put it on again. Three times. The evening was formal, Elliott had said, and the dress *was* formal. In fact it was the most beautiful thing she'd ever seen. She'd coveted it since it had sashayed along the runway at Raf Simons's first show as creative director at the House of Dior. But now that she had it, did she have the guts to wear it?

It was another of the dresses from her grandmother's house, this time in a flame-colored scarlet: not a color to hide in. The skirt swept the floor and had been expertly designed so that it only began to flare out when it reached her hips rather than flaring from the waist—a trick that made it look sensuous rather than princessy. The bodice was strapless, or more than strapless; it was almost like a corset. The gown skimmed up and over her waist to a line just below her breasts, which were covered by shaped cups that certainly hid everything and were much less revealing than the plunging necklines favored by football-ers' wives but it was so much sexier than anything Kat had worn in a long time, or perhaps ever.

Her phone buzzed. Elliott had arrived. There wasn't time to change.

She sent a text to her daughters—even though she'd already spoken to them that day—so they would have a message from her when they woke up. Then she checked to make sure her lipstick hadn't smeared over her teeth, smoothed her dark brown hair, which she'd decided to wear long and straight so as not to overdo things, and caught the lift down to the lobby. She tried very hard not to fidget when she felt the other people in the lift staring at her bold red dress.

She saw Elliott in the lobby straightaway, even though his back was to her. There was something about the way he stood—confidently, but not overconfident, as if he was happy in himself—that she admired and even envied. He definitely hadn't taken his tuxedo on and off three times before coming here tonight.

The sound of her heels on the tiled floor made him turn around. A smile crossed his face the moment he saw her. While he might have looked handsome in the moody lighting of the bar the other night, out here in the well-lit lobby he looked even more gorgeous. His tuxedo, which she realized as she drew closer wasn't black but rather the darkest shade of midnight blue, deepened the color of his eyes still more—magnetically so. He leaned over to kiss her cheek and her breath caught.

"You look stunning," he said.

"Anyone would look passable in this dress," she said, deflecting the compliment and hoping her cheeks hadn't flushed to match her dress. "But stunning might be extending your authorial license too far."

"It's not just the dress," he countered. "And I write nonfiction, which means I always tell the truth."

The truth. It was the only thing she wanted from people now that she knew how much lies could hurt. She decided to try simply accepting the compliment. "Thank you then."

He held the door open for her, one hand lightly on her back, as she stepped outside. The twilight was delightfully warm, the lights of the city sparkled as they began to turn on, and the evening lay before her like a red carpet ushering her onward to adventure. How nice it was to be unshackled, to be with a person who didn't know her as mother, wife, conservator or any other label.

"Do you want to walk there?" he asked. "It's not far and the night is—"

"Perfect for walking," she finished. "Let's."

They strolled along Pall Mall, attracting the glances of passersby, which Kat attributed to Elliott's semi-celebrity.

"See, I'm not the only one who thinks you look stunning," he said.

Kat blushed yet again. "Two compliments in the space of five minutes is a little too heady for someone who's more used to a very biased five-year-old telling her she's pretty."

"Two compliments in five minutes is less than you deserve, but if it makes you uncomfortable I promise to wait half an hour before delivering another one." His voice was deadpan but he grinned at the end and Kat burst out laughing.

"I'll be sure to time you," she said, tapping her watch before turning the conversation away from herself. "Tell me about being a writer. How often do you publish a book? I imagine it must take a bit of time to research and write the kinds of things you do."

He nodded. "I try to write one every couple of years. The publishers would like one a year but I'd rather take the time and know that I'm happy with the book—that it's my best work."

"I'm lucky in that respect," Kat said. "People seem to accept that museum artifacts deserve time and patience."

"Whereas anything contemporary needs to happen quicker than you can click your fingers. Fortunately the last couple of books have sold well enough that I don't have to put out a book a year to keep my daughter in the manner to which she would like to become accustomed, or to pay the mortgage. Time really is the most precious and least treasured thing in the world, I sometimes think."

"You're right," Kat said somewhat wistfully. This past year, as she hurtled toward forty, all she'd felt were the pressures of time. That she would suddenly be eighty and alone because there wasn't time in her life to meet and fall in love with a man. That her girls would grow up and have families of their own and Kat would become like her grandmother, living alone in a remote house, telling the world it was what she wanted but feeling always a lack.

A car horn sounded on the street, returning Kat from the melancholic future and back to the present with Elliott. "How did you go from pop stars' biographies to history?" she asked.

He winced. "I was hoping you wouldn't know about that."

She laughed. "I confess to googling you last night after you left. I know you said that I should, back when we first spoke on the phone, but I hadn't got around to it. The fact that people actually stopped you in the lobby to get your autograph made me a little bit curious."

"Oh, brilliant," Elliott said wryly. "I was hoping you hadn't seen that either. I suppose now you know about my grubby past, you've decided not to tell me anything about your grandmother?" He ran a hand through his hair, the aura of self-assurance suddenly falling away. "You're right to ask though. I'm asking you a lot of questions, so you should do the same. And if I wasn't standing beside possibly the smartest woman I've ever met—I don't know anyone who has both a degree in medicine and science, and who's also studied at the Sorbonne—I mightn't mind so much. But okay, here goes. I studied history and languages at college. Do you know how many jobs there are for twenty-something history and languages graduates?"

"I suspect not that many," she said.

"Fewer than that. I took a writing job with *Smash Hits* magazine— I don't know if you had that in Australia?"

"Oh, yes," Kat said nostalgically. "I used to pull out the posters of A-ha and hang them on my walls. See, now I've confessed that, you shouldn't feel bad about telling me anything."

He laughed, and they crossed the road, heading toward Mayfair. "I wrote for them for a year or so, and then a mate of mine who was in a band had a top ten hit. Women around the country were throwing their knickers at him at concerts and he asked me if I'd write something about him. It was the nineties and every pop star who'd ever had a hit was putting out coffee-table books heavy on photos and light on text. So I traveled around Europe with him and the band for three months, sending pieces back to *Smash Hits* and writing a kind of tour diary. I was lucky: he went through the stratosphere, so a publisher asked if I'd turn my articles into a book. It sold a lot of copies and suddenly every pop star in the country who didn't already have a book wanted me to write one for them. I did two more and then I had to stop because I was becoming the world's biggest pop star cliché—drinking too much, marrying women in intoxicated escapades—and I wasn't even a pop star."

Kat couldn't help smiling. He was a natural raconteur. "I did notice you'd practiced the art of marriage a few times."

"You saw that too? Excellent. Google is fantastic for research but an utter bastard when you're trying to forget you ever had a past."

"Hey, I'm divorced too. I'm not criticizing you."

"Really?"

She nodded.

"But probably only once? Not three times."

"Only once. And never again."

"It's not fun, is it?" he said quietly as they reached Piccadilly. Alongside them, Green Park glowed emerald beneath the last evening sunlight. "Especially when there are kids involved. I'm guessing from your comment about five-year-olds that you have kids?"

"I do," she said. "A three-year-old as well. They're the loves of my life and probably the catalyst for the end of my marriage."

"I wish I could give such a reasonable explanation, but two of my marriages were in those awful years when I did anything that seemed like a lark and was usually anything but. The first time was literally a dare that I went through with to prove—I don't even know what." He grimaced. "That I was an idiot, I guess. The second was because my then girlfriend was pregnant, but as I'm sure you can well understand, a child is the last thing to bring together two people who aren't really suited. I thought I'd better grow up and make a reasonable and considered choice about four years ago, but . . ." He shrugged. "I tipped the scales too far on the side of reasonableness and forgot about spark. It ended last year."

He stopped outside a brown brick building with a pillared portico, above which hung a flag. Windows bordered in white paraded regimentally across the facade.

"This is us," he said, indicating the building. "But now that I've filled you in on my sordid past, you might prefer to go back to the hotel. I can always email you the rest of my questions."

Kat offered him a smile. He'd made mistakes, but he genuinely sounded as if he regretted them. He'd obviously made himself a new life; he was the kind of father who'd leave a bar to help his daughter with her homework. And he'd been honest about his past failings.

So she said, "It must be hard, having to be on show like that, knowing anyone can look you up online and form an opinion about you based on what they read there."

He shrugged. "I knew when I first met you at the Savoy that you had no idea who I was and it was great because it meant that I *could* tell you that you're smart and beautiful. If you'd heard anything about me before we'd met, you'd have thought my compliments meant I was fitting my own stereotype. The thing is, it would have been fake if I hadn't said it. And that's what it's like: so many people have a fixed idea of who I am, and I try so hard not to be that, which means I end up not being me either."

"You should be you all the time," she said, then decided to try her own compliment. "I quite enjoy spending time with the real Elliott Beaufort."

Elliott touched her arm. "Thank you."

Somehow, even though they were standing in a street and people were stepping around them, all Kat could see in that moment was Elliott, looking at her with admiration in his eyes, and something more. Trust, she thought. It wasn't something she'd seen in a man's eyes for so long and she rather liked it, even though she knew it was a momentary dusting of magic prompted by her dress and the intimacy of the conversation they'd shared.

A man clapped Elliott on the back as he passed by, saying hello, and the moment ended.

Kat gestured to the stately mansion before them. "What is this place?"

"This," he said, "is the Arts Club."

"Wow," Kat said as they followed a line of beautifully dressed people inside. "Is it one of those very British private clubs?"

He laughed. "It *is* a private club. You'll have to tell me how very British it is at the end of the night."

She laughed too. "I will. I'm hoping there'll be no hunting souvenirs hanging on the walls."

"We're down in the basement, at the supper club, where you'll find enough plush curved sofas and low lighting and intimate booths to make you feel like you've just stepped into an episode of *Mad Men*."

"This is going to be fun, isn't it?"

He smiled at her. "You were doubting that before?"

They passed through a fabulous hallway of rose-gold and smoky mirrors, and into a room that made Kat want to turn around, mouth open like one of her daughters, and drink it all in.

* * *

"Elliott!" a woman's voice called, and then Elliott was engulfed in the woman's arms and his cheeks were kissed. The man with her shook Elliott's hand. Kat judged from the palpable feeling of goodwill that these were Elliott's friends.

"Sorry," the woman said, beaming at Kat. "That was so rude of me—throwing myself on Elliott and not saying anything to you. I can throw myself on you too if you like, but Josh is always telling me I should save the kisses and hugs for people I actually know." She grinned at the man beside her.

Elliott laughed. "Kat, this is D'Arcy Hallworth and Josh Vaughn."

"Nice to meet you, Kat." Josh, who had dark hair and beautiful blue eyes, held out his hand and Kat shook it.

D'Arcy linked her arm through Kat's and led her over to a curved banquette with the most incredible orb-shaped oriental paper lamp-shade above it, handprinted with a riot of flowers. Kat felt like she really had stepped onto the set of a terribly à la mode television program.

"I had the waiter reserve this for us," D'Arcy said. "We'll be out of the way and Elliott can actually enjoy himself. Although this crowd is too suave to show that they care about celebrities."

"D'Arcy, I'm a long way from being a celebrity," Elliott protested.

"Too modest," D'Arcy mock-whispered.

"Is that an Ossie Clark?" Kat asked, indicating D'Arcy's dress, which was also red but with bell sleeves and a low-cut neckline that looked sensational without being too much. In fact, D'Arcy was the one who should be called stunning: she had long blond hair in wild curls, and eyes that expressed everything she felt. It was impossible not to warm to her immediately.

"It is," D'Arcy said. "How could you tell? Although we both clearly have excellent taste. Your accent tells me you're Australian too, we've both chosen red and your dress is, I know, a Dior that I've salivated over ever since it hit the runway."

Kat laughed. "I'm a fashion conservator at the Powerhouse Museum so I recognized the style of yours. It's beautiful."

D'Arcy turned to Elliott. "A fashion conservator wearing my favorite Dior gown. It's lucky I'm married to Josh otherwise I might have to marry her instead."

"Well, you seem to have more luck with marriage than I do," Elliott quipped and everyone laughed.

Josh slipped his arm around his wife, who leaned back into him with a honeymooner's smile, as if she truly believed that she couldn't possibly be happier. Kat stopped laughing, wanted to tell them to leave now, to go far away to a magical place where love survived.

She realized she was staring as if she'd never seen a couple before, so she asked, "How do you all know each other?"

"We met Elliott a few years ago," Josh said. "D'Arcy's grandmother was Jessica May, the photographer?"

Kat nodded. During an adulthood spent working at various museums, she'd certainly heard of Jessica May.

"Elliott wanted to look at her war photography for a book he was working on, so he came to France for a couple of days to look through the archives," Josh continued.

"We had to throw him out after a fortnight," D'Arcy finished with a smile.

"Josh forgot to mention that the archives are kept in what used to be Jessica May's chateau," Elliott added. "And that he and D'Arcy live there. We had too much fun drinking calvados every night and eating amazing dinners in the gardens. It's an extraordinary place. I forgot to go home."

"You'll have to come with Elliott next time," D'Arcy said, snuggling in even closer to her husband's side.

"Oh no," Kat said, suddenly flustered. "Elliott and I aren't . . . I'm just helping him with some research."

"Come anyway," D'Arcy said mischievously. "Everyone who crosses the drawbridge at the chateau falls in love, don't they?" she asked Josh.

He smiled and took her hand. "We're going to get drinks for everyone before D'Arcy completely embarrasses you, Kat. I'll make sure she relocates her social graces while we're gone. What would you like?"

"Negroni?" Elliott asked Kat, which was just as well because she seemed to have lost the power of speech. Falling in love with Elliott was so far in the realms of fantasy that it belonged in the movies. She nodded.

Josh and D'Arcy walked to the bar with their arms wrapped around one another, and their love and happiness was so obvious that Kat could almost see a cartoon heart draw itself above them.

She heard herself exhale audibly.

"See what I mean?" Elliott said. "Overwhelming."

"They are. If they weren't so nice, you'd hate them. How long have they been married?"

"Six years. And they have four-year-old twin boys."

"You're kidding."

"I'm not."

"Wow." Kat shook her head. "They're amazing. This place is amazing. And in return for all the amazingness, I hope I can answer the rest of your questions. Did you . . . ?"

She didn't have to finish her question. Elliott reached into his jacket pocket. "Does this look like her?"

He produced a black-and-white square photograph. The quality was excellent. Pictured there was a beautiful woman, a model, a little on the thin side—her waist in particular was tiny—standing in a salon beneath a chandelier. She wore an extraordinary bridal gown that Kat suspected was a very early Dior—the salon certainly looked like Dior's. The bodice of the dress was like the one Kat was wearing now in the way it elongated the waist, emphasizing the body's curve down to the top of the hips. The model smiling for the camera could easily be, with just a little imagination, a much younger and very glamorous version of Kat's grandmother.

"Where did you get that?" Kat asked slowly.

"From Josh. He's an agent. He represents Jessica May's estate. I was in France a fortnight ago and I spoke to him about what I was researching. When I mentioned Margaux Jourdan's name he said he might be able to help me; he has an encyclopedic mind for his clients' work. Anyway, I was supposed to be meeting him tomorrow to see what he'd found, but I got your text and went straight over to his hotel. Jessica May took this shot of Margaux Jourdan at Christian Dior's first showing in 1947. It was published in *Vogue Paris*. Luckily May had kept the program notes for the showing too and in them it says that Margaux worked bravely for the WAAF in England during the war and returned to her homeland of France in 1945. That makes this woman my Margaux."

Kat stared at the photo. Because it also made the woman her grandmother, her Margaux. It was not possible to imagine that there might, somewhere in the world, be two different women named Margaux Jourdan who had worked for the WAAF during the war and who had a connection to Christian Dior.

Her grandmother was the woman Elliott had been searching for. Her grandmother had, therefore, been a spy.

NINETEEN

Kat couldn't look away from the photograph. Because, while it seemed to answer some questions, it created still more.

"But," Kat tried to protest. "How did a spy become a model for Christian Dior? She's wearing the wedding gown."

Elliott frowned, obviously not understanding her point.

"The wedding gown is always the showstopper," Kat explained. "It would only be worn by the very best mannequin. And this was Christian Dior's first-ever showing. So he would have chosen a mannequin who was even better than the best—he would have wanted the show to finish in a way that made everyone gasp."

And, of course, being a model for Christian Dior in no way accounted for the dresses in the cottage: sixty-five of the premier pieces. The Met museum had a Venus dress, for God's sake. The V&A held a *Soirée de Décembre* gown in its permanent collection. Both of those pieces were also in her grandmother's wardrobes. A model would never have been able to afford them. And couturiers, especially long-dead ones like Christian Dior, did not pay their models in gowns.

Kat realized that Josh and D'Arcy, unentwined now due to the drinks they were carrying, were nearly upon them. She knew she had to say it despite how much it hurt to acknowledge that she knew nothing at all about her grandmother. "My grandmother has a cottage in Cornwall. I'm going there on Saturday." She stared at the magazine picture of Margaux Jourdan modeling in Christian Dior's salon. "If you're free, you should come and take a look. Then I can tell you what I know of the Dior link—which isn't much."

"That'd be great," Elliott said. Then, before D'Arcy and Josh sat down, he asked Kat, "Are you all right?"

She nodded, although she wasn't sure if she really was.

But in the swirl of stimulating conversation that followed, Kat pushed her grandmother's secret past to the back of her mind. She even found herself laughing and having more fun than she'd had in a long time, especially when D'Arcy began to quiz her about her work.

"My job is basically to make sure that all the fashion objects held by the museum—fans, clothes, shoes, hats, wigs—deteriorate as little as possible, while still ensuring they can be displayed to the public whenever and wherever possible," Kat explained. "One day I might be reshaping a mannequin—literally cutting off its breasts and thinning the waist to make it the right shape for the era and the dress to be displayed on it. Or I might be taking a mold of a button to have a new one made as a replacement for one that's damaged. Or I might be in the lab analyzing a plastic that a contemporary acquisition is made from to work out if it needs to be stored in a moisture-and-temperature-controlled environment. Everyone thinks it's the oldest garments that require the most care, but actually cotton and wool and silk are very stable. It's the modern designs, made of everything from polyurethane to balsa wood, that are the most challenging to preserve."

Soon, the negronis had disappeared and Elliott stood up. "I'll get more drinks," he said. "And show my face to everyone on the way." He grimaced.

"I only had about a dozen people ask me where you were when I went to the bar," Josh said. "So be prepared."

As Elliott walked away, D'Arcy leaned over to Kat. "Elliott is a thoroughly decent human being, one of the best—besides my husband, of course." She smiled at Josh. "He regrets everything he did when he was younger, except having Juliette, his daughter. I also have a past I somewhat regret, so I know exactly how it can make one a better person. He stays with us in France twice a year to run writing work-shops for which he charges attendees only enough to cover costs, and each time there are several women who would willingly give up their writing practice to enjoy a fling with Elliott. But he never so much as flirts with any of them. He is a consummate professional, even though his past would suggest otherwise, and not at all the kind of person to engage in random affairs simply because he can. I was amazed—and very pleased—when Josh told me he was bringing someone with him tonight."

"But . . ." Kat protested. "I'm just . . ."

"Helping him with research." D'Arcy smiled. "I know. But from my side of the table, the way he looks at you is as more than research material."

"It's the dress," Kat said dismissively.

"It's you," D'Arcy replied.

"D'Arcy," Josh said, shaking his head but with a half smile on his lips, "leave Kat alone. She's a grown-up and can form her own opinions about people."

"But sometimes even grown-ups need a little help," D'Arcy said, bestowing an intimate smile upon her husband.

"Excuse me," Kat said, deciding now would be a good time to find the bathroom and leave Josh and D'Arcy to themselves.

On her way past the bar, Elliott stopped her. "You're not leaving, are you?"

"No . . ."

He reached out a hand, which found its way into hers. "Good. I don't want you to leave."

Someone squeezed past and she had to step in a little closer to him, close enough that she could feel the thrum of heat from his body, close enough that her own body began to behave in an alarming way. It was hot suddenly. And there wasn't enough air, or her lungs weren't functioning the way they ought.

"Kat," Elliott said, voice low, and she had to lean her head in even closer to hear him. His eyes were fixed to hers with the kind of intensity she'd just, not coveted, but yearned for, she now realized. He touched her cheek. "Kat . . . I'd really like to kiss you but I can't tell if you want me to. You're very hard to read."

Her stomach leapt and her mind fluttered wildly: *I haven't kissed a man since I separated from Paul; and, before that, I hadn't kissed any man other than him for nearly fifteen years.*

She shook her head, then realized Elliott might interpret the gesture as a no, when all she was trying to do was banish the killjoy voice in her mind. For once it would be nice not to be sensible; nice not to behave the way she thought a responsible mother should. She didn't reply, just tilted her head up and moved her mouth onto his.

That first kiss was so slow and so soft and so good that she stepped in still closer, snaking her arms up to his neck, deepening the kiss. It took only a moment before she lost herself in it so fully that the room and the people and the party fell away. Her stomach clenched and she felt his hand at her back tighten, as if he too wanted it to go on forever.

"Are you still after drinks, mate?" The barman's voice, coming from behind Elliott, made them both reluctantly disentangle.

"I'll see you back at the table," she whispered before continuing in search of the bathroom. Once there, she sank onto one of the very comfortable chairs in the anteroom. Her mouth was incapable of doing anything other than smiling. Before she left the privacy of the bathroom, she tried to settle herself into a slightly less exhilarated state but her face refused to comply.

Back in the supper club, D'Arcy was laughing at something Josh had said and Elliott was distractedly scanning the room. His eyes met Kat's with a delicious friction: silk on skin. She slid in next to him and he wound his arm around her shoulders, drawing her in. D'Arcy beamed as if the whole thing had been her doing.

Josh took his wife's hand as if worried she might punch the air with delight, and began to ask Kat more questions about her work, which she answered gratefully.

All too soon it was after midnight and D'Arcy looked reluctantly at Josh. "We have meetings tomorrow, as well as two sons who love to get up at five in the morning, so we should probably go."

"We should," he agreed. "I don't suppose the babysitter will have found a way to magically make them sleep in until seven."

"If she has, give me her number," Kat said. "I have two who wake up with the sun as well."

"Hopefully you'll have something more enjoyable to wake up to tomorrow morning," D'Arcy said cheekily, at which Josh groaned and stood up.

"It's definitely time for us to leave," he said. "Thank you, Kat, for being so good-humored in the face of D'Arcy's very unsubtle attempts at matchmaking. And, Elliott, we'll see you soon, I hope? You know there's always a room for you."

There was a flurry of kisses and handshaking, and then it was just Kat and Elliott, alone. She was very aware of his leg against hers, the drift of his hand on her shoulder, the way he made her feel: bold, alive and even desirable.

He leaned over and, without asking this time—which was fine with Kat—kissed her again. It was all the better the second time, and even though the booth was relatively private, the kiss was quickly becoming something inappropriate for a public place.

Kat forced herself to move away and leaned her forehead against his. "That's just a little bit too tempting."

"It is," he breathed. "Why is it that when you're grown-up and these things should be so much easier, it actually becomes so much harder? I mean, when you're twenty you don't really care how inappropriate it is to kiss someone in a bar; but when you're an adult, there are all these rules. Now that I've kissed you twice, I really want to do it again, but I absolutely cannot kiss you the way I want to here. And if I suggest going back to your hotel room, it sounds like I'm suggesting something else entirely, and it's the same if I invite you back to my house." He laughed. "And now I'm talking too much."

She laughed too, aware that neither had let go of the other, that they were sitting close and whispering like lovers. Then she confessed.

"This is going to make me sound like a boring old maid, but you're the first person I've kissed since I separated from my husband. Having a three-year-old and a five-year-old and working full-time doesn't allow much time for kissing," she added lightly, pulling back, embarrassed now by her candor.

"You're definitely not a boring old maid, Kat. You should ignore anyone who's made you think that."

"Let's go for a walk," she said impulsively. "Surely there must be a sheltered path somewhere outside."

It took far too long to extricate themselves from the party—everyone wanted to speak to Elliott—but they finally achieved the footpath, where he took her hand. "How about we cut through Green Park? Then we can walk up Pall Mall and I can drop you back at the hotel."

She liked the way he didn't assume anything, while at the same time being disappointed at the thought of him going.

They walked hand in hand and she asked him more about the book he was working on. He told her he was at an outline stage, where he planned each chapter and started to conjure up a story to go with the facts.

"I thought storytelling was for fiction," she said.

"I try to write history in a way that makes people feel as if they *are* reading a story. Anyone can list facts and figures, but that's not what history is about. It's about . . ." He stopped walking and looked around, eyes settling upon St. James's Palace. "Take the palace there. Anyone can tell you who built it, how long it took, when the kings first lived there. But I want to tell you what it was like to be the man straddling the tower as he hung the clock right at the top, most likely without even a rope to harness him. I want to tell you how wondrous it might have been, but how dreary and backbreaking it most likely was. I want to make you see the palace as animate, rather than just an assemblage of red brick." He stopped and Kat thought he might be blushing. "Now I'm ranting."

"Not at all," she insisted. "I could listen to you talk all night."

Elliott lifted his hand to her face and stroked a finger lightly along her jaw, tracing the bare skin at the top of her back. This time when he kissed her, their bodies molded into one another. She shivered.

"Cold?" he murmured.

"No. This just feels very . . . good. Which is an exceptionally poor choice of words when in the company of a writer."

He laughed softly. "I'm not sure I'm capable of anything more erudite at the moment." His fingers kept moving, running over her collarbone now, and then lower, to the top of her dress. "Kat, I'm not sure I want the night to end yet. But I'm also happy to drop you back to your hotel and see you again on Saturday if that's what you'd prefer."

She knew what he was asking her. And she wanted to say yes, so much, but she also wanted to be honest and give him the chance to reconsider.

"Elliott, I look much better in this dress and with makeup on my face than I do naked and without adornment. Nearly forty-year-old women who've borne two children can be a little underwhelming at close quarters." He started to speak and she held up her hand. "You're a very good-looking man who attracts a lot of female attention. I'm not saying this because I think you're shallow but because I'd much rather have you say goodnight now than be disappointed by what you will find hiding under this glorious red dress."

Instead of replying, he kissed her even harder than before. "Kat, I don't even need to see you naked. I'm attracted to *you*, not naked-you. Although I definitely wouldn't object to seeing you naked."

He grinned and she laughed in spite of herself. And that moment of lightness decided her. She took his hand and they hurried back to the hotel.

When they stepped into the lift, she prayed that nobody else would enter so she could kiss him again, but a whole party of people raced in, taking up all the room. Elliott had to shift back against the wall and he pulled her into him, the back of her body held tight against the front of his. She could feel the fast beat of his heart, the way his hands gripped her hips, that he really did want her and she decided that was the best thing of all: to be wanted.

Once inside her room she placed a hand on the light switch and then stopped, still thinking that darkness might be the most flattering option for her once her dress had been removed. But Elliott reached out a hand too, covering hers, turning on the light. She could see his face now and the way he was looking at her made her stomach swirl extravagantly and her hand fly up to touch his face.

"Elliott." She whispered his name, mouth near his, the most tantalizing space of about two inches separating their bodies.

"I'm terrified of ruining your dress if I try to undo anything," he murmured, keeping that gap between them, letting the anticipation smolder there.

She smiled and solved the problem by unfastening it herself and letting it fall to the floor. Then she kissed him exactly the way she'd wanted to but hadn't been able to in the bar. It was the best kiss she'd ever had in her life. As was everything that followed.

* * *

She expected that, afterward, Elliott would jump out of bed, get dressed and leave. But he didn't. Instead, he kissed her slowly and incredibly sensually, as if even after everything they'd done, he wasn't ready for it to be over.

She was even more surprised when he said, "That was definitely the best night I've had in a very long time."

"Really? I find that hard to believe."

"Don't go anywhere," he said. "Please? I feel as if you're likely to run away, even though it's your room. I'll be back in a minute."

He rolled over and went to the bathroom, and she still expected that he would get dressed and leave when he returned. But he climbed back into bed and gathered her up in his arms. "Is it your ex-husband's fault or is it just you? You should have much more self-confidence than you do. Yes, I had a very good night—and I hope you did too?" He looked almost worried now.

She couldn't help laughing. "I may be low on self-confidence but I'm definitely not as good at faking things as Meg Ryan. I enjoyed myself. A lot."

And she had. Elliott had been unafraid to take his time, to ask her what she liked, to talk to her rather than follow a set pattern of moves designed to bring the thing to an end as quickly as possible—which was how she remembered sex during at least the last year or so of her marriage to Paul.

"I guess I've always been a high achiever," she said, trying to explain, "so having my marriage fail was a shock. It dented my self-confidence. Like I said, I haven't started seeing other men yet. I haven't had time. No," she corrected herself, "I haven't made time. Don't want to fail again, I guess."

Before he could reply, his phone buzzed. He apologized as he retrieved it. "I want to make sure it's not my daughter. She's staying with her mother tonight but, like I told you before, they haven't been getting along. If it is Juliette at two in the morning, then something's very wrong."

"Don't worry," she said. "I'd do the same."

He laughed when he looked at his phone.

"What is it?" Kat propped herself up on one elbow.

"It's D'Arcy. Read it if you like."

The message said: *Josh and I are up with vomiting four-year-olds, so I'm desperately hoping that you and Kat are having a better night than we are. Please tell me you are? Josh told me not to send this but he's in the laundry washing the sheets so I'm safe! D x*

Kat laughed too. "She's hilarious."

"I hope you don't think she's annoying. I love her and Josh, but I know that her propensity to say exactly what she's thinking is a bit too much for some people. My ex-wife couldn't handle it."

"I think it's refreshing. So what are you going to tell her?"

Elliott dropped his phone on the bedside table. "Nothing. I'll let her simmer on it all night just for fun."

He reached out for Kat, drawing her in. She was still laughing, hadn't laughed this much in a long time, had hardly thought about her children and didn't feel horribly guilty about it either.

She curled into Elliott and he kissed her as she drew her hands up over his chest, which was lean and muscular and altogether very irresistible.

"Do you have an early start?" he asked. "I suppose you want me to leave."

"I don't want you to leave," she said. "I think we should make absolutely sure this really is the best night you've had in a long time."

TWENTY

K at didn't tell a soul what she was doing. She didn't want anyone's judgment or opinion; she just wanted whatever was happening to be all hers, and Elliott's too of course. She saw him again two nights later: an impromptu visit that was supposed to be a late supper but ended up in her hotel room without any food at all. Afterward, he asked her about her family, and told her more about his, until being naked in a bed with him became too distracting.

Everyone should have a fling at least once in their life, Kat thought on Saturday morning as she waited at dawn for Elliott to pick her up. It was definitely good for the soul. So good that she had managed not to think about the mystery of Margaux Jourdan very much at all, reasoning it was best put off until she went to Cornwall. But now that day was here, and so was Elliott.

He jumped out of the car and kissed her properly. "Good morning," he said with a smile.

"Good morning yourself," she replied, grinning. It was the first time she'd seen him dressed casually, in jeans and a navy-blue T-shirt that once again deepened the brown of his eyes to nearly black. That, combined with the way his body felt beneath the soft fabric as her hands moved down his back made her grin turn to a sigh. "You should wear this all the time," she said.

He raised a teasing eyebrow at her. "All the time?"

She laughed. "You're right. All the time in public places, I mean. But when it's just me, you're allowed to take it off."

He laughed too. "If I'd known you were this feisty in the morning, I'd have come earlier."

"Mornings are my metier, don't forget. Three-year-olds have no idea what sleep-ins are." She gave a wry grin. "And I'm sure sleeping isn't what you had in mind, which just goes to show how bad I am at flirting."

"You're perfect," he said, kissing her forehead.

She tried not to blush but knew she hadn't succeeded when Elliott touched her cheek and said, "You are."

They climbed into the car and Elliott drove along Pall Mall and then onto Piccadilly. The streets were quiet, most people still sleeping, Hyde Park a field of gold in the sunrise. Elliott glanced over at her and Kat knew he wanted to ask more about where they were going but that he was waiting for her to bring it up. She took a deep and steadying breath.

"In my grandmother's cottage in Cornwall there is one Dior gown for every year from the very first showing in 1947 until now," she began. "I found them last month."

Elliott's eyes flicked over to her again before he returned them to the road. "That's . . ." He shook his head. "I don't even know what the right word is. It's more than strange . . ."

"I know."

"And I suppose she won't talk about that either."

"Other than telling me I need to wear them, no. She said she'd thought she could tell me but then . . ." Kat paused. "That was when she looked so, so scared."

"Kat, do you want to do this?" Elliott asked gently. "I can turn the car around and we can go back to London. I'll somehow get on with my research and not bother you with it. I don't want to mess things up with you and your grandmother."

Kat's exhale filled the car and she stared at her hands, spinning her vintage Deco ring around and around on her finger. "I don't know if I can just forget about all this now. If there's something out there, some history that made my grandmother look the way she did that night," Kat felt herself shiver, "then shouldn't I find out what it is so I can make sure it never—I never—hurt her like that again?"

"Kat . . ."

The way he said her name made Kat the one who was scared now.

"There's something I need to tell you," he said.

She braced herself, but said lightly, trying to shrug off the dread that had woven itself tightly around her, "You have a fourth wife locked in your attic?"

He shook his head emphatically. "Definitely not. I wanted to tell you this at the party but it wasn't the right place—I thought you wouldn't want people around when you heard. And then after-ward . . . well . . ." He sighed. "Maybe I should have told you afterward but that didn't feel like the right time either. It's just that, if your grandmother really is my Margaux Jourdan, then it means your mother . . ." Another pause. "Your mother was born in a concentration camp."

Bright sun. Much too bright. Green fields lurid beneath the rays. A sunbeam glaring off a sign for a hideously quaint English pub called the Nobody Inn.

Was Kat now a nobody? If her grandmother really had been a spy . . . And her mother had been born in a—Kat blanched, cutting off the thought.

A piercing toot roused her, followed by another. Elliott had stopped the car by the roadside and was saying her name.

"I shouldn't have told you," she heard him say. "But I couldn't not tell you. If you'd somehow found out and discovered that I'd known . . ." He reached for her hand and she saw it wilt into his. "You look like you might faint or be sick or both. Do you need some air? Or can I get you a coffee?"

She shook her head. The thought of entering the Nobody Inn and hearing people laughing over coffee made the nausea rise. How could her mother have been born in a concentration camp? It meant that ...

"My grandmother was sent to a concentration camp?"

Elliott nodded. "She nearly died there, Kat. So did your mother. I can tell you more about it, if you want. Or I can shut up and regret having said anything."

She saw that his own face looked bloodless and understood what a conflict he'd faced: knowing something so appalling and deducing that she had no idea. Of course he hadn't wanted to tell her at the party. Or afterward. He'd been right not to. She hadn't wanted anything other than pleasure that night.

And now ... She didn't want to know it now either. But she also knew that behind his words—*your mother was born in a concentration camp*—lay a terrible story that she would have to face. A story that she must face, just as her grandmother had had to by living through it. No wonder her face had paled. No wonder she'd looked so frightened.

"Can you tell me more when we get to Cornwall?" she said. "I don't think I can deal with it right now. But I want to. Later." She felt tears fill her eyes. "Poor Margaux."

"Kat ..." Elliott reached for her and kissed her forehead. "If I say sorry for the millionth time, I know it won't help. I'll tell you whatever you want to know whenever you're ready to hear it."

They spent the rest of the drive talking about other things, and slowly Kat felt herself relax. By late morning, they reached Porthleven and the turnoff to the house. As they bounced along the track, the cottage, transformed by brilliant sunshine from the brooding creature of her last visit, looked almost picturesque.

Elliott drew the car to a stop, hopped out and whistled. "This is amazing."

"I suppose it is," Kat said as she joined him, taking in the undeniable beauty of the cottage's position, the uninterrupted view across the sea. The water moved smoothly and lustrously like a swathe of blue velvet, a bodice of sun-washed sky blooming out of it. Gulls circled, wings unflapping, soaring without effort. "I didn't really notice how pretty it was when I was here last month because I was so confused about why my grandmother had a house she'd never told me about. I thought I should convince her to sell it but . . ."

What if she didn't? What if she brought the girls over for a holiday? How they would love building sandcastles and exploring rock pools and searching for shells. But she knew she would only be able to do that if she let go of her unease over the house and uncovered what it meant to her grandmother, what the dresses meant too—and what her grandmother had hidden away behind her fear.

"Don't sell it," Elliott said. "That would be sacrilege. Not that I'm trying to tell you what to do," he added hastily. "But it's extraordinary."

"The outside maybe," Kat said. "The inside, not so much."

She slipped her hand into his and led him into the house. Dust rose to surround them the moment they entered.

"It's a bit neglected," Elliott said as his shoe crunched on the skeleton of a spider, "but I like it. It feels . . ." He stopped and smiled.

"What were you going to say?" she asked as they moved into the front room with its matchless view of the ocean.

Elliott walked over to the window seat, clearly unable to resist the lure of the water. "Something horribly pretentious: that it feels like an unopened book. Luckily I stopped myself before you had the chance to think I was an idiot."

She managed a wry laugh. "Tell me the story has a happy ending though."

"How could it not, set in a place like this."

"Let me show you what's upstairs first. You might change your mind then." She led him to the bedroom where the bounty of dresses hung in the wardrobes. "See?"

He stared at the rainbow of silk and she knew he was, like her, thinking of the *Vogue* image of Margaux Jourdan modeling for Dior in 1947.

She reached out to touch one of the dresses: Le Muguet, a white knee-length dress adorned with hundreds of intricate and perfect lily-of-the-valley flowers. May lilies. Lilies of happiness. Or the lilies that bloomed from Mary's tears at the foot of the cross. Now, in her grandmother's house and with her grandmother's dresses before her, all Kat could think of were the words: *concentration camp*.

"Let's go for a walk," Elliott said, obviously sensing her shift in mood.

She nodded. Perhaps the balm of sea and sky would restore her spirits and make her less afraid of her grandmother's secret past and what it all meant.

They walked down to the cove. Crabs scurried out of their way and over the sand. The shore stretched all the way to a rocky wall that almost hid the town of Porthleven from view. Kat wondered if there was a way through the wall, or if it created a dead end, making the beach truly private.

Before they reached the wall, the breeze picked up, flinging sand at them, so they decided to walk over the moors behind the house instead. After almost half an hour, they reached a wall at the far boundary of the property. On the other side she could see a beguiling mix of tall and elegant trees. She pulled herself up and sat atop the wall, peering down into wonder.

It was a garden that stretched for acres, in some ways formal, and in some ways completely wild. In the far distance a house was just discernible, almost hidden by a jungle of ivy, vines and grandiose trees. There were several greenhouses nearer to Kat, topiary hedges, a vegetable garden, a lake with a rope bridge curving across it and a meadow dotted with flowers like a striking pointillist painting. She was so awestruck that she leaned forward to see more, lost her grip and tumbled over the other side.

"Kat!" she heard Elliott call. "Are you all right?"

Within seconds he had scrambled over the wall, dropping far more elegantly than she had to the other side.

Kat sat up and smiled ruefully. "Luckily I managed to land in this." She indicated the mound of freshly mown grass that had cushioned her fall.

She stood up, grass stuck to her clothes and, she imagined, all over her. Sure enough, Elliott leaned over to pick some out of her hair.

"You look like a wild creature from myth," he teased.

They were interrupted by a harsh voice. "There's no getting in for free. Make your way to the front and pay like everyone else. Although when you arrive an hour before closing time, I don't know what you expect to see."

Kat drew back from Elliott and saw an elderly woman with long white hair that had faded like aged cotton to yellow near the ends. She was pointing a finger at them.

Kat shivered. "I'm so sorry. We didn't mean to sneak in. I fell off the wall."

The woman stared at her accusingly. "How did you get onto the wall? The only way to do that is to trespass on the property behind this one."

"Oh no," Kat said. "We weren't trespassing."

Elliott stepped forward and offered his hand. "I'm Elliott Beaufort. This must be the Lost Gardens of Lysander. I've heard of it, that it's a beautiful place, but I've never had the chance to visit. I can see that was a mistake."

The old woman smiled and shook his hand, clearly charmed by both his manner and his words.

Kat offered her hand too, and said, "And I'm Kat. It really is breathtaking."

"Do you own the gardens?" Elliott asked.

"Yes." And then the old woman said, "I'm Margaux Jourdan."

Kat's gasp ricocheted around them. She shook her head and stepped backward. It was only Elliott, putting a hand on her back to steady her, that stopped her from running away.

He said to the woman, frowning, "I called you months ago. You told me you were fifty years old and couldn't be the woman I was looking for."

"I lied," she said unapologetically. "Who wouldn't want to be fifty again? Besides, I never thought anyone would come looking for Margaux Jourdan."

Kat froze. The gardens vanished from her vision. Everything disappeared, in fact, except the woman. And the knowledge that her grandmother had said exactly the same thing to her back in Australia: *I never thought anyone would come looking for Margaux Jourdan.*

PART SEVEN
SKYE

The first thing I would like to make clear is that we women members of the Air Transport Auxiliary do not regard ourselves as heroines . . .

—Joan Hughes

TWENTY-ONE

ENGLAND, JUNE 1943

Over the next two months, some malevolent god ensured that Skye ferried planes to RAF Tangmere more often than she'd ever done for the entire year previous. On one of those occasions, she saw her sister's back slinking away but Skye didn't let her escape.

"Liberty!" she called out.

A grinning face whirled around and Liberty came over to greet her, at least having the sense not to lie and say, *Sorry, I didn't realize it was you.*

But even though Skye had forced the meeting, she didn't know what to say. She knew nothing about her sister now, so conversation came hard. "What does your new job involve?" she settled on, thinking that would be safe ground.

Liberty lit a Sobranie, smoothed a hand over her dark brown hair and said, faux-serious, "Flirting."

"Very funny." Skye waited, not for one minute thinking that was all her sister would say.

But Liberty blew out carefully formed smoke rings as if she'd been learning the art of irritation-by-cigarette from Margaux and elaborated with only one word: "Typing. You're the Penrose sister doing all the exciting things. Just like always."

"You were given every opportunity to fly. You never wanted to."

"No," Liberty agreed. "I never wanted to be Vanessa Penrose in the way that you did."

There was something about the way she said their mother's name—something hostile—that had Skye momentarily wishing one of those smoke rings might strangle her sister. "Have you been home since you've been back in England?" she asked.

"My home is up here with people rather than down there with crabs," Liberty said coolly.

"You say that as if you don't like Cornwall at all."

"It's a lonely place."

Don't leave me alone. The voice of Skye's nine-year-old sister insinuated itself into the present.

"It wasn't lonely," Skye objected. "You had me and Nicholas."

"No, you had Nicholas. And Nicholas had you."

"You had Mother."

Liberty's laugh was bereft of humor. "Nobody had our mother. She gave herself away long ago."

Don't leave me alone. That echo again. Even though Skye wasn't sure she wanted to see the conversation through to its end, given the peculiar direction it was turning in, she made herself ask, "What do you mean?"

"The world turned its back on us the moment we were born, Skye. That's what it does to illegitimate children." Liberty spoke serenely, one arm crossed over her body to support the other arm that moved her cigarette in and out of her mouth. "All she gave us were things that made the world turn its back on us even more. Flying lessons. Fortune-telling—"

"She gave us the courage to do anything." Skye interrupted her sister.

"She gave us the burden of disreputability."

It was Skye's turn to laugh, as if Liberty were just fooling around. "Well, I wouldn't change any of it."

"I would. Our childhoods, while parallel, were nothing alike."

"They were exactly the same," Skye said, temper flaring. "I have to go. I have work to do."

That afternoon, as she flew through a sky the color of the Cornish sea—a deep, fathomless blue—one thought whirled through Skye's head like a blizzard: she and Liberty told two such different versions of the same story. Whose was right? Perhaps Liberty was just trying to take away the one thing they shared beyond their surname—their history. But if they didn't even have a past, then what would tether them together now and in the future?

Don't think about it, she told herself. Liberty's childish kicking had simply been replaced by exasperating behavior designed to goad the other party into lashing out. And as usual, Skye had managed to do something she regretted: storm off. There was no point dwelling on it. The next time she saw her sister, Liberty was sure to have moved on to some other provocation.

* * *

Thankfully for Skye's jumbled emotions, she didn't see O'Farrell, Nicholas or Margaux for quite some time. It meant she was able to put off discovering whether what she felt for Nicholas was written all over her face, no doubt mortifying him, Margaux and most especially herself.

Then, unbelievably, Liberty wrote to Skye to tell her that she'd met O'Farrell and, when he'd discovered she was Skye's sister, he'd invited her to join them in London. She added a postscript that Skye didn't trust: *He's exceptionally charming*!

So it transpired that Liberty met Skye and Rose at Southampton station and caught the train with them to London. Joan was now training to fly four-engine bombers and couldn't join them. At the

Dorchester, O'Farrell and Richie met them in the lobby with eager smiles.

Richie kissed Rose's cheek and, blushing endearingly, gave her the key to their room so she could freshen up and stow her overnight bag there.

O'Farrell, of course, didn't blush or prevaricate; he took Skye's bag from her, and Liberty's too, and led the way upstairs to their rooms.

Liberty took one look at her cramped single, and at Skye and O'Farrell's much larger and more luxurious accommodations, sniffed and said, "I thought I'd be able to spend time with my sister this weekend."

O'Farrell's face contorted.

"We'll have plenty of time to chat over dinner," Skye said to Liberty.

But Liberty wasn't to be thwarted. "What if the Germans bomb us?" she said, eyes round with fear or mischief—Skye couldn't be sure which. Liberty took her bag from O'Farrell and deposited it on the double bed in Skye's room. "I think I'd best stay here with Skye."

She smiled beseechingly at O'Farrell who, realizing he had no choice other than to forcibly remove her from the room, took his own bag to the single next door.

"Thank you for ruining my evening," Skye said to her sister as soon as O'Farrell had gone.

"You don't look all that upset," Liberty observed. "Perhaps I've saved your evening?" With that, she flounced out of the room.

O'Farrell came back and enveloped Skye in a hug, his lips lingering on hers. "We can come up early, before Liberty," he said. "Maybe we'll have time—"

"Skye!" Liberty's voice screeched down the hall like an air-raid siren. "The others are waiting downstairs."

"Is she always like this?" O'Farrell asked. "I thought I was doing something nice by inviting her."

"Yes," Skye said grimly. "She is always like this." And only just managed to refrain from adding that "nice" and "Liberty" were two words that didn't really go together.

* * *

Nicholas, having succeeded in irritating both himself and Margaux with the constant drumming of his fingers on her chair back, took himself to the bar to order drinks. While he waited, he surveyed the room. Rose was snuggled into Richie's side on one of the settees, and Nicholas felt himself grow cold and very still at the thought that Skye might soon be doing the same with O'Farrell.

In the mirror behind the bar, he caught sight of his reflection: another man in uniform, so like every other man at the hotel. Yet Skye had called him handsome. Once. At no other time had she spoken of the way he looked, of the physical. But when they'd danced at the airfield, and swum together at Hamble, he'd felt something so intensely physical that it was as if the magnetic charge of an aurora— that startling and magical collision of particles—had fallen from the sky, lighting the water between them so vividly that its energy clung to him still.

And she wasn't even in the room. She didn't need to be. Just thinking of her in that swimsuit was more than he should allow himself to recall.

He leaned an elbow on the bar and rubbed his forehead. But she was inerasable. His eyes strayed toward the elevators, and when finally she emerged with O'Farrell and Liberty, he couldn't stop the smile that lifted onto his face.

Margaux caught him, and smirked. He rearranged his expression into blankness, but found himself wanting to punch the air and whoop when Skye came over to his side.

"What can I get you?" he asked. "More whiskey?" His wry smile prompted one of her own.

"I had a headache for three days after our misadventure with your whiskey flask," she said. "I should stick to water."

Liberty's voice, close by and loudly relating something to O'Farrell, made Skye frown.

"If I get you water, you won't be living up to your reputation," Nicholas said very seriously, trying to distract her from her sister. "The story passed around by the pilots is that your friend Rose is the practical one, Joan is the delightful one, Pauline is the terrifying one, and you're either the," he paused as if flicking through a list, "the mysterious one, the fun one or the wild one."

She was laughing now, the force of it like a mountain wave of air almost lifting him from the ground.

More bodies crowded around the bar and he moved aside to let them in. As far as he was concerned, he'd happily stand there all night, never placing an order for drinks, because then he wouldn't have to move away from her and she wouldn't return to O'Farrell.

He was standing much closer to her now, her smile all he could see, and he wanted, suddenly, to slip his finger into the collar of her shirt, to undo the top button. To touch the skin of her throat.

He turned his head away. He needed Margaux. He needed to re-instate the barrier between him and Skye; he'd let things go too far and now his thoughts were running down what could only ever be a dead end.

As Skye responded to his jest by saying, "You know my wild-ness is limited to illicit swimming," Margaux thankfully arrived, her dispassionate expression thrusting him back into his role.

Liberty's voice again pierced the conversation. "How about one of those drinks you bought for me at the pub the other night," she said airily to O'Farrell. "What was it called? Started with an 'n.'"

"Negroni," O'Farrell replied.

"Yes, our dear friend O'Farrell has been as busy as ever, entertaining young ladies in public bars," Margaux said coolly.

Nicholas stared at Margaux. Why was she telling Skye that?

He saw Skye shiver as she caught the glance that passed between him and Margaux, most likely seeing how formidable it was—the weight of all their secrets contained within it—but not what it meant. He didn't even know what he wanted to convey to Margaux; he'd kill O'Farrell if he broke Skye's heart by taking WAAFs out on the sly, but he also knew he had no right to interfere in Skye's life.

Now Liberty was whispering in O'Farrell's ear and if Skye turned her body a little to the right, she'd be able to see it too. "I'll be back in a minute," he said.

He passed O'Farrell, who had stopped at the bar to get Liberty's drink. When he reached Liberty, he took her arm and drew her away. She wore the same expression as when she was nine years old and kicking Skye under the breakfast table.

"What are you doing?" he asked.

"Flirting," she said with a laugh. "I told Skye that was what my job entailed. So she shouldn't be surprised."

"Don't mess it all up."

"Which part?" She eyed him over her cigarette and for the first time ever he wished he had a crab to put in the back of her shirt.

"I don't think Skye's especially interested in O'Farrell," Liberty added, eyeing him the same way Margaux had just done.

"Talk to her, Liberty," he said.

"You know I can't."

And that was the trouble: none of them could tell Skye anything.

* * *

"O'Farrell's been as excited about this weekend as a trainee pilot taking his first flight," Margaux observed to Skye after Nicholas had left.

Skye's hand clattered against a glass on the bar. Although her experience with men was limited, she knew what to expect and that O'Farrell was probably good enough at it to make her feel something. But that didn't help to ease whatever it was she felt in the pit of her stomach. Nor did it help to answer the question that was ringing persistently in her ears: did she really want to sleep with O'Farrell, and, if she didn't, shouldn't she let him know?

"Perhaps I'll have a whiskey after all," she said. But the drink only made her feel more detached from what was happening, rather than offering up a solution.

Soon it was time to walk to the Empire Cinema in Leicester Square. They arrived in time for the newsreel. The audience cheered at the good news, of which there wasn't much, and became silent at the bad, of which there was rather a lot.

Liberty chattered relentlessly to O'Farrell. Margaux smoked. Nicholas said nothing. The whiskey in Skye's stomach churned.

Given the difficulties of communicating with a pilot on another base whom she hadn't seen for two months, Skye didn't know a lot about what O'Farrell had arranged for the evening and she certainly had no idea what movie was playing. When it began, she was distracted with lighting a cigarette from a pack Nicholas had passed to her, but her eyes flew to him when he said in a strange and compressed voice, "Skye."

A blond head in an airplane appeared on the screen, and the words *They Flew Alone* scrolled across it in ominous white. Amy Johnson's face—or rather the face of the actress playing her—was all Skye could see. Amy Johnson, the first female pilot to fly from England to Australia, beating the record set by a man. Amy Johnson, whose triumphs in the air had spurred Skye's mother to fly to her death. Amy Johnson, who had died herself in 1941 after joining the ATA.

On the screen, she was still alive. Her ATA overalls were uncomfortably familiar—like the ones Skye wore each day—and the actress had Amy's mannerisms just about right.

The airplane took off, clouds descended. Then the blindness Skye knew all too well: the blindness of bad weather. The feeling of not knowing if you had flown right out of the atmosphere and into somewhere so foreign and so far away it seemed impossible that you would ever return. Amy's face: fearful, disbelieving that this could happen to her when she was so experienced. And the sudden and acute sweep of understanding that this was all there was: a woman alone in a plane in the clouds and that life had meant nothing at all.

"Are you all right?" Nicholas asked in an urgent whisper, and Skye realized that her breathing was terribly, audibly fast, her cigarette had burned down almost to her fingers and white ash was falling around her like teardrops.

"Excuse me." She jumped up, hurrying for the exit, not even stopping to see if Liberty was similarly distressed. She knew only that she had to get away before she started to cry in the way she'd only ever cried once before—on the day she found out her mother had died after her plane had entered that same cloud-filled void.

She had never cried like that again because Liberty had caught her sobbing on her bed in Paris and, in one of the rare tender moments they'd shared, had begun wailing herself. "No, Skye," Liberty had howled. "*You* can't cry." She was inconsolable for hours, repeating those three words in the tiniest of whispers—you *can't cry*—as if it were Skye crying that made their mother's death a terrible and acutely felt thing.

Skye had swallowed her sobs, wiped her eyes and held her sister, an orphan at age thirteen.

Now, a decade's worth of tears burst from her like a tempest the moment she made it out into Leicester Square. The reality of how vulnerable to death she was—and Rose was, and Joan, and Nicholas, and O'Farrell too—hit her. It could be any of their faces on that cinema screen.

But what a terrible place to be while in the midst of the worst kind of emotional storm. Service men and women swarmed around her as she wept, some of the men good-naturedly calling out that they'd buy her a drink before realizing that her face was soaked and hurrying away before they caught whatever grief had infected her. It was in that bewildering swirl of people and noise that someone took her arm and led her toward a wall, out of the hubbub.

She heard Nicholas say, "O'Farrell's coming and I know you'll prefer him helping you, but I just had to make sure—not that you're all right because I know you're not—but whether there's something I can do?"

O'Farrell's distinctly displeased voice broke in. "What did you do to her?"

Skye shook her head, meaning to indicate that nothing was Nicholas's fault, but Nicholas interpreted it as an answer to his question. He kicked at the ground with the toe of his boot and said, "I'm going inside."

"He didn't do anything," Skye said to O'Farrell, swiping at her cheeks as Nicholas left. "My mother . . . died in a plane crash. Like Amy Johnson."

O'Farrell didn't bother to ask her a single thing about her mother. Instead he said, "I know I already asked you this, but what is the story with you and Crawford?"

"The story," she said evenly and honestly, "is that I haven't had a mother since I was fourteen. I try not to think about that very often. Because it hurts like lying down on a runway and letting a squadron of Spitfires run over you. Nicholas knew my mother. And he knew how the movie might make me feel."

She expected he would leave it at that and they would go back inside, even though she didn't want to, and she would shut her eyes through the rest of the movie.

But he kept on. "I didn't know. But of course your *friend* did."

She blinked away her tears and shot the words at him. "This is the first time you've shown any interest in me beyond kissing. If you wanted to know about my past, all you had to do was ask."

"I told you I only wanted something casual," he said belligerently. "But that doesn't mean I want someone who kisses my boss in an alley right before she sleeps with me."

Don't cry, Skye told herself. *Not in front of O'Farrell.*

She remembered what Liberty had said about drinking negronis with O'Farrell, and what Margaux had murmured about the smiles he gave away so freely to every WAAF. O'Farrell wanted something casual for himself but resented Skye seeking comfort from a friend.

She knew then that she didn't want to be just another woman to smile at, another woman to share a drink with, another woman to bed. She wanted someone for whom she was the sea and the sky and the entire universe as well.

"You should find somebody else to be casual with," she said. "I'm sorry."

She walked back into the theater and sat at the back, away from the group. She saw O'Farrell return too and take a seat next to Liberty— who didn't seem at all distressed by the movie—and saw her sister lean into him. Skye closed her eyes. She knew exactly what was about to happen.

TWENTY-TWO

At the Embassy Club after the movie, Skye found a table in a dark corner where she could sit and smoke and drink and restore her equanimity. She didn't want to put a dampener on the party, didn't want to be annoyed at O'Farrell, just wanted to pretend that she wasn't sad, and that outside the club's doors everything was brightly lit and intact and so too was her heart. She tried to smile, but couldn't feel the happiness implied by the gesture, couldn't help wondering how one could dance and laugh and drink when the world was at war. And was it wrong to do so?

She seemed to be the only person who had such thoughts. On the dance floor, Liberty was twirling around with a drink in hand, spilling most of it on O'Farrell. Rose and Richie were locked in an embrace that could end in only one way; and even Margaux was smiling at Nicholas as they danced, not closely like Liberty and O'Farrell, but with something more of a shared understanding. Perhaps that was what happened to love once comfort set in: it quieted to a less explosive but more reliable intimacy. How Skye wanted both: the explosion, and the sweet quietness that followed.

A short time later, Margaux joined her. "Do you miss France?" Margaux asked abruptly, and in French, as she lit her usual Gauloise.

Skye considered her answer and then replied in the same language. "In some ways, yes. Although it's probably not simply France I miss, but the freedom. The lack of war. Which I wouldn't find if I was to return there now. And you? When did you come to England?"

"I was sent to boarding school in London when I was thirteen. My parents wanted me to speak English equally as well as French. They had some idea of what the world was coming to."

"Are your parents still in France?"

Margaux shook her head. "They were working with the Resistance. They haven't been seen or heard from for almost a year. My two brothers also."

"I'm sorry." Skye reached for Margaux's hand but only touched it lightly as she wasn't sure how Margaux would respond. "They must be very brave people."

"It's not bravery," Margaux said tersely. "It's necessity. Nobody wants France's heart to be invaded in the same way her cities have been."

Skye heard in Margaux's sharpness the shadow of anger and grief and impotence. They were all doing whatever they could here in England, but it must look like nothing to those in France. Besides the fighters and the bombers that went out every night to Germany, where was their Resistance?

Margaux signaled to the waiter for more champagne. "Why is O'Farrell dancing with your sister?"

Skye gave a short laugh. "You know, they should make you an interrogator. You're rather good at getting right to the point."

Margaux's answering smile was odd. "Nobody here ever asks anything that matters. Everyone's too busy avoiding the subject and any kind of emotion. It's a wonder you don't all explode from the pressure."

"Perhaps that would be a good way to frighten off Hitler," Skye said. "Have everyone in England simultaneously detonate their stiff upper lips. It might create a blast big enough to reach all the way to Germany."

She began to laugh at the ridiculous image of the stoic British people putting their pent-up emotions and the things nobody talked of to good use, creating a bomb so powerful it might defeat the Nazis. Margaux laughed too, and soon, whether because of the champagne or their own pent-up emotions, they were both laughing so hard they couldn't speak.

Nicholas approached them, looked from one to the other, and then over his shoulder at Liberty. "This isn't exactly how I thought I'd find you," he said.

Behind him, Skye could see that Liberty was attempting to kiss O'Farrell, who was halfheartedly discouraging her. He glanced over to where Skye sat as if even he knew it would be poor form to kiss the sister of the woman he'd planned to spend that same night with. Skye felt irritation more than hurt, and at Liberty rather than O'Farrell.

"Why don't you dance with Skye?" Margaux said to Nicholas.

The look Nicholas flashed Margaux—a kind of appalled shock that one might feel if asked to dance with a hideous monster—punched Skye in the gut. She stood up, hand pressed to her chest, pushing the pain back inside where no one could see it.

As she hurried away, she stumbled into Liberty, who had broken away from O'Farrell and whose face was as green as the grass of England. Skye took her sister's arm and felt her deadweight sag against her. They needed a bathroom.

Once there, Liberty managed to deposit her negronis into the basin, which was better than the floor. Then Skye found herself doing something she'd seen other women do for their friends, women who'd had too much grief to keep inside them and who were emptying it out into the toilets of a nightclub. She gathered up the strands of Liberty's dark hair and held them out of the way while her sister heaved over the basin.

She rubbed Liberty's back and whispered, "What are you doing? What are we both doing?"

Liberty didn't respond.

Skye passed her a napkin to wipe her mouth and told her to splash water on her face. Then she bore almost all her sister's weight as she took Liberty to their room.

Once there, she deposited Liberty on the bed, poured her a glass of water and found a wastepaper bin that Liberty would put to good use during the night ahead. Finally, Skye lay on her back beside her sister, hands folded on her stomach, and stared up at the ceiling. "I'm sorry," she whispered.

She felt Liberty roll over to face her, saw that her sister's eyes were still open, that she hadn't yet passed out. She reached out for Liberty's hand, just like those nights in Paris after their mother had died when they'd shared a bed and found solace in the simple act of lying next to one another.

"Isn't this better than being with O'Farrell?" Liberty mumbled.

Hot tears trickled over Skye's cheeks. "Yes," she said, squeezing Liberty's hand. "Yes, it is."

* * *

Not long after Rose and Skye returned to Hamble, Joan made a surprise visit to the cottage. After they'd engulfed her in hugs, the three of them sat squashed together on the front step enjoying the late-afternoon warmth. Joan produced a bottle of sherry, which was the only vaguely celebratory substance she'd been able to find in the whole country.

As Joan poured out three glasses, Skye asked, "What are we celebrating?"

Joan beamed and rested her head on Skye's shoulder. "First I have to thank you for making it possible. As of today," she raised her glass, "I'm officially an instructor for Class V planes!"

"Oh, my goodness!" Rose exclaimed.

"An instructor," Skye repeated with equal amazement.

All three forgot their sherry and laughed and hugged and cried. Because the unthinkable had happened. After Skye's conversion course for Class V planes, a handful of other women had been allowed to do the same. And now this: a woman would be instructing both men and women in how to fly the largest planes in the RAF. It was akin to a miracle.

Nobody was able to say anything coherent for quite some time, until Joan added, voice low, "It's better this way. I'm too full of things I can't talk about. Being an instructor will mean not having to . . ."

Farewell so many friends to that place somewhere over the rainbow. Skye heard her own shaky inhalation, and Rose's too.

"I sometimes talk to Richie about those things," Rose said quietly. "I know I used to say talking won't bring them back, which is still true, but I've discovered that being listened to brings me back from that place where there are too many clouds."

I was so scared, Skye had said to Nicholas. *I know*, he'd replied, bringing her out of her own leaden sky. Except Nicholas had Margaux to do that for him. He didn't need Skye.

Then Rose blushed, which she never did, and said, "I have something to celebrate too."

Rose's discomposure brought Skye out of her reverie. "What on earth is it?" she asked.

"Richie asked me to marry him and I said yes." Rose ducked her chin, unable to meet her friends' eyes.

"Marriage!" Joan exclaimed. "I thought you were wedded to diversions? Who'd have thought you'd be the one getting engaged . . ."

"And you'd be the one instructing men to fly Halifaxes," Rose finished. "War changes everything."

"It does," Skye said feelingly. "But this time for the better. Congratulations."

She kissed Rose's cheek, her eyes wet with tears, but glad she could get away with it in this instance. Rose's joy in love was as blindingly painful as staring at an eclipse. And Skye knew that love should be that easy, should create such radiance. Love certainly wasn't one person looking at another the way Nicholas had looked at her at the Embassy Club after Margaux had told him to dance with Skye. She withdrew her scarf from her neck and tied it over her hair, screening her face.

"Now we just need Skye to get what she most wants," Joan said.

Skye froze. Nobody could know what she felt for Nicholas. It was unforgivable for her to be in love with a man who was promised to another woman.

"I have what I want," she said, too sharply. "Flying. That's all I need."

Joan sighed. "War changes everything except Skye," she said, and Skye realized that Joan hadn't guessed anything of her feelings but was simply trying to find the romance in the situation.

Skye shifted closer to Joan and put her arm around her. "But it means you'll be leaving us," she said, and even she could hear her voice wobble.

"I will," Joan said, a smile on her face and tears in her eyes reflecting that this moment was both joy and sorrow, bittersweet.

"Remember the furs?" Skye said quietly. "From that first winter?"

Joan nodded. "I remember the furs."

"And the cashmere," Rose added. "We were like flying princesses."

"If princesses wore overalls," Skye said.

They all started to laugh at the same time, knowing they were far from being princesses, but that the richness of their friendship was worth more than a kingdom.

* * *

Summer turned to fall and there were more and more planes to deliver. They were so busy that Skye was surprised to hear her name and Rose's called over the tannoy at Hamble one morning, directing them to Pauline's office rather than to the hatch to get the delivery chits. There, they found Joan, who'd been recalled for what Pauline told them was a special operation. She handed Joan and Rose a chit to deliver Mosquitos to a nearby RAF base.

"Stay there for lunch," she told them. "You only have this one job today. Take as long as you need at the base."

"Why?" Rose asked, which was exactly what Skye was wondering. There was never time for lunch.

"I've chosen you both for this job because of your looks and manners," Pauline said, answering the question obliquely. "You have time to touch up your makeup before you leave. Efficient and pretty, please," she finished.

Joan and Rose hurried out, Rose looking bemused and Joan looking thrilled at being given express permission to beautify herself for the job.

Skye turned to Pauline. "I can see why you didn't choose me."

"If it were for looks alone, you'd be going with them. But I have another job that requires aptitude rather than manners."

"So I'm to take that one?"

"Yes, please."

"What exactly are Rose and Joan doing?" Skye asked, unable to keep the suspicion from her voice.

Pauline sighed. "Politicking," she said. "The squadron they're delivering the Mosquitos to has lost most of its men. As soon as new men join, they lose them too. Their CO asked if the ATA women could do something to boost morale. I wasn't sure your principles would allow you to provide the required bucking up."

Skye felt something surge through her: she wasn't sure if it was anger, despair, or if she was going to be sick. She'd thought Joan's new position as an instructor of the very largest planes meant that all the barriers between the men and the women had fallen. That they were being judged on talent alone now, not on whether they wore a skirt. But no; as well as flying every single plane in the RAF, often with very little training, and in all weather and without instruments, the women must also pretty themselves up to console the men. She *was* going to be sick.

As soon as she'd had the thought, she wanted to slap her own face. She was an awful person to begrudge the pilots who were fighting the war something that might make it a little easier to get back into an airplane tomorrow and face the prospect of death.

"Why?" she asked bleakly. She wasn't even sure what she was asking: why can't I be the same as everybody else, happy to flutter my lashes for the greater good; or, why does nothing ever change?

"Because it will buy us another month or two of simply getting on with the job," Pauline said. "It's *my* job to do whatever I can to make that happen. Yours is to deliver a Beaufighter to a squadron in the north. You don't have to smile. You just have to do a tight turn onto the airfield and take it down slowly. Make it spectacular, and easy."

Skye nodded, even though she knew there was more to it than what Pauline was saying. She took the delivery chit, found the Beaufighter and then she flew north, thinking only about roads and railways and landmarks and clouds—the substance of her days.

Once she'd found the base, she eased off the throttle and entered the circuit over the runway with a perfectly executed sharp turn, just as Pauline had requested.

There were no other planes flying there that day, and the pilots were sitting in a dejected clump close to the runway. Pauline had asked her to bring it in slow, so she dropped into a stall turn, coming in low over the men's heads, let down the flaps and the wheels and deposited the plane onto the ground as delicately as a butterfly.

As the roof was slid back and someone reached down to undo her straps, she heard a voice say, "Bringing in an ace test pilot to show us how to handle a Beaufighter isn't going to convince us to fly those beasts again."

"No, but *she* might," another voice said as Skye jumped to the ground.

All heads turned her way. It was something she was too used to now to be bothered by, but this was different. Two men were facing off over something. One was a squadron leader and another was the station commander. The station commander was smiling; the squadron leader speechless.

"I expect there won't be any problems flying Beaufighters now," the station commander said to the squadron leader. And to Skye, "Thank you, my dear."

My dear. If she was in the RAF, he'd never be able to call her that.

"Thank you for what?" she asked.

It took one of the engineers to tell her. Beaufighters, with their propensity to stall and their unpredictable behavior in tight turns, were notoriously difficult to handle. This particular squadron had found them so difficult that they'd refused to fly them. So Skye had been called in to show them that even a woman could manage it.

Even a woman.

Every one of her worst experiences at the ATA scudded across her vision: the test flight she'd had to undergo to prove she could fly, despite her logbooks; the medical examiner asking her to remove her clothes; the freezing flights to Scotland in open cockpit planes; the ten circuits she'd had to do in her Halifax just because she was a woman. For a moment, she hated flying, and never wanted to do it again.

She asked for directions to the bathroom. Once there, she stared at herself in the mirror, hands gripping the sides of the basin.

Why was she still fighting it? Nobody would ever look at her and see a pilot. They would see long hair, red lips and a skirt. And there were too many other things to fight right now. Her feelings for Nicholas. Her sister's continual attempts to push her away.

So she said nothing to Pauline when she returned to Hamble. The next morning, she didn't bother to pin up her hair so it sat at regulation length; she let it fall in long waves down her back. She just shrugged when a new engineer asked her where the real pilot was hiding when he slid back the roof of her plane. She went to a party with Rose and kept herself busy with eager pilots. It was so much easier to be what everyone wanted her to be: just a woman.

It went on like that for a few weeks until there was another night of movies and dancing at RAF Tangmere. As Skye walked into the sports hangar with Rose, a group of pilots charged like throttled-up Spitfires toward her.

"What are you doing?" Rose asked her.

"Enjoying myself," Skye said, unsmiling.

"Are you?" Rose snapped.

"Of course," Skye said, and quiescently accepted the hand of a pilot who led her onto the dance floor.

Nearby, Liberty and O'Farrell were dancing together. The way Liberty wriggled her body into his and kissed him insistently left nobody in any doubt that they were sleeping together.

Was her sister happy? Skye tried to examine Liberty's face as she swung around every three beats, but she was as hard to interpret as British weather was to forecast. The only thing Skye could be certain of was that Liberty either hadn't noticed her, or was doing her best to ignore her.

While Skye was dancing with perhaps the dozenth pilot, she saw Nicholas and Margaux enter the hangar. At the same moment, Skye realized that her mouth was being claimed in a kiss that tasted like surrender, and that she didn't even know the name of the man she was dancing with. Her head spun on a merry-go-round of champagne.

"Excuse me," she said, pulling back, but he didn't let go. So she continued to dance with him, held too tightly, because she couldn't recall how to escape.

That was the moment Liberty chose to look over at her. Their eyes clung together before Liberty turned back to O'Farrell.

When the music stopped, Skye was able to get away. She hovered at the side of the room near Liberty, hoping her sister might exit the dance floor too. And she did, nudging O'Farrell over to the bar and walking over to see Skye alone.

"I thought I'd come and stay a couple of nights with you next week," Liberty said by way of greeting.

Skye waited for the punchline. It didn't come. She said, "Why?" when she should have said, *That sounds great*.

"Why not?" Liberty said as she lit one of her black Sobranies.

"I'll make up the bed in the attic."

"I'll be just like Cinderella: relegated to the attic while my ugly sister has a room all of her own."

"I'm not giving up my room for you, Liberty," Skye said, suddenly so tired of these pitching and yawing conversations.

"Just your men," Liberty said, indicating O'Farrell. "Do you want him back?"

"I don't care about O'Farrell." As she spoke, Skye found her eyes drawn to Nicholas.

Liberty grinned. "I thought so."

Skye walked out of the hangar, knowing she'd just revealed too much to her sister. She didn't want to wait around to see what Liberty would do with the knowledge.

TWENTY-THREE

The anniversary of her mother's death the following week made Skye feel the same way it always did—as if she were falling off the earth, tumbling into a storm of sadness. She was thankful for only one thing—that she had the day off, because nothing hurt more than being in the sky on the day her mother had died.

But an empty day was so hard to fill with anything other than images of Vanessa Penrose: making porridge at the old stove in the kitchen, soothing Nicholas's blistered hands with aloe vera, giving Skye her old flying goggles as a parting gift before she left her daughters in Paris. Eventually, Skye closed her eyes in an attempt to stop the slideshow and sat on her porch and smoked.

Not long after, she heard footsteps approaching. Two sets. She opened her eyes to see Liberty and O'Farrell turning in at the cottage.

Liberty waved gaily and stepped onto the porch. "I could murder a cup of tea," she said before she let herself into the house.

Skye was about to say, sarcastically, *Hello. And, please, help yourself* when she saw Liberty turn and give O'Farrell a firm nod, as if prompting him to do something. In response, O'Farrell gave Liberty a sheepish smile. Then he dropped himself down to sit on the step beside Skye.

"I know that none of this makes me look good," he said.

Skye waited, curious to know what was going on.

"Back in New York I had a girl, you see," O'Farrell went on, voice low. "She and I would always invite my best friend along when we went out. They were close, but I thought it was good that they got along. It turned out they did more than get along. Seeing you and Crawford together that night..." He looked at Skye, humble for the first time since she'd known him. "I know there was nothing happening between the two of you. But it brought it all back. Which doesn't make it right. And then Liberty..." He stopped, and stared in bemusement at the door Liberty had disappeared through.

Skye almost felt sorry for him. He'd been swept up in Hurricane Liberty, a force it took great effort to extract oneself from. "You can say no to her," she told him gently.

"I've tried that. But she doesn't hear me. So it's easier just to..."

He didn't finish his sentence, and Skye felt a sharp twist in her stomach at the realization that so many of them were doing whatever was easiest because everything else was so damn hard.

"Besides," he continued, smiling a little now, "she's fun. And there's definitely a shortage of that around."

"There is." She touched his arm. "Come inside."

"I was going to wait for her at the pub. I thought you might be mad at me."

"I'm not mad."

He leaned over and kissed her cheek. "You're one in a million, Skye." She led him into the house and the three of them sat in the kitchen while Liberty told stories about people. Skye pretended to listen while at the same time marveling that her chameleon sister had come to visit on the anniversary of their mother's death and they were now gathered around a table and drinking tea, as if they rubbed along just fine together.

"Thank goodness the Ice Queen won't be around for a while," Liberty concluded.

"The Ice Queen?" Skye inquired.

"Margaux," Liberty said impatiently, and Skye thought she saw O'Farrell shake his head.

"She's been blessedly absent," Liberty went on, "so I haven't had to put up with any of her reproofs. I'm either too loud, or I'm in the way. Once she even tried to tell me I'd smoked the room up too much, when everyone knows she's the one who smokes more than every chimney in London."

"I didn't realize you had that much to do with her—" Skye began.

"Liberty doesn't have that much to do with her." O'Farrell broke in. "And especially not lately as Margaux's been assigned somewhere else for a while. Are we going to eat?" He stood up, stretching, and Skye watched Liberty devour his body with her eyes. "How about the Bugle? Come with us," he added to Skye.

"You go without me," Skye said. "And have a nice dinner together."

O'Farrell excused himself to the bathroom, and Skye took the chance to say one thing to her sister. "You're being careful, aren't you? A war isn't a good time to have a baby."

"We were both conceived during a war and we turned out all right," Liberty said glibly. "Well, you did. No one's quite sure if I have. Not even you."

Then, before Skye could get exasperated with that uninformative and provoking reply, Liberty said quietly, "Maybe I'd give all this up for a baby, Skye."

Never had her sister surprised her more, and that was saying something. Skye couldn't think what to say, knew only that her mouth had dropped open, and she was staring.

But as if it had all been a joke, Liberty added, "Maybe not. I was never the selfless one."

O'Farrell reappeared and the moment was lost. Skye knew only that Liberty hadn't answered her question, and it probably meant she couldn't answer it in a way that would please Skye.

Soon the cottage was quiet; too quiet, and Skye's thoughts were too loud. Had Liberty been serious? She couldn't have been. Why had she come if she'd meant only to have dinner with O'Farrell? And why had she chosen today to visit and then not spoken about their mother?

But nor had Skye said anything about Vanessa. Perhaps they'd both been waiting for the other to broach it. And Skye had squandered another opportunity to mend their relationship. *Tell me what to do*, she said silently to her mother. But no answer came. Vanessa had always preferred to let them work things out for themselves rather than offer advice. For the first time, Skye wished her mother had been different, as perhaps Liberty often did. What would it have been like to have had that fabled shoulder to cry on? What if Skye had given her shoulder to Liberty more often than just those nights in Paris?

Skye shook her head. She couldn't change her mother or the past and she was tired of asking herself unanswerable questions. So she went outside, hurrying down School Lane to the deserted beach. She sat on the sand and wrapped her arms around herself. The night was cool and she'd forgotten to bring a shawl. If only she could make a fire, as she'd always done on the beach at night as a child, when she knew nothing about blackouts or war.

Around her, darkness dropped slowly and then all at once, like the long fall of a dramatic evening gown. After a time, she heard footsteps and frowned. Surely Liberty and O'Farrell hadn't come for a romantic stroll by the water? It was hardly Liberty's style.

"Skye?" A voice she'd know anywhere.

And there was Nicholas, holding out his leather RAF jacket for her. She had to lift her head to see him properly and it was like the sudden and spectacular shock of seeing a moonbow—that once-in-a-lifetime phenomenon that only happened when the sky was a solid and unrelenting black, the moon full and low, and a mist of rain came in behind. Nicholas, her lunar rainbow, an accidental arc of brilliance set against her own dark secret.

"You're cold," he said, the gentle concern in his voice too heady for her.

She couldn't speak so she nodded, accepting the jacket, and then had to close her eyes against the warmth of his body still in the leather, the scent of him all over her.

He dropped to the sand beside her. "My op was canceled. I knew tonight would be hard for you. I had a petrol ration, so . . ." He shrugged. "I've always done something on this night to remember your mother. Once, I even made a bowl of porridge the way she used to make it." He stopped and ducked his head as if he were embarrassed.

If the tantalizing embrace of his jacket around her wasn't enough, his words just about undid her.

She risked a glance at him and regretted it instantly. He needed a shave and he looked as tired as she'd ever seen him, but it only made him more handsome, more Nicholas, more hers, and so much less the RAF wing commander who was engaged to another woman. How she wanted to place a hand on his cheek, to feel both stubble and warmth tease her palm, to stroke away his tiredness with her fingers. To curl up beside him while he slept.

She took off his jacket, no longer needing the extra warmth, and placed it on the sand beside her.

"Last year, I had to fly on this day," she said. "It was perfect weather. Too perfect. An hour into the flight, the clouds descended and I thought: this is it. Two of us vanishing into the clouds. But after only a minute I came out the other side. What had looked never-ending was only temporary. Right in the middle of it I saw St. Elmo's fire and it was like . . ." She faltered, unable to say it: it was like her mother. Vibrant. Alive.

"I've only seen St. Elmo's fire once," Nicholas said wistfully. "It was otherworldly. I remember Margaux said—" He halted.

"What did she say?" Skye made herself ask.

"Nothing. I've forgotten."

But he said it in such a way that Skye knew he hadn't forgotten. He didn't want to share whatever small intimacy had passed between him and Margaux in that moment in the sky watching something divine.

The warmth was gone now. In its place was the kind of coldness that embedded itself in one's bones and never thawed. Her toes ached with it. Her heart too.

And she saw it again, the thing she hadn't let herself remember: the flash of distaste on Nicholas's face when Margaux had told him to dance with Skye.

So she had danced with everyone else instead, trying to forget his recoil.

It was only fair that she explain.

She stood up quickly, so she could leave the instant she said it.

* * *

That night in the sky, Margaux had said to him: *When sailors saw St. Elmo's fire appear as tongues of flame atop their masts, they thought it was a good omen. Perhaps that's what it means for you too. That the war will end. That you and Skye will be together.*

The way she'd said it had made Nicholas believe, foolishly, that she was making a prediction. That, like Skye's mother, she was telling the future. The startling blue flame *was* like a promise. But of course he couldn't tell Skye that, which was why he'd stopped so abruptly.

And now Skye was standing up, his brusqueness driving her away again. He was about to reach out a hand, to apologize, to ask her to sit back down, when she spoke.

"I'm about to utterly embarrass myself," she said, eyes looking out to the horizon. "But I can't see you again and I need to explain why."

Nicholas stiffened. He wanted to stand up, to protest, but his limbs were bloodless. Not see Skye again? The idea was insupportable. He stared blindly at the horizon too, that fixed point by which one could tell if they were the right way up, just as Skye had always been his fixed point, keeping him the right way up. "Skye . . ."

She looked down at him and gave him a smile so sweet that his heart stalled.

"I know you won't want to hear this," she said, "but I don't think of you as my childhood friend anymore."

The minute she said those words he knew for sure that she'd seen him flinch when Margaux had suggested he dance with Skye at the Embassy Club. He'd hoped she hadn't because he realized it conveyed the exact opposite of what he'd meant. But if she no longer thought of him as a friend, it must be that she thought of him as something less than that. As a person who'd rebuffed her.

He wanted to tear the moon from the sky and extinguish it in the sea so she wouldn't see the agony on his face. "I was just—" he started to say. *Just trying to do the right thing*. The right thing in a wrong world. A world he alone couldn't change.

But she kept talking.

"I think of you as so much more than that. And I shouldn't." She stared ferociously at the sand. "Margaux, rightly, would never speak to me again if she knew. And neither will you once I tell you. Because the way I think of you now is . . . as a man. A man who I . . ." Her voice faltered.

Nicholas forced himself to stand, slowly, not wanting to do anything that might make her stop, or leave. The distance between them now was mere inches, the heat between her body and his was scorching. He willed her with his eyes to keep talking. It felt as if every single thing in the world had stopped and was waiting, breath held, for this moment that had been meant to come, that was here at last and was much too big for either of them to handle.

A long silence except for the sound of the water, clamorous against the sand.

Then she said, not blushing or whispering, her voice strong, her head high, every bit Skye, magnificent Skye, "I think of you as a man I want in a way I shouldn't want someone who's engaged to be married. A man I love more than anything. So I can't see you anymore. It hurts too much."

She breathed in sharply, then pressed on. "Goodbye, Nicholas. Be careful. And stay alive."

The moonlight falling on her face laid every part of her bare before him. And he saw it then, the pain. He had *hurt* her. Jesus, how could he?

"Skye," he said wretchedly.

Goddamn everything. He was always saying her name and then nothing else, keeping everything hidden just as everyone in bomber command and SOE expected him to. So many sentences started but never finished. So many moments with her over the past few months— the whole-body shock of finding her sunbathing on a plane in her brassiere, the torturous dance on the airfield, that exquisite second in the water when he thought his eyes had told her everything and she had maybe understood.

He almost cried with relief when she stretched an arm toward him, but she was only returning his jacket. He took it from her wordlessly, wanting to clasp the hand that had passed it to him. Wanting to utter some essential and unknown word that could undo all of this and redo them, together. But he said not a thing because he had signed the Official Secrets Act and truth was forbidden.

Faced with his muteness, Skye turned and ran back to the road.

The only thing left on the beach was the sharp and abrading sound of his breath in the otherwise silent night.

"Fuck." He threw the word into the void around him, but it relieved nothing.

He strode to the edge of the water and unbuttoned his shirt, took off his trousers, throwing everything onto the sand. Even the sea thwarted him; he wanted to dive straight in but it was too shallow. He strode out until it was deep enough that he could swim away from the sting of tears in his eyes, away from the feelings that she had and he had and which they could do nothing with, away from himself and away from her. His head hammered. The ache in his chest was diabolical.

He kept swimming. If he returned to the shore, he wouldn't be able to stop himself from going after her. From kissing her. From leading her back to her cottage, and up to her room and into her bed.

It was after midnight when he swam back in, put on his clothes and sat, wet and exhausted, on the sand until dawn.

PART EIGHT
KAT

TWENTY-FOUR

CORNWALL, 2012

Kat didn't know what to think as Elliott managed to get them both invited back to this other Margaux Jourdan's house for a cup of tea. She could barely take in the swashbuckling rope bridge over the lake, a bridge she knew her girls would love to adventure over; or the reclining stone maiden who looked so peaceful, as if she had exactly what she wanted; or the sundial surrounded by sunflowers and daisies, like miniature suns themselves. That there were two Margaux Jourdans who were most likely the same age and who had both said exactly the same thing made Kat feel as though she had walked out of reality and into a nightmare. The only thing that felt normal was Elliott's hand, gripped tightly in hers.

Inside Margaux's house, Kat perched on a chair and sipped a cup of horridly strong black tea. Margaux sat on the sofa, before leaning over to take a cigarette from a blue packet emblazoned with the word *Gitanes*.

As the woman smoked, Kat stared. There was something about the way Margaux held the cigarette that fired up the electrons in her brain, but not quite enough that they communicated a complete message. Words swirled in her head: furious words—*You're a liar*;

confused words—*That can't be your name*; sad words—*Who are you really, Margaux Jourdan?*

Thank God for Elliott, who was still capable of conversation.

"Can I ask you a few of the questions I wanted to ask when I called you last year?" he said to the woman.

Margaux moved her head—Kat couldn't tell whether she acquiesced or flinched—but her eyes didn't shift from Kat's face. Nor could Kat look away from her, even though she desperately wanted to disentangle herself from anything to do with this woman.

Elliott sat beside Margaux. "Were you commissioned into the WAAF as cover for your work with SOE during the war?" he asked gently.

Margaux inhaled deeply on her cigarette and scrutinized Elliott. "Is she your assistant? You've chosen a beautiful one."

Her voice was like Kat's grandmother's, accented indeterminately, but with more of an English circularity to her vowels.

Elliott didn't rise to the bait. "Of the two of us, Kat is the one with an assistant. We're spending the day at the house that adjoins your property. A house owned by Kat's grandmother, also called Margaux Jourdan. What a coincidence."

Kat waited for the woman to react, which surely she must. But it seemed as if the news that another Margaux Jourdan happened to own the house next door was a matter of unconcern.

The woman stubbed out her cigarette, reached for another, then seemed to think better of it. "The property adjoining mine is abandoned, has been for decades. But in answer to your question: yes, I was commissioned into the WAAF. I did work for SOE. That's hardly worthy of a writer's interest."

Kat was suddenly relieved. This must be the Margaux Jourdan who'd had the life Elliott had almost made her believe had been her grandmother's. But . . .

It really had looked like Kat's grandmother modeling Dior gowns in the photo Elliott had shown her and the program notes said that mannequin Margaux Jourdan had worked for the WAAF. And her grandmother had admitted her own connection to the WAAF when she talked about packing parachutes. So perhaps the woman sitting in front of Kat now had stolen Kat's grandmother's name? And her history? But which history? The one Elliott had described or the one Kat had grown up with?

"Where were you born?" Kat asked sharply.

"Where were *you* born?" the old woman said. "Why do you have the right to find out about me when I know nothing about you?"

"Australia," Kat replied, hoping her truth might force the same from the woman's mouth.

"Australia," Margaux repeated. "So far away." The way she said it implied more than distance.

"What do you mean?" Kat said pleadingly.

The woman frowned. "It's late. You've taken me by surprise. Come back tomorrow at ten. I'll talk to you properly then."

* * *

Kat's mind was spinning as she and Elliott walked away, past a yard full of chickens, then a row of beehives, and finally alongside the lake with the rope bridge.

"That was unbelievable," she said at last. "What's going on?"

"I don't know," Elliott admitted. "Do you think we can make ourselves comfortable at your grandmother's house tonight so we can be here again in the morning? I'll go into Porthleven and buy some food. And I'll definitely get us a bottle of wine. Then we can talk about it properly."

Kat nodded, grateful that Elliott had come up with a plan. All her mind could focus on right now were those shocking words: *I'm Margaux Jourdan*. She managed one question. "I don't suppose two women called Margaux Jourdan worked for the WAAF?"

"The records only show one."

Of course.

As Elliott drove away, Kat climbed the stairs and told herself to forget about both her grandmother and the woman next door until dinner. Instead, she inspected a couple of rooms before settling on one with an incredible view over the ocean.

In a wooden box still smelling of lavender she found sheets that, once she'd taken them outside and given them a good shake, were relatively free of dust. The bed had been covered with an old bed-spread, which had kept the mattress clean. She tore up another sheet and used it to wipe over everything, even giving the windows a rub. As she worked, she heard Elliott return and soon a delicious smell of food filled the house.

At last she sank into the window seat and admired the room, which looked cozy and inviting now. The window was gently curved and let in the smell of the ocean. The bed was decades old but, set against the floorboards and the antique dresser with its comb and mirror set, and made up with the clean white sheets, it looked like something from an interiors magazine.

Why do you have this house? her mind asked over and over, as if her grandmother could somehow hear her. Who had owned the brush and mirror set, the jewelry?

On impulse, she stood and opened one of the wardrobes in which the Dior gowns were kept. She searched until she found the one she wanted. A soft red this time, carnelian, its brightness tempered by the satin, which caught the shadows, deepening the skirt's hue to garnet. Aladin the dress had been called when it was first shown in 1947. It had perplexed some with its apparent simplicity, its echoes of a housecoat, but its deep V-neckline was anything but homely and its belted waist and full skirt were undeniably feminine.

She changed into it, wanting to feel closer to her grandmother after the day's events had made it seem that Margaux was moving further away.

Kat jumped when she heard Elliott. "You look like you're miles away," he said, leaning in the doorway and smiling at her.

"I was," she confessed. "Sorry, I've left you down there cooking while I've been daydreaming in window seats and trying on dresses as if I'm Cinderella."

"I mean this as a compliment: you're no Cinderella." He walked over to her and stroked her hair.

In jeans and T-shirt, barefoot, with dark stubble on his face, relaxed and so obviously and unselfconsciously himself, Elliott looked even better than he had in his tuxedo the other night. Or perhaps that was just because Kat knew him more intimately now, knew that everything inside matched or bettered the promise of his striking good looks.

She slipped her arms around him, smiling too, running her hands up his back. "I suppose we should eat," she said. "I don't want to ruin the dinner you've made."

"I suppose we should," he murmured reluctantly. "But we are definitely coming back up here after dinner. And I am definitely taking off my T-shirt."

She laughed. She loved the way he always tried to make her feel better, while at the same time accepting her confusion and her fear, loved the way he sensed and sensitively considered her feelings.

She took his hand and followed him downstairs where she found he'd done the same as she had in the bedroom: wiped down the table, washed the old crockery and cutlery, and set everything out in such a way that it looked like something from a magazine spread.

She sat down, sipped the wine, then tried the lamb salad, which tasted of coriander, ginger and a hint of chili.

"It's very good," she said appreciatively. "Almost good enough to make me forget what happened this afternoon."

"It must be good then," he said, sipping his wine too. "I'm kicking myself for not coming down here earlier in the year. When I called her she told me she was forty years too young to be the woman I was looking for, and I believed her. Why would anyone lie? But if I had come, I wouldn't have found your Margaux. Which means I wouldn't have found you," he added with a brief smile that made Kat's stomach leap.

She realized that, in spite of the attraction she felt for him, they'd passed the whole afternoon and evening attuned to one another in a tender way rather than a sexual way. For a relationship that she'd thought simply a fling, it confused her. She'd liked coming downstairs and seeing how thoughtful he'd been about dinner. She liked sitting with him now, talking. She liked that he was with her while she was feeling so unnerved about her grandmother. But those were the kinds of things that happened in a relationship, and what she had with Elliott was anything but, surely—she was only in the UK for ten days.

She touched his hand and he threaded his fingers with hers, waiting, giving her the space to think and to say whatever she needed to, not letting his research and the questions he must have take over from her feelings.

"I guess the question is: which one *isn't* Margaux Jourdan?" she said quietly.

He nodded.

"Part of me wants to believe the woman we met today is lying," Kat said, trying to sift through the worry and apprehension she felt. "Then my grandmother can remain who she's always been to me: Margaux Jourdan. But that still isn't a satisfactory answer because the Margaux

Jourdan I believed my grandmother to be and the Margaux Jourdan you've described are two different people. So, either way, it means my grandmother lied about something. And I don't know why."

"Maybe your grandmother didn't lie. Maybe she just couldn't talk about the past."

"Because of the concentration camp," Kat heard herself say, even though she was afraid to know more. But if there were women in her past who had spied for their country, risking their lives, didn't she owe it to them to be a little bit brave? "Can you tell me about it now?"

Elliott clasped his hands under his chin and leaned his elbows on the table. "Margaux Jourdan was captured by the Nazis in July 1944. Just after D-day, in the most bitter irony. Freedom was so close, but not for her. At the time, German outrage against the Resistance was at its height and Margaux was sent to a place where she would never be found. Ravensbrück concentration camp. Have you heard of it?"

Kat swallowed and nodded. "I don't know much about it though."

"Most people associate concentration camps with the Holocaust. But this was a camp for women." Elliott spoke slowly and quietly, as if he understood how hard it was for her to hear this. "Some were Jewish. Many were resistants, or other so-called undesirables: gypsies, communists, prostitutes. There were Poles, Frenchwomen like Margaux, just twenty British women and a few Americans too. It was a very long time before anyone realized the camp existed, and even longer before they realized SOE agents had been held there. The women in the camp were gassed, beaten, shot, worked to death, and deprived of almost everything a person needs to survive. It was a place of slow extermination, a historian once said."

"That's awful," Kat whispered. "Why...why were the SOE women sent there?"

"Some because of bad luck, and some because of their superiors' incompetence. It wasn't until September 1944, not long after Paris was liberated, that the section of SOE responsible for agents dropped into France knew it was missing one hundred agents out of the four hundred it had sent over."

"But that's a quarter of them." Incredulity rang in Kat's voice.

"I know. The Executive Director of SOE said, not long before D-day, that it was inevitable that the organization would suffer a huge number of casualties in France."

"But they sent the women over anyway?"

"They did." Elliott frowned and pushed his wineglass away. "And, what's worse, they dropped the women into circuits known to be compromised."

"What do you mean?" Kat asked tremulously.

"SOE ignored suspect radio transmissions from their agents, which should have alerted them to the fact that the Nazis knew of the circuits' existence and that some of their agents had already been captured. SOE kept deploying men and women into France, letting them walk into what was, in effect, a trap. Some of the women caught by the Germans were taken to Ravensbrück."

Kat studied Elliott's somber face. "What else? I have a terrible feeling there's more . . ."

He nodded. "It gets even worse. You're sure you want me to keep going?"

It was Kat's turn to nod.

"Everyone at SOE thought the missing agents would be held by the Nazis in regular prisons," Elliott continued. "That after France was back in Allied hands, they'd be set free. In the case of the women, it was a crazy assumption to make because the women had been commissioned into civilian organizations in Britain—not military—meaning they had no wartime status. The Nazis had no obligation to treat them as prisoners of war so of course they didn't. In the meantime, SOE convinced itself that if they just waited long enough, the agents would turn up somewhere in France. None of them did."

Kat shivered. "They didn't go looking for them?"

"Not only that, but they refused for a long time to publish the names of the missing or to alert the Red Cross to look out for them. Margaux's name, and Liberty and Skye Penrose's names, would have been on that list if it had been compiled. But circulating the names would have meant admitting women had been used as spies. It was apparently more important to hide that fact than to find them. And when Vera Atkins—who was in charge of SOE's women—asked the Foreign Office for information about a camp she'd heard of called Ravens-brück, the only information they gave her was that Ravensbrück was relatively unknown and there were no British prisoners there. This was in April 1945. One month later, the first female British prisoner from Ravensbrück arrived at Euston Station. All those blunders meant that Ravensbrück and its victims were left out of our war history."

"Which is why I don't know much about it."

"It's one reason why." Elliott looked across at her, checking again to see whether she wanted him to stop.

Kat finished her wine. "And the other reasons?" she asked. "I need to know."

"Let's sit over there." Elliott indicated the seat by the window through which the ocean rolled inexorably on. "I feel like you're too far away across the table."

She followed him to the window seat, curling into his side, feeling his arm hold her tightly to him. She rested her head on his shoulder as he spoke.

"The French and British women at Ravensbrück were young, mostly in their twenties," he told her. "The commonly held belief was that *men* were the lifeblood of the Resistance so, after the war, people didn't understand why these women had been taken to a camp. The other commonly held belief was that women in camps were raped by the Germans—which many were—and no young woman in her twenties wanted to be seen as 'soiled goods.' Ravensbrück had taken so much from these women; they didn't want it to take their reputations too. So they said nothing.

"Then the Iron Curtain came down and Ravensbrück was trapped on the wrong side. Nobody—historians, journalists—could reach it. Research became impossible; all the records were burned after the war. The Germans even threw the ashes into the lake, so eager were they that nobody learn what had happened behind the electric fence, hidden in a pine forest. I've been there and it is haunted. You can hear the dead crying out their despair—and their anger."

Kat saw, suddenly, water, drowned ash, a scream rising from the lake. She shivered.

Elliott had stopped speaking. He cleared his throat, perhaps seeing something similar to Kat's strange vision. She couldn't imagine what it must have been like for him to have visited the place where so much violence and injustice had been inflicted upon so many women.

After a moment, Elliott began again. "Since I visited Ravensbrück, it's been my personal mission to write about the women who were held within the camp walls. I've been using Vera Atkins's scant records. Unfortunately she kept most things in her head, not on paper, but she was the only one who tried to find the missing. And even she wasn't allowed to go to Germany for her investigations until December 1945—months after the war was over. So much information was lost between the end of the war and her trip to Germany. Luckily, I've been able to speak to a couple of the women who were imprisoned at Ravensbrück—most of them are dead now, so it's difficult to get firsthand accounts. At first, they denied they were there. Then they begged me to write about something else. They all say Ravensbrück was too horrific to ever be written about."

Too horrific. Oh God.

"And my grandmother was there?" Kat's voice was as thin as hundred-year-old voile.

Elliott nodded, and Kat tried her hardest not to cry. Margaux needed her strength, not her tears.

"Margaux Jourdan, along with a baby, was saved in April 1945 when the camp commandant let the Swiss Red Cross into Ravensbrück," Elliott said. "That was almost a year after Margaux was imprisoned there. The Red Cross were able to take some of the French prisoners out to safety. Being French-born, Margaux and the baby she'd given birth to in the camp were handed over."

Kat tried to picture having a baby in a place like the one Elliott had described, but she couldn't. She remembered the births of Lisbet and Daisy; both had taken place in a hospital, with midwives and doctors in attendance, essential oils burning, everything clean and sterile and with all of the medical equipment needed should anything go wrong. She'd had her own room, with a double bed, and Paul had stayed with her for a night or two.

"Vera Atkins recorded a visit she made to Margaux Jourdan in France in July 1945." Elliott kissed the top of Kat's head, but shifted his focus to the window and Kat could tell he was seeing the words he'd read about her grandmother, rather than the view beyond. Then he looked down at Kat, compassion in his eyes.

"Like the other women from Ravensbrück who Vera saw at that time, Margaux was terribly changed," Elliott went on. "Vera wrote that she estimated Margaux weighed around seventy pounds. Her head had been shaved in the camp, and scurvy and other . . . things . . . had left her body bruised all over. But what you have to remember, Kat, is that despite being imprisoned in a camp built for the sole purpose of stealing one's spirit and then destroying the body left behind, Margaux left Ravensbrück alive. One hundred and thirty thousand women passed through Ravensbrück. Up to ninety thousand of them died. Margaux didn't."

"Oh God," Kat said, wiping her eyes, trying to imagine her grandmother so deathly thin. And ninety thousand women dead. How must her grandmother have felt, witnessing death on such an inconceivable and colossal scale? How could it ever have been allowed to happen?

She stood up, walked to the far windows and touched a hand to the glass. Behind it was near-darkness: dusk and a dark blue sea.

"My mother died a week after giving birth to me," she said, and hardly heard Elliott's sharp intake of breath. Even though she had no real affection for her mother—how could you have affection for someone you had no recollection of?—the story was still hard to tell. The story of a mother who could have been, if only.

Kat made herself continue, going back further in time to a safer part of the story. "She was a doctor, doing her residency at a hospital in Sydney. She fell pregnant with me—a fling with a doctor who wanted nothing to do with a child. He's never been in touch with me, and my mother never told Margaux his name—I suppose she thought she'd have plenty of time to do that later, after I was born, if he decided to become involved. Anyway, she worked right up until the birth, trying to prove herself, which was what you had to do if you were a woman in medicine, especially back then. So I thought maybe it was overwork and excessive fatigue that caused it." Kat pressed her lips together, breathed in, pushed away the tightness in her throat and the sting of tears in her eyes, then kept going.

"She died of cardiovascular complications from childbirth. I became obsessed with it for a time when I was studying medicine, looking up all the risk factors—she had none besides the fact that pregnancy puts the heart under more strain. But women with congenital or other preexisting heart conditions are far more likely to have cardiovascular complications. And there's so much research now that shows a link between fetal malnutrition and heart disease in adulthood. I'm guess-ing a baby born at Ravensbrück wouldn't have been well-nourished. Margaux always said that my mother was somewhat sickly, not as strong as others. She took her to lots of doctors, but sometimes heart problems are overlooked if there are no obvious symptoms. And now all I can think is that she probably died because she spent the first months of her life in a concentration camp." Her voice trailed off.

"Kat, I'm so sorry." Elliott was beside her now, arms trying to shelter her from the unrelenting past. "I can't believe you're still speaking to me. All I've done is throw your life into chaos, and you've already had more to deal with than most people ever will. I should let all this go."

Kat shook her head. "How would you even begin to do that? You have to write about Ravensbrück. And Margaux. And the others—the Penroses. It's all connected somehow. There's a reason why there are two women who live virtually next door to one another using the name Margaux Jourdan. And as one of them is my grandmother, I need to know what that reason is."

She paused, took a deep breath and pointed to the photos laid out at one end of the table. "What are they?"

"Something I was thinking about while I made dinner," Elliott said.

Kat followed him back to the table, where he gestured to a picture. "This is the one I showed you already, of Margaux Jourdan dancing with O'Farrell. And this," he passed her a different image, "is another taken that same night, of Liberty Penrose dancing with O'Farrell. One of the things I've been trying to work out is whether Liberty was at Ravensbrück too. On her last mission into France for SOE, she went missing. In Vera Atkins's interviews with Ravensbrück prisoners, Liberty Penrose's name is mentioned by a couple of women. The British were kept quarantined and separate so Liberty wouldn't have had much contact with others. But when Vera asked Margaux if either of the Penrose sisters were at the camp, Margaux said no. That they were both killed in France on the night Margaux was taken. But that doesn't make sense. Liberty wasn't working with Margaux, and she went missing at least a month before Margaux did."

"I imagine being at Ravensbrück would make anyone's mind a little hazy on the details." Kat examined the picture of the smiling woman and saw that her body was pressed against O'Farrell's in a manner that suggested a definite intimacy.

"One of the women I spoke to can recall with absolute clarity what she saw at Ravensbrück," Elliott said, leaning against the sideboard, hand rubbing his jaw as if he were thinking something through. "And she mentioned Liberty Penrose. That might be important to us because Liberty's mission to France would have been her last, even if she hadn't been captured: she was pregnant. Vera Atkins's records show that she told Vera the father was a pilot."

Elliott picked up the photograph of Liberty and O'Farrell. "After you and I spoke at the Savoy, I went back to a memoir written by an ATA pilot, Rosemary Rees, who was friends with Skye Penrose. She talks briefly about O'Farrell throwing Skye over for her sister. Rosemary's somewhat brutal about Liberty; she says Liberty flaunted her relationship with O'Farrell more openly than was the custom back then, leaving no one in any doubt that it was sexual. And she says nothing about a relationship between O'Farrell and Margaux Jourdan."

Elliott paused before he reached the conclusion his words were hurtling toward.

Kat felt herself being drawn in to the picture of Liberty. Blurred and faded as it was, Liberty's face looked vaguely familiar. And Kat had always been told that her grandfather was an American pilot called O'Farrell.

"You're going to tell me it's possible Liberty could have had a baby in January 1945, aren't you?" Kat said. "That it was actually Liberty and her child who were rescued by the Red Cross, and Liberty took another woman's name."

She couldn't make herself say the rest: *That my grandmother might be a woman called Liberty Penrose.*

TWENTY-FIVE

Which was the worst outcome: that her grandmother was Margaux Jourdan and she'd omitted to ever mention that she'd once been a spy who was imprisoned in a concentration camp? Or that she had never been Margaux Jourdan at all?

Kat desperately wanted the first of those statements to be true now in a way she never had when Elliott had first proposed it to her. Somehow, in seeking to prove that her grandmother was a different Margaux to the one Elliott was looking for, Kat might now have uncovered a far greater deception.

She braced herself against the table and felt Elliott's hand on her back, offering solace. But solace was unattainable.

"We should find out if the Margaux next door has children," Kat said forlornly. "If she does, then *she* could be Liberty."

"Come here." Elliott wound his arms around her and she buried her face in his shoulder, trying not to cry.

"We can ask her tomorrow if she has children," Elliott said, thumb stroking Kat's cheek. "But I didn't see any photos of children in the house."

And nor had she. Most people had pictures of their kids on prominent display.

Kat drew back a little, enough that she could speak but not enough to leave the circle of Elliott's arms. "What about Skye Penrose?" she said, searching for both a distraction and further information that might lead them down another path. "You said she went missing too, so what happened to her?"

"That's the biggest mystery of all. Nobody recalls a woman called Skye Penrose at Ravensbrück."

Of course. More questions without answers. She tried one final path. "How does any of this have anything to do with the dresses upstairs? The House of Dior and concentration camps are as opposite as heaven and hell."

"I've been thinking about that," Elliott said. "When you're researching, everything you read goes into your head but if you don't think it's relevant to what you're doing, sometimes it takes a while for you to make a connection. I'm almost sure I came across the name Catherine Dior in the list of Ravensbrück prisoners. It didn't mean anything to me at the time, but I'm wondering now if . . ."

"Catherine Dior was Christian Dior's sister. That I do know."

"Well, maybe that's our connection. I can look through my papers in London and see what I have. Or do a quick Google now if you want."

Kat shook her head. "I feel like my brain is about to explode right now."

Elliott touched a gentle hand under her chin and kissed her. "Let's go for a walk."

It was a good idea, she realized, as they picked their way down to the sand in the moonlight. A breeze was blowing, not too strongly, but enough to whisk away some of the worry and the fear that had lodged in her stomach.

They walked hand in hand for a while, not really speaking other than to comment on something that caught their eyes: the gentle dance of the waves, the opening of what looked like a cave in the cliff face, a bird racing home for the night.

The sea air cleared Kat's muddled head somewhat, enough to

make her ask one of the questions that was nagging at her. "Is it really possible to become someone else? You certainly couldn't do it these days."

"I think it might have been possible then. The end of the war was chaos. There were two million Allied prisoners returning from POW camps, and processing and thoroughly interrogating them was the priority. There's a story that just one debriefing used nine pounds of paper. Imagine if, in the middle of that, a woman appeared without any papers and said she'd worked for a secret British organization that nobody knew about. Remember that hardly anyone knew the British were using women as spies. The U.S. Army picked up one of the SOE women who'd escaped from Ravensbrück and they wrote in a memo that she was unbalanced and must be impersonating somebody. Luckily Vera Atkins saw that memo and knew it was one of her women."

Elliott stopped walking and faced the ocean. "But what if there was another memo Vera didn't see? What if another woman turned up with a story that a different army unit thought was 'unbalanced'? The camp commandant at Ravensbrück went on record as saying that no British women were at his camp. What's an Allied officer supposed to think if a woman like Liberty appears, claiming to have been sent to France, to have been at Ravensbrück, and to be British? Maybe it was easier to pretend to be French. Some of the SOE women used their French code names at Ravensbrück. They were used to pretending to be someone else. Their lives depended on it."

A wave crashed noisily near their feet and clouds robed the moon, stealing all the light, as if the night were grieving for the women Elliott spoke about too. "At least one of the women was misidentified for some time," he continued. "Sonia Olschanesky, who died at Natzweiler concentration camp, was for a long time thought to have been another agent, Nora Inayat Khan. Quite a few survivors looked at Vera's photos of Nora and confirmed that Nora had been at Natzweiler, and that she had died there. But it turned out to be Sonia, not Nora. Much later, Vera discovered that Nora was shot at Dachau in 1944."

Kat closed her eyes. So many concentration camps. So many women who'd lost their lives trying to end a war. And so much confusion over who they were, and the part they played in the defeat of the Nazis in 1945.

"Okay. So maybe it was possible." Kat opened her eyes and stood beside Elliott as the full moon reappeared, gently lighting both their faces and the sea. "But why keep up the deception once everything had settled down?" Now she was searching, not just for a way to disprove the hypothesis that Liberty Penrose was her grandmother, but also to understand: not just what these women had done, but why they had done it.

"Some of the Frenchwomen tried to speak of and write about what had happened to them at Ravensbrück," he said. "But publishers told them nobody was interested in reliving those miseries, that everyone wanted to move on. To forget. Relatives accused them of making up stories, insisting such things couldn't possibly have happened. I'll never forget reading about an American diplomat who visited the women when they returned to France; he wrote that they were 'a convoy of martyrs, frightfully mutilated, skeleton-like—a terrifying spectacle.' So the women held on to everything that had happened to them, either because nobody wanted to hear it, or because it was too terrible to say aloud."

The empathy in Elliott's voice caused tears to fill Kat's eyes again. He cared about these women he'd never met; he felt for their silence, their trapped and unspoken horrors.

"Imagine discovering, after you'd returned from such a place," he went on, "that the Allies had decreed in 1944 that no camps should be liberated because it would mean too much confusion, too many displaced people who would get in the way of winning the war. Imagine discovering that you could have been rescued earlier except you were considered to be an inconvenience."

Elliott drew Kat toward him, the back of her body anchored against the front of his, his arms around her waist. She leaned her head back against his chest as he spoke again.

"And imagine trying to reconcile living for months in a concentration camp—being tortured, starved, beaten—with what came after the war," he said. "The government propaganda insisting that women must return to the home and cook roast dinners for their men. That they need only be decorative. Then the New Look. It must have seemed unreal. Imagine trying to fit back into that world."

Kat understood what he meant. Christian Dior's New Look—those feminine dresses, the punishing corsetry—was her metier. She remembered telling Annabel about the women whose twenty-inch waists had been a grim result of rationing throughout the war. What of those women who hadn't had the luxury of rationing; who'd been at the mercy of a camp commandant, and given the kind of food nobody would contemplate eating today?

She and Elliott turned to one another at the same time, not just embracing but holding on, their bodies so close that Kat could feel his heart beating against her chest, could feel something so deep and profound pass between them that it both awed and frightened her. She reached up and kissed him, hoping he wouldn't think she was forgetting the women they were speaking of; she could never do that. But right now she needed to remember that, as well as hate and pain and despair, other things existed in the world.

He seemed to understand, because he gathered her in, hands gripping her back, mouth moving against hers as if this moment was all there was. As if history and the past did not, for now, exist.

They returned to the house with the intensity of their embrace on the beach still blazing between them and they didn't even reach the stairs before Kat's dress had dropped into a pool of red silk on the floor, with Elliott's clothes beside. They made it as far as the window seat before Elliott sat down, drawing her onto his lap, and she braced one hand against the window as she made love to him with a passion she'd never felt before.

* * *

Kat woke the next morning with her head on Elliott's chest. Diamond light, almost colorless, a brilliant silvery-white, spilled through the window. The clock on the bedside table, which she'd wound the night before, told her it was nine in the morning. Nine? She never slept in until nine. And she'd never slept on anyone the way she must have slept on Elliott if the location of her head was anything to go by.

She felt a hand stroke her hair and realized that he was awake too; that he hadn't been moving because he hadn't wanted to disturb her.

"Sorry," she said, about to roll away.

"Stay," he murmured. "Just where you are. It's nice."

And it was. So nice to lie in a quiet house beside a man who caressed her back with one hand and her hair with the other. But they had somewhere to be. "Aren't we due to see Margaux at ten?" she asked.

"We are," he said reluctantly.

They climbed out of bed, and Kat pulled on another of her grand-mother's delectable dresses: the Zelie cocktail dress from 1954. It was plain enough for daytime, its collared neckline and the six buttons on the bodice mimicking a jacket. The waist was typically accentuated, before the silk fell into a simple flared skirt. Kat wanted something that would give her the courage to ask the woman next door the questions she was too afraid to ask her grandmother.

But Margaux, relaxing in a chair with a cigarette and a cup of tea, the blue and white Gitanes packet balanced on the arm, pounced first.

"You said yesterday that your grandmother has my name. Isn't that a crime?" she said, hardly waiting for Kat to sit down.

Kat froze. What if it was? What if her grandmother really was, as Elliott had hinted last night, Liberty Penrose, and she had stolen this woman's name? Kat had no idea what to say.

"Should we go to the police?" Elliott asked, and the way he asked it made Kat understand that he knew Margaux would refuse.

"No need for that," the woman said. "Your grandmother wanted to be someone else after the war. I sympathize. Do you have a photograph of her?"

Kat scrolled through her phone and found a picture of her grandmother holding her two great-grandchildren.

Margaux gave it a glance, nothing more. "I've never been to Australia. Never likely to. I suppose that's why."

"Why what?" Kat asked.

"I'm old," Margaux said, answering a different question. "Too old to go flying around in planes anymore."

Elliott stared at her. "Anymore? You've flown a lot then?"

Margaux stared back like an owl, unblinking, marking its prey. "No more or less than most people my age. I have been on holidays, you know."

This time it was Elliott who pounced. "You were friends with Skye and Liberty Penrose."

There was the smallest of pauses, but Kat noticed it and she was sure Elliott had too. Margaux squished her half-smoked cigarette into the ashtray.

"I knew them," she said.

"You knew them well, I understand," Elliott continued. "Rosemary du Cros, formerly ATA pilot Rosemary Rees, wrote in her memoir that she often went out with a group that included an English pilot, Richie Jenkins, two American pilots called O'Farrell and Nicholas Crawford, and Skye and Liberty Penrose."

Kat sat forward in her chair. Margaux's demeanor had changed; she was prickling with ... what? Definitely alertness. Fear too? Curiosity?

Margaux shrugged. "What if we did? They're all dead."

"Nicholas Crawford isn't dead," Elliott said.

"So, two of us survived. But we haven't kept in touch. Like passing clouds: fair-weather friends brought together by storms and circumstance. Now, it's high time you two left. I have work to do. A tourist attraction like these gardens doesn't run itself."

"But you haven't answered any of our questions," Kat said, her frustration ringing through the room. "You told us yesterday that you'd worked for SOE. But who are you, really?"

"Have you asked your grandmother that question?" was Margaux's well-aimed counterstroke.

How can I do that? Kat thought desperately. *How can I hurt the person I love most in the world?* Yet she'd been happy to ask the question of the woman sitting opposite her. To dig into the sediment of painful things long buried because of her own selfish curiosity. How many people was she hurting? Herself, her grandmother, this woman too.

Then Elliott said, "Can I take a look at this?" He picked up a gold pocket watch that sat on the mantel above the fireplace.

"No, you cannot," Margaux snapped, snatching it from him. "It's time for you to leave." She shooed them out of the house.

Neither Kat nor Elliott spoke on the way back to the cottage. She was lost, and she supposed Elliott was too, in a skein of thoughts that unraveled into too many loose threads.

Back at the cottage, Kat packed the blue dress, whose twin she had at the museum in Sydney, into a box lined with acid-free paper. Then she and Elliott collected their things and began to drive back toward civilization.

Not long after they left, Elliott said slowly, "She talked about flying. About clouds. As if she knew them better than most."

Kat tried to remember that part of the conversation. "I'm not following."

"Skye Penrose was a pilot. A pilot would know about flying and clouds."

"You're not..." Kat groped for what Elliott was trying to say. "You're not trying to suggest that the Margaux we've just spoken to is really Skye Penrose? I mean, did she really say enough to make her a pilot? Aren't clouds often used as a metaphor? *I wandered lonely as a cloud* ... See, even a scientist like me remembers that."

Elliott sighed. "You think I should stick to nonfiction, rather than trying to make up stories where there are none?"

"I honestly don't know. Yesterday we thought one of them was lying. Now you're saying..." Her voice trailed off.

"What if they both are?" he mused. Then he added, "I don't think lying is the right word. Like I said last night, maybe what happened to your grandmother and the woman we saw today was so awful that, afterward, neither of them wanted to be who they were anymore. It's possible that Cornwall Margaux is Skye Penrose and ..."

He paused, and she knew he didn't want to hurt her by saying it aloud, just as he'd held back from saying it last night.

"And my grandmother is her sister, Liberty," Kat finished bleakly. "They own houses side by side, after all."

She stared out the window, at the dreariness of the motorway and the cars. "What happened to the real Margaux then?" she said. "You told me her boss, Vera Atkins, interviewed Margaux Jourdan after the war, so did she disappear after that or before? And if it was before, wouldn't Vera Atkins have noticed she was talking to a different woman? It's a long bow to draw that this other Margaux in Cornwall is Skye Penrose just because she said something about clouds."

Or that my grandmother is Liberty Penrose just because she was pregnant with a baby at the right time. But Kat knew that the bow in that case was about the right length.

"There's something else," Elliott said. "It's the pocket watch. I think that watch once belonged to a man named Nicholas Crawford. I have a description of it, and the one on Margaux's mantelpiece seems, from the quick glance I had of it, to be the same. I mentioned Nicholas Crawford earlier—he and Skye Penrose were . . . very good friends. Such good friends that it's entirely possible she might have his pocket watch."

"But why would sisters be so estranged?" Kat asked. "Why would this Margaux seem so indifferent to a photograph of my grandmother, a woman you're saying is her sister, Liberty?"

Elliott rubbed his jaw. "I've dragged you into this mess and all I have are more questions than answers. I don't suppose asking your grandmother if she's Liberty Penrose is a very sensible idea?"

"Does it make me a complete coward if I say that I don't want to? My grandmother is more than ninety years old. Sudden revelations over the phone are all very well for the stout-hearted but . . ." Kat shook her head. "I'll ask her when I'm back in Australia and I can be there for her, especially if it unearths memories of somewhere like Ravensbrück."

"I understand. I have a grandfather I'm very fond of and I'm not sure I'd feel comfortable asking him those kinds of questions over the phone either. Let me think about what to do next. I'll look back over everything I've gathered so far and see if I've missed something."

For the rest of the drive, Kat felt something turning over in her mind; something that had been bothering her since the day before when they'd first met Margaux. She couldn't say what it was, just that she felt as if something obvious had been shown to her and she hadn't been paying sufficient attention. But no answer revealed itself.

* * *

When they reached the outskirts of London, Elliott asked, "Do you need to get back to the hotel? I have a standing arrangement to have lunch with my mother most Sundays, and Juliette, my daughter, comes too. We've missed lunch but I have to pick Juliette up from my mother's—she stays with me on Sunday nights. But I can drop you back to your hotel first if you'd prefer."

"I don't mind," Kat said truthfully. She had nothing else to do in a hotel room by herself except fret over her grandmother.

Not long after, Elliott parked the car outside a home in Hampstead. They both climbed out, glad to stretch.

The door opened when they were halfway up the path and a woman appeared, beaming. "Elliott, darling." She embraced Elliott with warmth and affection.

"Hi, Mum." Elliott turned to Kat. "This is Katarina Jourdan, but I think you can call her Kat."

Before Kat could hold out her hand, the woman swept her into an embrace too. "It's a pleasure to meet you. Please call me Aimée."

Kat smiled. "I hope you don't mind me coming along."

"Of course not. I have far too much cake inside and I need someone to help me eat it."

As they entered the house, Elliott asked his mother, "How's your hand?"

"Almost there. Only another week of this blasted thing." Aimée pointed to a cast poking out from under her sleeve. "I broke my wrist," she said to Kat. "A silly fall. I've had to do everything with my left hand and it's driving me mad. I can't wait to get back to being right-handed."

Something flashed in Kat's mind again and she almost saw it this time, except a teenage girl stepped in front of her and stared.

"This is my darling granddaughter, Juliette," Aimée said.

Juliette rolled her eyes and Kat couldn't help smiling.

The girl flung herself at her father. "Dad! You've been ages. I had to have lunch without you."

"Yes, it's been a trial of Tudor-ish proportions," Aimée said mock seriously. "Someone's ready to lose their head after having to make it through lunch without Elliott there to interpret Juliette's various facial antics and monosyllables."

Elliott laughed and Juliette glared. "So, you've been pleasant company then," he said to his daughter, kissing her cheek, and Kat saw Juliette's mouth twitch at her father's joke, then quickly straighten before anyone could see.

"Yes, I must brush up on my knowledge of *The X Factor*," Aimée said. "After your last visit, I've been listening to nothing but Pink and Beyoncé, but now it seems I must progress to reality television."

Kat laughed. "I'd give anything to be listening to Pink instead of the Wiggles," she said. "I have a three-year-old and a five-year-old."

"How delightful." Aimée beamed again as if she didn't have the slightest problem with her son dating—was that even the right word to describe their relationship?—a woman with two very young children. "You must show me a picture of them."

With that, Kat was swept into the parlor, which was all paneled wood walls and antique sideboards and delicious Louis XV settees, and a cup of tea—herbal and delicate rather than muddy and awful— was placed before her. She exchanged more pleasantries with Aimée while Juliette regaled Elliott with a story that involved a lot of expressive arm waving and a roller coaster of vocal expression.

"She should definitely be an actress," Aimée said, glancing at her granddaughter.

Juliette's eyes rolled so wildly that Kat wondered if they might fall out. "The *last* thing I want to be is an actress," she said scornfully. "I want to be able to eat."

"Kat has degrees in science and medicine, and another in conservation," Elliott said to his daughter. "You should chat to her about science careers. Then you might be able to put something more specific in your careers assignment than you want to do 'something science-y.'"

"Conservation?" Juliette's expressive eyes widened. "Does that mean you get to touch mummies?"

"Only their clothes," Kat said. "I'm a fashion conservator, so my expertise in Egyptian artifacts is limited. But I'm very happy to chat to you if you want to."

Juliette shrugged, the moment of interest gone, and her fourteen-year-old aloofness reasserted itself.

Aimée stood up. "Juliette, give me a hand to bring out the cake."

"I'll do it, Mum," Elliott said.

His mother batted him away. "You have children so they can wait on you," she said. "Talk to Kat. Juliette can help me."

Aimée reached for the teapot with her right hand, then stopped herself and switched to the left. And the thing that had been eluding Kat finally sharpened into focus.

As Juliette and Aimée walked into the kitchen, Kat spoke. "Right-handed," she said slowly. "Margaux Jourdan is right-handed."

Elliott shook his head, clearly puzzled. "What do you mean?"

"Your mother," Kat said, trying to explain, "she went to pick up the teapot with her right hand. Most people are right-handed. But Margaux—Cornwall Margaux that is, not my Margaux—smoked all of her cigarettes with her left hand. In the photograph you showed me of Skye Penrose, she's brushing her hair back from her face with her left hand. If she were right-handed, the natural instinct would be to use her right hand. And in the photograph you showed me of Margaux Jourdan in 1944, she's smoking a cigarette with her right hand."

"I left the folder in the car," Elliott said, anticipation in his voice. He paused, as if thinking. "You've just made me remember something else. In all the oral histories where Margaux is mentioned, everyone talks about her refusal to smoke anything other than Gauloises. They were a symbol of patriotism for the French people during the war. Whereas Rose, Skye Penrose's friend, said that Skye preferred Gitanes even though they were hard to come by in England. The woman we spoke to today . . ."

"Smoked Gitanes," Kat finished. More evidence that the woman they'd spoken to that morning in Cornwall might once have been called Skye.

"I'll have to see what other photographs I have of Skye Penrose. Perhaps they'll confirm that she *was* left-handed. But what about your grandmother? Is she right-handed? Or left?"

"She's always used both," Kat said. "We used to laugh about it: she sews right-handed, writes with both, but eats the left-handed way with her fork in her right hand and her knife in the left." Then she added hopefully, "So maybe my grandmother really is Margaux Jourdan and not Liberty Penrose. Maybe she did have a love affair with O'Farrell, even if nobody can recall it."

"You know," Elliott said, reaching for her hand, "it doesn't matter what your grandmother's name was. None of it changes the fact that she raised you and loved you and that you love her. She's still the same person."

Kat tried to blink her tears into submission. Elliott was right. Her grandmother was still the wonderful person she adored, even if her past was a story she'd never told Kat.

As Elliott stroked away a tear that had escaped, Kat felt her heart squeeze at the way he put her feelings ahead of delving into this new line of inquiry for his book. Without thinking, she said, "I'm going to miss you when the mystery is solved."

He kissed her, so softly, so exquisitely. And Kat felt something shift. It was as if the knowledge had dropped over both of them that they hadn't talked about their end, but it was coming.

Elliott touched his forehead to hers. "Kat," he said, "I need to show you something. Something I should have shown you before now." He stood up. "Let me arrange for my mum to have Juliette for a bit longer."

He disappeared into the kitchen, leaving Kat to wonder what on earth he meant.

TWENTY-SIX

The drive to wherever they were going was awkward. Was there a word for the anticipation of bad news? Elliott would know. But she didn't want to ask him, not when he looked so serious.

They drew up outside an aged-care facility.

"Why are we here?" Kat asked at last, unable to bear the silence.

"I need to show you something."

It was what he'd said to her at his mother's house, but it told her nothing. At least he took her hand, for which she was grateful.

At the front desk, the nurse smiled at Elliott. "He's in his room," she said. "He'd had enough of the noise in the sunroom."

"Thanks."

Elliott led the way down a clean and sunny corridor lined with colorful paintings and dozens of snapshots of children and dogs and family groups, and black-and-white pictures of brides and grooms. Everything was bright and cheery, but Kat could somehow sense sadness.

He pushed open a door and said, "Hi, Grandpa," to a man in a chair.

The man looked at him blankly.

"I brought you some cake." Elliott held out a container, which Kat hadn't even noticed he was carrying. He handed it to his grandfather, along with a fork. The man smiled as if it were the best thing he'd seen in a year.

Kat ached that he hadn't had that same look on his face when he'd seen Elliott.

"I'll put the telly on for you," Elliott said and his grandfather nodded.

While his grandfather ate cake and the television roared applause for teams of footballers, Elliott indicated to Kat that she should sit in one of the other armchairs.

He sat beside her and said, "This is Nicholas Crawford, my grandfather. He has dementia. He's had it for quite a few years now."

"I'm really sorry," she said softly.

"I've been looking for Skye and Liberty Penrose, and Margaux Jourdan, for selfish reasons too," he continued. "I'm hoping to find Skye Penrose in particular, for my grandfather."

"Why?"

"My grandfather and Skye were in love during the war. Really in love," Elliott said, emphasizing that last word as if he were expert in the emotion. "The once-in-a-lifetime, cinematic-type love that you don't think exists until you see a couple like Josh and D'Arcy. But Skye was captured during the war and she vanished. And my grandfather, Nicholas Crawford, had a child with someone else."

"Then he obviously wasn't as in love with Skye Penrose as you think," Kat said, anger building in her as she began to understand that Elliott had lied to her. It was the one thing she never wanted a man to do to her again.

"I'm not explaining this very well." Elliott ran his hand through his hair, awkward for the first time ever, as if he could see not just her anger, but her hurt and her disappointment too. He tried to take her hand but she pretended she needed it to smooth the collar of her dress.

"When I was young," he went on quickly, "just a little kid, Grandpa would take me out every Sunday. We spent the mornings together, often at the seaside, digging in the sand, collecting shells, searching for crabs. We also went to air shows and Grandpa would tell me what it was like to fly. One day when we were watching an air show, the sky filled suddenly with old airplanes, ones that were used during the war. And Grandpa looked so sad I thought I must have stepped on his toes. I couldn't think of any other reason, back then, for anyone to look so sad other than physical pain."

Elliott's grandfather interrupted. "You don't have any cake," he said to Kat. Then, to Elliott, "Let me hug you."

Kat saw Elliott's eyes shine and understood that, in the one sentence, his grandfather had returned.

But no sooner had Elliott stood up to embrace his grandfather than Nicholas Crawford said to Kat again, "You don't have any cake."

Elliott hugged his grandfather anyway, despite the fact that he had vanished. Then he sat by Nicholas's side while he picked up his story.

"When I asked him why he was sad, he told me about a woman called Skye whom he'd loved more than he'd ever thought it was possible to love anyone. That she'd flown planes too, but she'd died during the war. After that, every time we went out together he'd tell me something else about Skye. That she was the best swimmer he'd ever seen. That she could cartwheel like a falling star. One day, when I was older, around twelve, I asked him how she'd died. He told me about the war. That SOE believed Skye had been caught by the Germans, but nobody knew if she was killed when she was captured or if she was sent to one of the camps. Nicholas spent years searching for her. Eventually he came to believe that Skye was dead, because if she were alive she would have come to find him. They'd promised themselves to one another. He cried then. You can't imagine what it's like to see your grandfather cry."

Elliott stopped talking and Kat felt her throat tighten with sorrow despite her disinclination to be drawn in by the story. Yes, she could imagine exactly what that might be like. Her grandmother had cried in front of her only that one time and it had almost broken Kat's heart to witness it.

"As I got older I spent less time with him," Elliott continued slowly, as if managing the emotion behind his words. "I didn't visit him every Sunday because I was busy and more interested in my mates. I forgot all about Skye. When Grandpa started to show signs of dementia, I tried to see him as much as I could, but it wasn't until he moved in here and we spent a weekend clearing out his house, going through his things and deciding what to keep and what to throw away—God, how does anyone ever decide which pieces of a life to throw away, especially a life you can see slipping away before your eyes?—that I found something. It was like a diary he'd written about the war. And I suddenly understood that what he'd felt for Skye was that rarest of all things: true love. And I wondered if perhaps he was wrong, if maybe Skye hadn't died, if there was any chance at all that she might be alive. I'd done enough research by then to know how many people disappeared after the war and were thought dead but were later found alive."

He paused, eyes fixed on his grandfather's face. Even Kat could see his eyes held in them another kind of true love.

"You can see what he's like," Elliott went on. "A body without a mind. But sometimes he has flashes of lucidity. It's not that I ever thought finding Skye would heal him, but if he was to see her and remember her for even five seconds, wouldn't it be worth it? Doesn't a man like him, who has so little happiness, deserve five seconds of it?"

Kat felt her eyes spill over, tears running down her cheeks. How could anyone not be moved by what Elliott had said?

But there was also the knowledge that everything he'd done had been for his own reasons. His personal crusade to find a woman called Skye Penrose in the scant hope that his grandfather, a man with clearly advanced dementia, might remember her. On the one hand it made Elliott a sweet and loving grandson. But it also made Elliott a man who had seen how much Kat was hurting from the revelations of the past few days and who had still lied about his reasons. She'd told him from the start how much she couldn't stand to be lied to. So why hadn't he just told her the truth from the outset?

She knew the answer to that: because gathering information for a book celebrating brave and courageous women had seemed important and essential. Now his motives seemed self-centered and insensitive.

You hurt me, she wanted to say. Instead she stood up, swiping more tears from her face. "I'm going to catch a cab back to the hotel."

"I didn't mean to lie to you, Kat," he said, standing up too. "I didn't know that this—us—would happen."

I didn't mean for any of this to happen: that was what Paul had said to her when she'd asked him for a divorce. She was, yet again, an unintended consequence of a man's thoughtlessness. The worst part was that she'd thought Elliott was different; honorable. But perhaps he wasn't.

"Have you actually written any of this book you told me you were writing?" she asked. "And do not lie to me again."

"No," he admitted.

Kat walked out.

She'd reached the footpath when Elliott caught up to her. She spun around, prepared to let fly with exactly what she thought of him right now when, rather than offering more excuses, he pushed something into her hand—an old book, its cover dog-eared, its binding split.

"Will you read this?" he said. "I know there's nothing I can say right now. I've hurt you so much and I'm so, so sorry. But if you read this—the diary my grandfather wrote about him and Skye and the war—then you might understand."

"I will never understand why you did this, Elliott," she said. Then she walked away.

PART NINE
MARGAUX

Will they ever know how I died? A dress riddled with bullet holes, stained with blood, one more name crossed off the camp list: that is how we learned the fate of the others who disappeared into the night.

—Geneviève de Gaulle

TWENTY-SEVEN

The Dior family home—Villa Les Rhumbs—is pink and gray. The gardens are pink and gray too, matching the house like a debutante and her partner. Blooms of pink hydrangea, the silvery leaves of lavender, the delicate pearl-gray of snow-in-summer flourish beside the external walls of the house, which are blush pink—the color of the sun's first morning kiss upon the sky. But the gray is—as gray can only ever be now—brutal, the color of hunger and loss, the echoes of screams trapped in its spectra.

The sea laps timidly at the edges of the cliff below the house. Yesterday—Margaux's first at Les Rhumbs—it was, thankfully, blue. Today it is gray and she has to avert her eyes.

Then gray dusk reaches down from the sky and stains the air all around, so Margaux sits, shivering, on the floor in the baby's room, wishing she too could release everything in a violent paroxysm of infantile screaming. The mirror on the wall hurls her reflection back at her: skin eaten away by lice and draping strangely over her bones with no layer of fat beneath. She is all angles and protrusions, as meanly shaped as a truncheon. Her head is shaven; only a scrape of dark brown covers her round and startling baldness. Her legs are so bruised from scurvy that they are colored purple and her eyes bear the hemorrhages of that same disease.

On the way to Les Rhumbs, people turned from her as they would a monster. She is inhuman; it is impossible to imagine she might ever have been loved.

Only Catherine Dior understands, because she feels the same. Her brother Christian, is kind too, kinder than Margaux could ever have imagined a man might be when faced with two such as she and Catherine have become.

Thankfully Catherine—or Caro as Margaux and Christian call her—comes to find Margaux before the shivering takes her over and she plummets back into the past that she cannot believe is really over.

"*Chérie!*" Caro cries, rushing over, huddling close to her the same way they had crowded together on the bunk for eight long months—although there had been three of them then. "*Chérie,*" she says again, this time in a whisper. And then she holds Margaux despite the fact that Caro's head is bald too, her body similarly lacking anything besides skin and bone and bruises, despite the fact that Caro shivers at night too.

Margaux remembers the laughing woman she had met in Paris who used to always speak of flowers and she hopes that Caro will one day describe a lily-of-the-valley to her again: how small and fragile and white it is. Not because it will make Margaux feel better, but because it will mean that Caro is better. If Caro gets better, then perhaps Margaux will also.

"I'm sorry," Margaux says as the shaking lessens.

"I didn't keep down any of my lunch today," Caro says in response and Margaux understands what she is saying: that she too has failed at being normal.

The shivering stops at last.

"We will build a pyre in the garden, on the clifftop," Caro says in the most solemn of voices. "We'll burn everything."

Margaux nods and follows her out to the clifftop overlooking the

Chausey archipelago, where islands scar the surface of the ocean and the sky is bruised by livid clouds.

They gather wood, so much wood, and they strike a match to it. Flames leap hungrily upward.

They cannot burn anything physical from Ravensbrück because they left behind them in Switzerland what little they had. Instead, they place their memories onto the fire—everyone tells them, insistently, that they must forget, that their story is too weighted down with pain to be held within the fine contours of language. But memories are as insistent as the lice at Ravensbrück: puncturing the skin, burrowing in, emerging with renewed vigor at every attempt to fight them off.

So the pyre is the means by which they will reduce the past year to ashes. Onto the fire go the peacocks, the red flowers, Block 10, the Bunker, the canisters of Zyklon B, the Kinderzimmer, the children playing the game of gas chamber selection, the sound of a shovel striking a skull.

They throw on the predawn roll calls, and death by *appell*—the slow freezing to death of bodies during the long winter roll calls— and *la chasse*—the daily hunt down the Lagerstrasse for anyone offensive—which was everyone—to satisfy the target set by the Nazis of two thousand dead each month.

They add to the flames the ferocious jostle each morning for the very few latrines, and the smell of those latrines—fetid and overpowering at first, then hardly discernible amid so much that was rank.

They throw on the ash and odor of scorched flesh billowing from the crematorium, their hunger—not even hunger, the craven emptiness— their hunched shoulders, the need to be small, tiny, invisible.

They stoke the fire still more with the terrible understanding that nobody knew Ravensbrück existed, that they really had been as lost and invisible as Camp Commandant Suhren had said.

Catherine and Margaux hold hands, their two bald heads like

pagan moons attesting to their lack of faith and trust and hopes and dreams. They cast the wishes they once had onto the pyre.

The fire spits, not yet sated.

The first person they give to the flames is Skye. The smoke rises immediately, taking off, letting her fly up and up to the place that was always her home.

Nicholas is next. What he did to Skye goes on the fire too, followed by Skye's broken heart.

On goes O'Farrell, and the baby he never had a chance to be a father to.

They pause when they get to Liberty. Does she deserve to be swallowed at last by fire? Or should her reckoning be to have no epilogue, but to forever bear the soul-breaking burden of what she did?

They turn from the fire, which, like them, will forever remain unsatisfied.

PART TEN
SKYE

A handful of heartbeats. That was what life was. A heartbeat followed by a heartbeat. A breath followed by a breath. One moment followed by another moment and then there was a last moment.

—Kate Atkinson, *A God in Ruins*

TWENTY-EIGHT

ENGLAND, MARCH 1944

Over the long stretch of months into 1944, as more airplanes were built and mustered for an invasion of Europe, for Skye there was only one thing: flying. But so much flying meant so much time alone, time for her to recall the strict politeness, or even boredom, on Nicholas's face when she'd poured out her heart to him. His silence had been the worst thing of all.

Each morning, she put on a shirt under her flight overalls, then her scarf, then a coat buttoned up to the neck, trying to replace the skin Nicholas had peeled away with his disinterest. She piled blankets on her bed at night and woke up stifling, but at least she wasn't so monstrously exposed. When she flew, she wished for an enveloping canopy of lenticular cloud to surround her, but the skies were blue and clear.

Nicholas did exactly what she'd asked him to: kept as far away from her as he possibly could, probably to save both himself and her from any more embarrassment. But she carried with her the everlasting wound of his indifference.

Until one day in March 1944 when Pauline told her she'd been asked to report to a War Ministry building on Portman Square in London.

"What for?" Skye asked despairingly. "What have I done now?"

"I don't know," Pauline said, concern apparent in her frown. "I've done my best to find out but nobody's talking. Try not to worry. Surely you know by now that I won't let anything happen to you."

Skye managed a small smile. She supposed she did know that. But it didn't make her feel any better as she caught the train to London and the Tube to Marble Arch and walked to a columned mansion house on Portman Square, apprehension coating her nerves like high-altitude frost.

She was promptly whisked down a hallway, past rooms with closed doors, and then behind another closed door, where she found Air Marshal Wylde, of all people, waiting for her.

"Captain Penrose," he said, nodding at her. "Please take a seat."

Skye did so without a word. She had none at her disposal.

"Tea? Coffee?" Wylde asked.

"Tea, please," she managed.

They waited, both silent, for the tea to be made and poured and for the woman to leave.

At last Wylde seated himself too, but instead of speaking, he studied her. She did the same to him, noting that he had a severe face, not unattractively so for someone who must be close to fifty, but as if it would be a challenge for him to relax his countenance into affability. His hair was silvered and his bearing authoritative, but when he had sat down, he'd moved with an agility Skye remembered from when he had danced with her mother.

"It's come to the attention of certain people," he said at last, sipping his tea and then leaning back, eyes still on her, "that you could easily pass for a Frenchwoman. You speak fluent French, your gestures are French, and you lived in the country for years. You also have a cool head in times of trouble. Of course," he added thoughtfully, "I already knew all of that, but now it's been pointed out to others. Thus, here we are."

"What on earth has my latent Frenchness to do with anything?" Skye asked, bewildered.

Wylde's smile was sudden and warm, but quickly erased by melancholy. "You are so very like her. You probably don't know that—there isn't anyone left to tell you. Except me."

"You mean my mother," Skye said, voice a whisper.

"Yes. Vanessa Penrose. With whom I had the misfortune of having a similar conversation about twenty-five years ago."

Fortune-telling, feather-and-black-silk-nightgown–wearing Vanessa Penrose in a room like this? Skye shook her head. If she had never seen her mother dancing with this man, she wouldn't believe any of it.

"I don't suppose you have any whiskey to go with the tea, do you?" she asked hopefully. "I'm not sure where this conversation is going, but something tells me that tea won't have quite the kick I'll need."

Wylde actually laughed. "I'm sure I can find something to trick up your cup." He moved to a sideboard and held up a bottle of Scotch. "Will this do?"

Skye nodded. He poured a decent slug into her cup and she swallowed rather than sipped. "Go on," she said.

"You must be aware, especially after our last conversation, that the War Office organizes clandestine operations into France."

"What does that have to do with me, or my mother?"

Wylde sighed. "Vanessa was far too good at dissimulation. Or perhaps she really did become just a mother and a fortune-teller."

"Just?" Skye snapped.

"I didn't mean that the way it sounded." Wylde poured himself a Scotch, neat. "If you'd known your mother during the Great War, you might understand why I find it so hard to imagine her as content to parent two small children and predict futures for narrow-minded Cornish villagers."

"And what did my mother do during the Great War that was so very impressive?"

"She began her working life as a typist in the Intelligence Office. But Vanessa was always the kind of woman who attracted notice and it soon became apparent that she was smarter than most, that she spoke fluent French and could handle herself well. My . . ." He hesitated for the first time since Skye had entered the room. "My brother and I were intelligence officers. He felt she might be more useful to the war effort in a capacity other than typist."

"Is intelligence officer a euphemism for spy?" Skye asked, wondering if she'd drunk too much Scotch.

"In a way. And everything I'm telling you is still classified as most secret. Which means you cannot repeat it." He sipped his Scotch and added, "I suppose a lot of things would still be secret if there hadn't been another war."

"You're not suggesting that my mother . . ." Skye stopped. It was preposterous. Yes, Vanessa had always been elusive about Skye and Liberty's father, but that was the way of the world. It was utterly shameful in the eyes of almost everyone that Vanessa had borne two children out of wedlock; no one then expected her to broadcast the details of the swine who'd seduced her and abandoned her. Except that Skye had never quite believed that version of whispered events. Why would her mother have gone back to the so-called swine; why would she have taken the risk of falling pregnant again? Now Wylde was suggesting that the omissions and the mysteries ran far deeper.

"Your mother did some work in France for the Intelligence Office during the Great War, Skye. My brother, as well as teaching her to fly, was her liaison officer, and Vanessa worked with my sister, who lived in France. They were the golden threesome: the two women in France sent information to my brother in London, who passed it on to the War Office to make sure our military tactics were based on more than hearsay."

Skye wanted to drink the Scotch straight from the bottle. How was this possible? She shivered, trying to recall anything of her childhood, any conversation with her mother, that would indicate it was true.

"Are you sure you want to hear the rest?" Wylde asked, rather gently.

"No. But I think I have to. You should probably take the Scotch away though or I might soon be too drunk to listen."

He allowed himself a smile as he put the bottle out of her reach. "The thing of it is, Skye . . . you are, in fact, my niece."

Niece. Which meant . . . "Your brother?"

He nodded. "Sebastian was married. It was an arrangement, I suppose, the way things were done between families like ours. Select a woman with the right background and make a promise when the children are young, a promise that ends in marriage. Being the second son, such decisions weren't foisted upon me. But if I'd been the eldest and they had been . . ."

His last words were wistful and Skye's stomach contracted. She knew the sound of a person who loved someone they couldn't have.

"You were in love with your brother's wife," she said. "And then he took up with my mother. While he was married, I assume. How you must have hated my mother."

Wylde didn't hold back. "I did. I didn't care that she was helping to save our country; she was also ruining a marriage. A marriage that was, I now see, already ruined by bringing together two unsuitable people, and made worse by Marie—Sebastian's wife—proving to be barren. There wasn't even the distraction of children."

"Except for those your brother had with my mother. Two more reasons to hate her."

"Yes."

Skye tried to picture this other version of her mother: in love with a married man; not scrupling to think of his wife, or to remove herself from temptation; throwing herself headlong into an affair that had resulted in Skye and Liberty. How history repeated itself. Here was Skye, in love with a man who had promised to marry another. But Skye hadn't done what her mother had; Skye had acceded to temptation only in her mind. Maybe living with the kind of danger her mother had lived with made one take whatever one could from life—what would be the point of dying if one had never loved?

Skye shut her eyes for a moment, before refocusing on Wylde. "You never looked as though you hated my mother when you came to our house in Cornwall. What happened to your sister? And your brother?"

"My brother," he said, and she could feel the weight of the word on his tongue. "Vanessa and Sophie, my sister, went missing. It was thought they'd been captured. Sebastian flew his own airplane into France to find them. I didn't know at the time, but Vanessa had already given birth to you and was pregnant again with your sister. Whenever she was away in France, you were cared for by a nurse Sebastian had employed."

So Sophie really was Skye's aunt. But... "Your brother died on the way, didn't he," Skye said, knowing that was how it must have happened. Everyone involved with her died in the great blue sky.

"He did. At least, he vanished. The weather was filthy. He most likely got lost in the cloud and was shot down somewhere. The day after he disappeared..."

Wylde stopped, and Skye sensed that he was capable of deep emotion, and he was feeling it in that very instant.

"Your mother and Sophie reported in," he went on. "They were fine. The nearest wireless transmitter had been blown up and they'd had no way of communicating with us. Sebastian needn't have gone after them. I imagine he would have waited a few more days if he hadn't known that Vanessa was..."

"Pregnant again with his child," Skye finished for him. "How you must hate us too, his children, for costing him his life."

"I did hate you both, just as I once hated Vanessa—but hate doesn't get you anywhere, does it?" He sighed. "After the war, Sophie stayed on in France. She'd been very close to your mother, as close as sisters, and didn't blame her at all for what had happened. She told me that Sebastian was his own man and made his own decisions, that he was the one to blame, not Vanessa."

"And she promised my mother to look after me and Liberty if anything happened."

"Quite right. After spending several years being angry at Vanessa, I went to stay with Sophie in France for a week or two. She neglected to tell me that Vanessa and her children—you and your sister—would be there also. I was furious at first. But then I realized Vanessa was one of the only people I could speak to about my brother—she'd known him properly. So after that, I went to see her occasionally, to remember. I should have done more for you and your sister though. You're my nieces, for Christ's sake."

He touched Skye's arm, then withdrew his hand uncertainly. In that gesture, she understood that she now had another family besides the women at Hamble. It almost made her smile.

But there was, still, the most important question, which lay all around them unanswered.

"Why are you telling me this now?"

He stood, moving away, and spoke with his back to her. "It's thought you could help the war effort the same way your mother did. I'm not at all sure that I shouldn't try to dissuade you. But we need more women. It's getting harder and harder to send men over; they're too conspicuous. Most Frenchmen have either been prisoners of war since 1940 or have been sent to Germany on forced labor programs. Women attract far less suspicion. It's just damned hard to find ones who speak French well enough, and who seem French enough not to give themselves away within five minutes of being over there. We've had to take on a couple whose trainers raised doubts about their emotional control but, as their Frenchness was beyond doubt and we can't lose this bloody war . . ." His sigh expressed his frustration. "Well, nobody could afford not to use them."

He turned to face her, his expression troubled. "I have no doubts about your self-possession; you've more than proved yourself in the ATA. If you agreed to all this, you would join the Special Operations Executive, or SOE as it's known. Duties generally involve sabotage, working with Resistance circuits, and gathering and passing on information between those Resistance circuits and HQ in London. The agents are flown into France on full-moon nights by Lysanders, whose pilots are based at Tempsford, where you arrived by accident eighteen months ago. I'm responsible for all the Special Duties squadrons in the RAF, of which that is one."

Nicholas. Her breath stopped, her heart clenched like a fist. Nicholas flew spies into France. If something went wrong with his plane and he was captured by the Nazis . . . She shuddered.

"You look as if you need more Scotch," Wylde said. "I didn't mean to shock you quite so much. You can certainly refuse."

"It's not that." She shook her head and, unbelievably, the words came out. "Nicholas Crawford is . . ." *The man I love.* She caught herself just in time. "A good friend. I had no idea he was in so much danger."

"Ah." Wylde took up the bottle and poured her the healthiest slug yet. "I didn't know that."

He was kind enough not to press her, but she knew she hadn't hidden anything from him. Which would make her a terrible spy.

He waited while she drank deeply, as if the Scotch were water. Her head was already spinning so much the Scotch did little more than burn her throat.

"Would you like to meet someone who can tell you more?" Wylde asked.

Could she give up flying for this? How could she not? *We can't lose this bloody war*, Wylde had said. What kind of person would it make her if she refused to give the kind of help that was most needed?

The heat from the Scotch was suddenly doused by ice-cold fear and she felt that same terrifying immobility suffuse her just like it had when the Messerschmitt had shot at her. No breath. No pulse of blood. Nothing beyond her eyes riveted to Wylde's face. And one thought: there were a hundred ways to die in an airplane in the sky. But there were a million ways to die as a spy in Nazi-occupied France.

But Nicholas flew there all the time. He didn't sit like a mute and self-centered idiot thinking only of himself. Her heart just about burst right then with how much she loved him.

She managed one long, deep inhalation. What of all the people who had died since 1939, all the people who were yet to die with every day the war went on? "Do you think I can do it?" she asked Wylde.

He didn't hesitate. "Yes. And part of me wants you to do it because if you're as good an agent as you are a pilot, I have no doubt we'll win. But I also know that if I let you go, I might never see you again. And I would," his lips pursed as if the words hurt to say, "regret that very much."

Skye felt her hand reach out to take his. He squeezed it, holding on, and her own mouth skewed to the side, everything inside her hurting too. "I think I have to," she said.

He nodded. "I think you do too." He let go of her hand and stood up. "I'll take you to meet Vera Atkins. You'd report to her if you choose to work with SOE."

Skye's limbs unfolded and she managed to stand, despite the quantity of Scotch she'd consumed, the new history she'd learned, and

the new future that threatened like a distant thundercloud, and walk
in a relatively straight line behind Wylde.

He was about to tap on a door along the corridor when it opened
and Nicholas and Margaux walked out.

Skye stared at them.

Margaux smiled.

Nicholas stopped still. His eyes, dark blue with sudden fury, blazed
at Skye. She flinched.

"No," he said, face hard.

Wylde stared at Skye, and then at Nicholas.

"No," Nicholas said again. "No."

* * *

Seeing Skye again, so close he could reach out and touch her, almost
had him staggering backward at the realization that everything he felt
for her had only intensified over the months of absence, and also fighting every instinct in his body that wanted to draw her in and kiss her
like he'd never before kissed anybody. Even breathing was difficult;
the shock of being just two feet away from her like flying into a fire
rainbow—dazzling.

Then it hit him: a body blow against his heart. She was at SOE headquarters. Which meant only one thing. They wanted to recruit her.

"No," he said. Because then it might be Skye shot dead on a field in
France right before his eyes, and he would have to climb back into his
plane and leave her body there. He would *never* be able to do that.

"No," he said again. It came out even more forcefully and he saw
Skye step away. He had never punched anything in his life, but right
now he wanted to punch the wall.

Then he caught sight of Margaux's face and he knew. She had
brought them all to this place.

He hadn't understood why he'd needed to come with her to SOE headquarters today. He never went there; his dealings were all through the RAF. But Margaux had said it was to do with their cover story so he'd driven them both down from Tempsford. But Vera Atkins hadn't seemed to know why they were there and Margaux had apologized and said something about having the wrong day and he had been about to ask her what the hell was going on when she'd opened the door and there was Skye.

"You can't," he managed to say. *Take my hand. Let's go. Anywhere. Together.* And he saw his hand actually reaching out to take Skye's, before he caught himself and recoiled, just as he'd shied away the night at the Embassy when Margaux had told him to dance with Skye.

Skye's face twisted into an expression he'd never seen on her and never wanted to see again: hard and hostile, as if he'd stolen all of her joy. He stood silently watching as every one of her feelings for him erupted into loathing, one more beautiful thing ruined by war.

"I can," she said, and she stalked into Vera's office and shut the door.

TWENTY-NINE

On the train back to Southampton the following day, Skye thought about two things. That she now had an uncle. Someone to perhaps spend Christmas with. To talk about her mother with.

Her mother. She was the other person Skye thought of. She imagined the life Vanessa Penrose had led: a life of secrets and danger and excitement and, obviously, love. Then, once the war ended and her services were no longer required, she had moved to Cornwall with two daughters and a broken heart, which must have been one of the most difficult things of all.

And now here was Skye, nursing a similarly broken heart, but she had only herself to care for, not two small and needy children who craved love and attention. And the man she loved was still, for now, alive.

It was only as she cycled back to Hamble that she thought of Margaux emerging from a room in a building that obviously housed intelligence workers. If Skye's suspicions were correct, Margaux had recommended her to SOE. For them to have taken her recommendation seriously, it meant that Margaux wasn't working for the Women's Auxiliary Air Force, but for SOE.

None of it changed the fact that Margaux was engaged to Nicholas, who had spoken to Skye at SOE headquarters with so much anger, as if he hated her. Perhaps telling him she loved him—giving him that burden—had been unfair of her. He certainly, at best, seemed to resent her for it.

She cycled faster, along the pathways of frail England and away from the remembrance of Nicholas's annoyance. She arrived at the cottage in Hamble to find she'd forgotten about the dance being held that night at the country home of the Tangmere station commander who wanted to celebrate Easter 1944 and the fact that they'd all made it this far. A time of sacrifice and then resurrection; even Skye could see the symbolism.

The dance was being held a week early because, after next week, everyone had had their leave canceled and they all knew it meant that the rumored invasion was soon to sweep them up in its deadly wake. That everything until now had been a rehearsal, and this was the finale: an extravaganza of blood and battle and broken bodies.

It was also why SOE needed more agents. The next few weeks in the lead-up to the invasion, and the months thereafter, would be the most crucial time for bolstering Resistance networks, and for sabotage. Skye had two days' leave before joining that fight. No more flights for the ATA, but a training course, which she'd been told she mightn't pass. If her superiors' reports were favorable, then she would become someone else, a Frenchwoman, and take her place in a plane like the ones Nicholas flew, heading off to fight the Germans.

I never wanted to be Vanessa Penrose in the way that you did. Strangely, her sister's words floated into Skye's consciousness and she stood and held them in her mind as she propped her bicycle against the wall of the cottage. Was that why she was doing this? Was her whole life some kind of duplicate of her mother's: a history repeating on and on, leading only to death and heartbreak?

Skye shook her head. She thought of Amy Johnson dying while ferrying planes, Honor too. She thought of every other ATA woman who had lost her life, all of them her fellows. This had been going on for four and a half years. It had to end. No, this was one thing she wasn't doing for or because of Vanessa. But for so many others instead.

Skye felt a tear on her cheek and then another. She brushed them away and composed her face into an expression Rose would expect to see. A little bit of anticipation about the dance, a little bit of excitement. No fear, no sadness. A mask she would wear from now on as her life became a lie that she lived.

"I've been looking forward to this all month!" Rose cried, erupting out of the cottage.

Skye turned to her with a grin behind which she hid what she knew about Rose's fiancé—that he flew spies into France like Nicholas did. She hid also the prayer she offered up right then: that Richie would survive, and that Rose would always be this happy.

Rose, unknowing, continued her enthusing. "We're allowed to wear civvies!" she whooped. "Pauline said I could make a detour this morning to Mummy's so I gathered up a few dancing dresses for us. They're prewar but I think they'll do."

"Show me what you have," Skye said.

Rose's dresses were lovely. Skye coveted one in particular; a Vionnet she discovered with a gasp when she saw the label. It was a shade of pinkish red she couldn't quite describe—magenta possibly, or fuchsia, or perhaps just the deepest pink of a sunset sky. Two pieces of fabric wrapped up over her bust to form a softly draped neckline, and then tied at her back, and the bias-cut skirt caressed her hips before falling with a little swirl—but not too much—to her ankles.

"It's too bright though, isn't it?" Skye said, wanting Rose to disagree but also worried that showing up at a party in a color so blazing might be offensive when grief and mourning were the ordinary way of things.

"If anyone's earned the right to wear a dress like that, you have,"

Rose said. "Enjoy it. Who knows how much longer we'll all be smiling for? Besides, with your dark hair, you're the only person it would suit. It never looked any good on me."

So Skye did wear it, curling her hair and putting on only a touch of makeup because the dress didn't need any embellishment.

Then she and Rose hoisted their finery onto their bicycles and rode to the train station, and were grateful to find two cars organized by the station commander to collect everyone in Chichester.

At the house, tulips and hyacinths—in defiance of war, like Skye's dress—stood proudly in the garden beds and buds thrust their stubborn heads out from rosebushes. The last candle flame of sun was waiting to be extinguished by night as Rose and Skye stepped inside, where lights shone and music played and everyone laughed and was merry, and Skye tried her hardest to be as well.

Until Liberty wound her arm drunkenly around her sister's neck. "Guess what I just heard?"

Skye sighed and removed the glass from her sister's hand. "I don't want to have to clean you up tonight," she said.

Liberty snatched the glass back and, eyes on Skye, took a large sip. "Guess what I just heard?" she repeated.

"What?" Skye said, thankful for an approaching pilot who looked as if he would ask her to dance and save her from her sister's gossip.

"Margaux and Nicholas are no longer engaged," Liberty said triumphantly.

Skye shook her head at the pilot, who veered off, disappointed. "Pardon?" she said.

"Nicholas is free to do what he likes. He and Margaux had a huge row this afternoon. Then Margaux strolled into the mess like she hadn't a care in the world and announced to all the men that she was now available for dates. Within ten minutes she was sitting on someone's knee!"

"That's not true," Skye said. She'd seen Margaux and Nicholas yesterday morning and they were very much together.

"It is," Liberty said, suddenly insistent and serious and focused on Skye as if the drunkenness were only an act and she was, in fact, extraordinarily sober and knew just what she was doing.

Isn't this better than being with O'Farrell, Skye remembered Liberty saying that night at the hotel when they were lying in bed and Skye had thought her sister was drunk and babbling. Why, of all the men in the RAF had Liberty been so intent on O'Farrell if indeed she thought Skye was better off without him? Then, like a finger snap, the moment was gone and Liberty was back to her scandalmongering.

"It looks as if the Ice Queen has definitely come here to have a good time," Liberty said, nodding toward the dance floor.

Skye followed Liberty's gaze. Margaux, wearing a spectacularly revealing backless dress in cobalt blue, was leading O'Farrell out to dance, the closeness of her body to his suggesting that dancing alone wasn't her intention.

Liberty thrust her glass at Skye. "Here." Then she strode off in the direction of the dance floor and Skye didn't know if she was planning to separate O'Farrell and Margaux, or if she was going to lure another pilot into her arms to show O'Farrell that she too could flirt with the best of them.

Suddenly, Skye couldn't bear to watch whatever was about to happen between Liberty, O'Farrell and Margaux. She also didn't want to know if Nicholas was at the party, didn't want to brace herself in expectation of more hurt. So she crept outside, where a waning moon shone, silvering the house, spotlighting the gardens, defeating England's attempts at blackout.

Skye picked her way across the lawn, past the hopeful flowers, far away from the house. But she couldn't be alone even there. She'd no sooner kicked off her shoes and dug her toes into the velvety lawn when she heard a voice she didn't want to hear say her name. *Go away*, she tried to whisper. Her whole body contracted—even her skin, even her breath—as if she were made of glass.

If Nicholas spoke again, the sound of his voice against her heart would make it splinter. If she said nothing, perhaps he wouldn't either. Perhaps he would leave.

But he crossed the lawn and stood far closer to her than she wanted. "I'm not..." he began, then broke off, swore under his breath and started again. "I'm not engaged to Margaux."

"But you were happy to let *her* spy for our country," Skye said, testing.

"That's not—" He stopped and she knew that her guess about Margaux had been right.

She rounded on him, her voice dangerously quiet. "Do I really seem that inept to you? Margaux is cool and elegant and self-controlled enough to spy, but I'm young and foolish and would make a mess of it with my devil-may-care attitude. How about you try thinking of me as something other than a child?"

"Believe me, I do that far too often."

It was his peculiar smile that did it. It made her shout as if he were someone she loathed.

"I'm so tired of all the riddles! Why the hell is it all right for Margaux to do what she does, but not me?"

He shouted back, his voice even more vehement than hers. "Because I fucking love you, Skye."

I love you, Skye. I love you, Skye. I love *you.* She shook her head. Stared at him, her mouth a well-rounded "O" of shock.

"What?" she managed at last.

"Without the obscenity this time." He gave a wry smile, his tone gentle now. "I said I love you. I'm not engaged to Margaux. I never was. I've never even kissed her, except on the cheek. It was part of her cover." He shook his head as if trying to comprehend something. "I was sworn to never say anything. But this morning, after I saw you at Portman Square, Wylde told me that, given you'd most likely guessed Margaux wasn't working with the WAAF, I could tell you that much and he wouldn't court-martial me. And that since they'd had more female agents start, they weren't using cover stories like mine and Margaux's anymore. So we could end the pretense."

Skye's forehead creased into a frown as she did her best to piece together his words. He'd never been engaged to Margaux. Never kissed her. Had appeared to say that he loved Skye.

He spoke again, when it became apparent that she could not. "From the moment you jumped out of the Spitfire at Tempsford, I have loved you more than you can possibly know. I know you hate me now because you think I keep acting like I have a right to tell you what to do, but it's just that every time I so much as contemplate you doing something dangerous and maybe . . . dying," she heard his voice crack, "I go a little crazy. I can't bear the thought of losing you again. I can't bear it," he repeated, his eyes on her and his hand moving toward her now, as if all he wanted was to touch her.

She reduced the distance between them to nothing.

"Will you dance with me?" she said. "Properly. The way I've always wanted to dance with you."

Then she was in his arms and he wasn't holding her away from his body but as closely as he could, both his hands on the small of her back, both of her arms entwined around his neck. Their cheeks touched as they danced, her barefoot and in a beautiful dress, him in a tuxedo, and every dance from the time she was ten and he was eleven enfolded itself into that one moment, unraveling the friendship they'd forged and built and treasured into something more beautiful and dangerous than a storm over a Cornish sea.

At last he moved his mouth down to hers.

* * *

It wasn't the way you were supposed to kiss somebody for the first time, tentatively, a shy unfurling of lip against lip. Instead it was her mouth pressed hard against his, his opening to drink her in, his tongue brushing hers, furious, almost as if they were fighting. And they were, in a way, fighting to not lie down on the grass right there and take off each other's clothes and allow their skin to be as close as their mouths.

Her hands moved down Nicholas's neck to his back, sliding under his jacket so she could feel him all the better with only his shirt in the way, feel every exquisite muscle. His mouth slipped from hers, running along her jawline and then down her neck, making her whole body ache. She couldn't breathe and could hardly speak but she managed to gasp out his name, indistinctly.

"What?" His voice was a mere whisper as he took his lips away from her neck.

That action alone almost made her cry out—that he shouldn't stop kissing her—but anyone might come out of the house and see them beneath the moonlight.

He looked at her, eyes telling her unmistakably what he wanted, his hands on her back ungovernable now, dropping down to the curve of her hips, drawing her in, and her breath caught as she felt every inch of him speak of the hunger that she felt too.

"The folly," she managed to say, pointing in the direction of a more private space, thankful that the night was forgiving rather than freezing. "Do you have . . ."

He nodded, understanding the question. Neither of them wanted to risk a baby now.

She took his hand, hurrying them down the path, wanting the folly's walls around them. As soon as they were inside, one of his hands tangled in her hair, bringing her mouth back into that fierce kiss, his other hand holding her tightly as if he thought she might run away. She was dimly aware that she was quite capable of curving her leg around him and unbuttoning his trousers and having it happen right there, but she also knew that she wanted more than a quick extinguishing of desire.

"There might be blankets," she spoke against his lips, "in the box over there."

She felt his forehead nod against hers, and the wrench as he pulled away. While he searched the box seats that lined one wall of the folly, she reached around behind her neck and undid the knot of silk so that her dress slipped off.

When he turned back to her, she stood in just her knickers and brassiere, the one he'd seen her in that day when he'd caught her sunbathing on a plane. He stopped, and almost dropped the blankets.

She couldn't help smiling. "This wasn't what you were expecting," she said mischievously.

"God, Skye. You are . . ." He swallowed, but it didn't help to steady his voice. "There isn't a word that can possibly describe how you look right now."

"I think it's only fair that you take something off too," she said, smile growing. "It's been a long time since I've seen you in your underwear."

He laughed, threw the blankets onto the ground and shucked off his jacket. "You certainly didn't look like that the first time I saw you in yours. Which is good, because if you had I would have been terrified."

"Are you terrified now?"

He unbuttoned his shirt and slid it off before he answered, and it was Skye's turn to swallow as her eyes roamed the muscled expanse of his chest, his dog tags moving up and down in time with his uneven breathing.

"Yes," he said. "Terrified and so damn turned on. Skye, you are magnificent."

As a reward, she unhooked her bra and let it drop to the floor. The folly wasn't completely dark; star shine and moonlight filtered through and she knew that he could see her, almost naked. He drew in a sharp breath and let it out slowly.

"Trousers," she said, voice strangled.

Once his trousers were gone and they both stood in their underwear, Skye saw that Nicholas had grown into a very fine man. She watched his eyes travel over her body, up and down, sweeping across her breasts, lingering, falling down to her legs, crossing to her hips, resting there.

"Skye."

The word was the faintest whisper and then he strode across to her, taking her back into his arms, and they were kissing again, a clash of mouth on mouth, a skirmish of tongues, the unbearable agony of his hand moving to her breast to stroke, ever so gently, too gently, her nipples. Her leg lifted to wrap around him, and one of his hands dropped to her hip to slide inside her knickers.

"Skye," he said again. "I have to stop kissing you for a moment." He drew back, and if she'd thought his breathing was fast before, now it was ragged. "I don't want this to be over," he said. "I want this to take forever, but if you kiss me like that it won't last more than a minute."

He was right, she knew, so she took his hand and drew him down onto the blanket. He lay on his back, and she tucked her hair behind her ear, one arm bracing her body above his. As she sat astride him, she moved her hands to his underwear, suddenly uncertain.

"Can I?" she asked softly.

He grinned. "It will be much trickier to do this if I keep them on."

She laughed. "You're making fun of me," she said, fingers coming to rest on his hip bones.

"I've just never seen you nervous before," he said, running his thumb over her lips. "Even when you jumped out of that plane at Tempsford after the Luftwaffe chased you, you barely raised a sweat."

"I'm not nervous. It's just . . ."

She studied him: that face, so familiar, but also unfamiliar, overlaid with the man he'd become. And everything else about him unfamiliar too—his chest, the line of hair traveling down to where her hands were now.

"I feel as if everything," she continued hesitantly, "everything since the moment I cartwheeled in front of you has been leading to this. As if the future's been waiting for us to kiss. And now here we are, and there's so much at stake."

His response was to reach up and kiss her again, and in that kiss Skye knew that the moment was there at last, and they were going to sink bodily and sensually and with their entire beings into it. So she did reach down and remove the second-last piece of clothing between them, and he did the same to her, and then she lay beside him, more aroused by his thigh against hers, her chest grazing his, their lips almost touching, than she'd ever been by anything she'd done with a man before.

"If it feels this good just to lie next to you . . ." she said.

"I can't even imagine how it's going to feel very soon," he replied, his words a whisper in her ear as his hand dropped to explore her.

He slowed time then, his fingertips drawing a soft circle in the hollow between her collarbones, another between her breasts, and then around her navel and back up to trace that same light and sensual path around one nipple, again and again, and then the other.

Skye felt her back arch, and arch still more when he stopped using just his fingertips and stroked each breast with his hands. All she could do was say his name and reach up to kiss him, rolling him onto his back, straddling him, doing the same to him but with her mouth—

kissing one shoulder and then the other, his chest—and she hadn't even reached his navel when he said her name, more loudly even than she'd said his. Then she was on her back and his mouth and his eyes told her that he wanted her, and she told him the same thing in just the same way.

He slid inside her and she braced herself, used to this part being somewhat uncomfortable and rather a disappointment, but he lifted her hips a little, moving tenderly, unbearably slowly. She felt her legs wrap around him tightly, felt too much all at once, until she gripped his back and he smiled at her and that was it—she was falling into St. Elmo's fire but this time she wasn't alone. Nicholas was with her, in the explosion of her body and his, her mouth and his, her soul and his.

THIRTY

They didn't stop kissing for a long time after, not until their breathing settled and their hands unclenched. Eventually, Nicholas reached across to wrap the edge of the blanket over her, mistaking her shivering for cold, but it was impossible to be cold when he was still so close to her, chest against chest, leg against leg, forehead against forehead.

"That was worth waiting for," he whispered.

"It was very surprising," she said, and he looked suddenly worried.

"You didn't like it? I'm sorry—"

She smiled and kissed him again. "Nicholas, for someone who knows me as well as you do, you say some very strange things at times. Did I look or sound as if I didn't enjoy that?"

"No, but—"

"I just meant that on the other two occasions when I've done something similar, it wasn't like this. It was at best interesting and at worst uncomfortable."

He drew back so she could see the intensity on his face as he said, "There is so much more that we will do together, Skye." She shivered again at the prospect. "And it damn well won't be either interesting or uncomfortable. If it is, you have to tell me because I want you to love us being together like this as much as I do. Every single time."

"Every time?" She smiled. "It sounds as if you plan to do this rather a lot."

He grinned. "As much as you want to."

"So all the time then."

He laughed.

"I loved it," she said. "I promise."

"And I love you, Skye. So much."

It almost hurt to hear those words, so longed for. She clung to them, turning them over and over in her mind with the wonder of a person seeing the moon for the very first time.

"I didn't know what love was when I left Cornwall at fifteen," Nicholas said, kissing her forehead, her cheek, and then her lips, "but I loved you then and I've never stopped. Not ever. It was the hardest thing I've ever had to do to not tell you I loved you over this past year and a half. Every time I saw you, I wanted to hold you or kiss you; do anything except be the person I had to be."

She blinked and buried her head in his chest, but he lifted her face to his so he could see her eyes.

"Are you crying?" he asked gently, bringing the pads of his fingers up to sweep away, so softly, the tears that she was indeed weeping.

"I try not to do it very often," she said with a faint smile. "But I've cried more tears over you than you know."

She lay with her head on his chest then, his arms firm around her, her leg wrapped over his. Until the sound of voices, closer than the general waft of noise from the party, threatened.

"We need to get dressed," she said reluctantly.

They stood up, which meant seeing him naked once more, and she couldn't help kissing him as if she intended to do all over again what they'd only just finished.

"Skye," he said, fingers dancing along her back, "you can't kiss me like that if you want me to get dressed."

"I don't really want you to get dressed," she confessed with a grin and he laughed.

But the voices sounded again, closer.

"Damn," he said, and this time they both grabbed their clothes and fumbled into them.

Even so, it was impossible for Liberty and O'Farrell to interpret the scene in any innocent fashion when they walked into the folly and saw the blanket on the floor, Skye's hair a tangled mess around her shoulders, her cheeks flushed, and Nicholas with his jacket off and shirt unbuttoned.

"You two have been having a reunion," Liberty said with a grin.

"Perhaps you could give us a few minutes," Skye said to her sister.

"Oh, I'm sorry. When I suggested to O'Farrell that we go for a walk, I didn't realize I had to avoid the folly in case of possible debauchery. I was actually planning my own debauchery, but I can see I'll have to find another location for it."

"Let's go," O'Farrell said, turning around and striding off.

"Not back to the party," Liberty called, hurrying after him. "Or Margaux. I have to talk to you."

Nicholas sighed. "I should explain to him."

Skye shook her head. "I don't think he's mad. He chose my sister months ago. And he and I never shared more than a few kisses."

"Really?"

"Really. I just couldn't . . ."

Nicholas drew her back into his arms and she forgot about Liberty and O'Farrell as he whispered in her ear, "I can't bear it if I don't see you again for weeks. Can you get leave for the weekend, before it's all revoked?"

"My leave started tonight. I have the next two days."

"Let me arrange my own two days," he said. "I haven't had leave for six months, and full moon's over. It shouldn't be too hard. Especially as there won't be any more for the foreseeable future."

"Let's go to Cornwall. To the house," she said, knowing that the place where they'd first met was where she wanted to be with him.

* * *

Nicholas stepped out of the car at Porthleven and whistled. "It's exactly the same as I remembered," he said.

"It is," she agreed.

They stood together, staring, as sunrise set the sky aflame, rendering the cottage a silhouette. Its shape sent him tumbling back into the past, to the first time he'd stood there with Skye, awestruck by this amazing cartwheeling girl who'd shared her cove with him, and with whom he'd shared his father's pocket watch.

An absence of weight had him reaching into his pocket, only to discover that the watch wasn't there; it must have fallen out in the folly. It didn't matter. He'd find it before he next went flying—O'Farrell might have picked it up. Besides, he had Skye now and she was a more powerful good luck charm than any timepiece.

He reached down to touch her cheek, marveling that he could do that now; that the restraint of the past year and a half had vanished, never to return.

The smile she gave him stole his breath and he couldn't do anything other than kiss her, arms circling her waist, already regretting the end of these two days.

They hardly moved from the bed all that day, finally falling into sleep toward evening, a sleep Nicholas awoke from near midnight with a nightmare fading behind his eyes. Somehow, Skye sensed it because she stirred and reached out for him.

"What is it?" she asked sleepily.

"You're going to do it, aren't you?" he said, certain of her answer.

She understood the question. "I have to."

Of course she would. She had been asked to help her country, and it wasn't in her nature to refuse.

He saw his nightmare now: the SOE agent who'd been shot in front of him blurring into a Nazi leading Skye into a hotel room, and her having to do what Margaux did. They wouldn't ask that of her, surely? He would never know—she wouldn't be allowed to tell him anything: not her code name, not the details of her missions, nothing. For the first time in his life, he knew the heart-pounding sickness of real terror. He closed his arms around her so tightly that he thought she might pull away, but she only held on.

If only he could be the one to fly her into France. But if Wylde had known enough about Nicholas and Skye to give Nicholas permission to tell her what he had, there would be a note on a file somewhere that Nicholas Crawford and Skye Penrose were never to go on a pickup operation together.

He'd make sure it was O'Farrell who flew her over. But once she was on the ground in France, what then?

There was also the matter of Liberty. Nicholas wasn't allowed to tell Skye about that either, unless for some reason they crossed paths at the cottage in Tangmere. The risk of a captured agent giving up everyone else in the organization was too great so SOE tried to keep meetings between agents and knowledge of who else worked for the organization to a minimum. What would Skye say when she found out about Liberty, and that he'd known all along?

"All I want is this," he said vehemently, needing her to understand. "The dreams I had before the war, which seemed so large and important, are nothing now. All I want is you, here. Alive."

"That's all I want too," she said.

He shut his eyes. It was almost April 1944. War had been declared four and a half years ago. Surely it must end soon?

He opened his eyes and kissed her, using his lips to study the terrain that was Skye Penrose. He began with her back, so tiny now, rations and hard work making her almost too thin. He followed each ridge of her spine with his lips then he turned her onto her back and moved his mouth to her breasts.

"Nicholas," he heard her say, and he kissed her mouth quickly, one of his hands clenched in hers, his other hand drifting down to the flat expanse of her stomach, then down lower to her thighs.

He felt her hips arch toward him and as much as it was almost torturous to delay, he wanted to, because to watch her like this—naked, body crying out for his touch—was the most sensual thing of all.

He let one hand graze lightly between her legs, and she whispered, shakily, his name once more. Then he kissed one thigh softly before moving slowly upward, his hands a little ahead of his mouth. He glanced up and saw that her eyes were closed, her head tipped backward, her legs open, and he finally let himself do what he'd been wanting to do since the moment they'd lain together naked on a blanket in the folly. He placed his mouth where his hand had been and heard the sharp and sudden intake of her breath, felt her body move urgently toward him, and then he saw her tremble, heard her cry out once, twice, three times—and it was the most perfect moment of his whole life.

When she'd recovered enough to open her eyes, she stared at him, then grinned. Her hair was spread across the pillow like the dark strands of evening, her cheeks were flushed, and she looked as wild and beautiful and utterly Skye as she ever had before.

"Your turn," she said, drawing his hips toward hers, legs circling his waist.

"Maybe yours again too," he said.

"Twice in five minutes," she said incredulously.

He smiled and nodded. "Maybe."

"Well," she said, drawing his mouth down to meet hers, "you've never once broken a promise."

The way she said it made his heart squeeze. "You have no idea how much I love you," he said.

"But I do," she said. "Because it's as much as I love you."

He slid inside her, making sure to lift her hips again as he'd done the night before, and it wasn't long before he saw an expression traverse her face that he was coming to understand and to adore, an expression that told him she was on the threshold of a pleasure so intense it had to be taken with their hands threaded together, their mouths too, him breaking away for just one quick moment to say, "God, Skye," before they fell together into the only place he ever wanted to be.

As their breathing gradually settled, she bestowed on him again that brilliant smile. "Luckily for you, you still haven't ever broken a promise."

He could do nothing other than laugh.

* * *

Nicholas was soundly sleeping when Skye woke the next morning. She lay for a long time watching him, seeing all the new things. The stubble along his jaw, the long curve of his beautiful eyelashes, the faded freckles just discernible in a patch on his nose. The breadth of his back, the sound of his voice when he'd said her name the fourth or possibly fifth time they'd been together—she'd lost count. Every moment of their lovemaking rolled into the next, making her feel like a hedonist, addicted to this bed and to Nicholas naked within it.

A sudden howl of wind made her look across to the windows. She edged out of bed, slipped on Nicholas's shirt, and was greeted by a day born disconsolate, the sky smudged a sunless gray. She shivered, picked up the blanket from the end of the bed, wrapped it around her shoulders and walked out of the house and down to the sand. Once at the cove she was sure she would see it: a flicker of blue, a ribbon of optimism hiding somewhere in the sky. But the wind tore brutishly at her blanket, the sea tossed itself recklessly at the rocks, and the rocks pushed back so hard that each wave disintegrated into tear-sized droplets that drowned in the mass of ocean.

"No," she said, shaking her head, refusing to allow this grim and fateful morning to have any power over her. But she knew, because she carried it in her bones like the fossil of a shell caught in a rock, that this was the kind of day on which her mother had died.

As on that day, a dreadful presentiment tumbled down upon her, and she wondered suddenly if the reason her mother had never told Skye her future was because it was too sad to speak of.

"Skye."

She heard Nicholas's voice behind her and she fell into his arms. She almost wished that this love hadn't happened, because then the loss, if it came to pass, wouldn't be so catastrophic. But she would never give back last night and yesterday, not for anything.

"You're crying," he said. "What is it? Tell me."

He held her so close it was as if he were part of her, inseparable. But she knew it was only his soul—that flimsy, insubstantial thing, unable to be held on to or spoken to or seen—that was inseparable from her. His physical body, the self her hands clutched at now, was subject to the whims and ways of war, as was hers.

"I love you," she managed at last.

He bent to gather up a strand of seaweed, which he twisted and wrapped to form a circle. He picked up her left hand and slid the band onto her finger.

"It's impossible for us to be officially married in only two days of leave, but I am yours for the rest of your life, Skye. I hope you'll be mine for the rest of my life."

"Of course I will," she cried, and she kissed him vehemently, her passion outdoing the gale around them. "Do you think it's strong enough?" she asked, drawing back to study her wedding ring. "Strong enough to beat everything we have no control over?"

"Yes," he said, kissing her finger and then her lips. "We will live here, Skye. You and I and our brood of fearless girls. We'll teach them to swim and to fly and to know that the world has no real limits except the ones we make. And we are boundless."

"We are boundless," she repeated, as if they were in a church and he had said a prayer and she had given the response.

And they were, in a way, in the only holy place she believed in: *en plein air*, with everything she needed surrounding her. Wind and water and sand and rock and air and Nicholas.

PART ELEVEN
KAT

THIRTY-ONE

B ack at the hotel, Kat lay in bed unable to sleep and stared at the ceiling. That morning, she had woken up with her head on Elliott's chest. That afternoon, she had started to believe that her grandmother was a woman named Liberty Penrose whose sister, Skye, lived at the property adjoining the Cornwall cottage. That evening, Elliott had admitted to deceiving her and he had become, in that instant, someone she could no longer trust.

And Kat's grandmother had obviously been untruthful too.

When Paul had lied to her, Kat had wanted to scream, to tear her outrage from her chest, hurl it at the wall and watch it shatter in a grotesque splendor of red. But now she lay perfectly still, hardly even blinking, not angry at all, but sadder than she'd ever been in her life.

Because she adored her grandmother, who had suffered a pain so great she'd never been able to tell her granddaughter about it. A pain so great that her grandmother had perhaps decided to become someone else, for decades wearing a mask as her life became a lie that she lived, in order to forget.

And Elliott . . . How had Kat felt about him? She blinked now as tears trickled over her cheeks. She had made herself vulnerable to him and he had hurt her. She had given him her trust and he had not respected it, nor understood how significant a thing it was to her.

Perhaps it wasn't his fault; perhaps it was hers for giving him a heart as delicate as Venetian lace. It was bound, at some point, to tear. She swiped her cheeks but the ache inside didn't lessen.

She wished she could stay in bed, but that was the thing about being a mother. You got up even if it was one in the morning and you were so tired you could hardly walk. Your body was more attuned to obligation than to self-comfort. So at five, Kat rose and went for a pounding, punishing run. This was physical pain she could enjoy because its source wasn't someone she had trusted too much.

Back in her room, she put on the black New York afternoon dress that Yves Saint Laurent had designed during his tenure at Dior. She hoped the unusual silhouette that billowed like whimsy over a slim pencil skirt might elevate her mood from listless to functional. Then, with a carefully packed box in hand, she caught a cab to the V&A Museum, hoping that Celeste would be able to distract her with information about the mysterious blue gown. On the way her phone buzzed. Elliott. She ignored it.

She arrived early, made herself a coffee, opened the box and laid the dress colored a shocking and extraordinary blue on the worktable.

When Celeste hurried in only ten minutes later, she halted by the dress and said, "Mon Dieu!"

"It's incredible, isn't it?" Kat said.

"Even for Monsieur Dior, it is incredible," Celeste agreed. "And I have good news."

For the first time since she'd left Elliott, Kat felt something like interest ripple through her. "Good news would be marvelous," she said, managing a smile.

"Oh no!" Celeste said. "You are sad. Trouble with a lover?"

Was Elliott her lover? The term, used casually nowadays to signify a person you had a physical relationship with, actually implied so much more. It held within it the word *love*.

Kat willed fresh tears away. "No," she said. "It's nothing."

"Well, *this* isn't nothing," Celeste said. She laid a photograph of a woman on the desk. "This," she said, "is Catherine Dior, Christian's beloved sister, in 1948. As you can see, the photograph is, unfortunately, black-and-white. But this one," Celeste produced a color image now, "taken fifteen years later isn't. It's from the Dior-Charbonneries archive, which is why I couldn't find anything about the dress at first. That archive holds items from Catherine's life with her late partner, Hervé."

Kat stared at the photograph. The gown Catherine wore in the photograph was a brilliant azure blue, of a color and style that was epoch-making, almost too magnificent for a princess.

Celeste continued to speak. "We've always had the black-and-white image in the archives. The dress Catherine wears in it has proved something of a mystery until now. It was never made for production. Our hypothesis was that it was a trial, and Dior did not like it so he did not include it in the Envol line in 1948."

Envol.

Flight.

Kat's mind grasped onto the word.

Celeste sighed. "Poor Catherine—or Caro, as Christian called her. Do you know her story? Almost nobody does. She worked for the Resistance during the war and was imprisoned at a concentration camp called Ravensbrück, from which she emerged barely alive. She was awarded the Croix de guerre and the Légion d'honneur for her work with the Resistance."

Which meant Elliott had seen Catherine Dior's name on a list of Ravensbrück prisoners. The connections were all there at Kat's fingertips but she was missing the thing that made them fit perfectly together, that gave her the answer to who her grandmother really was.

Celeste was still talking. "So Christian Dior made two dresses in exquisite blue: one for his beloved sister and one for another woman. But who? Someone in Australia? And one of those dresses found its way to your museum and the other to a collection owned by one of your relatives. It is incredible."

"Incredible," Kat murmured, unable to enter properly into Celeste's excitement.

"I have a letter written by Catherine in 1948, and one written by Christian." Celeste produced some more carefully protected items from her bag. "We will analyze the ink under the spectroscope, and you can have them do the same with the ink on the label of the dress in Sydney. I want to know if the dress in Sydney was perhaps a gift from Christian or Catherine. As the Dior archivist, I also want to know which dress was Catherine's. It's a long shot, but worth doing, I think. Do you agree?"

Kat nodded, itching to call Elliott and blurt it all out to him.

"You must come to the archives for a few months," Celeste said. "Take up a fellowship there. We'll write a paper about the dresses together. Organize an exhibition."

"I can't," was Kat's automatic response. "I have two kids."

"Wouldn't they like to spend a few months in Paris?"

What if she did take Daisy and Lisbet to Paris? Kat wondered. What if she did work at the Dior archives with Celeste for a short time? What if, instead of always apologizing to Paul for her job, instead of letting her work become a nuisance that had to be fitted in around her daughters, she embraced it—like she had used to? What if she had a conversation with Paul where she anticipated his assent rather than steeling herself up front for an argument and exhibiting a wariness toward him that he must be able to feel?

What if she saw Celeste's invitation as an opportunity rather than an impossibility?

Perhaps her grandmother would come to Paris too. And they could all go to the cottage in Porthleven for a holiday together.

Kat smiled suddenly at Celeste. "I'll talk to my boss about it." Then she touched the photograph of Catherine and said, voice quiet, "Shouldn't Catherine be more famous than her brother for her bravery? We remember dresses more than we do a woman who almost gave her life for her country."

Celeste touched Kat's shoulder. "She should. Let's make her famous with our paper."

For the rest of the day, Kat let excitement take precedence over sadness. She emailed her boss straightaway and Celeste did too. Her phone buzzed with another message from Elliott, which she again didn't read. Her boss replied to her email and said she could organize a six-month fellowship in Paris. Kat grinned. She couldn't wait to call Daisy and Lisbet that night to tell them.

Then she busied herself with an analysis of the ink on the two letters, and sent it to Annabel. She knew she wouldn't hear anything back from Australia for hours yet. All she could do was wait.

She returned to her hotel room, and finally read Elliott's messages. The first said: *I miss you, Kat. I'm so sorry.* The second said: *I told you the truth because I care about you.*

She ran her hand over the cover of the book he'd given her to read. It was so old. Why had he given it to her? As a plea for forgiveness? To distract her from his lie?

Her phone beeped again. Another message from Elliott, a long one. *The worst part of it is,* she read, *Nicholas Crawford isn't really my grandfather. Not by blood. My real grandfather was a Nazi and he raped my grandmother. I used to think it defined me: being related to a man who would assault a woman, a man who would abuse a country. That I must have violence in my blood, violence I had to run from. I found out the truth in my early twenties, and it prompted my extremely immature behavior back then.*

But what I'm trying to do now—although you might not believe me— is to show that despite the many despicable acts by men like my true grand-father, they did not destroy women like Skye and Liberty Penrose, and Margaux Jourdan. They mattered. Their courage outshines everything.

If you read the book I gave you, you'll see what I mean. Nicholas Crawford is my grandfather in the only way that means anything. Which is what I was trying to say to you, Kat. It doesn't matter who your grandmother is. She is your grandmother. And you'd do anything for her because you love her. I would do anything for Nicholas Crawford too. There is nothing quite the same as the love of a grandchild for a grandparent.

PS—I still miss you.

Kat opened the book Elliott had placed in her hand. Tiny writing, as if the writer hadn't been sure he would have enough paper to say all that he needed to say.

Margaux Jourdan's name caught her eye, and Kat found herself sinking into a chair with the book and beginning to read.

* * *

The first few pages of Nicholas Crawford's diary were lovely: recol-lections of a childhood spent locked in the kind of ferocious friendship only children are capable of; sigma bonds, unbreakable. Cartwheels and dancing on clifftops and learning to swim, and Nicholas's pocket watch. Kat shivered, remembering the pocket watch on Cornwall Margaux's—Skye's?—mantelpiece. Flying lessons and discovering lost gardens by falling from walls.

Here Kat looked up. The past rushed in to the present and she saw a dark-haired girl fall from the same wall she had fallen from, then another dark head appear at the top, laughing.

She shivered, and almost didn't continue, almost called Elliott to ask him to sit beside her while she ventured on to the next part of the story.

But she made herself turn the page and read on: about two people who had shared the kind of love that was, as Elliott had said, true. Love that endured, and which had reached its zenith, Kat realized now, on that same stretch of beach in Cornwall upon which she and Elliott had walked.

This was not manipulation or a plea for forgiveness. This was a story of love. Love shattered by war.

PART TWELVE
SKYE

You couldn't let them see you weep. The women who wept at night usually were dead by morning. You couldn't give in.
> —Virginia D'Albert-Lake, *An American Heroine in the French Resistance*

THIRTY-TWO

S kye's intensive training for SOE, in everything from using a gun, to deciphering codes, to sabotage, to the terrible art of killing silently, took place during April. The impending Allied invasion of Europe meant SOE was intent on readying their agents as quickly as possible, and soon Skye was ready for her first mission.

She arrived at the cottage in Tangmere from where the agents departed feeling almost like a rainstorm, as if she were a collection of individual beads—her head was given over to a make-believe person with the code name Odette Legrand, her heart belonged to Nicholas, her soul was Skye Penrose's—all of them tumbling headlong to earth and how did she know which droplets would slide harmoniously into the river and thus move easily onward and which ones might shatter to pieces on the sharp point of a rock?

She smoothed her hands over her skirt; it didn't need smoothing but her palms were damp. Then she stepped hesitantly into the cottage.

She hadn't seen Nicholas since they'd returned from leave but now there he was with Margaux. She wanted to run straight into his arms, the one place where her apprehensions might settle, but there were other people around. All she could do was follow him with her eyes, the same way he was following her with his. Soon before dinner was served, he indicated with his head that she should follow him and she did, into a momentarily quiet hallway.

He placed a hand on her cheek and drew her in close, whispering, "Are you all right? You look so pale."

"I'm terrified," she admitted, words she wouldn't say to anyone but him.

I was so scared, she'd said to him once before when the Lancaster had nearly crashed into her in the sky. But that fear was nothing compared to what churned though her now. If that plane had run into her, there would have been an explosion, and then death. A certain outcome. But what she was facing now had no certainty to it at all: if she were caught by the Nazis, all she knew was that death might be something she would pray for because what they would do to her would make her understand for the first time what pain really was.

She touched the locket at her neck. Inside it was the cyanide capsule she'd been given along with French occupation money and identity papers. Cyanide to bring death on quickly so that she wouldn't suffer.

Nicholas drew her hand away from the locket and held it. "You know it's normal to be scared?"

She breathed out, and the rainstorm inside her pushed back so that, for the first time since she'd been briefed on what she was to do in Paris, she felt like she knew who she was, and who she needed to be.

"You're the bravest person I know, Skye," Nicholas said, voice a murmur in her ear, "because you do what needs to be done even when you're scared. And remember, you promised me you wouldn't fucking die, so you won't."

She hadn't thought it would be possible to smile at all that night but she did, remembering their handshake at the pub in Hamble. "Thank you," she said, reaching up to kiss him, just once, because she knew they were running out of time.

"I love you," Nicholas said against her lips and Skye said the same. It was their past and their present, and it would be their future.

Her mother had been wrong. *The future isn't a promise yet to be kept*, Vanessa had said. But Skye and Nicholas had made their promise. And even though one part of it was yet to be kept—*I will marry you*—everything he told her now, his gaze locked in hers, said that it would be.

* * *

After a dinner she could hardly eat, Skye and Margaux climbed aboard a Lysander piloted by O'Farrell. All the way to France, Skye could feel Margaux's eyes on her and she tried not to fidget, tried to take solace from being in the sky, tried to remember only Nicholas telling her he loved her, tried not to think about where she was going— Nazi-occupied Paris. Then the plane landed and it was time to climb down the ladder.

"Wait," O'Farrell called to her before she did.

She stepped up to the cockpit.

"Liberty's pregnant," O'Farrell said, his obvious joy almost out-shining the moonbeams around them. "We're having a baby."

"A baby," Skye repeated, nerves fleeing in the face of this news that was, she now realized—and despite what she'd said to her sister—the best thing she'd heard in a long time and just what they all needed. She kissed his cheek, knowing why he'd told her now, right before she walked away with the reception committee. "I can't wait to meet my niece."

O'Farrell grinned at her, and it was the kind of grin that meant everything would be all right.

And it was. The reception committee was ready and waiting, grate-ful for the supplies they'd brought, and quick to send the two women on, in the morning, by train to Paris. Margaux went to have lunch with her Nazi target and Skye met Catherine Dior, a somber-faced woman with startling eyes—like dewy blossoms, but dark now with secrets. Catherine worked with the Resistance circuit Skye was to join as a courier.

At first, few words passed between the two and Skye wasn't sure if Catherine's reticence was just her nature or if she didn't trust Skye yet. She supposed that was sensible: when so much was at stake, how could trust ever be given freely?

But their friendship cemented itself that first afternoon when they were walking together to the *Métro* station. Skye carried a basket covered with a cloth as if she'd just purchased the day's rations; it really held money and guns. She almost froze when a German soldier approached, could feel Catherine's aghast eyes on her and knew the other woman thought Skye would fail this, her first test, because she'd been in France for less than a day.

Instead Skye thought of her promise to Nicholas and her sister's baby, a child she wanted to meet, and she smiled at the German.

"What do you have in there?" he asked, unaffected by her smile.

Catherine went to speak but Skye interrupted. "Why, things to spy on you with, of course. Who wouldn't want binoculars to see you up close, a radio to eavesdrop on everything you say?"

She laughed and the German did too. Nobody in their right mind would tell a Nazi they had such equipment in their basket. So she got away with it, in exchange for a promise to meet him later at Fouquet's.

He checked her papers so he knew her name—Odette Legrand—and her address. She would have to go. She waved goodbye with her smile still on.

"What will you do at Fouquet's?" Catherine asked gravely. "You know what he wants."

"Drink enough of the champagne he'll buy me to ensure that I'm incapable of anything other than throwing up on his boots at the end of the night."

Catherine smiled and the sorrow in her eyes retreated, and she looked, for a moment, like any woman in her mid-twenties: a little too thin, brown hair not as glossy as it should be due to soap rations, a distinct elegance hiding under the serious face. "I'll come with you," she said.

And she did, improving on Skye's plan by pretending to have drunk too much herself, thus saving Skye from a hangover and allowing Skye to leave early to look after her supposedly drunken friend.

"Thank you," Skye said once they were far enough away from Fouquet's to speak properly.

Catherine shrugged and Skye thought it would be left at that but then Catherine added quietly, "Thank you."

From that night on, Skye and Caro and Margaux, in between drinking too much champagne as a salve for their abraded nerves, did everything they could. Margaux gathered information from her Nazi; Catherine collected intelligence on German troop movements; and Skye, as soon as she discovered that the circuit leader she was supposed to report to had gone missing, found herself managing the Resistance cell—around two hundred people and all of the money— and recruiting more and more French civilians to the cause. Within just two weeks, they had sent vital information back to SOE about the German defense system in Paris and its points of weakness; and had armed and prepared dozens of small groups of fighters who would erect barricades and help take the city when the Allies were ready.

"We might win," Skye whispered to Caro and Margaux, believing for the first time that it was possible.

It was almost dusk and they were walking along the Rue Royale. A heavy wooden door opened and, from the courtyard behind, the scent of jasmine bloomed into the street.

Caro inhaled deeply, closing her eyes. "Childhood and summer," she said.

"And hope," Margaux added, smiling a little as she spoke.

Catherine darted into the courtyard and plucked a handful of blooms, passing some to Skye, some to Margaux and keeping some for herself. "To remember," she said simply and Skye knew what her quiet, flower-loving friend meant: that every time they smelled jasmine from then on, they would think not of Nazis but of hope.

*   *   *

Three weeks later, Skye and Margaux were in a field in L'Aigle, standing by to be taken back to England. D-day had, unbelievably, just happened; but all of France, beyond a strip of beach, was still in German hands. The two women were to be apprised of new targets and new plans, and would then return to Paris within two days to help the Resistance wreak havoc with sabotage to support the Allied advance.

As Skye waited with Margaux for the pickup, she felt her excitement at the prospect of perhaps seeing Nicholas buzzing out of her like radio waves.

"I hope the Germans aren't tuned in to your frequency," Margaux said drily as a Lysander circled overhead.

The plane landed and O'Farrell stepped out, which he wasn't supposed to do. He hurried over to them, face white, and Skye knew. Nicholas. Margaux fumbled for Skye's hand.

"He's not dead," O'Farrell said emphatically. "He just didn't come back."

No! That one word, keening inside her, was all Skye allowed herself of heartbreak. She did not weep. She pushed away the memory of the sky she and Nicholas had stood beneath in Cornwall, the one she'd feared because it had seemed without mercy. She remembered instead that he'd wrapped her finger in seaweed and convinced her of a future. It was up to her to make that future happen. She would find him.

"I'll tell them it was too cloudy," O'Farrell said. "That I couldn't land. Then you can stay and find him. He went down near Orléans."

"I'm staying too," Margaux said.

Margaux's words made Skye's throat ache. She didn't look at her friend, knew Margaux didn't want her sacrifice acknowledged; that to her it wasn't even a sacrifice, but an inevitability.

Then O'Farrell said, "Liberty's missing too. She's with Nicholas. You have to find them both."

Comprehension had Skye reeling as she watched O'Farrell climb back into his plane and felt Margaux draw her into a tight embrace. Liberty must have been working for SOE too. Her sister's drunkenness, her search for solace in O'Farrell's arms, her spiky attitude to Skye had most likely been the only way she could manage all of the emotion, emotion Skye understood because she felt it now too. The knowledge that death was around every corner; that anyone might betray you; that you would shoot and kill someone if you had to. Liberty had always had difficulty expressing even the most ordinary of emotions. How else could she have handled the constant peril of living life as another person in Nazi-occupied France?

And now Liberty was pregnant. A baby would only magnify everything: the danger, the threat, the sense that one must do whatever one could to survive.

Skye heard Margaux whisper in her ear. "I'm sorry I couldn't tell you about Liberty."

Then a sound. A terrible roar from above, loud and brutal, as if someone had taken the sky in their hands, ripped it open, and let hell fall out. O'Farrell's plane, a ball of fire, screaming to earth, shot down by a flak battery nobody had known about.

"No!" Skye wept now. "No!"

O'Farrell, hair as blond and shiny as hope, a man who'd come to England to fly planes at a time when he could have turned his back on the war, a man who'd rivaled the moonbeams when he'd told Skye about his baby—he was gone. Another soul to carry inside her. How many could she bear?

She cried, and so did Margaux, on each other's shoulders. Liberty's child, if it even survived, was fatherless now.

* * *

But they couldn't stand and mourn for long. That was war: a too-short explosion of grief, which then had to be buried inside, covered over with determination. There were two people and an unborn child to be found. That night in her bed, Skye pressed a new spray of jasmine flowers to her face and hoped harder than she ever had before.

But there was no longer a Resistance circuit operating in Orléans; everyone had been captured and tortured and killed. Despite that setback, Margaux and Skye didn't stop any of the work they'd been sent to France to do, but they added to it the task of finding Nicholas and Liberty.

They got so close. They heard a tale about a man and a woman hiding in a cellar. A priest had seen them.

Then on the sixth of July, one month after D-day when the Allied troops were still far from Paris, as Skye, Margaux and Catherine walked along a street, three men in Gestapo-gray approached. None of the three friends faltered. But the men did not pass by. They pounced, and Skye knew immediately that somebody must have betrayed the women. Perhaps Margaux's Nazi had become suspicious. Perhaps

Catherine had been seen transmitting messages. Perhaps one of the men Skye had recruited hadn't been as loyal as she'd thought.

Margaux managed to bite one of the Gestpao agents, Skye to scratch another's cheek and Catherine to land a well-placed kick. Skye didn't even consider the cyanide she wore in the locket around her neck. She had to stay alive.

But the building on the Rue de la Pompe where she was taken was not a place devoted to life.

There, a redheaded French girl sat on the edge of a bathtub transcribing everything Skye said into a notebook while a German man injured every part of Skye's body in ways she had never imagined. The bathtub, full of water, was the means by which Skye thought she might die as her head was pushed into it time and time again.

Nicholas. She thought of Nicholas. And her sister. She prayed that no Nazi had done any of these things to her sister.

She was so grateful when she finally passed out.

When she woke, she was not in a better place but lying in a cell in Fresnes prison. Another place known for torture. Her head spasmed with so much pain she was sick. But at least she was alive.

That night, she heard tapping on the wall. Morse code. Prisoners were talking to each other in the only way they could. Skye wept when she heard the taps that spelled out Caro's name. And Margaux's. She crawled to the wall and tapped out her own name: Odette Legrand. She wept still more when Margaux and Caro replied.

Days passed. So many days, each of them the same. Her head in water. Her body disfigured. Her throat raw from vomiting. And then the nights and the blessed relief as she discovered that Catherine and Margaux had each survived another day too.

Throughout Skye held firm to her story of being a French girl caught up in the thrill of danger. And the Germans appeared to believe she was Odette Legrand, and that she had been working for the Resistance—which was bad enough, but not as bad as being discovered to be a British spy. She prayed they believed the same of Margaux.

Finally she was moved again. To a train station: Gare de Pantin. There was no possible way to stop the tears when she saw Margaux and Caro on the platform too. Skye did not look at their bruises. She looked only at their eyes, which were the loveliest things she had seen since the sixth of July, full of tenderness. She had almost forgotten that humans could love, and be kind.

"They don't know?" Margaux whispered. *That you're British?* she didn't add, but Skye understood.

Skye shook her head. "No."

"Thank God."

So they were three French girls who'd foolishly been caught up with the Resistance, not one French girl and two spies working for the British government.

The signs of imminent Allied victory were everywhere that day, lessening the ache of Skye's injuries somewhat. The Gare de l'Est had been destroyed by an Allied bomb, said Margaux, whose specialty had always been information. And there was no longer any electricity in Paris.

The Allies were at Rambouillet, the Red Cross workers at the train station told them, not quite forty miles from Paris. That distance could be broached in a day!

"You'll be free before they can take you to Germany," the Red Cross volunteer called as she was pushed away by a Nazi.

Skye squeezed Caro's hand, and Margaux's. They would make it. They just had to be patient.

But they were pushed into cattle wagons on a train that left Paris with 2,200 prisoners on board. The brutal August heat poured down upon the wagons and breathing became almost impossible. The train moved slowly, no faster than a person walking, stopping constantly to let through the German troop trains that had priority.

The women's spirits rose when the Resistance tried to stop the train at Dormans. But they were fought off by the Germans. Dead men lay like railway sleepers all around.

"Dormans is hardly more than sixty miles from Paris," Caro told Skye. Her voice was the barest whisper through her parched mouth. "It's taken two days to travel such a short distance."

"The slower we go, the better chance we have of the Allies catching up to us," Skye said, and Margaux nodded.

They must think like that. They had to, despite the fact that the latrine buckets were so full they slopped filth onto the floor, the sweat of fear emanating from the crammed-in bodies was choking and the women around them had begun to die from the diabolical heat.

"Not us," Caro said, gathering Skye's and Margaux's hands in hers.

But Skye saw that her eyes had wilted, that Margaux's ordinarily composed face was set hard over a clenched jaw. And Skye's hands were twisting at her neck, seeking out a cerulean scarf that she'd had to leave behind in England.

Then Caro sniffed the noxious air. "I can smell jasmine," she said, pulling a dead bloom from her pocket.

She passed it to Skye to press her nose against, and then to Margaux. Skye's hands settled, as did Margaux's jaw, and Caro's eyes bloomed once more with hope.

"*Bon courage!*" they heard villagers shouting at the next station, where the Red Cross pleaded with the driver to stop the train.

Perhaps Caro had been right. "You see?" Skye said determinedly, taking her turn to lift their mood. "We won't reach Germany."

But she couldn't meet Caro's eyes, or Margaux's, when the train started up once more. She summoned the strength to stand and peer through the wagon slats and saw that the signs were written not in French anymore, but in German.

Le dernier convoi that train was later called: the last train out of Paris. It arrived at Ravensbrück concentration camp on the twenty-first of August 1944.

Paris fell to the Allies just four days later.

THIRTY-THREE

Ravensbrück concentration camp, on the far eastern border of Germany, was a place beyond description. Skye, Margaux and Caro's arrival coincided with an influx of prisoners moved from other camps nearer the western borders as the Germans tried to hide their monstrous deeds from the Allies in this place too far from anywhere to ever be found. There were so many women to house that they were kept outside the gates for days, patrolled by guards and dogs. Over that time, the ground beneath them turned into a mud of excrement.

Eventually, they were sent inside in ranks of five prisoners, marching down the Lagerstrasse between two rows of hulking gray blocks. A voice boomed *Achtung!* from the loudspeakers in the Appellplatz as they were herded into a bunker. There, they were washed and stripped and shaved, and dressed in rags with wooden clogs, a headscarf, and a red star that denoted them as political prisoners.

The only spark of something other than terror came when Margaux, Caro and Skye—or Odette as everyone called her—were allocated to the same accommodation block, one of the French ones.

Margaux had already heard, somehow, that there was a handful of British women at the camp, and they were kept "in quarantine" by the Nazis, because the only possible explanation for a British woman to be in France was that she was a spy. From the way the word was spoken, Skye knew she did not ever want to be kept in quarantine.

In the French block, they slept three to a mattress in the triple tiers of bunks but this suited Skye, Caro and Margaux because it meant they could always find one another come nighttime. In her bunk on that first night, Skye remembered shaking Nicholas's hand across a table and both of them making a vow. *You promised not to die*, she whispered. *And you've never broken a promise. So stay alive. And I will too.*

It took Skye several weeks to comprehend what Ravensbrück was. Then came a week in October when she realized that she no longer flinched when she saw a woman licking up a morsel of spilled porridge from the ground. She didn't groan when the sirens blared at four in the morning and the vigorous jostling for what was called coffee began, and starving woman elbowed aside starving woman because the only thing that mattered was survival. She forgot to recoil when she saw a woman mauled to death by one of the dogs; forgot again when a guard murdered a woman with a pickax in the Appellplatz because she didn't respond when her name was called; didn't shudder when the guards made a woman dig a tunnel through the sand until it collapsed on her and she was buried alive. She could no longer smell the scent of the dead disgorged by the crematoriums into every crevice of the camp.

Only when she saw the tiny body of a dead baby did Skye tremble. How much worse it was, she thought, not to react. How much worse that such unimaginable things had become quotidian. All around her were women whose souls had died but whose bodies lived cruelly on. She touched the finger that had once worn Nicholas's seaweed ring. She could not let her soul die here too.

"We have to do whatever we can to stay alive," she said when Caro refused to drink a bowl of liquid that was soup in name only. Skye took the bowl and pointed to the tiny lump floating in the liquid. It was the first time she'd seen anything that indicated that what they were eating might actually be food. "Look. There's a piece of turnip. It's not just water. All we need is to find one thing every day that the guards have missed and that makes this day better than the one before."

Margaux nodded resolutely, nothing glamorous about her now, nothing glamorous about any of them. But in that nod Skye recognized the Margaux whose poise always turned heads, who was always composed. Caro's head lifted too and, despite her baldness, she looked like the determined woman Skye had met that first day in Paris, a woman whose beautiful eyes were as yet undiminished. The relief Skye felt then had her brushing away a tear. She knew she wouldn't survive without Caro and Margaux. But she also knew that now, each day, they would all find a reason to survive.

One day it was a handful of herbs that Caro managed to pick and pocket before anyone noticed as they walked five abreast through the pine-scented woods with shovels over their shoulders to begin their twelve-hour work shift.

"The herbs have vitamins in them," Caro whispered. "Vitamins will keep us alive."

Another day Margaux discovered that Geneviève de Gaulle, Charles de Gaulle's niece, was in Ravensbrück too. "The Allies will come for her," Margaux said firmly. "And they'll find us too."

For one incredible month it was the revelation that resistance still lived in all of them. Skye, Caro and Margaux were sent to a sub-camp at Torgau along with a group of Frenchwomen. The three women held hands as they marched there, terror-stricken at having the known horror that was Ravensbrück taken temporarily from them, dreading what unknown horror they might find at the end of their journey.

On arrival they discovered they were to make munitions. Bullets for the Germans to fire upon the French and the British and the American and the other Allied armies.

"*Non*," Skye whispered to Caro and Margaux. Because what if one of those bullets killed Nicholas, or Liberty?

Their fellow-prisoner Jeannie Rousseau said to the German officer in charge of the factory what everyone assembled there was thinking. "I won't make arms for the Germans. I cannot. Asking us to do so is in direct contravention of the Geneva Convention."

Caro's hand tightened around Skye's and Margaux's. They stepped in behind Jeannie. Many others did too. They hadn't enough food, they were, all of them, bleeding or bruised from some German violence or other, their smocks were damp from rain and their bodies shivered with cold, but they would gladly accept all that and more in order not to make the weapons that would murder their fathers and sisters and friends and lovers.

They were lucky. The officer was so shocked at their refusal—a refusal nobody had ever dared to make before—that he placed them in the kitchens to work, where they made food for the women who did not protest, the women who made bullets instead.

How much easier it was to work in a kitchen, where the ovens provided warmth and where crumbs could be easily stolen, than it was to dig sand for twelve hours for no purpose whatsoever except to exhaust them all to an eventual death.

Of course it couldn't last. The women who'd protested were sent back to Ravensbrück.

"I don't know if I can go back in there," Margaux said as the gates loomed before them.

It was the first time Skye had ever seen Margaux vulnerable and it frightened her more than reentering the gates of hell.

"You can," she said. "I need you." She placed Margaux's hand on her stomach, and Margaux nodded.

It meant that the next day they had to find something that would make Margaux's day better than the one before. Skye and Caro spent all day collecting what they needed from wherever it could be found. By evening, they had enough.

Crumbs. That was what they had searched so painstakingly for. Crumbs which, molded together, made a birthday cake for Margaux. And while marching through the snow-whitened forest on their way to work, Skye had gathered twenty-six twigs for candles. Caro had found a Christmas rose to place atop the cake too.

Margaux cried when she saw it. Skye and Caro held her, crying too. Skye tried to sing "Somewhere Over the Rainbow," but the bluebirds would not fly. They got stuck in her throat instead, beating their trapped little wings.

The very best day of all was when Margaux was moved to the Effektenkammer, where prisoner possessions were stored, and she stole a piece of cardboard from which they cut out tiny playing cards. How many precious hours were spent thereafter in a game of bridge or rummy, which made time actually pass rather than stall.

On the days when they found nothing, especially those bitter November days when they were made to lay slabs of sod in the snow at Königsberg—sods that iced up one day and had to be hacked free, or that thawed another day and turned into an arctic mud that froze the women despite the straw they had stuffed in their clothes for warmth—they would share stories of the past, of their childhoods. So Skye and Margaux knew all about Caro's brother Christian and the family villa, Les Rhumbs, at Granville by the sea.

"Christian and I both love it there, but he's always hated the dining room," Caro told them, smiling a little. "The lions and chimeras fighting on the dresser have always frightened him. When he was younger, I'd tell him to come with me into the garden because there were definitely no dragons in a place filled with flowers."

Skye pictured a small and serious Catherine giving her brother a posy of blooms, just as she'd once given Margaux and Skye those hopeful jasmine flowers.

Then Margaux spoke about her childhood in Lyon, her years

in Paris, and school in England. And Skye described her magical Cornwall summers, how she'd learned to fly, and everything about Nicholas. Always Nicholas: the day she'd found him again on an airfield in England, the moment she realized she loved him, what they'd said to each other when he'd placed a seaweed ring on her finger.

They didn't, ever, share their dreams. Everything they spoke of was from the past—a time that was real and beautiful and couldn't be taken from them, unlike the hypothetical future and the phantasmagorical present. Occasionally, when her courage was failing, Skye wondered if it meant that none of them had any dreams left.

Abandon all hope, ye who enter here, Dante had said. Words meant for Ravensbrück, even though they were written centuries before. But then Margaux would deal out the playing cards, or Caro would describe the pink roses at Les Rhumbs, or Skye would tell the story of Nicholas bringing cowrie shells to her when she was lonely, and they would think only of that moment. And because of that, Skye Penrose, Margaux Jourdan and Catherine Dior came to be more than friends. They were the currents of air holding one another up, keeping each other alive.

* * *

By December, freezing December, the Appell began at half past three in the morning and women froze to death as they stood waiting for their names to be called. Skye, Caro and Margaux's most important job became not to search for that one life-giving thing every day, but to find out more about the Kinderzimmer—Block 11—where the babies were kept. Because, between the three of them, they would soon have a baby to care for: Skye and Nicholas's child.

Before Skye had arrived at the camp, any pregnant women had been taken away and their babies murdered. But with the influx of prisoners in August and September, the rules had been changed. Births were now permitted, but Skye knew that just because something was allowed, it didn't mean it was desired. And so it proved to be.

Margaux, who had cleverly managed to be moved from the Effekt-enkammer to the camp administration block where she could find out the things that might keep them alive, told Caro and Skye that she had news.

"Six hundred babies have been born since October. Only about forty are still alive," she said.

Skye sank to the ground. It was worse than she'd hoped.

"The babies are kept five across one side of a mattress and five along the other," Margaux continued. "When the mothers are allowed into the block to feed their babies, they can't tell which one is theirs. Each baby is given only one rag, which is to serve as both nappy and blanket. The babies are locked up alone in the block each night, and one of the nurses maintains that a window must be kept open, regardless that it is December, to allow for ventilation. Rats thrive in Block 11," she finished.

"Skye's baby cannot go there," Caro said firmly.

"No," Margaux agreed. "Nobody knows you're pregnant, Skye. It's impossible to see anything beneath that smock. We'll keep it that way, and keep the baby with us when it comes. It's becoming possible now."

And it was. In the hoar and frost of winter 1944–45, it was well known that the Allies were moving through Europe—although to the women in the camp it felt as if they must be crawling on their hands and knees, so long was it taking them to reach Germany. Many of the guards no longer cared what their prisoners did, and sometimes didn't even bother to make them work. They were simply marking time until the inevitable occurred. In such circumstances a baby might not be noticed.

But then Margaux came to them with another warning. "Camp Commandant Suhren has been told to clean up this mess by making sure two thousand women die each month. It is retrospective: he must catch up to his quota. I've heard they're building a gas chamber and will take the weak and the sick first. You must never go to the Revier. Besides, the doctor told me that they keep women with typhus in the same bed as those with a simple foot infection, hoping the one with the infection will catch the typhus and then she will die too."

Skye touched a hand to her stomach. Never go to the Revier, the camp's infirmary. Which meant having a baby and seeking no medical help. For the first time she felt all hope slipping away.

"It won't survive, will it?" she said hoarsely, unable, on that bitter day in late December when she'd forgotten that Christmas had ever existed, when all she wished for now was the end of winter, rather than something as uncertain and undependable as the end of the war, to find the sliver of turnip floating in the soup of her hopelessness.

She coughed, the spasm lasting so long her hands scratched at the dirt beside her, clawing onto life, such as it was. She knew she probably had pneumonia, that Margaux had dysentery, and that Caro most likely had both.

But Margaux paid no heed to the crippling stomach pain that accompanied her dysentery. She stood up straight and tall despite her spindly legs and gestured toward the truck that had pulled up by the Revier. It tipped to the ground a pile of newly arrived bodies that were to be sorted into those who were, thankfully, dead, those who were, unfortunately, still alive, and those whose minds had departed their bodies. Then Margaux moved her hand to encompass the bones stacked against the washroom wall; to the ash of the crematorium graying the snow at their feet. "If anyone had told you a year ago about this, would you have believed that you could have survived for as long as you have?" she said.

"No one will ever believe this, will they?" Caro said, staring at the truck.

Skye shook her head. She didn't believe it and yet she could see it.

"Would you have ever believed you would carry a baby to full term in these conditions?" Margaux demanded, standing in front of Caro and Skye, blocking their view of the wretched bodies. "It's a miracle, Skye."

Now, Skye saw only Margaux, unwavering in her belief that they still had, somehow, one last scrap of wonder. Something precious. And Skye couldn't believe that she'd once looked at this woman on an airfield in England and tried to dislike her. Margaux was the bravest of them all.

* * *

When the day came, Skye ignored the pain at first. Pain was normal now; its absence so disconcerting that she had seen women reopen their wounds in order to feel its reassuring presence again. Indeed, Skye's lungs burned with disease unrelentingly now and she hardly noticed it. But the tightening of the skin on her stomach and the clutch of her insides told her this pain was different. It was a sacred thing in this most unsacred of places.

Caro and Margaux knew the instant they caught her eye, because the three of them were closer now than sisters; they were each the same person. If one was kicked by the guards, the others gasped too. If one's dreams were cauterizing, the others awoke and embraced the dreamer before she even realized she was in the grip of a night terror.

"Inside," Caro hissed, taking Skye's hand and leading her into their block.

"I'll keep the guards at bay," Margaux said, and she let Caro stay by Skye's side while she herself moved between Skye's bed and the block entrance, keeping a lookout, using her obdurate presence to conceal what was happening in one of the bunks.

Instead of medicines, Caro used stories of her family home, Les Rhumbs, to anesthetize Skye. "Pink roses," she said, sniffing the air as if flowers, not evil, bloomed beside them. "And peonies all through the garden. Jasmine so thick you feel dizzy when you first walk outside. I would use a bucket to collect all the petals and buds that fell off the bushes and I'd lie on the ground and tip them all over me. Have you ever felt a shower of flowers? It's something a child would love to feel."

So Skye imagined her baby lying on green lawn by the sea, a deluge of pink peonies and white jasmine falling down around her.

As much as she could, through fits of coughing alternating with the shuddering contractions of childbirth, Skye held on to that picture. She wished she could smell salty air sweetened by rose, but she hadn't the strength to push away a stench so powerful as Ravensbrück.

Luckily for all of them, the birth took only a few hours: a baby reared on air and love did not grow like a normal child. She slipped out, a tiny blue thing that Caro rubbed with all her might, while Margaux held Skye's hand and watched for the afterbirth.

Then Skye held her child, Nicholas's child, the first of the brood of fearless girls he had promised her, and she wept. Nicholas had no idea he was a father. He had no idea where Skye was. She had no idea where he was or how to tell him about their miracle. And Skye had no idea how fierce love could be until she touched her daughter's cheek and saw her tiny mouth open, felt the flail of a little fist against her breast. She knew right then and there that she would kill anyone who came between her and her child, that she would give all she had left to protect this baby.

Nor had she any idea how devastating love could be until she tried to feed her daughter. The baby nuzzled her head in frustration, a pitiful cry coming from her mouth as Skye's breasts refused to produce more than a drop or two of milk.

"I'm sorry, *chérie*," Skye whispered, understanding now she was so depleted that, even if she could give her all ten times over to her daughter, it still wouldn't be enough. Her weeping turned into body-wracking sobs, which then turned into a paroxysm of coughing that made the baby pull back in fright and begin to howl.

Skye looked up at Caro and Margaux. Their cheeks were wet too. Skye had tried not to abandon hope but it had abandoned all of them.

Margaux erased her tears with the back of her hand. She tried to draw herself up tall as she spoke but the dysentery had, over the past month, made her concave inward. Still, her voice was unwavering. "Some of the women make teats from the surgical gloves in the Revier," she said. "I'll steal some. Then we can at least give her water."

"I'll take some powdered milk from the kitchen," Caro added in her quieter but equally determined voice.

Skye wanted to shake her head, to say *No, you can't put yourselves at risk like that*, but she knew it was useless. She would do the same if Caro or Margaux were in her position.

That night, with the sliver of baby tucked soundlessly beside her—it hadn't cried again; it didn't have the strength—Skye, in the embrace of sleep, fell heedlessly into the past.

Nicholas was there. *My watch*, he said to her, as he had on their last morning in Cornwall, *it's not here. I must have dropped it in the gazebo. Kiss me again for luck and I won't need it.*

She kissed him, smiling, and said, *Perhaps Liberty saw it and picked it up.*

Then the dream tipped and she was screaming and something was crying.

She woke with Margaux's hand over her mouth. Caro was shushing a bundle that Skye knew was her baby. She tried to lift her arms to take her daughter, to hold her beside her heart so she would hear in that still-beating thud that Skye loved her no matter how her useless body let them both down, but her arms didn't work. The sheets were wet. There was too much blood for it to mean anything good.

Then there was only blackness, and the thought that Liberty couldn't have found the watch because she'd had no luck; she was missing too.

In the dream, Nicholas smiled sadly at Skye, turned his back and walked away.

THIRTY-FOUR

The next month was one long and appalling hallucination. Skye didn't know what was real and what wasn't, just that every morning in the dark she was, somehow, dragged to the Appellplatz for roll call where she leaned against Margaux and Caro, the blood still running down her legs. The guards paid no heed. Blood on prisoners' legs was nothing to remark upon; the very few women who still had their monthly cycles, despite the starvation, had no rags to use.

Caro, shivering, wrapped Skye in her cape and Margaux, shivering too, gave Skye her blanket to obscure the bundle strapped against Skye's chest. The bundle that had hardly grown at all, the bundle that would, Skye knew, die before she did.

The guards had given up enforcing labor, but still used the stick freely during Appell, and both Caro and Margaux stepped in front of Skye and took blows meant for her in order to protect the baby—*ma petite chérie*, as they called her. Skye felt each whack of the stick on her friends' bodies but it was too cold to cry; instead her tears froze on her cheeks, burning her skin.

"If the guards are agitated, the Allies must be near," was all Caro whispered after one particularly hard blow to the shoulder that had her coughing blood, not blaming Skye, still trying to find the splinter of sunshine to warm the bitter winter.

Besides that, all Skye remembered was the constant need to hide as general Appells were called more and more often, and the women were made to walk naked past the guards. Those with sores on their legs, or legs too thin to have any strength left, were herded to one side and taken to the death-buses parked in the woods outside the camp gates, buses from which the rumor of gas escaped. Buses from which nobody returned.

Skye couldn't walk naked past the guards because then they would see her baby, would see the blood still running down her legs and the fact that she was almost too weak to stand. So, during the selections, Margaux and Caro handed her over to the French doctor, Loulou Le Porz, who hid her in Block 10—the infectious diseases block— because no guards ever went in there. It was the biggest risk—that the baby would catch something and die—but she would certainly die if the guards saw her so it was the only risk that held within it a grain of hope.

So abrasive, those grains of hope, Skye thought as she sat on the floor of the death block with her baby, waiting for the Appell to be over. They had scoured her away almost to nothing. She tucked her finger into her daughter's fairy-sized fist and whispered over and over about houses on clifftops, a soft blizzard of petals, and a dark-haired man whom the baby would one day call Daddy.

Then the largest hallucination: Liberty. She appeared on the Lagerstrasse one day, smiling a vicious smile at Margaux.

Margaux stepped in front of Skye. "How long have you been here?" she asked Liberty.

"I've been in quarantine since June," Liberty said.

Quarantine. One of the camp's darkest places. Skye shivered.

"Why did they let you out?"

The suspicion in Margaux's tone was apparent even to Skye in her disordered state. She tried to speak, to tell Margaux to look behind the smile and hear what Liberty was really saying. But the effort made her cough, a sound so familiar to the baby that she didn't flinch at all now when she heard it.

The noise caught Liberty's attention. When she saw her sister, her smile collapsed. She flung herself on Skye, embracing her in a way they'd never embraced before, squashing the baby, which yelped. Liberty's eyes grew large.

Where is your baby? Skye tried to ask but it was hard enough to draw in breath let alone force out words.

After that, Liberty appeared on and off for days. Skye overheard snatches of strange conversation: Margaux telling Caro she'd discovered, in the administration block, that Liberty *had* been in quarantine because the Germans knew she was British; that she'd been let out because she was helping the guards, telling them who were the most powerful members of the Resistance, and which women in the camp had lied about who they really were.

She's a spy, Skye wanted to say. *She's just pretending*.

But when Margaux leveled her accusation at Liberty, Liberty admitted that she had given the guards two names.

"They were so sick they were to die soon anyway," Liberty said, her voice cold. "And they'd been feeding information to the guards themselves. You should be glad I gave them up before they had a chance to tell the guards anything about the two of you." She indicated Skye and Margaux.

Skye passed the baby to Caro before she threw up bile. How much longer could it go on: the bleeding, the coughing, the fever, the threat of Liberty?

That was the start of the worst time: hours of delirium during which she heard Margaux and Caro telling her her own story, about Skye and Nicholas on a Cornish beach with cowrie shells beneath their feet. Sometimes Liberty was there too, smiling too nicely at the guards and trying to feel Skye's ferociously burning forehead, but Skye turned her head away.

Never, during all those delirious days, did she see Nicholas again.

* * *

Then came Good Friday: a day of more death, heralded in Ravens-brück by a whipping of sticks. A rumor tore through the camp that there were more vans parked in the woods, and the rounding up of the women began. Just the Frenchwomen though.

"Hide," Margaux told Skye, and Caro as well this time because Skye could no longer move without help.

Then Liberty was there, pointing Skye out to the guards, her voice strident. "You should take her to the Revier. She's sick. Feel her head. See the blood. She had a baby and you didn't know."

The Revier. A place where people went to die.

Skye managed the only sound she'd been able to make in days. It was supposed to be a scream; it came out as a moan. Anger, violent and ferocious, roiled through her. Liberty wasn't pretending. She was everything Margaux had feared.

And Skye remembered that she'd been waiting, ever since Liberty had turned up on her doorstep at Hamble, for her sister to strike. She had finally done it.

Skye looked at Liberty properly for the first time since Liberty had appeared at Ravensbrück and she thought she saw her sister flinch. She would never, ever, forgive Liberty if, by her words, Skye and her baby were taken to the infirmary, where the baby would certainly die.

"I'm staying with Caro and Margaux," she whispered, and reached out for the hands of her true sisters.

They held on to her and Skye knew they would thwart Liberty. The guards, weak themselves from lack of food and from apathy and fear, would hardly bother with a woman who was going to fight when there were so many who could not. Liberty would have to choose someone else to send to the infirmary.

Liberty's eyes flashed with an emotion Skye did not recognize; an emotion that made her squeeze her own eyes shut so she might never see it again.

She heard Liberty hiss, "Nicholas has married a Frenchwoman. He has a child with her. Even if you and his bastard child get out of here alive, you can't have him. He has someone else now."

You thief of love! What, have you come by night / And stolen my love's heart from him? The lines Skye had once declaimed on a wall thrashed like the guards' sticks against her heart.

The nightmares, the hallucinations, whatever those things were that plagued her every waking and sleeping moment, vanished. Blackness, infinite, descended. She felt her body lifted from the ground and carried away and knew she was being taken to the infirmary but she no longer cared.

Beside her, she heard a loud scream. A gunshot.

Was the baby still with her? She scrabbled desperately for her daughter but knew nothing for certain except that, behind her, Liberty would still be smiling that awful smile.

PART THIRTEEN
NICHOLAS

*I always thought "missing presumed dead" to be such
a terrible verdict.*

—Vera Atkins

THIRTY-FIVE

FRANCE, MAY 1944

Nicholas flew Liberty into France one night in May, soon after he'd said goodbye to Skye and watched her fly away with O'Farrell.

As soon as they landed, Liberty scrambled up from her seat and to the ladder of the plane before Nicholas had made eye contact with the operatives on the ground.

"Wait," he barked at her.

Being Liberty, she didn't.

She'd been a bundle of jittery energy for the whole flight. Nicholas had tried to talk to her, to calm her, recognizing too well the signs of an agent pushed too far. He'd nearly circled around and returned to England, but there was no reason to do so beside his misgivings, and his superiors would scoff at those and accuse him of partiality. And perhaps they would have been right.

He caught sight of one of the men from the reception committee in the light of the flare path and his insides contracted. It was no one he knew.

The Germans must have found out which field they were coming to, and which was the right Morse code letter to flash. They'd suspected for weeks that there was a traitor among them, one of the field operatives, perhaps.

"Liberty!" he shouted, breaking all the rules by using her name so she would know there was trouble.

Liberty turned and he saw, sweeping across her careless face, the realization of danger.

Jesus, he was supposed to fly off and leave her there. But how could he leave Skye's sister with the Germans?

He took his gun and climbed out of the plane.

They were lucky because the Maquis were hiding in the trees on the perimeter. Gunfire sounded from those trees, aimed at the Germans.

They were lucky again because, somehow, everyone except the Germans shot true, and soon he and Liberty were being taken to a safe house.

"It's not the best place to spend a night," one of the men warned. "The mother is nervy and would most likely crack if questioned too closely by the Boche. But the daughter is charming. And it's the closest place we know of."

Nicholas wasn't worried. "There's a pickup operation tomorrow night not far from here," he said. "We only need to stay until then. If we can get a car to the field—it's near Orléans—late tomorrow, we can be out of everyone's way within twenty-four hours."

But it wasn't to be. The car never came. Nicholas guessed, after the previous evening's events, that the Resistance circuit had been captured and dismantled.

He tried desperately to make other arrangements with the woman, Madame Beaufort, and her daughter, Adèle, but they didn't have a car. And with the circuit gone, they didn't have access to a radio to send any messages to SOE to tell them that he and Liberty were alive and needed a Lysander to come and get them.

Madame Beaufort, desperately frightened by the fact that they were going to be in her cellar for longer than expected, barely spoke to them. It was Adèle who brought them food. She told them she was trying to find another Resistance circuit who could move them on to safety. Nicholas's guess, she told him, had been correct: the only one in the area had been decimated. She could only make discreet inquiries of people she hoped she could trust; inquiries that had, so far, come to nothing.

Three weeks passed by in a state of extreme tension. Neither he nor Liberty could leave the cellar. The space was cramped and they barely managed a civil word to one another. He tried his hardest to be patient, to bite his tongue, to tell himself that Liberty was probably scared too.

Occasionally Adèle joined them in the cellar and Nicholas told her about Skye. Even Liberty was silent then, her face as peaceful as it had once been in childhood when she'd stared at the stone maid lying on the ground in the lost gardens.

By early June, the lack of Skye was excruciating, as was the seemingly never-ending wait for help. He and Liberty actually agreed on something: they ought to take their chances and leave that night under cover of darkness.

They both knew that, before they'd left England, the Allied invasion of France was imminent. Which meant they might find another Resistance circuit themselves, or discover that the invasion had taken place and they could meet up, somewhere, with the Allies.

When Adèle next brought food down to them, they told her of their plan. She nodded and said she would organize supplies.

Ten minutes later, two sets of footsteps sounded on the stairs. Madame Beaufort appeared with Adèle.

"We have looked after you both for some time," Madame Beaufort said, strain evident on her face, hands clasped tightly together in front of her. "By having you here, we have . . ." Now she sought for her daughter's hand. "We have exposed ourselves to danger."

Nicholas put down the plate of food Adèle had given him and stood up from his place on the floor. The things that French people like Madame Beaufort and Adèle had done for people like him made him feel small and very humble. To risk imprisonment or death in order to shelter two strangers—a British pilot and a spy at that— took courage beyond anything. And more so if you were as terrified as Madame Beaufort obviously was. Yet she had done it in spite of her fear.

"Thank you," he said. "I know you could have turned us in. You've had our lives in your hands. If I can do anything for you, I will."

"There is something," Madame Beaufort said, tears in her eyes, tears in Adèle's eyes now too.

She told Nicholas, haltingly, that Adèle was pregnant with a Nazi child. That she hoped Nicholas would marry her daughter to give the child a name, to make sure nobody ever thought her daughter had collaborated with or formed an attachment to a German soldier. The timing would be about right. Adèle had only found out she was pregnant the day before Nicholas and Liberty had arrived. The villagers knew Madame had a pilot hidden in her cellar; it was entirely believable that the pilot and her daughter might fall in love, and marry. Then Adèle and her child would be safe.

"I have a priest here," she finished, gesturing to a man who now came down the stairs.

Nicholas knew it *was* a believable story—he'd heard about more than one Allied pilot marrying the Frenchwoman who'd sheltered and saved him. He wondered whether Adèle had been raped, or if she'd fallen for one of the Germans billeted nearby. Both scenarios were equally likely, and he understood the way villages worked.

Neither story would be palatable, and even the possibility that Adèle's child was of German blood would mean she and her mother would be ostracized, or perhaps even subject to a kind of tribal justice. He closed his eyes against the image of Adèle cast out of her village, with nowhere to live, and a baby to feed.

Liberty stood up beside Nicholas and was the first to speak. "Nicholas isn't going to do that," she said angrily. "You can't make him feel guilty like that."

Nicholas felt not anger, but a deep and desperate sadness. How could he resent Madame for wanting to protect her daughter? "Tell everyone it's my child," he said. "I don't mind. But I can't marry Adèle. I'm sorry."

"Nobody will believe us without proof," Madame said wretchedly. "It must be marriage."

"I'm already married," Nicholas said.

Liberty stared at him.

"I made a vow to Skye and she made one to me," he told Adèle and Madame. "We mightn't have paperwork but I married her bodily and utterly and with a strand of seaweed to prove it."

The priest conferred with Madame. Adèle wept silently beside them.

"The man who fathered the child," Nicholas asked Adèle, carefully, quietly, "did he . . ." He paused. How could he ask her if she'd been raped?

"When you're starving, and your mother is starving, you do things you might not otherwise do," Adèle said simply.

Nicholas felt his jaw clench. Adèle had given herself to a Nazi in exchange for food for her mother, but it was rape all the same. Just as Margaux gave her body to a Nazi in exchange for information. Right then he hated, truly hated, the world he lived in: a world in which women's vulnerability was used so appallingly by men. He thought of Skye, in France somewhere, vulnerable too, and he had to turn around and hold on to the wall, swallowing down the urge to be sick.

Madame Beaufort spoke then. "We will leave you to think about it. The priest will come back this afternoon." She took her daughter's arm, but before she left, she said falteringly, "You said you would do anything at all."

Nicholas slid his back down the wall and sat on the floor, hands covering his face.

After a few minutes, he felt Liberty sit down next to him. "Does that mean you're my brother now?" she said.

He looked across at her and she was smiling, beaming, actually. Nicholas nodded and managed to find a smile too.

"Thank God," she said. "Short of locking you and Skye in a room together, I'd just about run out of ways to make sure you ended up together."

"What do you mean? Are you saying you and O'Farrell . . ."

She grinned. "The thing with O'Farrell started so that Skye wouldn't convince herself to fall for him in an effort to forget about you. But now . . ." She touched her stomach. "Now it's a lot more than that. We're having a baby in January. As soon as I get back to England, we're getting married."

Nicholas stared at her. Liberty married and with a baby. Liberty maybe even in love.

"You look about as gobsmacked as if I'd told you I was marrying an elephant."

He laughed. "Sorry. I'm really happy for you both." He reached over and hugged her and she hugged him back.

"Maybe we can get married together," she said. "In Cornwall. You and Skye. Me and O'Farrell."

"I think Skye would love that." Nicholas could barely say the words. Skye in a wedding dress. Skye his wife. The forever that was meant to be theirs, that would be theirs the minute he got out of France, the very second the war stopped.

"All we have to do is get back to England. And make sure neither Skye nor O'Farrell do anything stupid. You don't think he's . . ." She stopped and for the first time ever, Nicholas saw that her eyes were damp and that it wasn't from fury.

"If my mother could see the future, then wouldn't I have some of that clairvoyance?" Liberty went on, swiping a quick hand over her eyes. "I don't feel anything telling me he's dead. So that means he's fine, doesn't it? I don't think I could bear it if he abandoned me too . . ." Her voice cracked.

Nicholas gripped her hand. "O'Farrell's alive."

He needed to believe his words because he'd also tried, each night, to sense Skye somehow. And all he'd felt was an urgent need to get home, never any message telling him to lie down and die because the love of his life was gone.

"We'll still leave tonight," Liberty said determinedly.

"We will." He rubbed a tired hand over his forehead. "I just wish there was something I could do for Adèle given she's risked her life for us."

Liberty shrugged. "There are some sacrifices, like hers with the Nazi, that are never repaid. It's the way of the world."

He thought of Luc sacrificing his life on that lonely field in France. Surely that was for freedom. And Margaux, sleeping with a Nazi—that was for freedom too. "Meanwhile, I said I'd do anything for them but it turns out I'm a liar," he said bitterly.

Liberty's voice hardened and she repeated her last, wretched sentence. "It's the way of the world. You can't always do the right thing, Nicholas."

* * *

Madame came back that afternoon with the priest and Adèle.

"I really am sorry," Nicholas said to Adèle. "Like I said, go ahead and use my name. Say we're married. I don't mind."

Liberty frowned at him: her earlier foray into empathy was evidently over but damned if Nicholas wasn't going to at least apologize to Adèle for not being able to give her what she wanted.

Madame told Liberty that all the curtains were closed and she could take a bath upstairs, perhaps believing it would be best for Nicholas and the priest to be alone, without Liberty's influence.

It didn't matter to Nicholas. Whether Liberty was in the room or not, he was still going to refuse.

The priest talked for a long time about mercy and charity. Nicholas was polite but steadfast. Liberty's bath went on forever.

Just after dusk, Madame Beaufort and Adèle appeared, both of them with frightened eyes.

"She's gone," Adèle said shakily.

"What?" Nicholas's voice was a crack of gunfire in the silent cellar.

Madame Beaufort told him that Liberty had crept out of the bathroom while Adèle and Madame were in the kitchen, had stolen some of Adèle's clothes, and had taken off into still-occupied France.

Fuck. Why the hell would she take off like that?

But the instant he asked the question, he knew the answer.

Don't leave me alone. It had been Liberty's refrain as a child. It was the same in adulthood, but unspoken and all the more heartfelt after being left alone by her dead mother, and after being, as Liberty had viewed it, abandoned by Skye in Paris.

You can't always do the right thing, Liberty had said to him—as if it were his especial character flaw—right before she'd gone upstairs to the bath, no doubt thinking the priest would talk Nicholas into doing that right thing and marrying Adèle and then Nicholas would abandon Liberty too. So she had left first.

He should never have told her that he wished he could help Adèle. She had completely misunderstood him. And he'd known from the time they'd stepped onto the plane together last month that Liberty was at her edge. Being stuck in a cellar with too much time to think was the last thing she'd needed and now she'd made the worst god-damn decision of all.

Nicholas hit the wall with his hand, but it was a futile gesture, like standing with a placard at Hyde Park Corner and denouncing Adolf Hitler.

"I have to go after her," he said. "Right now."

"Wait," Adèle said pleadingly. "I know you can't marry me. But you can come back here after you've won and take my child to England with you. Not me. Just the child."

"No, I can't," he said, shocked.

"I can give the child nothing. France has nothing now. I want my child to grow up in England where war hasn't destroyed everything." Her voice was anguished, pleading, urgent.

This was what war did to people.

Nicholas shook his head. "You'll change your mind when the baby comes," he said gently.

"If you leave the baby here, you're refusing it the chance to have a good life." She told him it would be years before France was anything more than a desecration. The fields were ravaged and empty, there was no food, thousands of people no longer had a home.

Even the priest nodded in agreement.

And Nicholas understood that Adèle had lived crushed in the fist of the Germans for years, and it had taught her to do whatever she had to. Who was to say that if their positions were reversed he wouldn't do something desperate too if it meant keeping Skye safe?

"All right," he said. "I'll come back. I promise."

He truly believed the promise would amount to nothing; that

she would keep her child once she had seen it and held it and loved it.

Then she said, "The English and the Americans are here. They've been in France for a few days, I think. Go north and west. You should find someone who'll help you."

He almost cried with relief. The invasion had happened!

"Thank you," he said, kissing her cheeks. "I'll see you soon." He said it because he thought he would find Liberty and they would get out of France and the war would be over in just a few weeks. The Germans couldn't possibly hold out for very long.

But then Adèle added, her face white, "My mother and I didn't come to tell you straightaway when we discovered your friend had gone. We thought . . ." She pressed her lips together and backed a little away. "We thought you might be angry."

He flinched at the realization that Adèle now thought all men, even him, were prone to violence and anger.

Her voice dropped to the faintest whisper. "I think they caught her. Someone from the village came around and told us that a woman had been found in the woods and taken away by the Germans."

Nicholas almost gave in to fury. Why hadn't Adèle told him at the outset? Because she'd had her own business to transact. That was how war worked. *Damn the whole world to hell.*

Adrenaline took over. "I'm going," he said. He made the priest give him his clothes.

He spent the night making slow and careful progress through the woods. At dawn in the nearest town, he saw a poster printed with Liberty's face. It boasted of the spy who'd been caught, and asserted that resistance was useless, that Hitler's people were always and forever victorious.

* * *

It didn't take long for Nicholas to be picked up by the Resistance. He cursed himself for having waited so long at Madame Beaufort's, but he hadn't known the Allies were in France. Things had changed so much in the time he'd been hiding in the cellar. Now, everybody wanted to help someone they hoped would be on the winning side.

It was still a dangerous journey back to the Allied lines; the Germans occupied most of the country. But he made it to Normandy, and then England.

As soon as he landed, he passed on the information about Liberty: that she'd been taken; that she must be sought and found.

They told him that Skye and Margaux were missing too. That O'Farrell was dead. That he was the only one left.

He found himself in a chair, unable to recall having sat, lungs not functioning properly, face soaked with tears. He remembered what he'd thought in the cellar at the Beauforts' house about Skye's vulnerability and his heart cracked violently inside his chest.

Vera Atkins, who was in charge of SOE's female agents, and Air Marshal Wylde stayed in the room with him, and all he could say, over and over, was, "You don't know where Skye is?"

Vera and Wylde just shook their heads.

For the first hour after hearing the news, he wanted to die. But then he wanted, more than anything, to live. To finish the war. To find her.

"Take leave," Wylde told him.

"Go to hell," Nicholas fired back. "Send me to France. Now."

Wylde acquiesced, saying only, "Find her." His eyes were damp too.

So Nicholas got himself posted to France, commanding a fighter squadron. He shot German planes out of the sky every day. And every minute that he wasn't flying, he spoke to the dozens of people he'd met on the Resistance circuits since he'd joined 161 Squadron and tried to discover what had happened to the woman he loved. And to Margaux. And to Liberty.

Some spoke of cattle trains filled with people that vanished into Germany. After he heard that, he spent the entire night so sick that he couldn't even cry.

With every day that passed, he grew more frantic. Sleep was something he barely remembered. He followed clues and gossip and rumor, and he checked in with Vera and Wylde each week, but he found nothing except exhaustion, and incredulity that this could have happened. Skye wasn't dead. He would know if she were.

Then, after almost a year, the war was over. But not the missing.

He went back to London to look through all the information Vera had. Somebody had to know something.

Before he left, he visited Adèle. She hadn't changed her mind. And he knew she was right. France *was* desecrated. It was no place for a child to flourish. So he took the child, a girl, with him. Her name was Aimée. She gripped his finger for the entirety of the plane ride to England, as if she needed to know he was there, keeping her safe. He stroked her cheek in reply.

In London, Vera told him she'd heard rumors of a camp full of women. Soon after, the first of the Ravensbrück prisoners arrived in Paris. Nicholas flew there and tried to speak to some of the women. He lost the contents of his stomach when he saw them; couldn't bear to think that Skye might be one of those unhuman-looking beings. But nobody knew of a woman called Skye Penrose. Nobody would even speak to him. Perhaps they were no longer able to speak.

Eventually, Vera crisscrossed Europe seeking her lost women. Thirteen of the thirty-nine women sent by SOE into France were confirmed dead. Almost half of them. As for Skye and Liberty and Margaux, Vera told him they had all disappeared, that they were missing, presumed dead.

Nicholas didn't return to New York. Skye would never find him there. He stayed in London, waiting for her.

After another year, Wylde told him he wanted to hold a memorial service for Skye and Liberty, but Nicholas refused.

He didn't need a service; it was impossible to do anything other than remember Skye Penrose. She was the sea and the sky and the entire universe as well.

PART FOURTEEN
KAT

THIRTY-SIX

I t was four in the morning when Kat finished reading. She put down the book, her cheeks wet. She'd been crying throughout—for people she didn't even know; for people she did perhaps know because one of them was her grandmother.

She understood now what Elliott had meant when he said that Nicholas wasn't really his grandfather. Elliott was the grandchild of the Frenchwoman Adèle and a nameless German. And Elliott's mother was the child Nicholas had brought back to England: Aimée.

Kat made herself a coffee and stood gazing at the sunrise over London, seeing something else. Because she also understood, after reading Nicholas's diary, why Elliott had wanted to forge a reunion between Skye and Nicholas. Their love was the real showstopper—the kind of thing all heads would turn to see, to sigh over, to wish for. The kind of love that was too magnificent for the terrible world that shaped it.

A buzz from her phone made her start. She glanced down to find a message from Annabel.

We looked at the writing on the label under the spectroscope, as you asked. The ink matches that from Catherine Dior's pen. She must have written on it. And I know you thought the letters on the label were "g" and "a." I'm pretty sure they're "y" and "e."

It took Kat a moment to recall what label Annabel was referring to. Then she remembered. The lapis blue dress. Catherine Dior had written something on the label. A word with a "y" and an "e." Kat shivered.

The first call she made was the easier one. Her daughters pulled faces at themselves on FaceTime, always more fascinated with their own moving image than with her. Until she said, "Let's have a holiday in Cornwall in England in September. All three of us."

"England!" Lisbet shouted, and Daisy, uncomprehending, repeated the word.

"Will we see Big Ben?" Lisbet asked.

Kat laughed. "We will."

Paul's face appeared on the screen too. Ordinarily, she would wince and expect the worst. This time, she didn't ask permission or apologize for having ambitions and aspirations of her own, and a career she loved. She just said, "I've been asked to work in Paris for six months. I think it would be great for the girls. And for me."

He studied her face and perhaps he saw that something had changed. His own expression was complicated and Kat, for the first time since their acrimonious parting, felt sorry for him. A busy emergency doctor, remarried to another doctor whose life must be equally frantic; a too-brief honeymoon before his new wife had fallen pregnant.

"I think it's a great idea," he said.

"Thank you," she said; and her emotions were still too overwrought because her eyes filled, and she thought perhaps his did too.

Next, she dialed her grandmother's number. "*Bonjour,*" she said as cheerfully as she could manage. Then she told her grandmother a half-truth. That a dress exactly matching one in the Cornwall cottage had been gifted to the museum. Given that she owned its double, Kat wondered if her grandmother knew anything about the Australian version. Kat told her to check the photograph she'd just sent to her mobile.

Her grandmother was slow to answer.

"I do know this dress," she said very carefully. "The one in Cornwall was left to me by Catherine Dior. But the other . . . it was mine. I sold it after your mother died and I knew I was to care for you. It was my nest egg: money for school fees. Or in case anything happened to me and I could no longer look after you."

"It must have been difficult to sell such a beautiful dress," Kat whispered.

"It was," her grandmother replied, words cracking on a sob, and Kat wept too.

"I love you," Kat said eventually.

"You are everything to me," was her grandmother's response.

And Kat knew what she must do for the woman who was, also, everything to her.

She hired a car and drove south. She needed to speak to the Penrose woman still living in Cornwall.

* * *

When Kat pulled into the sweeping driveway, the woman—Margaux, she wanted to be called—seemed to be waiting for her, leaning against a pillar on the porch, smoking a cigarette in her left hand.

Kat climbed out of the car. In honor of her grandmother—whoever she was—she wore one of the Dior dresses: strapless silk, knee-length, with Liberty blue roses printed on a deep sapphire background.

"You came back," Margaux said coolly. "I should have known you'd be stubborn."

"Why?" Kat asked. "Why should you have known that about me?"

"Let's go for a walk." Margaux set off, almost spryly, not waiting to see if Kat was following.

They walked to the lake, over which a rope bridge was strung like an upside-down rainbow.

"I met Nicholas Crawford," Kat said as they stared at the water.

She waited for the woman beside her to flinch, as she surely must if she were Skye Penrose. But perhaps she was made of tempered steel because neither her body nor her face moved in response to Kat's words. Or perhaps there was another reason for her self-control.

"I read his journal about the war," Kat pushed on. "It was heart-breaking. He had so much love for a woman named Skye Penrose. I'm rather envious because I don't think . . ."

Kat paused as, before her, she saw the transparent outline of two children in the lake, a boy holding on to a rope above him, and a girl in the water giving him courage. "No," she corrected herself. "I *know* that, until now, I've never loved anyone the way he loved Skye. Wholly. Overwhelmingly. As if his life depended on it. Which it didn't, in the end—because he lived on without her. But did she live on without him?"

Kat looked at Margaux. The other woman started walking again, so fast that Kat worried she might fall on the uneven ground.

She fired the question at her anyway. "Are you Skye Penrose? And if you are, does that mean my grandmother is your sister? Or is it the other way around?"

At last Margaux halted and turned slowly to Kat. "Bring your grandmother here to see me. Then I'll tell you who I am. And so will she."

* * *

When she returned to the driveway, Kat saw another car pull up.

Elliott climbed out. "I had a feeling you'd be here," he said.

Of course he did, Kat thought, because he understood everything about her that mattered.

He took off his sunglasses. He looked as if he hadn't slept, as if the rift between them were as devastating to him as it was to her.

"I wish I'd never lied to you," he said, face serious, intent on her and nothing else. "When I first met you at the Savoy, I never imagined you'd be the kind of person I'd lie awake next to all night long because you were sleeping on my chest and you looked so lovely that I didn't want to miss a moment. If I didn't care about you as much as I do, Kat, I wouldn't have told you I'd lied. I would have just let it go on, because it would have been easier."

Kat was transported back to that morning in bed with Elliott. She'd been happy in a way she'd never been before and had known, in the same way her body knew how to breathe—essentially, innately—that Elliott was happy too. Yes, he could have let the lie continue. It *would* have been easier. Perhaps then she would have continued to sleep with him until she returned to Australia, where she would have put their relationship down to a once-in-a-lifetime fling that had revived her and restored her but wasn't meant for the real world.

Paul had never confessed anything to her until after she'd found out something was wrong. Whereas Elliott had admitted his lie before she'd found out what he'd done, and while understanding the possible consequences. He had just told her that watching her sleep was precious to him.

The real world was both imperfect and wonderful. And Elliott was part of the real world: imperfect and wonderful too.

She walked over to him, ran her hand along the stubble of his jaw, and kissed him.

PART FIFTEEN
MARGAUX

Was it possible? We were returning from the other world.

It was true. We were still alive. We were free.

—Jacqueline Péry d'Alincourt, *Forgive, Don't Forget: Surviving Ravensbrück*

THIRTY-SEVEN

GRANVILLE, 1946

It takes time for Margaux's body to learn how to eat without purging the food; time for her hair to grow back; time to resume her body's ordinary monthly cycles. When her monthlies restart, she stares at the blood in horror, wondering what now is the matter with her. But then she remembers that this blood is normal.

Vera Atkins from SOE comes to see her once, to confirm that she is alive, to ask her to testify against the Nazis. Margaux refuses and begs her to tell no one of her existence—she can't bear the thought of people she once knew turning from her in horror. Even Vera hadn't been able to hide her distress.

But one day in 1946, when her hair has reached shoulder length and her external wounds have scabbed and healed and the bruises faded, Caro's brother Christian says to Margaux, "See this."

He passes her a drawing: a woman wearing a skirt as closely pleated as a clam shell, a jacket budding into efflorescence from the *très rapetisser* waist. The features of the woman's face are not drawn in, but she does not need eyes, a nose and a mouth to be arresting. The suit takes care of that.

Tian takes out his pencil, leans across and sketches a hat on her head, its brim so wide that it obscures the woman's face. Then he darkens the skirt. "Black can be violent or it can be elegant—more so than any other color."

Beyond them, the Chausey archipelago stirs, the water darkens from sapphire to midnight, bypassing gray entirely.

"Will you be one of my mannequins?" Tian asks Margaux. "You have healed here, among the flowers. And I want you to be happy. As you made Catherine—not happy, but resolute—at Ravensbrück."

Margaux shakes her head. She is still the creature who stepped off the train at the Gare de l'Est in Paris in July 1945; a creature from whom children cowered, adults too.

But Christian brings her a looking glass. "See," he says.

Margaux looks at herself. Behind her, in the glass, she can see the house, pink and glossy as a boiled sweet. The flowers, enveloping her in perfume. Her face, thinner than it used to be. Her eyes, larger than they used to be. And Margaux sees for the first time that she is not the monster she had imagined. The violence is gone. What remains? Surely not elegance?

Margaux imagines herself wearing the suit Christian has drawn. Its vast skirt would hide the scars on her legs, erase all imperfections.

A little girl toddles unsteadily across the lawn, hand held by the nurse Tian has employed. She doesn't walk as well as she should, not yet. But it is incredible that a child given the worst possible start in life can walk at all. And Margaux realizes that she never sees, as others do, a strange waddle. She sees a certain grace. A certain beauty.

Neither she nor her daughter are perfect. But they are, somehow, still alive. It is a gift that she once hoped for above anything. Why is she so determined now to leave the wrapping on? Why not reach out her hand and touch this life she is, despite everything, living?

Her daughter, Nicolette, smiles at her, an action that always makes Margaux's eyes flood, and all she can do is blink at the tear-blurred outline of this tiny miracle. She pats the lawn beside her and her daughter sits, then lies down on her back, eyes closed.

Caro tiptoes over and scatters a handful of rose petals and jasmine flowers over the little girl and Nicolette's laugh is the most exquisite sound of all. Margaux's hand tightens over her daughter's as Nicolette passes her a handful of jasmine—a handful of hope.

Margaux's eyes meet Caro's.

* * *

Several weeks later, Margaux stands completely still in Christian's couture house while fabric is draped around her. Christian decides that the cream silk tussore is best for the jacket, and the black wool is ideal for the skirt. The Bar Suit is created on Margaux's body, made especially to suit her measurements. She had never imagined there would be such affinity between a dress and a mannequin, had never realized that Christian's ideas require not just pen and paper and needle and thread, but a figure to inspirit them.

Christian watches as the suit comes alive. He alters the size of the collar; is unhappy with the flare of the jacket over her hips until Pierre Cardin, the young tailor responsible for the ensemble, has the idea of using surgical cotton wool in the lining, folded in such a way to achieve the required volume and shape.

Then it is done and it is, Margaux sees, eloquent. The colors: violent black and unwary white. The sloping brim of the hat that shadows her face. The winged contours of the jacket's peplum. The constriction of the waist, so tight that it is difficult to speak when wearing it.

Christian has seen what is inside her.

His show is, of course, an enormous success. When he tells her that some of his gowns will be shown in Australia, Margaux asks to travel there as one of the mannequins. She isn't sure why; just that, perhaps, in a country far away she might drink less champagne and allow fewer men to seduce her and not suffer from headaches in the morning.

It takes four days to fly to Australia on a private plane. Four days! It is extraordinary. They stop in Tripoli, Cairo, Karachi, Calcutta, Singapore and Darwin—so many strange and faraway places—before finally reaching Sydney.

As soon as she steps off the airplane, Margaux knows she has done the right thing. The light in Australia is scouring, abrading; it burns everything away. The seas are ferocious and can stop anything evil from coming too close. The people are happy; they have never heard of Ravensbrück.

She asks to return to Australia in 1948 when the David Jones stores present an entire show of Dior designs. She is much feted in the press. Upon seeing the photographs, Margaux does not recognize the woman depicted there. She has truly become someone else. It has been her goal, ever since leaving Ravensbrück.

So she decides to stay on in Australia, returning to France only once to pack up her things. There, Caro tells her, "Christian has made an arrangement to send you each year a gown he thinks will best suit you."

They are in Margaux's room in Christian's Paris apartment, where the gold-flocked wallpaper and Kentia palms are an elegant offset to the debris of packing for a long journey, which covers every Belle Epoque surface.

"The couture house will continue the arrangement forever, no matter what happens to Christian," Caro continues. "It's set down on paper. I hope you don't forget us all the way over there."

"You know I never could," Margaux says as she places her daughter's doll in a valise and looks at her friend. "Do you think it's ever possible to stop running from something like..." Margaux cannot bring herself to say the word: *Ravensbrück*.

"But now I am Miss Dior," Caro says, referring to the perfume Christian has named after her, a perfume whose scent saturates the air throughout the apartment, but that still doesn't block out the other odors Margaux wishes would stop following her.

"And I am a Dior mannequin," Margaux says.

The women reach out their hands to one another and the unspoken words echo between them: *Is that really who we are?*

"I have something for you," Caro says, breaking the silence. She gestures to the valise she has brought to Margaux's room.

It sits on the bed, innocuous, but Margaux can feel something inside it, something that yearns to be let out. She walks slowly over to the bed and opens the lid of the case.

Its contents are so brilliant that she steps backward, a startled "Oh" rushing from her mouth. For Caro has packed the sky into that valise, a Cornwall sky: the kind of sky that Skye Penrose grew up beneath, the kind of sky that blazed all around her and Nicholas Crawford as they first became friends, and then became lovers. The kind of sky that makes her break down utterly, in a way she hadn't known she was still capable of.

"Christian made one for me too," Caro says.

Margaux slides to the floor, one arm wrapped around herself, one hand covering her mouth, and she weeps.

Caro sits beside her and holds her, crying too. It is a long time before either woman can move.

"Will you put it on?" Caro whispers and Margaux nods.

She slides off the skirt of the Bar Suit she is wearing, and unbuttons the jacket. Caro holds up the dress and Margaux steps into it, not looking in the mirror until Caro has done up the many fastenings, and the silk and tulle have molded around her bones like another skin.

But this is not the skin of grief. It is the skin of memory, and it is a violent thing. She can see her hands shaking as she confronts herself.

She isn't Margaux Jourdan any more. She is the other woman still trapped in her soul.

"Do not forget her," Caro whispers, unfastening the top of the dress and pointing in the mirror to the name she has written on a label inside. "Take out this dress, as I will do, and think of her occasionally: of all the good she did, all the love she had. It was not nothing."

No, Nicholas, it was not nothing, the woman now known as Margaux Jourdan thinks. How could he have treated it as though it were?

PART SIXTEEN
KAT

THIRTY-EIGHT

CORNWALL, 2012

It took a month for Kat to get her grandmother onto a plane. Margaux didn't have a passport and she didn't want to go, and in the end Kat used outright lies and blackmail. She pretended the Dior archives had to meet with her grandmother, who was the current owner of Catherine Dior's blue dress before Kat's fellowship could begin, before any papers could be written, before the dress's provenance could be properly verified. She made sure Lisbet and Daisy moped around their grandmother's house, asking why they weren't going to France anymore until Margaux, exasperated, agreed to go.

Kat expected her to complain the whole way there. But her grandmother mostly stared out the window, as if fascinated by everything outside: the sunlight, the clouds, the unrelenting blue, even the deep black of night.

They stayed at a hotel near the airport when they landed. The following day, Kat drove them to Cornwall.

Her grandmother began to fidget as they drew closer to Porthleven. "I'm sure the old house doesn't need me to look at it," she said.

"I'm not changing my mind," was Kat's only reply.

Unexpectedly, her grandmother smiled. A youthful smile; it caught

Kat's breath and made her blink, hard, because for how long would Margaux still be smiling like that?

"Maybe it's time," her grandmother said. Then, "Maybe this is the future she never told."

"Now you're just being cryptic." Kat tossed her grandmother a smile.

Margaux returned it, beautiful suddenly, her face patterned with her life in the same way a hundred-year-old gown still held the shape of its wearer.

They diverted from the road at Porthleven and Kat turned in at the Lost Gardens of Lysander.

Her grandmother frowned. "I don't know this place."

"Perhaps it doesn't look the same as it used to," Kat said.

Elliott sat on the bench seat on the porch, looking as good as ever in navy shorts and a black T-shirt almost the same color as his hair. Kat smiled at him and resisted everything inside her that made her want to run over to him and feel his arms wrap around her. There would be time for that later. This moment was for her grandmother, and for the other Margaux too.

Her grandmother stepped out of the car, her eyes fixed on the female figure beside Elliott: the other Margaux Jourdan, who was, of course, smoking a Gitane.

Kat's grandmother didn't look shocked or surprised but rather resigned as she said to the woman, "You want my forgiveness. You want to sleep dreamlessly, untroubled by nightmares. But I can't. So why should you?"

Silence. Two women, eyes locked, poised as if to throw a punch. Or perhaps to defend themselves.

Kat frowned. She didn't know what she'd imagined but it wasn't this.

Suddenly the woman on the porch smiled, and it reminded Kat so exactly of the smile her grandmother had given her in the car that she froze.

"Your forgiveness isn't something I ever doubted, Skye," the woman said. "You always forgive. Your understanding, however, is something quite different."

Skye.

Kat's eyes met Elliott's and she saw that they were as watery as her own. Her grandmother was the cartwheeling girl who had turned Elliott's grandfather's life upside down. Which meant that the woman on the porch . . .

Her grandmother turned to Kat. "This is my sister, Liberty," she said quietly. "Margaux Jourdan . . ." Her voice withered and Kat barely heard the final words. ". . . is dead."

The words hit Kat painfully. Skye and Liberty Penrose. Sisters. And Margaux Jourdan . . . a life ended so terribly young.

"I knew the Red Cross was coming," Liberty said to her sister.

Kat shook her head, uncomprehending. "Can we go inside?" she said. The tension between the two women was suffocating.

As Liberty led the way into the house, Kat's grandmother—Skye—caught sight of Elliott for the first time.

"Who's that?" she demanded.

"Elliott Beaufort," Kat said. "He's Nicholas Crawford's grandson. Well, in a way he is."

"Nicholas Crawford's grandson," Skye repeated slowly. "Well, today is full of surprises, isn't it?"

* * *

Inside, the first thing Kat's grandmother did was to approach the mantelpiece and the gold pocket watch. She stroked the case, then enveloped the watch in her hand and closed her eyes. "You did pick it up from the folly," she said to her sister.

Then she opened her eyes and sat down suddenly, gazing at Liberty. "You want me to understand. Does it matter, after all this time?"

"You talked about nightmares, about not sleeping," Liberty said. "Which means you haven't left the past in the past. Until you set the ghost free, it will continue to haunt you."

"You sound like our mother."

Liberty laughed. "Yes, that is the kind of thing she would say. Perhaps I did inherit some of the good after all."

"Don't," Skye said. "Don't let's go back so far . . . to everything else. Just tell me what you need to, and then Kat and I can leave you . . ."

In peace. Alone. Kat waited for one of the standard endings to the phrase but none came. She subsided into a chair too, and Elliott perched on its arm. They threaded their hands together.

Liberty began to speak. "Those guards everyone thought I was too friendly with," she said, "one of them told me about the Red Cross. They'd been given permission to come into the camp and take away some of the Frenchwomen, on buses bound for Switzerland and then France. Catherine would be one of them, but not you or Margaux, as Commandant Suhren had doubts about you both. You were too ill to understand, and I knew that if I told Margaux or Catherine they wouldn't believe me. We all knew what the buses in the forest had been used for up until then. But I believed the guard—that these buses were different, not death buses; she told me in exchange for—well, we needn't go into that."

Liberty paused and Kat watched her grandmother's eyes fill with tears, as if Skye knew exactly what Liberty had done in return for the information, and that it was horrific.

"The guard also said," Liberty continued, staring at the window as if it had opened onto the past, to a time sixty-seven years ago when barbarity and shame were all these women knew, "that the Red Cross would take some extra women from the Revier. You wouldn't go there, but I knew it was the only way to get you and the baby—that tiny baby—out. So I told you . . ." Liberty blinked, as if she were trying to stop the press of the past into the present. "I told you that Nicholas had married. That he had a baby. It was the only way to make you go," she repeated. "But it was part-truth and part-lie."

Skye shook her head. "It was all truth. I read about his child in one of the War Ministry's postwar, chin-up, good news bulletins when I was in Granville. *Much decorated pilot Group Captain Nicholas Crawford has returned to London with his child,*" she quoted robot-ically. Her voice fell to a whisper. "I'm not sure I need to hear any more."

"You do," Liberty said forcefully. "The mother of the child had fallen pregnant before Nicholas arrived in France. The baby wasn't his. Taking the child to England was one of those desperate actions people undertake in wartime to save someone else." Liberty looked down into her lap, as if she wished to undo everything, but also as if she knew how futile and foolish the wish was.

Skye stared at her sister through an ocean of tears. Her face was so pale that Kat moved to stand up, to stop the flow of confessions and shocks. But Liberty spoke again.

"After the war," she said, "it was easy to become Margaux. As you know, nobody coming back from the camp had any papers. Nobody had registered with Margaux's name and birthdate here in England. I gather you got your papers in France?"

Skye nodded. "Vera didn't come to see you? She visited me."

"When was that?"

"July, forty-five."

"It took me a little longer to get back. I expect she thought it was simply a double-up when she saw the name again, an accident of paperwork."

Skye nodded again, mutely.

There was a long silence.

Liberty busied herself with lighting a cigarette, but Kat could feel—and she thought everyone else could too—the pressure of more words filling Liberty's mouth, needing at last to be spoken.

When they came, they were halting. "I was . . . I was too afraid to look for you at first. I didn't want to hear that you had died any-way . . . hating me . . . and that your child had died too. Then I made some discreet inquiries and was told that Skye Penrose was one of the women who did not come back."

Skye drew herself slowly up from her chair and walked over to stand in front of her sister, hands on hips. Kat could see them both as children, eighty years before, doing the same thing.

"I have felt a lot of emotions for you in my life," Skye said. "Frustration, confusion and, of course, love—but never hate. I did ask Vera Atkins if you were alive. She said you weren't, as far as she'd been able to discover." Skye's voice cracked. She took a deep breath and gave herself a little shake. "I can see why you chose that particular tone of voice and those particular things to say at Ravensbrück. They were very effective in getting me to the Revier. Now," she brushed quickly past the one mention of the camp, "tell me about the Gitanes. Don't tell me you developed a taste for them?"

"They reminded me of you," Liberty said starkly.

"Ah," Skye said. "I used to drink negronis for the same reason. But you forgot to be right-handed like Margaux."

Liberty managed a smile. "I couldn't smoke as many right-handed."

Skye smiled too. "I could never quite get the hang of eating right-handed. I managed almost everything else though." Then she touched her sister's shoulder. "And your baby?"

"A German boot to the stomach took care of that."

There was no emotion in Liberty's voice and Kat understood that was how she had lived her life since Ravensbrück: alone, away from the world, devoted to a garden that couldn't hurt her.

That she had chosen such a life made even more sense after the next exchange between the sisters.

"Were you there at . . ." *Ravensbrück*—they all heard the word Skye chose not to say—". . . until the end? When the Russians came?"

Kat recalled what Elliott had told her: that the victorious, conquering Russians had raped the women left behind at the camp, over and over, no matter that what remained of each woman was no more than a skeleton.

Liberty nodded, wordless.

"Then you were the bravest of us all," Skye said simply.

Liberty broke down at last.

Skye drew her into her arms and they cried together, true sisters for the first time in their lives. Sisters whom war and torture and lies and misunderstandings had not been able to tear asunder.

THIRTY-NINE

Later, after the tears had been wiped away, Skye told Liberty about what she'd done in the many, many years since they'd last seen one another. About modeling and selling dresses, about raising a child and then a grandchild.

And Liberty told Skye about wanting to be near their childhood home but not having the courage to step inside it. Instead, she'd bought the adjoining property and resurrected the lost gardens, naming them after Lysander, the Shakespearean figure they'd learned about at school whose moniker had been adopted for a series of airplanes.

They parted at last, Skye explaining to Liberty that she hadn't yet seen inside the old cottage, but very much hoped to take Liberty on a tour tomorrow.

"We'll walk along the cove. I'll even let you put a crab down my back if you must," Skye said mischievously and Liberty laughed.

As they made their way to the cars, Elliott whispered to Kat, "I'm going into the village to get some food for tonight. That'll give you and your grandmother time to talk. I'll join you for dinner—I'm cooking." With that he left the two women alone.

"You look happy when you're with him," Skye observed on the drive to the clifftop house.

"I am," Kat said. "Happier than I've ever been. I'm not just Kat-the-mother, or Kat-the-conservator, or Kat-the-granddaughter; I'm all of those things together. I've realized I don't have to keep the parts of my life so separate and nor do I have to apologize when one spills over into the other."

Skye nodded. "I'm looking forward to giving him the once-over at dinner."

At the house, Kat helped her grandmother up to the room where some of the dresses were still hanging in the wardrobes. "Will you tell me about these?" she asked.

Skye sat down on the bed and told Kat how she'd met Catherine—Caro—Dior while working for SOE, and how she, Caro and Margaux had become the fiercest of friends. Every time Skye said Margaux's name, her voice trembled.

"I didn't know," she said eventually, "and nor did Margaux, that they were Red Cross buses in the woods that day. Not death buses. We didn't know either that the Red Cross had always intended to take Caro. When I was being carried to the Revier, Margaux took out a knife she'd had hidden in her sleeve for months and she cut Caro's leg with it, badly enough that she was sent to the Revier too—so I would have someone with me." Skye's face crumpled. "Then the guards . . . they shot Margaux."

Kat sat down beside her tiny, frail grandmother, a woman whose body and mind had endured so much, and drew her close. Skye sagged against her like a dress robbed of its mannequin, or a woman whose everything had been taken from her by the Nazis at Ravensbrück.

"Only Margaux could have done such a thing," Skye whispered into Kat's shoulder. "She was the kind of person who could do all the brave and terrible things that must be done during a war. I miss her so much."

Skye wept again, and Kat did too, crying for a woman she didn't know but who had given her grandmother a name and an identity.

"Caro was a true heroine too," Skye said when her eyes had dried a little. "She wasn't just Miss Dior—a name on a perfume bottle. Long before any of that, she was precious. I named you for Catherine Dior. Margaux was my strength and Caro was my hope."

Kat gripped her grandmother's hand.

"Somehow, on the bus to Switzerland," Skye continued, as if determined to have it all come out, "I was recorded as Margaux Jourdan. I kept saying her name, because I knew she wasn't with us—so the Red Cross thought that's who I was. Then in France, when I read about Nicholas's child in the War Ministry newsletter, I assumed he had married, as Liberty had told me. I knew then I could never be Skye Penrose again. It was easy enough to change my identity. When you leave a place like Ravensbrück, you look—"

Skye pressed a hand to her mouth. Kat waited, silent, letting her grandmother recover. When Skye spoke again, her voice was thin, like water.

"We looked very different. When the Swiss doctors boarded the bus to decide who could go on to France and who needed to stay in Switzerland in hospital—which I did—they all cried when they saw us. And when Vera Atkins from SOE came to see me, she believed I was Margaux. I was unrecognizable."

Skye moved to the window overlooking the sea. "I never went looking for Nicholas. I truly thought he'd married, that he had a child with his wife. I couldn't have gone to him, in the state I was in, and told him I was alive. I would never have asked him to leave a wife and child for the monster I'd become. I couldn't look at myself, let alone bear anyone else's gaze, even my Aunt Sophie's. So I asked Vera not to tell anyone that Margaux had returned."

Kat remembered what Elliott had said about the American diplomat who had thought the Ravensbrück women were a "terrifying spectacle." Would she have had the courage, looking like that, to go to a man who had once loved her? She rubbed her arms, but the kind of chill she felt was impossible to warm.

"It was better, I thought, to not be Skye anymore," Skye said quietly, looking down at the Cornish bay where she and Nicholas had first met. "Some time later, Christian asked me to model for him. I didn't have to think or talk; I had only to smile. I agreed. I also drank, quite a lot. When there was to be a show in Australia, he sent me. I stayed in Australia. And I drank some more."

Skye fell silent then. Kat sensed there was more she wanted to say, and that she was searching not only for the words but the courage to say them. She sat in the window seat beside her grandmother.

"You named my mother for Nicholas," Kat said gently. "Didn't you?"

Skye drew in a long breath, then nodded. "I did. Nicolette Jourdan. It was the only part of her father I could ever give her. I should have given her more. I should have . . ."

Kat wound her arm around her grandmother's shoulders through another long and tear-filled pause.

"I didn't do the best I could by your mother," Skye managed at last. "After getting her out of Ravensbrück against all the odds, I had what would now be called post-traumatic stress. Ravensbrück lived in me. I could never be rid of it. It made me hallucinate at night. And drink. Only at night and never in front of your mother, but still. I adored Nicolette. But perhaps I was suffering too much myself to be the best mother to her."

"Don't say that!" Kat cried. "You were the best mother anyone could have had to me."

Skye interrupted her. "That was because the day your mother died I stopped drinking. I sold the blue dress that Christian made for me, and sent the rest of them to England so I could truly put the past behind me. I had a caretaker from the village store them in the house, and take delivery of the dresses that arrived from each new collection. When Caro died four years ago, she left me her blue dress and I had it sent to Cornwall too. I knew I couldn't look at that particular dress without remembering everything that happened."

"Did you sell your blue dress to someone named Madeline?" Kat asked. "She was the woman who donated it to the museum."

"I did. I met her at my very first showing in Australia. She loved Dior. It was she who gave me the idea of the little business I had when you were living with me."

"It doesn't look as if she ever wore the dress."

Skye smiled, just a little. "She understood it was special. She probably didn't wear it, merely safeguarded it. I'm glad she did."

* * *

The next day, Kat and Skye went down to the cove. They were both wearing one of Christian's gowns—Kat in the *Soirée de Décembre*, long and black, the same violent color as the revelations of yesterday; and Skye in white, the Venus dress, its skirt made of overlapping shells.

Looking out over the water, hands joined, they wished Kat's mother—Skye and Nicholas's daughter—godspeed to peace. They wished the same for Margaux Jourdan. And Catherine Dior. And O'Farrell too.

The waves rushed toward them, cresting into a salute and then withdrawing slowly, as if they understood that the names they carried were treasure of the rarest kind.

After that there was just one more ghost to lay to rest.

FORTY

Elliott drove Kat and Skye to the nursing home. Kat had explained to her grandmother where they were going and that Nicholas was, perhaps, unreachable. Skye had frowned and said nothing. Kat worried that her grandmother didn't understand the gravity of the situation, but she also knew the meeting must take place. Skye had been holding on to Nicholas for seventy years and it was time to wish him godspeed too.

Elliott led the way to Nicholas's room. "Hi, Grandpa," he said cheerfully, but Kat could tell it was forced, that Elliott was as worried as she about what might happen.

"I need my pills," Nicholas said, as if he thought Elliott was the doctor. He added to Kat, "It hurts," mistaking her for staff too.

He merely nodded at Skye, as if she were another of the residents at the aged-care facility. But Skye walked over to him, smiling.

Kat almost didn't want to watch what would happen. She felt Elliott's arm wrap around her shoulders.

Skye picked up Nicholas's hand and held it tightly. "Do you remember a girl named Skye?" she asked.

Nicholas stared at her, his eyes foggy, no light of recognition clearing away the mist. Kat waited, breath held.

"She liked to swim," Skye continued, not letting go of Nicholas's hand, not glancing away, even though it must be so painful to see the blank face of a man she'd loved so deeply, a man whose eyes must once have looked so very different whenever they gazed upon her.

There wasn't a sound in the room.

Then, "Cartwheel." One word from Nicholas.

One small word that wouldn't mean anything to anybody else, but Kat knew that to her grandmother it meant everything.

"Yes. She liked to cartwheel." Skye's voice was unwavering, not betraying any of the emotion she must be feeling.

Nicholas smiled. "Underwear."

A long pause followed. Skye didn't speak. Nor did she move. She just sat on the chair holding the hand of the man she loved, seeing again perhaps what she had beheld on a beach in Cornwall so long ago.

"Yes," Skye managed at last. "She pulled down your trousers and laughed at your underwear."

Kat could no longer watch Skye and Nicholas grasp at the edges of memory. She didn't want to witness the moment when Nicholas's memories faded and his eyes clouded and he became again a man without a past.

She turned around, buried her head in Elliott's shoulder and sobbed.

It was a long, long time before she was capable of speaking, of wiping her face and gulping air rather than bawling.

Elliott cradled her head against his shoulder. "Don't cry like that again," he whispered. "Nothing has ever hurt so much as seeing you cry like that."

Which only made her start crying all over again.

Eventually, her tears lessened and they both heard Nicholas say to Skye, "Who are you?"

Kat froze.

"Skye," she heard her grandmother say.

"Out there," Nicholas replied, pointing to the sky beyond the window.

"Yes."

"It's a pretty name."

It's a pretty name. As if Skye were nobody. Kat saw one lonely tear streak her grandmother's face.

"I don't want it to end this way," Kat said to Elliott. "Can't you . . . I don't know . . . rewrite it or something?"

She wished it were that simple; that a life could be changed in the same way words in a book could be recast into a different version, a better version. A happy ever after.

"Look at your grandmother," Elliott said, voice low. "Do you think she doesn't want this, even if it's all there is?"

Kat could see that Skye hadn't let go of Nicholas's hand. Hadn't taken her eyes off him. She was talking to him about Nicolette, in a soft and lovely voice Kat had only ever heard her use with her great-granddaughters, late at night when they were scared by a ferocious storm.

Somehow, Kat found a smile and she looked up at Elliott, the man she loved in the same way Skye loved Nicholas.

"Will you marry me?" she said. "I don't know how it'll work, other than I'll at least be nearby in France for the next six months, but I don't really care about the practicalities and the things I usually live by. I want every memory of you, from now until forever, to be mine."

He didn't answer. Instead he kissed her unrestrainedly and with far too much passion, obviously forgetting they were in a room with their grandparents.

Kat smiled against Elliott's lips. "Does that mean yes?"

"We'll get married in Josh and D'Arcy's chateau," he said, smiling too. Then he took her hand and drew her over to the bed. "Grandpa," he said, "I'd like you to meet my fiancée."

"Fiancée," Nicholas said. "I always wanted to get properly married." And then he looked at Skye.

Whether, for just a millisecond, he had remembered who Skye was and that he'd loved her, and with that look had wanted to convey that the only proper marriage would have been the one between her and him, Kat didn't know. But it was what she chose to believe.

Skye leaned forward and kissed Nicholas's lips. "We were always married, Nicholas," she said. "And it was magnificent. *We* were magnificent."

As Nicholas drew Skye's hand up to his cheek, Kat felt the years fall away. She saw a dark-haired man and a dark-haired woman on a beach, wrapped in a blanket and in one another's arms, the woman's finger wound with a seaweed ring. Across the sand, laughing, ran the ghosts of the girls they had wanted together; and around them all a vow that echoed through time: *We are boundless*.

Yes, Kat thought, smiling at Elliott. *We are*.

AUTHOR'S NOTE

The idea for this book came to me when I was reading Anne Sebba's book *Les Parisiennes: How the Women of Paris Lived, Loved and Died in the 1940s*. There, I learned of Catherine Dior—Christian Dior's sister: her work with the Resistance throughout the war until her capture by the Nazis and her imprisonment in Ravensbrück concentration camp. How had I never heard of this woman, other than as the person after whom her brother Christian named his perfume, Miss Dior?

I determined to find out more and was shocked to discover that there is, sadly, little information about Catherine Dior, who was very reticent about her wartime activities. I did glean some scant facts from Villa Les Rhumbs, the ex-Dior family home in Granville, now a museum, and some from Christian Dior's autobiography. Catherine risked her life by working for F2, a British-supported Resistance organization that primarily worked out of southern France. However, Catherine and her partner, Hervé Papillault des Charbonneries, carried out Resistance activities in Paris too, using Christian's apartment as a meeting place for the network. For her work during the war, Catherine was awarded the Croix de guerre and the Légion d'honneur by the French, and the King's Medal for Courage in the Cause of Freedom by the British.

As takes place in my book, Catherine was arrested on July 6, 1944, in Paris and sent on the last train to Ravensbrück. She spent some time doing forced labor at Ravensbrück satellite camps at Torgau,

Abteroda and Markkleeberg. I have only included Torgau here, rather than have the reader jump to several different locations in a short space of time.

Until mid-2019, I hadn't been able to find a consistent explanation about how Catherine left Ravensbrück in 1945. Most sources note only that she was "freed" or "liberated" near Dresden. Sebba, for instance, mentions only that Catherine was "released" in April 1945. In the absence of certainty, I chose to place her on one of the Red Cross convoys that took French prisoners from Ravensbrück in April 1945. But Justine Picardie, who, with the help of the House of Dior, is writing a book about Catherine Dior, published an immensely useful article in *Harper's Bazaar* in March 2019 in which she states that Catherine escaped while on a death march from Markkleeberg satellite camp in April 1945. By the time I came across this explanation in May 2019, my book was largely finished. Therefore you will have to treat as fiction the section of my book where I have Catherine leaving on the Red Cross convoy. I look forward to reading Justine's book and learning more about Catherine.

I find that stories usually come from two or three unrelated ideas suddenly colliding and this was certainly the case for *The Paris Secret*. While researching *The Paris Orphan*, I learned about the Air Transport Auxiliary, and the important role women played in that organization despite initial prejudices and difficulties. I also came across the story of 161 Squadron, who flew by moonlight into France to deliver SOE agents whose job it was to sabotage the Germans and to spy on them. I knew I wanted to write about both groups of pilots.

The final link that brought it all together came when I visited the Dior exhibition at the National Gallery of Victoria in Melbourne in 2017. There, I discovered that Australia was the very first place outside France to show Dior's gowns in 1947, that David Jones had organized a special showing of Dior's gowns in 1948, and that Australia thus had a strong connection with the House of Dior.

Many people in the book are based on real historical figures: Pauline Gower, Rosemary Rees, Joan Hughes, Vera Atkins, Amy Johnson, and Catherine and Christian Dior being among the most integral to the story. Wherever I have used a name of a female pilot in the Air Transport Auxiliary, that is the name of a real person. I had to change history slightly with regard to Pauline Gower: she was in charge of the women's section of the ATA, but Margot Gore was the commanding officer at Hamble, not Pauline. However, it didn't make sense to introduce another person after the reader had already become comfortable with Pauline; and besides, I already had a Margaux in my story and it would have been confusing to add another.

Many of the incidents I cover in relation to the ATA are based on fact. All the awful quotes from magazines and newspapers about the women pilots are real, as is the first press call, and the fact that the women flew open-cockpit planes to Scotland all through that first bitter winter. I borrowed ATA pilot Maureen Dunlop's image in the *Picture Post* of her stepping out of a plane, hand in hair, for Skye. Maureen's picture was taken at a later time than I have used in the book.

Many books that I read about the ATA referred to the nude medical examination the women were subjected to on joining the ATA—and I have moved the timeframe of this to suit my story. It was the new female American ATA pilots who refused to be subjected to such treatment, but I would like to think that Skye, should she have existed, would have objected too.

The progression of the women from trainer aircraft to fighters to bombers, and the opposition mounted against them at each stage, was also recorded in many of the books that I read. Margot Gore, CO at Hamble, did organize for two of her pilots to go to an RAF base and deliver smiles to a squadron that had suffered losses. The wording

I've given Pauline, "Efficient and pretty, please," and her asking the pilots to make themselves as attractive as possible, are both recorded in, among other sources, *Sisters in Arms: British and American Women Pilots During World War II* by Helena Page Schrader. In the same book is the story of a female ATA pilot being tasked with delivering a Beaufighter to an RAF base to show the men, who had refused to fly that aircraft type, that even a woman could fly it.

Skye's stay at RAF Leavesden and the attitude of the RAF toward women flying the largest planes, and requiring them to do more practice circuits than the men, is based on Lettice Curtis's experiences, recorded in *Bomber Girls* by M. J. Foreman. The grounding of all women for further physical and cognitive assessments after Mona Friedlander burst a tire on a plane is noted in *Spitfire Women of World War II* by Giles Whittell.

The lunch at which Skye speaks about allowing women to fly a wider range of operational aircraft to help resolve the pilot shortage in Britain is based on similar lunches at which Pauline Gower spoke on the same topic. The film *They Flew Alone*, about pilot Amy Johnson, that Skye sees in London is a real film.

All of the information about the difficult flying conditions faced by the ATA is based on fact: they did fly without instruments and radio, instead using visual navigation and dead reckoning, and avoiding clouds at all costs; and they were unarmed. Many of their pilots died on the job; and occasional attacks on the ferry pilots by German planes did occur.

Other sources I consulted for information about the Air Transport Auxiliary include: Diana Barnato Walker's memoir, *Spreading My Wings*; Rosemary du Cros's (née Rees) memoir, *ATA Girl*; *Brief Glory* by E. C. Cheesman; the Air Transport Auxiliary's *Ferry Pilots Notes*; and the collection of papers about the Air Transport Auxiliary held at the National Archives in Kew. The Imperial War Museum at

Duxford allowed me to see many of the different kinds of airplanes that Skye would have flown, and helped me understand the mechanics of flight.

The Dior family home, Villa Les Rhumbs, is a beautiful building set in stunning grounds atop a cliff in Granville, France. I visited the house, gardens and the Dior museum now located there in October 2017 and knew immediately that I wanted to use the house in my book. The only issue was that the Diors, who purchased the villa in 1905, were forced to sell it in 1932 due to money problems. It was purchased by the town of Granville in 1932, meaning the Diors were no longer living there in the 1940s. I hope you will forgive me for using the home anyway, as I just couldn't imagine that part of the story unfolding anywhere else.

All of the gowns Kat finds in the house in Cornwall are real Dior gowns. The four outfits bequeathed to the museum Kat works at are based on the four original Dior designs shown at the Paris Fashions For All parade at David Jones in 1947. The mysterious blue dress is a figment of my imagination.

For information about Christian Dior, I referred to *Christian Dior: Designer of Dreams*, published by Thames & Hudson; *Dior by Dior: The Autobiography of Christian Dior;* and *The House of Dior: Seventy Years of Haute Couture* by the National Gallery of Victoria. I also visited the Dior exhibition at the NGV in 2017, and the Dior exhibition at the Musée des Arts Decoratifs in Paris in 2017, and read many of the extant newspaper articles published in Australian newspapers about the Dior showings in 1947 and 1948, as well as copies of the David Jones newsletters from this time.

161 Squadron did conduct moonlight flights into France for two weeks every month, carrying secret agents and supplies for the Resistance; and operated out of the secret base RAF Tempsford, with forward operations carried out from RAF Tangmere. For this part of

the story I referred to *Lysander Pilot: Secret Operations with 161 Squadron* by former pilot James Atterby McCairn; *We Landed by Moonlight* by former pilot Hugh Verity; *RAF Tempsford: Churchill's Most Secret Airfield* by Bernard O'Connor; *Runways to Freedom: The Special Duties Squadrons of RAF Tempsford* by Robert Body; the collection of records of 161 Squadron held at the National Archives in Kew; and the collections of the RAF Tangmere museum, which I visited in October 2017. I also read former WAAF Doreen Galvin's memoir, *Arts to Intelligence*, to help me understand the role of the women of the WAAF at RAF Tempsford.

Another part of the story that I have manipulated slightly is to do with Margaux and Nicholas's cover story. Once several women were working for SOE, their cover was that they worked for the Inter-Services Research Bureau, a fictional organization. Female SOE agents were recruited from the WAAF, and several were commissioned as junior officers in the WAAF, like Margaux. I made Margaux one of the first women to work for SOE, before protocols for women were clear, so that I could create an engagement cover story. It's possible that this could have happened; as SOE was a secret organization, nobody knows everything about how it worked. As SOE expert M. R. D. Foot says in his book *SOE 1940–1946*, "the exact size of SOE has never been revealed . . . exactly who did and did not belong to SOE are questions so difficult and intricate . . ." Therefore, I went with what was possible.

Much of the information Elliott reveals to Kat about SOE is based on fact, including the mishandling of the search for missing agents— especially the women—toward the end of the war. I gleaned much of this from Sarah Helm's excellent book *A Life in Secrets: The Story of Vera Atkins and the Lost Agents of SOE*. In this book, I also discovered the story of the misidentification of agents Sonia Olschanesky and Nora (or Noor) Inayat Khan.

As well as the above-mentioned books, my research on SOE took me to the Imperial War Museum in London and I found, in particular, their *Secret War* permanent collection very useful. I also read through the SOE papers held at the National Archives in Kew, and referred to the book *The Women Who Spied for Britain: Female Secret Agents of the Second World War* by Robyn Walker and *The Heroines of SOE: F Section, Britain's Secret Women in France* by Beryl E. Escott.

Some SOE historians take issue with the use of the word "spy" in relation to SOE agents, preferring to call them secret agents. However, as Sarah Helm notes, the women were working for a secret service; they wore no military uniform and were thus liable to be executed as spies; they had no legal protection as, when the Hague Convention was drawn up, it had never been envisaged that women would be used as combatants; and they were performing clandestine work in enemy territory. If this doesn't make them spies, then I don't know what does!

The hardest thing of all to write about in this book was Ravensbrück concentration camp. Geneviève de Gaulle's memoir, *The Dawn of Hope: A Memoir of Ravensbrück*, is heartbreaking reading. I borrowed the story about the birthday cake made of crumbs and decorated with twig candles from this book. Sarah Helm's *Ravensbrück: Life and Death in Hitler's Concentration Camp For Women* was thorough, important and haunting, and I used many of the anecdotes that women recounted to Helm for my story, including everything relating to the Kinderzimmer, the death buses in the woods, the dumping of bodies for sorting outside the Revier, the retrospective order to Camp Commandant Suhren to kill two thousand prisoners each month, the Good Friday round-up of women, and Jeannie Rousseau's heroics at Torgau. Two further memoirs from Ravensbrück survivors, *Forgive, Don't Forget: Surviving Ravensbrück* by Jacqueline Péry d'Alincourt and *An American Heroine in the French Resistance* by Virginia

D'Albert-Lake, provided further detail and also the epigraphs on pages 437 and 381.

I am indebted to Suzanne Chee, fashion conservator at the Powerhouse Museum in Sydney, who invited me to spend a day with her so I could understand what her job involves, and who let me (with gloves on!) touch and examine some of the museum's collection of Dior gowns from the late 1940s. She also gave me a copy of Marika Genty's presentation on Christian Dior, which was very helpful. I also owe a big thank-you to Elizabeth Carter, manager of the Vibrational Spectroscopy Facility at the University of Sydney, who talked to me about how one might analyze fabric and inks, and showed me how spectroscopes were used for this kind of analytical work.

The lost garden that Skye and Nicholas find, and which Liberty resurrects, is based on the Lost Gardens of Heligan at St. Austell in Cornwall. Finally, I apologize to whoever lives in the house atop the cliff just outside the town of Porthleven in Cornwall for my clambering all over the surrounding land trying to take photographs. The position of your house inspired the Penroses' home in this book.

READING GROUP GUIDE

DISCUSSION QUESTIONS

Note that these questions might contain some plot spoilers.

1. Had you heard of the Air Transport Auxiliary and the women who worked for that organization before you read this book? Which of their experiences in dealing with the Royal Air Force and the male establishment did you find the most deplorable?

2. Why do you think women like Catherine Dior have been forgotten by history? Is it due to their gender, their reticence to speak about their wartime experiences, the nature of the savagery they endured, or other factors? What can we do to make sure the heroines of today aren't similarly forgotten in the future?

3. How much did you know about Ravensbrück, Hitler's concentration camp for women, before you read *The Paris Secret*? How difficult was this part of the book for you to read, and do you think the author achieved her aim of bringing to light the injustices and terrible acts committed against women in the camp? Why do you think the Nazis established a concentration camp solely for women?

4. Did Skye and Liberty do the "right" thing after the war? Can you understand why neither was in touch with the other afterward? How might things have changed if they had tried harder to find

each other? Is pretending to be someone else ever acceptable, and what did you think of their actions after the war?

5. How would the book have been different if it had been told from Liberty's point of view? In what way would the childhood sections of the book have changed? What did you think of Liberty, and did this perception alter as the book progressed? Would you have liked to have seen more from the perspective of any other character?

6. Take a look on the internet and see if you can find pictures of the Dior gowns referenced in *The Paris Secret*. Do you have a favorite? If you do, why do you think the author chose that particular dress for that particular moment in the book? Can fashion be art, and can it, as Margaux says, restore and revive the spirits? Can it have any meaning beyond providing protective covering, or is fashion merely frivolous?

THE STORY BEHIND THE BOOK

THE REAL HERO: CATHERINE DIOR

I expect that before you read *The Paris Secret* you had heard of Christian Dior. But had you heard of his sister Catherine? I certainly hadn't until I read about her in Anne Sebba's wonderful book *Les Parisiennes: How the Women of Paris Lived, Loved, and Died Under Nazi Occupation*. Sebba mentioned Catherine a few times, that she had worked with the French Resistance and had been captured by the Nazis and deported to Ravensbrück concentration camp. Her work with the Resistance was so heroic and so important that, after the war, Catherine was awarded a Croix de Guerre and the Légion d'honneur by the French, and the King's Medal for Courage in the Cause of Freedom by the British.

The terrible injustice of what and who the world remembers struck me immediately: the man who once made dresses is so famous that most people, if asked to name a couturier, would mention Christian Dior. But his sister, who fought for freedom for her country and who nearly lost her life in that struggle, had been forgotten.

I embarked on a quest to find out more, a quest that uncovered very little concrete information about Catherine, who rarely spoke about her wartime experiences after the end of the hostilities. Still, I wanted to find whatever I could, and my journey took me to

Melbourne and Sydney in Australia, and to Paris and Granville in France.

An exhibition about the House of Dior in Melbourne, besides allowing me to revel in the beauty of the gowns, revealed only that the perfume Miss Dior was named for Catherine. Christian had been uncertain about what to call his very first fragrance, and then, one day in 1947, Catherine had walked into a room while he was discussing that very problem. Someone said, "Ah, here is Miss Dior." And thus the perfume was named.

In Paris, there was another exhibition of beautiful Dior gowns, and, amid the glamour, one small piece of paper that caught my eye: a letter from Christian Dior to his father, advising the latter that Catherine had been liberated from Ravensbrück concentration camp. The letter was dated April 1945. But what had happened to Catherine in the preceding years, both at the camp and while she was working with the Resistance, and what had happened to her afterward?

More questions. Seeking answers, I went to Granville in Normandy, France. Villa Les Rhumbs, the ex–Dior family home, sits atop a cliff there and is now a museum dedicated to the Diors. Here I saw several photographs of Catherine, read a little about her life in the house as a child, and saw what was once her bedroom. But there still remained a huge gap of time between child Catherine and hero Catherine, the woman who, against all odds, left Ravensbrück with her life.

That gap has not yet been filled extensively by any writer or archive, but there is, thankfully, a biography of Catherine scheduled to be published in fall 2020. In the meantime, I had to use much imagination and some fabrication to work Catherine into my story because I desperately wanted people to know about this other, arguably more important, Dior sibling.

THE DRESSES

As you read through *The Paris Secret*, you'll see the names of many House of Dior gowns. All of these are gowns that I saw at the *Dior: Couturier du Rêve* exhibition at the Musée des Arts Décoratifs in Paris, *The House of Dior: Seventy Years of Haute Couture* exhibition at the National Gallery of Victoria in Melbourne, or on my two visits to Villa les Rhumbs in France.

My phone is almost weighed down with an excess of the photographs I took of so many of the gowns at each museum in order to refer to them during the writing of the book. I encourage you to go online, search the names, and take a look at them—and try to choose a favorite!

SEARCHING FOR SKYE'S HOME

After France, I went on to England and spent several days driving through idyllic Cornish villages, trying to find one that would be just right for Skye's home. St. Ives was too busy. Fowey was divine but lacked the kind of rugged coastline I had in mind.

I don't know what made me drive into Porthleven—a whim or an intuition—but as soon as I walked to the end of the pier, looked back at the small but pretty town, and then along the shore toward a clifftop on which perched a lonely house or two, I knew I had found Skye's home.

I walked along the beach and then clambered all over the clifftop, near the few houses there, taking lots of photos of the view and the surrounds. Luckily nobody came out and asked me what I was doing!

There is no cave on the beach at Porthleven like there is in the book—I stole that from the beach at Tintagel, also in Cornwall.

The moment I saw the cave there, I could clearly imagine Skye and Nicholas inside it, so I added an element of make-believe to Porthleven Beach. On my travels around Cornwall, I also visited the Lost Gardens of Heligan, which are truly delightful. I was fascinated by the idea of a lost garden that had been found and resurrected and knew I had to use that in the book too. Many of the objects in the lost garden in *The Paris Secret* are stolen from Heligan, including the rope bridge over the lake and the statue of the sleeping woman.

LEARNING TO FLY

Then it was time to learn about planes and pilots. This was the most difficult area to research, as I knew nothing about the mechanics of flight before I began.

Luckily, the National Archives in Kew, England, still has all the papers from the Air Transport Auxiliary and 161 Squadron. This meant I could look through photographs of all the women in the ATA, see how much they were paid compared to the men, and read the many letters Pauline Gower wrote exhorting those in charge to employ more women in the ATA.

In 161 Squadron's papers, I read through the Air Transport forms that detailed where in France each evening's pickup operation was to take place, how many agents were to be dropped off and how many collected, and how many containers of supplies for the Resistance were to be unloaded. Also on file were the reports after each mission that detailed weather conditions; problems encountered en route, such as enemy fire or planes; mechanical issues; and problems at the landing field. These papers were a treasure trove and, without them, much of the necessary detail would have been missing from my story. It was also quite thrilling to be handling papers stamped "Secret" and "Most Secret"!

From there I traveled to Tangmere Military Aviation Museum, located at the former RAF Tangmere, the base where Nicholas works in the book. So I was able to walk in the footsteps of my characters and climb into and out of Spitfires and Lysanders and see the L-shaped flare path lit by Resistance torches, signaling to the Lysanders in the sky.

I also visited Hamble, where Skye is based for much of the book. The air base is now gone and all that remains is a small and rather sad memorial attesting to the fact that women once ruled the skies there.

GETTING MY HANDS ON A DIOR GOWN

The very last stop on my research trip was back home in Australia, in Sydney. I wanted to touch a Dior gown from the late 1940s, to look inside it and really examine it. I also wanted to understand more about what a fashion conservator does so that I could write Kat's part of the book authentically.

I sent an email asking for help to a museum in Sydney called the Powerhouse, which has the best fashion collection of any museum in Australia. As luck would have it, at the exact moment that my email landed in the inbox of the fashion conservator at the Powerhouse Museum, she was reading one of my previous books, *The Paris Seamstress*! So she knew who I was and was more than happy to help me.

I donned a pair of rubber gloves and descended with her into the depths of the museum. She explained all the many different methods conservators use to store precious old gowns and items of clothing. Then the conservator pulled open a large drawer. Nestled inside in acid-free paper was the Christian Dior *Moulin à Vent*, or Windmill dress, from 1949!

The interior of the dress was an absolute marvel—I had no idea how many hook-and-eye closures were used by couturiers like Dior to ensure a dress shaped itself properly around a body, nor that covered lead weights were sewn into such pieces so they would hang correctly. It was just as interesting to see the internal construction of the dress as it was to marvel at its stunning exterior.

As a historical novelist, I'm indebted to archives and museums the world over—without them, my books would be much the poorer, and so much more would have to be imagined, rather than based on truth and fact. And I like to honor the past properly, by doing my research and drawing unknown and fascinating elements into a story that everyone can enjoy. I truly hope I succeeded with *The Paris Secret* and that you enjoyed reading the book as much as I enjoyed researching and writing it.

ACKNOWLEDGMENTS

I always thank Rebecca Saunders first but that's because she is such a big part of each and every one of my books. When I first told her I wanted to write a book about a collection of Dior gowns, and Catherine Dior, and female pilots, and a secret moonlight squadron, and everything else, she told me to go for it, so I did. Rebecca's inexhaustible enthusiasm and support is what every writer needs, and I'm very lucky to have her as my publisher.

Thanks also to Alex Craig who, as Fiction Publisher at Hachette Australia while Rebecca was on maternity leave, had to suffer all of my meltdowns when I thought that the book was too big, too vast, too complicated and beyond the scope of my abilities. Thank you, Alex, for always listening, for your sage advice, for your brilliant editorial eye.

I want to thank everyone else at Hachette Australia who had a hand in this book, but especially Sophie Mayfield, whose editorial skills are second to none, whom I trust beyond anything, and who helps me sort out all the intricate problems associated with a novel like this. And thanks to Dan Pilkington, who champions each of my books, and to the superb sales team too. To Fiona Hazard and Louise Sherwin-Stark, thanks for always being accessible and supportive as well.

Nicola O'Shea's copyediting skills made this a much better book, and I thank her for all of her advice and assistance.

My publishing team in the U.S. at Grand Central is the best

any writer could wish for and I owe a big thank-you to Leah Hultenschmidt and Jodi Rosoff particularly.

To my family—Russell, Ruby, Audrey and Darcy—I love you all and thank you for always being proud of what I do, for coming with me on weird and wonderful research expeditions, and for all the hugs and kisses.

Sara Foster always reads my novels for me and she has an especial talent for saying just the right thing at just the right time. Thank you for being such a wonderful writing buddy. And Louise Allan, thank you for our fortnightly writing catch-ups where we write a little, and talk a lot.

My readers are the nicest people in the world and I wish I could personally thank every single one of you. Thank you for coming along to my events, for sending me beautiful messages, for your enthusiasm and your joy, for loving my characters as much as I do.

Without booksellers we would have no books, so my last thank-you goes to everyone who has sold, recommended, displayed, promoted or supported my novels. Thank you!

ABOUT THE AUTHOR

NATASHA LESTER worked as a marketing executive for L'Oreal before penning the *New York Times* and internationally bestselling novel *The Paris Orphan*. She is also the author of the *USA Today* bestseller *The Paris Seamstress*. When she's not writing, she loves collecting vintage fashion, traveling, reading, practicing yoga, and playing with her three children. Natasha lives in Perth, Western Australia.

For all the latest news from Natasha visit:

NatashaLester.com.au

Twitter @Natasha_Lester

Instagram @NatashaLesterAuthor

Facebook.com/NatashaLesterAuthor

YOUR
BOOK
CLUB
RESOURCE

VISIT
GCPClubCar.com

to sign up for the **GCP Club Car** newsletter, featuring exclusive promotions, info on other **Club Car** titles, and more.

 @grandcentralpub

 @grandcentralpub

 @grandcentralpub

More sweeping historical fiction featuring extraordinary women:

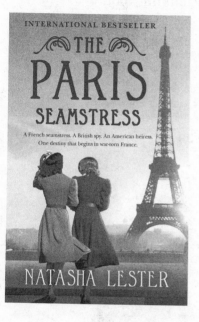

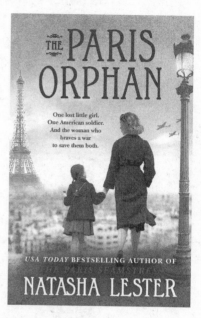

Discover bonus content and more on read-forever.com.
Find more great reads on Instagram with @ReadForeverPub

Follow @ReadForeverPub on Twitter and join the conversation using #ReadForever.

Connect with us at Facebook.com/ReadForeverPub

Journey to the past with more unforgettable historical fiction. Read the *USA Today* and *Wall Street Journal* bestseller everyone is talking about!

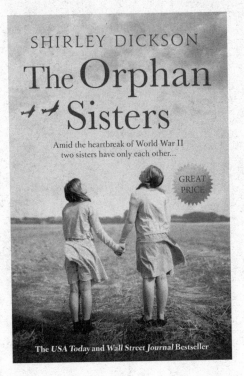